Victorian Dream

by

Gini Rifkin

Victorian Dream

Cover Art by *Debbie Taylor*

The Wild Rose Press, Inc.
PO Box 708
Adams Basin, NY 14410-0708
Visit us at www.thewildrosepress.com

Publishing History
First English Tea Rose Edition, 2013
Print ISBN 978-1-61217-727-4
Digital ISBN 978-1-61217-728-1

Published in the United States of America

"Have I missed the first waltz?" he asked, escorting her to the center of the room.

"No," she confirmed. "I've allowed none to be played, and my poor guests are near to the point of exhaustion from quickstepping about the room."

He chuckled, and took a step back, his gaze gliding over her from head to toe. "You appear to have held up beautifully."

As they stood before one another, a hush blanketed the room. It was one tiny moment, filled with a lifetime of anticipation. Coming to her senses, she caught Penelope's attention and nodded toward the orchestra. Her friend rushed toward the musicians, nearly tripping on the hem of her dress. The lilting strains of Tchaikovsky swirled through the air like a welcoming breeze, and her guests issued playful hurrahs as they hurried to find their partners.

Captain Garrison, male elegance infused with animal-like grace and strength, swept her into his arms—and into a dream come true.

When he placed his hand solidly at the small of her back, a tingling sensation shot straight up her spine to the roots of her hair. The resulting effect was more potent than wine. She was dizzy with desire, giddy with happiness. She must remember to breathe.

They stood so close—only their clothing and the heat of their bodies between them. What a glorious temptation, just beyond reach. Teasing and taunting, it was a fleeting taste of what she yearned to partake of fully.

"I've thought a time or two about holding you in my arms," he admitted, in a husky voice. "It feels even better than I imagined."

Praise for Gini Rifkin

Dedication

In memory of Mom,
who taught me to read and love books,
Estelle,
who read my books and encouraged me to write,
and Gary,
who was man enough to wear my pink baseball cap.

With thanks and gratitude to
The Wild Rose Press and
the amazing Amanda Barnett.

Dedicated to family who are friends—
and friends who are family.

I had a dream, which was not all a dream.
~Lord Byron, "Darkness"

Chapter One

1851, New Bedford Harbor, Massachusetts

Alone in the dark, Walker Garrison stood on the dock of the deserted waterfront, his shoulders hunched against the nor'easter blowing down from Wellfleet. How many hours had he stood just like this, only on the deck of a ship?

He usually found unrestrained nature exhilarating and conducive to clear thinking, but tonight nothing dispelled the nagging feeling something was terribly amiss. It was unwarranted of course. Lost in thought, he smoothed his mustache with thumb and forefinger then rubbed the palm of his hand across his clean-shaven chin. What could possibly go wrong?

He narrowed his gaze, and the ghostly outline of the *Alicia Elaine* came into focus. Evening mist, cold and sinister, wound around her rigging and mast, and the huge vessel quaked as if it too felt danger lurked nearby. Standing taller, he tried to throw off the unease creeping through his body like a fever. Foreboding was a sensation he'd felt before—disaster had always followed.

Maybe he was simply afraid of being happy. An infrequent visitor in his life, when happiness had come, it had never stayed long. Now it made him nervous when things seemed to be going too well.

A bell tolled out on the reef, the mournful clang heading straight for him, striking a lonely chord deep within his soul. Shreds of fog, twisting and dancing, joined hands to form a thick gray wall. It felt as if it cordoned off his heart as well as the horizon.

"Buy us a drink, luv?"

Startled, he turned in the direction of the voice and spied two women-of-the-night plying their trade along the wharf. Their girlish laughter was a welcome interruption.

"Not this evening, ladies," he declined, with a slight bow and a grin. "But thank you for the...generous offer." The last he added in response to the visual enticement the two well-endowed females boldly flashed in his direction.

With a snort of amusement, he watched their hips as the women sashayed down the cobbled street. Even if he was not inclined to book passage, he appreciated a well-outfitted ship. At present, the creation of his transport line was his only passion. He had no time for attachments, or even simple diversions. At least that's what he told himself.

Besides, it was safer to love a ship than a woman. You could depend on a ship. She wouldn't surprise you when least expected. You could be her master and trust her to be there when you needed her. All a ship demanded in return was your respect, and for you to know her limitations. Women were like the sea, unpredictable and hard to fathom. And even loving the good ones came at too high a price—when they were no longer there.

Hands clasped behind his back, legs braced wide, he fought the haunting thoughts of days-gone-by.

Tomorrow he would begin his new life, the culmination of many months of hard work, his last hope for salvation. His chance to escape the downward spiral into which his life had been heading. Now he had a reason for getting up in the morning—a purpose other than seeking forgetfulness. All the more reason there must not be one misstep.

In truth, everything had gone like clockwork. He admired and respected Philip St.Christopher, his new business partner recently arrived from England. Earlier this evening, along with Philip's wife, Ophelia, they had enjoyed a pleasant and leisurely dinner. The legal documents for the shipping line, signed and sealed, left only the ceremonial papers needing attention in the morning. There was nothing to worry about.

Besides, under no circumstances could he cancel tomorrow's proceedings. It would be monstrously unfair to his crew and all the people instrumental in this undertaking. They deserved a celebration before the *Alicia Elaine* took to the open sea on her maiden voyage. He could hardly justify ruining the dockside party and scheduled gaiety because of an attack of nerves. He needed to put these thoughts to bed, as well as himself.

With the warmth of a lover's caress, his glance slid over the sleek clipper ship. From keel to masthead, he'd watched her grow, watched her come alive.

"You're a proud free-spirited lady," he declared. "Unquestionable strength, tamed by grace and beauty."

He'd named his first ship after his mother. She had possessed similar qualities. So had his wife. Too bad neither had lived to see this day. Too bad neither would be at his side tomorrow to share in his achievement.

****

Twickenham, England, that same night

The scream that awakened Trelayne St.Christopher turned out to be her own.

Hair damp, nightrail twisted and clinging, she bolted upright in bed and gulped in great breaths of cold night air. The images, so vivid in her mind, were gruesome portraits of her mother and father. They were bloodied and injured, unable to move or talk, they were dying.

Shivering with fright as well as the cold, she gripped the covers, and drew them up to her chin. Her gaze darted from corner to corner of the dark room. It was all in her mind, not real. At least not yet.

"Trelayne, dear child, you've had another one of those beastly dreams."

Aunt Abigail entered the room, hurried across the floor, and sat on the edge of the bed. The flickering light from the candle she carried sent haunting shadows looming obliquely across the walls. The effect did nothing to calm Trelayne's nerves

"I'm all right, truly I am," she lied, as Aunt Abigail set the candleholder aside. Then, like a mere child rather than a grown woman, she sought the refuge of her aunt's embrace.

"If only your parents were here," the older woman fussed. "They would know what to do."

At the mention of her parents, she shuddered. *It was only a dream. A horrid wicked dream.* Maybe this one wouldn't come true.

"Darling, you're shaking like the last leaf of winter. What is it? Describe the vision. Perhaps it will help."

"No," she all but shouted.

4

To speak of the nightmare might give it life, setting it free into the night. Although in her heart, she feared nothing could truly stop its course. As a child, prophetic dreams had occasionally come her way, but they were happy illusions, portents of when people were coming to visit, or helpful information to aid someone in finding a lost object. Then during adolescence, the dreams had stopped. Now, since the advent of womanhood, they had come back, and not pleasantly so. Usually the people involved in her dreams were strangers, and she had no way of knowing if what she saw came to pass. But this was different—this time it involved her mother and father.

"Dear, dear child," the older woman crooned, rocking Trelayne to and fro. "Isn't there anything I can do? With your parents in America, and your brother Branwell jagging off to India, the family is scattered hither and yon. And you're stuck here with me, your old Aunt Abigail."

"You're not old," Trelayne defended, easing back in her aunt's arms. "And I'm not stuck, I'm unfettered. You're much more lenient than Momma and Poppa."

Ten years ago, when her older sister died of typhoid fever, her parents not only suffered most grievously, they also instituted desperate measures to ensure she did not follow suit. No outings in inclement weather for fear of pneumonia. Visits to town only for necessities and fittings. Small soirées to be attended only if the known participants were in apparent good health. At times, it was quite stifling.

In turn, most of the year, the family stayed at Royston Hall—breathing fresh air and eating a plethora of vegetables. And while her education, acquired via thoroughly scrutinized tutors, was extensive, she felt wrapped in metaphoric batting. Being insulated from the ugliness and hardships of the world was not the worst circumstance to be endured, but it eliminated the exciting adventurous parts—like the things she read about in books. Having Aunt Abigail stretch the rules on occasion was a boon to her existence

She eased her grip on the counterpane. "This past month has been wonderful," she insisted, as the wild thumping of her heart began to slow. "Our overnight stay at Amberley was especially enjoyable—exploring the ruins, stargazing at night, reading Byron by the light of the moon. And my mind is soaring with your suggestions for restoring the medieval dwelling." How she loved the old fortress left to her by her grandfather.

Aunt Abigail smiled, her expression enlivened by faraway memories. "As children," she reminisced, "your mother and I had splendid times there. It was more primitive of course, no modernized kitchen like there is now, and hardly any furnishings. But we loved living the gypsy life, not a care in the world as we dreamed of knights in shining armor and perfected our renditions of Shakespeare grandly performed for your grandfather."

"We should go back again soon," Trelayne suggested. "I shall take my charcoals and make sketches. And we'll bring more food and stay longer."

She must keep busy, be too exhausted to dream. If only she could stay up all night and not risk dreaming at all.

"It sounds like a good plan," Aunt Abigail agreed. "In hopeful preparation we can procure supplies tomorrow while we're in town for the lecture on the cause. Your mother will be green with envy for having missed the meeting."

Her mother was fine. She would be home soon. It was just a silly dream.

"At least," her aunt teased, "your father will be spared another bout of apoplexy generated by our support of scandalous activities. And heaven help us should the Queen hear of such wicked goings on."

"It would be the horrors," Trelayne agreed, making an effort to play along. "I find it curious Her Majesty never doubts her own ability to rule the greatest empire in the world, yet she accuses women who express liberated views of being feebleminded and maddish."

Aunt Abigail turned thoughtful. "Perhaps in order to govern a world dominated by men, the Queen need think like one. But lest we be dismissed as hysterical females, calm and decorum shall remain our watch-words. And," her aunt stressed with surprising firmness, "you must never confuse open minded with empty headed. I near had apoplexy myself when Merrick recounted how you'd wandered off near St. Giles in an effort to assist some crying little beggar-boy find his way home."

"Merrick wouldn't have let anything happen to me."

"Nonsense. You know better. He is a faithful family friend and employee—not a hired bodyguard. And he's getting old to boot. There are ruffians about the city, men who could lay him low in an instant, leaving you defenseless in a part of town where people disappear on a regular basis."

"But the little pip needed help. It's impossible to turn a blind eye to the suffering running rampant in the streets."

"I know, dear. But there are better approaches to addressing the problem. Openly crusading can be a bloody business—and a lonely one. I'll not see you end up like me, a spinster gone to the shelf. I spent far too much time gallivanting around the world fighting for one cause after another, all the while battling the will of society."

Trelayne hugged her aunt. "To be just like you would be a marvelous thing," she said and meant it. Her aunt was one of the most unconventional and interesting women she knew. But she must agree. Being a spinster was not what she divined for her own future. She dreamed of a dashing hero of a husband and a gaggle of children.

Intent upon straightening the bed coverings, Aunt Abigail stood and grasped the quilt. As she gave a good tug, several books tumbled from the downy softness onto the floor.

"Good heavens," she laughed. "No wonder you do not rest properly, your bed is full of Newgate novels."

Trelayne grabbed at the treasure-trove of books remaining on the bed. "They aren't crime fiction," she defended, "they're literature. See, I have Milton's *Paradise Lost,* and *Ivanhoe,* and *The Lady of Shallot.*" The poor Lady of Shallot, watching the world pass by in the reflection of a mirror. At times, she felt the same.

"And what is the one you are hiding behind your back?" her aunt insisted. "Hand it over, please."

Reluctantly, she offered up the forbidden material.

"Mercy me." Her aunt's voice rose an octave. "It's *Vanity Fair.* Wherever did you come by this…this…questionable publication?"

"You know my dear friend, Penelope?"

"Yes, a lovely well mannered girl. Go on."

"Well, you see, her brother is at Oxford now and he comes across the most intriguing material at school. And at home, Vauxhall provides pamphlets and tomes even more notorious. When he's not looking, Penelope appropriates the best ones for us."

"Penelope knows no bounds," Aunt Abigail said, with a raised brow. "One would think the works of Elizabeth Barrett Browning more edifying. It's a travesty she was passed over for Poet Laureate in favor of Tennyson."

Flipping through *Vanity Fair*, a mischievous smile reclaimed her aunt's lips. "As your guardian, I feel it my duty to peruse this one personally. I hear it does not end satisfactorily. At your age, you should only read stories with 'happily-ever-after' conclusions. The real world will soon enough strain your belief in such possibilities."

The real world. It seemed an obscure destination, a place she might never reach. Another London season was slipping away posthaste, and they had only stayed one week at Father's London flat. Life was passing her by at a dizzying clip. Just the other day, Penelope stopped by to relate the details of the Queen's outdoor concert. It sounded divine, and very romantic. There had even been one of those terrifying flying balloons soaring overhead, hissing like a dragon, with people dangling precariously beneath it in a wicker basket. To attempt such a feat was beyond her daring—but what a thrill to watch. Other than Penelope, they rarely had visitors. Except, of course, for Lucien.

She glanced at the books jumbled upon the bed—

her precious windows to the world. In an effort to rescue the remainder from confiscation, she shoved the books beneath the coverlet, and changed the topic of conversation.

"I do hope Captain Garrison accompanies Mother and Father on their return trip from America." *They could be homeward bound right now, safe and sound.*

"It would be a fascination if the good Captain did grace us with a visit," her aunt agreed. "He seems a curious mixture of contradictions. Determined enough to insist your parents travel all the way to Massachusetts to sign the official papers, yet sentimental enough to insist upon naming the partnership's first vessel after his mother."

"He's an American, Auntie. From what I've heard, they view the world through a different scope. Even his name is a bit odd," she pointed out. "Captain Walker Garrison. Who would give their son two last names? "

"I suppose someone with great pride in their heritage."

That gave her pause for consideration. The colonists had no titles to bequeath, so perhaps this was the best they could do. If ever she had a son, she would carefully consider the name he must carry for the rest of his life.

She heaved a sigh. Why didn't she have dreams about the good captain, this rugged man from a wild and savage land? A rush of desire streaked through her body, and lusty contemplations tripped through her mind. The errant tingling settled between her thighs, making her squirm, making her warm despite the ambient temperature.

"Over the years, I've crossed paths with several

Americans," Aunt Abigail mused. "They are an unusual breed. Rough around the edges, but bold as brass. It's no secret they cherish their independence, and like children, they seem ever eager for escapades. They're an intrepid lot, to be sure."

"You sound as if you admire those traits," she said, shifting around in the bed.

"I do. Always have had a penchant for a man with adventure in his heart. According to your father, Captain Garrison once lived with the Red Indians and fought in the territorial wars. Can you imagine that?" Aunt Abigail waived the book she held. "Men are always off having all the fun while we women are expected to sit at home reading and awaiting their return. But we'll not be sitting around tomorrow. So close your eyes and think pleasant thoughts." She glanced out the window. "Dawn is nigh, but after your upset you should rest a few more hours. We can't have you losing weight. Being pale-cheeked is desirable, but a boney symmetry is detrimental in attracting eligible young men."

"I'm afraid to go back to sleep."

She knew the nightmare still lurked in a dark corner of her mind. Precariously held at bay, it was there, hiding in the shadows, less visible, less threatening, yet waiting to rear its ugly head.

Aunt Abigail smoothed Trelayne's tangle of hair back from her brow. "Don't be afraid, darling. I shall sit sentinel at your side, and forbid Morpheus to allow any troubling elements to enter your sphere again tonight. And," she added brightly, "tomorrow after the lecture and shopping, we shall stop by Professor Fowler's. Perhaps he has returned from traveling abroad. An in-depth phrenology session could shed some light on these dreams of yours."

Her aunt took to a nearby chair, and began reading Thackeray's dark portrayal of human nature. Trelayne mentally tiptoed toward sleep, lamenting she did not have nice dreams, or erotic fantasies. Either she suffered some twisted wretched imagining, or no dreams at all.

Eyes closed, but far from sleepy, she conjured naughty images of Captain Garrison—a most welcome and enjoyable distraction. Would she ever feel the touch of a lover's hand? With all her heart she wished to be swept away by raw, overpowering, unstoppable passion—emotions like she read about in her purloined novels.

Lusty fantasies soon flooded her mind, blocking out everything else. Snuggling deeper into the downy mattress, a smile upon her lips, she wondered who danced through Captain Garrison's dreams.

Chapter Two

So far, it proved to be a glorious morning, the kind that made a man feel good to be alive.

Striding dockside, Walker drank in the heady smell of autumn mingled with the brisk sea air. Then misgivings from the night before struck home, worrying his soul and cutting short his innocent interlude.

Ignoring the disquiet, he moved on, tugging at the stiff collar of his linen dress shirt. He reached to unbutton the restrictive waistcoat then recalled the reason he had chosen such elaborate attire. Hand clenched, he lowered his arm to his side. Homespun fashion was more to his liking, but today he'd foregone comfort and practicality for style. His business partner, Philip, always looked so damnably dapper—it made him feel like a backwoodsman. Not something to be ashamed of, just an observation.

He slowed to a halt, and the warmth of the morning sun muscled aside his nagging pessimism and penchant for letting the past rule his future. Today, the *Alicia Elaine* seemed in high enough spirits. Her brilliant white sails snapped smartly in the mild breeze, and her brass gleamed and sparkled like jewels at the neck of a princess.

Calm reflection eased his concerns until the creaking of wood and hemp caught his attention. Like a bad omen, a shadow passed overhead. He glanced up and sidestepped out of the way. A cargo crate, suspended by one fragile rope, swayed alarmingly above the dock. Where the hell had that come from?

"Seaman," he barked to a man onboard ship. "Report dockside and secure that crate. And find out who was fool enough to put it there in the first place."

"Aye, Captain," the man saluted. "I'm on it, sir."

That damnable sense of foreboding gripped him again. Jaw tight with dismay he studied the skyline. In typical New England fashion, the weather was taking a turn. A squall was mounting a determined attack, heralded by a northerly wind blowing to portside. They were in for another blow.

Out maneuvered, the morning sun retreated behind a wall of fuming black clouds, and without its warmth, the air turned damp and discontented. Soon, an ethereal mist coated the lines and every strip of gleaming brass upon the ship. The crew and their families, gathering for the promised celebration, seemed unaware of the climatic change. They laughed and slapped one another on the back, but the *Alicia Elaine* took note and began to gently heave against the waves.

Too late to change course now… Mustering a cheerfulness born of necessity, he turned to greet Phillip and Ophelia.

"Good morning. I feared our weather might deter you, Mrs. St.Christopher." Concerned for her safety, he wished it had. His heart rate picked up speed as he listened to her reply.

"On such a grand day as this," she declared, slipping one hand into the crook of her husband's elbow, "'twould take more than a bit of blustering breeze to keep me from my Phillip's side."

As if to challenge her courage, a gust of wind battled Ophelia for possession of her bonnet. It took liberties with her cloak and skirts as well, but with a smile and good grace, she managed a victory in each instance. She appeared determined to tough it out with the men, and after meeting her last evening, he hadn't expected less. Heads down, they huddled together.

"I suggest we expedite the christening with all haste," Walker shouted, to make himself heard above the crowd and the inclement weather. "We can dispense with the ceremonial documents until another time."

"Splendid idea," Phillip agreed.

Allowing the St.Christophers the honor, he handed them the magnum of champagne. As they traversed the dock toward the prow of the ship, Walker was waylaid by a young child.

"Captain, Captain," the lad sang out, grabbing his coat sleeve and impeding his progress. "You be needin' any more cabin boys on this voyage? I got experience."

The boy didn't look old enough to have experienced his eighth birthday. "Not this time, son. But I'll keep you in mind for the future. I can see you'll make a fine sailor one day."

The child beamed with pride. Walker tousled the boy's hair then followed the St.Christophers. They were already in place. The bottle broke over the hull, and a great cheer rose from those gathered around. Caught up in the moment, Walker halted mid-stride, adding his whoop and holler to that of the crowd. Head back in jubilation, his expression froze, and the sound of joy choked off in his throat. His order hadn't been obeyed.

As if in slow motion, the crate tumbled downward. Bystanders screamed in horror. He lunged forward to push his friends from the path of the deadly freight. They were too far away. Aware of their plight, fear contorted their faces. They clutched at one another, and in a heroic effort, Phillip shielded Ophelia from the huge object as it crashed to the ground.

The cargo container smashed onto the dock, burst open, and spewed its contents in all directions. Thank providence it wasn't a direct hit, yet the couple was trapped beneath slabs and heaps of splintered wood.

"Send for a doctor," Walker shouted.

He pushed past panic-stricken people, ignoring the blur of comments about it being too late to save anyone caught beneath the mountain of rubble. With his bare hands he ripped and tore at the debris. Soon, others came to their senses and rushed forward. Employing a board and a barrel, they levered the accumulated weight off the pair. Their twisted bodies lay side by side, their hands still clasped together. Life barely flickered in either one of them. The unsigned ceremonial documents blew forlornly across the dock and into the sea.

In bizarre contrast to the grisly scene, flowers lay gaily strewn about. The murderous crate, bound for Queen Victoria's private garden, had contained a quarter ton of Vermont rose plants, all in full bloom, their pearly white petals spattered with blood. As if they were to blame, he crushed a pile underfoot and kicked them aside. How the hell could this have happened? Kneeling beside the couple's unmoving forms, he blocked the wind blowing with cruel disregard for circumstance.

"Give me your coats," he snarled, at the bystanders, rage replacing shock. "And find Seaman Barkley," he added, catching the eye of one of his men.

He covered Ophelia's trembling body with the cloaks and jackets tossed in his direction. A dark-suited man carrying a reticule made his way through the crowd and crouched down at his side.

"They might live," he declared, with rather feeble enthusiasm as he finished his initial examination. "Bad luck them being struck down like that," he observed, binding their most grievous wounds in preparation for transport to hospital.

"Luck had nothing to do with it," Walker growled.

Why had Seaman Barkley ignored his order to remove and secure the crate? He damn well better have a good excuse for not following orders. As his anger flared anew, a saber of guilt slashed through him as well. He should have taken it upon himself to make sure the crate was properly off-loaded.

The doctor gained his feet and motioned for the stretcher-bearers now on the scene. "I'll know more regarding their condition once I've check them over thoroughly."

"Thank you for coming," Walker acknowledged. "However, I wish my friends to go to the New Hope clinic, not New Bedford General. I would be grateful if you would accompany them in transit. When you arrive, ask for a Dr. Nathan Robinson. Tell him Walker Garrison sent you. He'll take over from there."

Discharged so quickly, the doctor appeared miffed, frowning he held his ground. Walker pressed two silver dollars into the man's hand.

"If this doesn't compensate for your expenses," he reassured, "prepare a statement, and I'll see you are paid in full."

With a nod, and a more cooperative expression, the

physician left with his patients.
$$****$$

The police inspector glanced around the dock. "Well, Captain Garrison, I must agree it appears to have been an intentional act. Most likely this missing seaman of yours was involved. Been having troubles with him? Seems odd him suddenly disappearing."

Walker shook his head. "I can't believe he would be party to anything of this magnitude. He's been with me for nearly two years. A fine dependable man, married with four children. It just doesn't figure."

"And you've no reason to think anyone would want to hurt you, or stymie your business."

"No," he answered, without consideration. Then he recalled the boy who had interrupted him during the ceremony. If not for the lad, he would have been standing directly beneath the falling cargo crate. Perhaps he was the intended target, the St.Christophers only unfortunate bystanders.

While the inspector busied himself elsewhere, Walker studied the neatly severed rope attached to the overhead beam. Unnoticed, some sonofabitch had stood right here and sliced it through, nice as you please. And that tiny action had changed several lives forever—including his own.

A discoloration on the rough hemp caught his attention. It resembled tar or resin. He touched the pliable matter, rubbed it between thumb and forefinger, then gingerly sniffed it. He even went so far as to taste it. Chocolate, by heaven, how curious.

He searched the ground, his gaze following the direction of the wind. Several shiny objects had blown into a crevice in the planking. He retrieved the small misshapen foil balls and uncurled one. The inside was coated with the same brown candy smeared on the rope. The outside read; *Chocolates and Confections by Fry and Son, Bristol, England, Established 1847.* His missing crewman didn't have the money or the nature to be eating imported bon-bons. Someone with connections to England had staged this murderous act.

"Inspector," he called, secreting away the chocolate wrappers. "I think we should encourage the notion the St.Christophers are dead. After all, if someone wanted them out of the way, it seems safest to let that someone think he has succeeded." He watched the wily little man mull over the idea.

"You might have something there, Captain," he agreed. "But I don't think the department can take the responsibility of feeding lies to the general public. We can't encourage theatrics when it comes to police business."

"Could you at least see your way clear to being noncommittal for a few days?" he bargained. "Perhaps if I were to release you from involvement and declare the occurrence an accident, you could turn a blind eye. It might make a difference as to the safety of my friends. Surely you can see that."

Generally speaking, lies and subterfuge went against the grain, but it would buy needed time, and give them breathing room before he left for England.

"May I remind you," he added, at the inspector's hesitation, "the St.Christophers are foreigners. An international incident would be most unhelpful in your bid for becoming Mayor."

Speculation shadowed the man's expression, and he fidgeted with the buttons on his frock coat. "I'll go along with your scheme," he conceded, "but the resolution of this matter rests with you now. Good day to you then. And good luck." Quick as a ferret, he scurried away.

Hands in his pockets, Walker glanced around uneasily. He was on his own—with hardly a clue as to where to start.

Chapter Three

At six a.m. on the second morning following the incident, Walker made his way to the clinic. This was his last chance before he took his leave to rouse Phillip from his coma. Loaded to the gills, the *Alicia Elaine* would cast off in two hours. As captain, he had no choice but to be onboard.

The diagnosis for both patients was a spontaneous return to consciousness with periodic relapses. And although this had yet to happen, he trusted Dr. Robinson completely. Nathanial was highly intelligent, had a good sense of humor, and never cheated at chess. In fact, Walker trusted Nate so completely, he'd dared to inform him of the details surrounding the situation.

Nodding to one of the guards hired to watch over the St.Christophers, Walker entered Phillip's room, strode to the bedside, and stared down at his partner.

"Can you hear me?" he asked, for what seemed the hundredth time. Breaking through the silent barrier separating him from his friend was paramount. "Damn it, man, wake up. Your very life may depend on it."

Downhearted, he paced the room, raking his fingers through his hair. *Come on, Phillip,* he silently prayed, *at least grant me some sign you're on the mend before I leave.* About to give up, he turned toward the door.

"Ophelia," Phillip croaked, his parched lips barely

moving. "How is my Ophelia?"

Surprised and relieved, Walker hurried to the bedside. "She's unconscious, but will recover. You were both nearly killed," he bluntly added. "Your injuries were not caused by accident, Phillip."

Having found Seaman Barkley's body stuffed in a trunk, the man was no longer a suspect, and murderous intentions were no longer in question.

"Do you understand what I'm telling you, Phillip? Have you any idea who would want to harm you, or destroy our partnership?"

For a moment, it seemed Phillip had slipped back into unconsciousness. Walker snatched up a damp towel, and wiped the man's face.

"Don't know who or why," his partner gritted, between raspy breaths. "You must go to Trelayne. Whatever it takes, you must keep my daughter safe. Trelayne is all that matters. Promise me." With a burst of strength apparently fueled by profound concern, Phillip grabbed the front of Walker's shirt. "No matter what it takes."

"I promise I'll protect her," Walker vowed, "if need be, with my life."

Phillip's grip went slack. He was unresponsive again, and no amount of encouragement brought him back to the conscious world. As Walker hurriedly took his leave, he nearly crashed into Dr. Robinson.

"Nate, Mr. St.Christopher was momentarily awake. That's a good sign, right?"

"An excellent indication," his friend agreed. "But I'm afraid the cat's out of the bag regarding their condition. It's common knowledge they both survived. One of the girls who works—or I should say worked—

in the kitchen spilled the beans. I let her go last evening when I found out what she'd done. Confounded silly female. She sneaked up here and was caught reading Ophelia's chart. Apparently she was swayed by some fellow doling out English chocolates."

"Chocolates? Where is the girl? May I speak with her?"

"Already packed up and gone I'm afraid."

"That's a bit of bad luck."

The person with the candy was likely the same person who had been on the wharf. He slipped his hand into his pocket and touched the wrappers nestled inside. He carried the tiny foils now as if they were his worry stone.

"Sorry," Nate apologized. "Is it important? We could try to track her down, but I believe she told one of the other girls she was catching the early train to Boston, and it's already departed. 'Had enough of this smelly whaling port,' she said. All around grating personality. Don't know how she got hired in the first place."

"No time now to worry over the girl, Nate," Walker said. "Hopefully, the St.Christophers will be up and about soon for all to see, so we couldn't have kept up the pretense much longer." He headed for the main entrance. "I appreciate all you're doing for them," he added, over his shoulder.

"Keep in touch," Nate called back. "And keep safe. You're the only one around these parts worth a darn at playing chess."

****

With no time to spare, Walker boarded the *Alicia Elaine*. Guilt booked passage at his side. Why hadn't he personally secured that crate? The injury to his friends, and Seaman Barkley's death, had occurred on his watch. He was responsible for them, just like he was responsible for his ship, crew, and cargo when at sea.

Only a twist of Fate had saved him from ending up like them. That was a sobering thought. As they came about and headed for open water, he grazed his finger across his chest, seeking the comforting feel of the St. Brendan medal tucked beneath his shirt. Giving thanks for keeping him safe in the past, he offered his gratitude to the saint then prayed for an uneventful and swift crossing. Like most sailors, there was a little superstition mixed with his commonsense—good luck and spiritual intervention were always welcome.

Tired and worried, he scrubbed one hand across his face then leaned stiff-armed against the starboard rail. It had been a less than auspicious beginning for his new venture. But concern over the reputation of his ship and the transport company must be put on hold. His most vital mission was honoring his promise to protect the St.Christophers' daughter. That and making sure the lowlife responsible for this nasty business paid in full.

****

Royston Hall, Twickenham, near London

Although not breaking any record, the clipper ship made good time, giving Walker nineteen days to formulate what he wanted to say to Philip's daughter. It seemed a lifetime, and yet not long enough, and now as he stood before the pillared entryway to his partner's country estate, he hesitated, unsure of his next step.

He was treading unknown territory—literally and figuratively. Whom could he trust in this foreign country, who might still have murder in mind? Relying on instinct seemed the best idea. One thing he knew for sure, delivering this heart-wrenching news to a delicate young woman wasn't going to be easy. Again, responsibility for what happened weighed heavily.

How old was she? He tried to recall his conversation with Ophelia from the night before the disastrous ceremony. Full-grown had been the impression he'd gotten. He remembered thinking it odd their daughter seemed a bit past the usual age for a society marriage. Perhaps she had not inherited her mother's striking good looks, or her father's quick mind. He prayed she had at least inherited their strong constitutions.

Employing the doorknocker, he waited for a response. About to try again, the door swung open revealing a rosy-cheeked, smiling maid.

"The Mister and Missus ain't home at present, sir. But if you be so inclined you're welcome to leave a card or message."

"I've come to call on Miss Trelayne St.Christopher," he explained.

The girl's eyes widened in surprise, and a blush deepened her milkmaid complexion. "Step in, sir. Who may I say is calling?"

"Captain Walker Garrison, from America."

"America?" The girl appeared confused.

He smiled at her reaction. "Yes. New Bedford, Massachusetts to be exact."

Her gaze traveled down to his boots then back up to the top of his head. He felt like a new species on Darwin's list of most recent discoveries. "As soon as possible would be appreciated," he prompted.

Her blush deepened. "Yes, sir. I'm beggin' your pardon, sir. I'll inform Miss Trelayne you're here." With that she scurried off, leaving him to stand in the foyer.

It was an impressive hall, attached to an impressive house, yet the feeling of down-home comfort and welcome was also present. With any luck, Phillip and Ophelia would soon be recovered and returning to their residence.

The maid returned and ushered him along. "This way, sir."

He kept possession of his coat and hat, and followed the girl to a dayroom.

Light flooded through the east windows, relieving the otherwise dim atmosphere of wood paneling, heavy-legged furniture, and Persian rugs. But the true brightness in the room was the young woman sitting demurely by the hearth, her attention directed toward the needlepoint frame upon which she worked. With a sideways peek, she noted his entrance, but for some reason did not deem to fully recognize his presence.

As he waited, he utilized the opportunity to study the delightful image she evoked. Her dress of pale yellow muslin, worn off the shoulder, revealed smooth ivory skin. And her hair—arranged loose and flowing—glowed with a reddish-brown hue implying warmth would be intermingled with the promise of softness. She sat straight, her tapered fingers nimbly going about the business of creating some masterpiece. The urge to draw closer, to lean over her tempting shoulder and slender neck, to drink in her fragrance, and examine that upon which she work so diligently, was a tangible ache in his chest.

"Captain Garrison, what an unexpected pleasure."

The voice jolted him from his reverie and he turned in surprise. Having been enthralled by the young woman, he hadn't notice the diminutive lady who also occupied the room.

"I'm Abigail Royston, Ophelia's sister." The woman stepped forward, taking his coat, indicating his presence was welcome. "And this is Trelayne.

The girl stood and turned in his direction. Of medium height, she appeared somewhat fragile, but her gaze was steady and intelligent, and her hazel eyes seemed to warm at the prospect of seeing her parents.

With a demeanor more bold than retiring, she reflected the strength Ophelia had shown. As if by rote, she reached up and touched the heart pendant hanging from a fine golden chain. Her mother had worn a similar piece. He had a desire to mimic the movement and seek the medallion he wore. Instead, he simply returned her perusal.

****

Trelayne studied the man who had fueled her daydreams over the past months. Captain Garrison was even more handsome than she had envisioned. Broad shouldered and oh so tall, he eclipsed her expectations and transcended all musings, the effect kindling unexpected physical sensations.

"It's a pleasure to meet the both of you," he said, with a fleeting smile.

His teeth flashed white in marked contrast to his tanned skin, and the crow's feet deepened at the corners of his eyes—heavenly blue eyes, tinted with enough gray to save them from childlike innocence.

"Are Phillip and Ophelia with you?" Aunt Abigail

27

asked, glancing around him toward the door to the room."

"No, I've come on ahead without them," he answered, with seeming reluctance.

When the man remained hesitant to move or speak, a spark of alarm flared inside of Trelayne. Something was amiss. Scenes from her nightmare roared through her mind, blocking out all other thought. Reaching for the arm of the settee, she eased down onto the seat, fighting to remain calm, forcing herself to breath slowly and deeply.

Without seeking permission, Captain Garrison folded himself into a nearby chair.

"Why aren't they with you?" she asked, dreading the answer.

"There's been an accident on the wharf in New Bedford," he began.

Then he told all, and Trelayne was lost to a world of disbelief.

Sympathy and sadness shown in his eyes, but nothing stemmed the heartfelt pain and fear rushing at her from all sides. Her hideous dream had come true after all. As the horror of his words clawed their way through the initial shock, the distinct possibility of fainting dead away seemed imminent. Overpowering darkness engulfed her, and even the sunlight streaming in offered no comfort. Rather than gaining warmth from the light, she felt as if she were melting into oblivion. Aunt Abigail slipped an arm across her shoulders, and they leaned against one another.

She swallowed hard, wanting only to run screaming to her room. But this was no time for panic or female swooning. She recalled the day her brother had fallen off the postern gate. Branwell had broken his leg in the worst way. Mother had paled for a moment, staunched the bleeding, tied pillows around his leg, and rode with him in the back of the supply wagon all the way to the town surgeon. That was the kind of courage needed now.

She gained her feet. "I must go to them," she announced, hands clenched in determination, "immediately."

Captain Garrison leapt from his chair, his taller stature especially apparent as he stood before her. "You most certainly will not," he ordered

"But they are alone in a strange country. They need me. Don't you see?"

"They are under the care of an extremely worthy physician, one I would trust with my own life. And what they need most, Miss Trelayne, is to know you are safe."

He grasped her upper arms, and gently urged her back down upon the settee.

"During your father's one lucid moment, he bade me promise to do whatever it took to keep you safe. I'll not break that promise, which means I'll not allow you to go running off to America. I have left instructions to establish ongoing communications. Every seven days, one of my crew will book passage to London carrying written information from the doctor, and hopefully from your parents. Soon we shall have weekly updates regarding their condition and anything discovered regarding the incident. By return ship, we can send them your personal notes and the confirmation of your safety."

She supposed that sounded logical, but knowing

they were suffering and so far away was pure torture. Good Lord, what if they grew worse, what if they died? And how could she take this man at his word, or trust the arrangements he'd made when he'd allow her parents to be in injured in the first place?

"Dr. Robson assures me they will recover," he prompted, "but it will be a lengthy process. He's a good man, well educated and forward thinking. I've also hired around-the-clock bodyguards to watch over them."

"Bodyguards." Her anxiety doubled. Seeking comfort and support, she grabbed the embroidered pillow at her side and crushed it to her chest. "You believe this to be necessary?"

"Until matters are sorted out, I must insist."

"Thank you, Captain Garrison," Aunt Abigail put in. "Under the circumstances, you seem to have done all we could hope for."

She wanted to agree, knew she should agree, should thank him for his efforts, but anger and fear overrode good manners. She was back on her feet, pillow in hand. "How could this have happened?" The words were out of her mouth before she could stop them, and to her own astonishment, she threw the embroidered cushion at him.

The Captain dodged the harmless missile then appeared crestfallen, but he held his ground and her gaze. "I shall never forgive myself for not ensuring their safety," he acknowledged.

"For heaven's sake, Trelayne." Surprise was evident in Aunt Abigail's voice as she rose to stand at her side. "The man is not a clairvoyant. No one could have foreseen such a turn of events."

Now it was her turn to feel guilty. She had known there would be a catastrophe. Was Captain Garrison any more at fault than she? Anger and fear twisted together in a knot in her chest, threatening to stop her breathing. Perhaps all the resentment was for her own inability to stop what had happened, not for him.

He studied her for a moment, genuine sadness tempering his expression. Then with surprising quickness and determination, he collected his hat and coat. "May I please speak with whoever is in charge of matters during Phillip's absence?" he requested.

"Yes, of course, Captain Garrison," Aunt Abigail replied. "That would be Merrick. I'll notify him at once."

"Thank you," he said. "And please, call me Walker. Unless protocol dictates otherwise, I should think using our Christian names might be allowed. I've a feeling we shall be spending a great deal of time together."

His words imparted a feeling of comfort as well as a shiver of anticipation, adding confusion to the list of emotions running rampant through Trelayne's mind.

****

Leaving the women to their privacy, Walker opted to wait for Merrick in the immaculate white kitchen. Sitting now at the long wooden table, he watched Cook knead bread dough, a previous batch was baking in the oven. It smelled good, it smelled safe—it made it difficult to believe what had transpired back home was real.

Thank goodness, their first meeting was behind them. He thought it had gone fairly well. They had taken the news with minimal hysterics and no fainting.

And while Miss Trelayne's anger and mistrust were not unexpected, nor misplaced, she seemed of a sound mind and disposition. She was also beautiful, even more so than Ophelia, and again he wondered why she wasn't married.

He smiled, remembering the pillow she chucked his way. She had a bit of pluck and temper. Qualities he appreciated in a woman, not that it should matter. And where were these thoughts coming from anyway? Watching Trelayne as she embroidered, and being near her, had reawakened raw emotions deeply hidden since Katie's passing. The resurrection of these feelings put him off balance. Not a good position to be in. He needed to get a grip. Clenching one fist, he rested it upon the table. He wasn't here to make friends or instigate romantic liaisons—especially not with Phillip's daughter.

"I'm Merrick Hawkins," the man entering the room announced. "I was told you wished to speak with me."

Walker rose and offered the older man his hand. "Yes, thank you. I'm Captain Garrison, Walker if you please. They explained to you what happened to Phillip and Ophelia?"

"Aye, they told me." Although the older man's face was a map of wrinkles, his eyes were sharp, and his handshake firm. "Dreadful business. What can I do to help?"

"Is there somewhere we might speak more comfortably?" he suggested, lowering his arm to his side.

"Certainly. My quarters are this way."

Merrick led the way through a door, down a hall, and into a secluded section of the east wing of the house. "This is my wife, Wynona," he introduced, as they entered a small yet comfortable sitting room.

"Have you eaten, lad?" Merrick asked.

Walker shook his head. He'd come directly from the ship to the estate, the fullness of his concern outweighing the emptiness of his belly.

"Fix Captain Garrison a plate, please, Wynona."

"Of course, dear. Right away." The kindly woman smiled, and hurried off toward the kitchen they had just vacated.

"Will they be all right?" Merrick asked. There was true apprehension in the man's eyes, the kind of concern one held for friends, not just for one's employers.

"Yes. But only by the grace of God. Have you been with the St.Christopher's long?"

"Grew up with Master Phillip. My father worked for his father. When we were young, we got into some fine troubles," he added, with a chuckle.

Walker smiled in understanding. "Regardless of the fact that they are far away, Merrick, you're the man he needs to watch his back. And you're the man I need to help keep Trelayne safe as we figure out why this happened. Can you think of anyone who would want to cause harm to them or the company?"

"Not as I could say. Mr. St.Christopher is kind to all his employees. From me at the top," he said, with pride but not vainglory, "down to the youngest footman and cabin boy. And the Missus is generous to a fault, what with them bazaars for the needy and all those church socials. The only one with his aristocratic nose out of joint lately is Mr. Lucien."

"Who's that?"

"Lucien Lanteen. Mr. Phillip's solicitor. For some reason he was against the partnership. And he's got designs on Miss Trelayne, if you know what I mean. But overly protected though she is, the lass is also of an independent mind, and nobody's fool. Leads him a merry chase, but ain't ready to be caught."

It should not matter to him who Trelayne favored, or with whom she kept company, but Merrick's revelation regarding her nature pleased him. The idea this solicitor was interested in her, did not.

"Tell me more about Mr. Lanteen."

"Ain't much to tell. He's a bit of a loner. Been Master Philip's legal council for some time now, and he oversees the books. He ain't a bad sort that I know of, just a tad wild like so many young folk now days. Likes the ponies and a bit of elbow shaking. Plays the dice," he added for clarification. "Joins in anything he thinks might make him look a station or two above his calling."

"And you don't believe he would be involved with anything as underhanded as this?"

"Well, he's a bit of a scoundrel, to be sure. And there ain't no telling what he gets up to when he's not here mooning over Miss Trelayne. But I have no evidence he harbors a cruel streak necessary to do what you described. And I seen him around here within the last week, so it hardly seems likely he was over on your shores at the time of the incident."

Merrick's wife returned with a tantalizing plate of roast beef and gravy, browned potatoes, and a fresh loaf of Cook's earlier achievement.

"Thank you, ma'am," he said, as they retired to a dining area. "I can't tell you how much I needed a good home-cooked meal."

"You're welcome, Captain," Wynona sliced the bread, and poured tea for him and her husband. "Don't make yourself scarce around here," she added. "We enjoy visitors. Especially handsome ones." With that, she gave him a wink and busied herself elsewhere.

"We lost our boy in '47, in South Africa," Merrick said. "He would have been around your age, had he lived. She likes to see a young face at the table."

"I'm sorry for your loss, Merrick. It's never right that a man should bury a son."

"I'm sorry too. I don't hold with all this foreign fighting. If you ask me there's plenty rebellion here in this country needin' our attention. You ever been to war? Is that why you go by Captain?"

"My title is due strictly to the good fortune of commanding a ship," he revealed, between bites. "But yes, I've seen battle. The Mexican war, '46 to '48."

Merrick nodded his head thoughtfully, then both men fell silent. Walker cleaned his plate, and tried not to visualize in too great a detail the bloody memories stirred by their conversation. Other than being a grim training ground for life, war was a brutal useless phenomenon.

Chapter Four

The next morning, ignoring the kidney pie grumbling around in his belly, Walker left the hotel dining room. What he wouldn't give for three eggs sunny side up, a rasher of bacon, and coffee—dark as sin and strong as Atlas. Anything but this blasted tea. Some of the food here was as disagreeable as the weather.

A dirty mist hovered over the city. They needed a good thunderstorm to wash away all the grit and grime choking the breath out of London Town. At least he'd had the foresight to pack utilitarian clothes. Who cared if they marked him a "Yank" and garnered sideways glances? They were practical, which to his way of thinking counted for much.

After a few blocks, soot-infused moisture beaded on his black canvas duster, and mud spattered his knee-high boots. He gave an amused smile. A few of the English women out and about seemed nonplussed by the elements. They discreetly hiked up their skirts and tiptoed through the worst of it. You had to give them credit for that.

Following the directions given by the hotel clerk, he arrived at J. S. Fry & Sons just as the storefront shutters opened to patrons. Several people were already waiting for custom—chocolate was evidently in high demand here. As he waited his turn, he retrieved one of the precious candy wrappers, and flattened it as much as possible.

"You're up next, sir," announced the young man behind the counter. "What might we offer you today?"

"I'm interested in this particular item," he said, handing over the foil.

"A most excellent choice sir." There was surprise in the lad's voice as he studied Walker more closely. "This particular lot came from our Bristol establishment, although we do have a limited supply available here as well."

"I take it you don't sell many of them."

"They *are* top of the line. And being a favorite with the Royal Family, quite expensive as it were"

"Who besides the Queen has a taste for them?" he probed.

"William Clarke always buys a box for his All-England Eleven when they win."

"When they win what?" He'd never heard of the man or the group.

"When they win the match."

"Boxing match?"

"Heavens no, sir. They're high-class cricketers."

Of course, cricket. The New York City newspaper frequently touted the St. George's Cricket Club. "Who else?" he encouraged, doubting this group had any interest in his shipping line.

"Well, there's the Ladies Temperance Organization. They may be against the drink, but they do love their sweets. And lately one of our rather frequent customers is a Mr. Lanteen. I don't believe he buys them for himself, the gentleman is trim as fashion demands." The young man fell silent as if realizing he may have slipped beyond sales-pitch to gossiping.

Mr. Lanteen. This was getting interesting. Figuring no further information would be forth coming, he eased up on the questioning. "Sounds like esteemed company. I'd like to purchase a small box if you please."

He planned to give them to Miss St.Christopher. The feeling he had much for which to atone regarding the condition of her parents still bothered him. And although a rather meager start, the chocolates would show his personal interest in her comfort. Was Lanteen also plying Trelayne with sweets on a regular basis? That put a bit of tarnish on the uniqueness of the gift.

"Thank you, sir. That will be Ł10."

Ten pounds...He quickly worked out the monetary conversion in his head. Good Lord. That was nearly a month's wage for a sailor.

"The papers are made with gold-leaf," the clerk added, at his hesitation.

"Well, that makes all the difference then," Walker said, working to keep the sarcasm from his voice. He handed over the coinage, took the small decorative box, and slipped it into his pocket. Personally, he'd rather have a piece of blueberry pie.

****

"Lucien, what a surprise. Had we an engagement I've overlooked?"

Trelayne rose to meet her ardent suitor. What, she wondered, would be his excuse for showing up unannounced this time?

"No, darling, we made no arrangements. I was overcome by the most curious sensation straight from out of the blue, and I thought you were in some sort of trouble. So I set out immediately to reassure myself all was well."

This was a new twist on his usual fabrications. Now he was being inspired by communication from the ethereal realm. Yet how could she complain about his perseverance and attention? Although a bit overwhelming at times, it was flattering to be doted upon, and it wasn't as if ardent admirers were beating down the door. Mother was from old money, Father was not, and their combined fortune was far from vast. Therefore, over the years, the number of acceptable suitors had been sparse, and viable marriage proposals even more paltry.

"I'm perfectly healthy and sound, Lucien. But there is news regarding Mother and Father. News of which you must be apprised." She took a seat on the divan, and Lucien followed suit. "They've suffered a most grievous accident in America."

"Your parents? Oh, my dearest. I am sorry." He scooped up one of her hands and held it to his chest. "You're bearing up magnificently, my brave girl. Tell me everything."

"It happened in Massachusetts, during the christening of the partnership's new vessel. There was an incident on the wharf. Mother and Father are both in hospital, under the strictest care and protection. Their recovery has been assured, but apparently it will be quite some time before they are able to return home."

"And you will remain here rather than making for America?"

"Yes. Since we do not know if it was a true accident or a malicious act, Captain Garrison felt it more prudent for me to remain in England."

Dropping her hand as if it had sprouted warts,

Lucien sprang to his feet. "Garrison. He was not injured?"

"No, Lucien. He's perfectly fine, and stopped by yesterday."

"He's here? This is outrageous. How dare he bother you at a time like this?"

"But he's been no bother, Lucien. He's arranged for weekly reports from the doctor and has offered to help me with the shipping business until my mother and father return."

"I'm sure he has been most helpful indeed."

The cold anger in Lucien's voice was near palpable, and the expression in his pale blue eyes did nothing to warm the atmosphere.

"Next he'll be pressuring you for money, and seeking your family name to back his enterprise. You must not sign any papers regarding the formation of the partnership concocted by him and your father."

"You are full of presumptions today, Lucien. Captain Garrison has done nothing of the sort. He has acted the gentleman in every respect."

Although there was not a reason in the world for it, unquestionably defending Walker seemed the correct thing to do. She had not forgiven him for his part in her parent's misfortune—still she couldn't bring herself to malign him in front of Lucien.

"Fortunately," she added, "all the papers were signed prior to the accident. The partnership is in full-swing."

Lucien turned pale as cream, and couldn't have appeared more stricken had she announced the permanent closure of the Ascot racetrack. He paced about like a caged animal, grinding the fist of one hand into the palm of the other.

"This is preposterous," he stormed, coming to a halt before her. "You know nothing about this man. How can you blithely trust his intentions or his ability to run your father's business? You should have consulted me before handing the reins to this…this American."

"Goodness sakes, Lucien, do calm yourself. Captain Garrison has been around ships and transport lines for a good portion of his life. I'm sure his intentions for the partnership are to see it prosper and grow. Besides, while you are fabulous at overseeing father's legal affairs, you hardly know one wit about the day-to-day running of the shipping business. I have spent more time on the docks with Poppa than have you."

What was wrong with Lucien? The only time she had seen him this distraught was following a three-day losing streak during Derby week. She should ring for tea, perhaps a cup would settle him down. She gained her feet, and was about to reach for the bell pull when the maid entered.

"You've another visitor, Miss Trelayne. 'Tis Capt. Garrison." The girl blushed like an ingénue, barely suppressing a giggle, her mannerisms a far cry from those she exhibited when announcing Lucien.

"Should I show him in?"

"Yes, of course. And Bitsy," she added, "please arrange for tea."

Heart racing, Trelayne patted at her hair and smoothed her skirts. What a frantic morning. Another unannounced visit. Had the world gone mad? Yet somehow, she didn't mind Captain Garrison's intrusion.

She glanced up. There he was, as tall as she remembered, and so commanding, his broad-shouldered visage seeming to fill the doorway. A long black duster draped over his left arm, he gripped a very large black hat in his hand. The other clothes he sported were modest, and more suited for genteel labor than for visiting.

Form-fitting brown trousers hugged his muscular thighs before disappearing into rugged knee-high boots. His shirt, of fine linen, sported a band collar disallowing for a cravat, and his top jacket made of thick wool appeared warm and inviting. She gripped her hands together, but what she really wanted to do was ease them up inside the garment.

Their gazes locked. Like the needle on a ship's compass, she felt a magnetism drawing her in his direction. It urged her forward, but she held her ground.

He remained unmoving as well, boldly staring at her. Not wishing to shatter the moment, she stared back in silence, noting how his dark hair, thick and abundant, curled over the top of his collar. He possessed a strong nose, nicely balanced and refined by an equally strong chin. But what truly fascinated her was his mustache. She had wicked thoughts of touching it. It was not a foppish pencil-thin affair, but a full-fledged, well-groomed healthy accumulation, and it aroused some primal response in her soul.

Lucien had tried growing a mustache. It had been a scraggly failure, soon shaved off and never referred to again. Captain Garrison's facial hair seemed an integral part of his being, adding a hardy no-nonsense air to his countenance. It was difficult to imagine him without it, but it was easy to picture him upon the sea. He appeared entirely capable of commanding a ship—or a woman—to do his bidding.

"Good morning, Miss Trelayne," he finally said, jogging her thoughts back to her surroundings.

"Good morning, Captain Garrison," she returned, with a little shake of her head. "How fare you so far in London?"

"I'm doing quite well. Thank you."

With a none-too-subtle cough, Lucien reminded her of his presence.

"Oh, I *am* sorry. Captain Walker Garrison, may I present Lucien Lanteen."

To her surprise, Walker's gaze narrowed and a muscle jumped along his clenched jaw as he took stock of Lucien.

"Pleased to meet you," he finally said. Ambling forward he extended his hand. His words were cordial, but there was a hard edge to his expression and manner.

"Indeed." Offering little enthusiasm, Lucien returned the gesture with a limp shake of the proffered hand. "If you need the services of a tailor while you are here, I could put in a good word for you with mine. I'm sure he would make time for someone so desperately in need of his skills."

Walker stepped back, amusement turning up one corner of his mouth. "Why thank you, Mr. Lanteen. And you let me know if you're ever interested in being outfitted in clothes suitable for activities more energetic than tea parties."

Covering her mouth with one hand to hide her smile, she fought not to laugh. Score one for Captain Garrison.

Lucien appeared positively livid. The air between

the two men seethed and crackled with unchecked emotion. Had it been visible, it most definitely would have been blood red. The awkward situation was saved when Aunt Abigail sailed into the room. The maid followed in her wake, carrying the tea service.

"Good morning, all," she greeted. After kissing Trelayne on the cheek she took up her post at her side. Her cheerfulness lightened the atmosphere, and the two men came to attention and eased back into metaphorical neutral corners.

"To what do we owe the pleasure, Captain?" her aunt asked, ignoring Lucien. Apparently she figured he was present for the usual non-reason. "Any news from abroad?"

"Nothing to report regarding Phillip and Ophelia," Walker began. "And do please pardon my unscheduled arrival. If it would not be too inconvenient, I was hoping to check the inventory at the warehouse and perhaps familiarize myself with Philip's accounts."

"I am responsible for the bookkeeping, as well as Phillip's legal concerns," Lucien growled.

"Then I'm sure all will be found in good order," Walker countered.

"Today is not convenient. I thought to take Trelayne to see the Crystal Palace."

"Lucien, we talked about going next week, after my new dress and hat have been completed. Let us accommodate Captain Garrison. I'm sure it would be most helpful for him to become acquainted with the business he has graciously offered to oversee."

"As you wish," Lucien deferred, but the contempt in his eyes never wavered as he aimed a heated glare at Walker. "I'll have the books available, and inform the clerk at the office of your impending visit." Rudely, he turned his back on Walker. "Now what might I do for you, my darling?" he asked.

"Nothing. Thank you for your concern and for coming to visit." She added the last by way of dismissal and prayed he would oblige.

After a moment of awkward silence, Lucien took the hint and stalked across the room. Walker shuffled sideways to avoid being winged by the man's determined exit. Then the front door slammed shut.

"Shall we have our tea before it cools?" Aunt Abigail cheerfully offered, ignoring the incident.

At the suggestion, Walker appeared disappointed, his expression not holding a dram of enthusiasm. She pictured him more comfortable with a mug of ale or some such brew rather than a teacup. He seemed so earthy and genuine in an overwhelmingly masculine sort of way.

He gave a quirky good-natured smile, however, set aside his outer wear, and wedged himself into a chair. As she poured, he retrieved a small package from his jacket pocket, and set it upon the silver-serving tray.

"I happened by a shop selling these this morning," he explained, "and I thought they looked enticing."

She stared at the little box and wondered why he had just lied to her. Fry and Son's was a far cry from conveniently located between the hotel at which he stayed and Royston Hall. How curious.

"Thank you, Captain Garrison. These are my very favorite chocolates."

"I thought we agreed you were to call me Walker."

"I promise to do so in the future," she amended.

Her heart warmed to the idea, and her cheeks

warmed to the way he looked at her. Yes, she longed to do just that, call him by his Christian name—unusual as it was. But she dare not. She must keep some semblance of proper distance between the two of them. After all, she hardly knew the man, and he had a perilous effect upon her mind and body. She had only seen him twice, but she wished to see a great deal more of him. He was an intriguing foreigner, and unduly handsome. He seemed a hot spark, and she felt like dry tinder, lying in wait.

****

Lucien rode posthaste to the office. He must review the books, both sets, and make sure everything appeared as it should.

Had there ever been a more frightful morning? It was beyond belief. One set of shocking news following upon the heels of another. The partnership papers already signed, sealed, and delivered, and that meddling bastard Garrison healthy as a horse and here in London.

He'd seen the *Alicia Elaine* docked at St. Katherine's harbor, but never dreamed it brought such disastrous cargo. The finalizing of the partnership would severely hamper his control over the situation, offering too many opportunities for interference and prying eyes. Damnation...he raised a fist and railed against the heavens. Maybe the contract papers were forgeries. He should have demanded to see them.

Months ago, he tried to kibosh the partnership, but that had not worked. Philip thought teaming up with this uncouth American a grand idea. It was an outrage. Barely thirty-five years had passed since England had been at war with these Yankee upstarts, yet Philip welcomed them with open arms. Then before he knew it, the St.Christophers were sailing for New Bedford. Another personal affront. He hadn't even been asked to go along to handle the paperwork.

He kicked his mount into a faster pace. He could still salvage the situation. Everything would be all right if Garrison only scrutinized the second set of books. Even if he compared them to the bank transactions, they should prove out. And once he sold the opium coming into Brighton, he could replace the money borrowed from the company to cover his gambling debts. Who would imagine one could lose a near fortune in only three days at the track and a few nights playing whist at the club.

No more gambling, he silently promised. At least not for a while, and after he remedied this current catastrophe, he must concentrate all his energy on securing his future with Trelayne. Whatever it took, convincing her to become his wife was what mattered. Now more than ever, it would appear time was of the essence. His guts tightened into a knot, and chaotic thoughts pounded through his brain. He did not fancy the behavior she exhibited around the American. The man was an uncouth barbarian, yet he brought an enamored glow to Trelayne's face—a reaction he had yet to garner.

All in due course. He mustn't ruin years of planning by panicking now in the eleventh hour. First he would make arrangements at the dockside office. Then he would speak to Bartholomew, and try not to strangle the incompetent fool.

Chapter Five

The floorboards creaked as Walker made another turn around his hotel room, anything to forestall lunch as long as possible. After three days of hotel food, maybe he'd try a local pub. At least today, there was good news regarding the St.Christophers. The most recent communication stated they were making steady progress—which was more than he could say for himself.

It was proving harder to find his "Candy Man" here in London, than tracking a desperado through the entire Colorado Territory. And he should know. That's where he'd finally caught up with the turncoat who betrayed him and his men as they fought alongside Zach Taylor. Fourteen American Marines died at the battle of Dominquez Ranch because of that man, and it had taken over a year to find the traitor and bring him to justice. Things were different now. There were other people to consider, and no luxury of unlimited time— no new clues either. But the answer had to be here in England, tied somehow to the man who liked chocolate.

The business ledgers he'd seen the other day appeared to be in order. Still something about them didn't ring true. The information contained within went back several years, but the books looked almost new— no ruffled edges, no wear and tear on the cover or deep creases in the spine. Perhaps the original tomes were damaged, and the information recently transcribed. Perhaps, but not likely.

He raked his hands through his hair, and tried to ease the kinks and knots from his upper back. The lack of progress was wearing on him, so was the hustle and bustle of the city. It was hard to think straight amidst the cacophony of sound blasting forth from every corner.

He stepped to the second story window, and glanced out at the commotion down below. Carriage after carriage clamored down the cobbled street, the vibrations rattling the panes of glass in the windows. So many people scurrying about with serious intent, their purpose defined, their expectations waiting to be fulfilled. He felt as if he were on the outside looking in, marching double time and getting nowhere fast.

The same reaction dogged him in Hong Kong and Bombay. Chaotic, closed-in surroundings set his nerves on edge. He preferred wide-open spaces, like the sea, where a man could breathe deep and see forever. Even his emotionally charged visits to Royston Hall had been refreshing in comparison to London.

Truth be told, he felt adrift in life, not just here, but in the world in general. His shipping line acted as his professional anchor, but his private life was without attachment or commitment. Freedom, he called it. But was it really? He felt more lonely than liberated.

His gaze meandered the street then locked onto two familiar figures. Trelayne and her Aunt, their arms laden with recent purchases, strolled up the avenue. His senses quickened. Something about Miss St.Christopher captured his fancy. Besides being lovely to look at, she stirred his protective instincts, and not just because he'd been charged with the duty. He didn't blame her for being reticent and not trusting him completely—hopefully, not a condition that would last forever. Merrick said she was headstrong and a bit impetuous, but also kindhearted and quick to laugh. All characteristics he had loved and admired in his wife, Kathleen.

Katie…she was on his mind a lot lately. Why? Because his heart skipped a beat at the sight of this woman similar in size and demeanor?

Since Katie's death he'd had no long-term associations with a female. There had been a fair share of passionate interludes, but nothing meaningful, nothing of substance. He wasn't sure he wanted that again—until now.

On impulse, he shrugged into his duster and headed for the door, grabbing his practical headgear on the way out. For his money, the towering top hats other men wore served no purpose whatsoever. They were unstable as a torn sail in the wind, provided no relief from the sun, and in foul weather funneled the rain straight down a man's collar. Settling the wide-brimmed hat he'd grown accustomed to in America securely on his head, he smiled. Just wearing it made him feel closer to home.

At the curb, he located the two women, then hung back and discreetly followed, telling himself it was for the two ladies' protection and not for his desire to be close to Trelayne.

They paused to accept a handbill offered by a rather angry looking woman on the street corner. After they moved on, he grabbed one as well, receiving a startled look followed by a penetrating glare.

For Ladies only.
Meeting Thursday next.
2:00 P.M. sharp
at Miss Bonnie Rutherford's.
Bring ideas for letters to Parliament
Long live the Cause.

What was all this about? Ah yes, *the Cause*. There were similar activities going on in Massachusetts. Women seeking the right to vote, own property, have dominion over their children. They were marching in the streets. Or in the case of Amelia Bloomer, riding on bicycles and initiating a whole new trend in female clothing. Although often in the minority, he admired their spirit.

The womenfolk he knew stood by their men, suffering the cruelties of war and the hardships of settling a new land. Why shouldn't they reap the advantages so hard won? He supposed unflagging devotion to misguided ritual, and unbending tradition outweighed logic.

A short distance up the street, Trelayne and Abigail entered a shop. While occupied within, he drew closer to see what commerce the store offered. The sign read "L.N. Fowler & Co." and a large nondescript porcelain rendering of a head stared unseeing out the window. The replica was crisscrossed with demarcations, each one offering a written notation. It was a phrenology shop. How intriguing. In his travels, he had come across many a curious notion and philosophies. What a pleasant surprise to learn Trelayne enjoyed some of the more outlandish wonders of the world.

Not wishing to be caught spying, he ambled up the street to the tobacconist shop, and lounged against the outside wall. As he waited, a young lad hawking a supplemental issue of the *Times* caught his attention.

"Extra, Extra, take a gander. Spring Heeled Jack strikes again."

People rushed at the boy from every side, shoving coins into his hands and grabbing copies of the tabloid. What was all the commotion about? An older gentleman halted nearby to peruse the news. Walker levered away from the brick wall and peered over his shoulder.

Miss Lucy Scales, daughter of a local butcher, was attacked as she walked home following a visit to her brother's house. As she approached Green Dragon-alley, an unnamed assailant, enveloped in a cloak, spewed a blue flame right in her face and knocked her down.

Miss Scales, of Narrow-Street, Limehouse, stated it could only be Spring Heeled Jack as the man not only emitted fire from his mouth, but flung it about as he bounded away over a high wall and into an adjacent walkway.

"Who the devil is this man?" Walker asked in surprise.

The old man glanced up. "Devil indeed. Ain't you never heard of Spring Heeled Jack? Where you from, mister?"

"America."

The man looked him up and down, a spark of curiosity brightening his rheumy eyes and wrinkled face. "Yes, well, he attacks foreigners and English folk alike so you best watch your step if you be out after dark."

"Why haven't they caught the ruffian?"

"They had him cornered once, but they don't call him Spring Heeled Jack for nothin'. According to the police, as they bore down on him, he clawed the air with gruesome silver talons, and let loose with a keening howl—crazy as the deuce. Then he lobbed a fireball at the befuddled officers, and leapt over a fifteen foot hedge."

"Sounds a monster from a nightmare."

"Tall and thin with a hideous face sporting glowing red eyes, I'd say he's a right proper bogeyman."

Here was another reason to worry over Trelayne's well-being. Did the creature haunt vicinities as far afield as Royston Hall? Cold concern gripped him, and he wished again he wasn't obliged to stay in a hotel so far from the St.Christophers' to facilitate his search.

"Does he only prowl about the city?" he asked.

"Our boy Jack harries folks all over the countryside," the old timer enlightened. "Some say he hides out in the marshes down by the Lea River east of here, near Bromley by Bow. Lately, he's been sighted on Clapham Road and Lavender Hill."

"You seem to know a lot about this fellow," Walker pointed out.

"Hard not to. Been readin' about his antics since '38. The penny dreadfuls had their turn at him, too. There was even a play what featured him called *Terror of London.* Don't know how much is fact, and how much is fiction, or just plain hysterics, but it keeps this old man entertained." With a chuckle and a shake of his head, he tottered on down the street.

As Walker digested the information, Abigail and Trelayne exited the shop. He eased back into the shadows of the alleyway until they passed then followed at a prudent distance.

Good Lord, they just turned up Lilac Lane. He quickened his step closing the distance. That's where the newspaper said Spring Heeled Jack had been operating. Or was it Lavender Lane? Now he wasn't sure, remembering only that it had some damnable flower name. The town was a maze of juxtaposed streets and alleys, all with seemingly irrelevant names and no proper numbering system.

Unable to stop himself, he drew ever closer, hoping to grab a bit of conversation.

"How fortunate Mr. Fowler returned yesterday from Edinburgh," Trelayne said. "I was so disheartened at having missed him the last time we were in town."

Abigail nodded. "And to offer you a personal phrenological examination was most generous, and unexpected. People wait months for an appointment with him. No doubt your pretty face had something to do with his enthusiasm."

Walker balked at the thought of some man freely exploring the shape of Trelayne's head and running his fingers through her hair—lustrous strands he'd yet to savor. It was unsettling and unfair for a stranger to touch her so intimately, while he must suffer self-imposed boundaries and admire her from afar.

"It was impossible to write down all the information," Trelayne put in. "And Mr. Fowler spoke so softly at times I could barely hear him, yet I feared to request he speak up or repeat himself."

"I remember he referred to each area of the head as a *brain organ,*" Abigail recalled. "It seemed such an odd term it stuck in my mind."

"Yes, that was it. And he mentioned my sensitivity

to ethereal spirits and veiled imaginings. Very intuitive as we hadn't told him about my dreams."

What was this about dreams? For a moment, Walker wished one of them might have been about him. How ridiculous. Yet the idea she might devote a few moments of her nighttime wanderings or even a daydream to him was nice. He often thought of her. It made him feel younger than his thirty years of age. Younger and in fine fettle, but those were dangerous feelings. A man was bound to lose his edge when a female occupied too much space in his brain.

"He hit the mark regarding your well-developed sense of color and love of music," Abigail said. "You enjoy needlepoint and playing the piano."

"I do," Trelayne agreed, "but had he actually heard me sing, he might have reconsidered. I best liked his comment predicting I was to fall in love with a tall stranger from a foreign land." She gave a quick peek over her shoulder.

Nearly caught trailing the women, Walker turned aside and stood staring into a shop window. Had she been referring to him? He snatched the hat from his head and continued his pursuit. He had to hear more.

"When did he say that?" Abigail asked.

"Right before he requested payment."

"Surely you misheard him, dear. He's not a palmist or a gypsy. Too bad they outlawed fortunetelling. I do know a woman who dabbles in the black arts…"

Trelayne shifted her packages all to one arm, and slipped the other around her Aunt's waist, giving her a hug. "Of course you do. But we've no time for that today if I'm to have my final fitting for my new dress. Lucien is ever so persistent about taking me to the

Crystal Palace. How sad Mother and Father aren't here to attend.

"Regardless of their cheerful letters, I know they must be lonely and suffering terribly from their injuries. I feel guilty taking in amusement when I know they are in pain and bored to tears in dreary dull America."

"You must stop fretting. They're safe and on the mend, and your father is giving Dr. Robison a run for his money at the chess board."

"And Mother promised to send each of us a pair of those shocking bloomers all the rage there. Penelope will be over the moon when she learns there is to be a set included for her."

"Precisely," Abigail encouraged. "They want us to soldier on, and not mope about on their account."

"The after-hour gala at the Palace would be a boon to my sensibilities," Trelayne admitted. "How romantic to see it at night—the stars and moon shining through all that glass-work But it's very select, by invitation only."

"I can't believe the Queen is to make an appearance just to bestow her royal sanction on some Amazonian flower named for her," Abigail mused.

"But it isn't just another water lily," Trelayne countered. "It's very rare and blooms only after sunset. What a thrill to be part of such an entourage."

Walker smiled. Here was the perfect gift for Trelayne. One Lanteen couldn't match.

Chapter Six

Leaves of russet and gold pirouetted across the floor of the ancient ruin. Overhead a string of snow geese cheerfully honked their way south. Autumnal delights did not serve to brighten Lucien's world.

In this section of Amberley Abbey, the roof was missing and glancing up, he shielded his eyes against the glare of the fierce blue sky. Where the hell was Bartholomew? He'd been waiting here for two days, and still the man had yet to arrive.

In a huff of impatience, he shifted about and leaned one shoulder against the crumbling wall of the medieval structure. A woman sat upon a heap of nearby stones. His gaze raked the familiar contours of her form. Beatrice's face was far from comely, but she was well endowed, kept fastidiously clean, and was wanton as a Lime Street harlot.

When he was bored, such as now, he concocted scenarios for severing their relationship, for surely one day it was wont to come to pass. Or perhaps, after he was married, he could keep her on the side. Either way, it never hurt to be prepared. Unfortunately, she was Bartholomew's sister, so eliminating Beatrice from his life would mean terminating a perfectly good business relationship with Old Barty.

At present, things were best left as they were. A bottle of gin and a few opium cigarettes, and he could do as he willed with Beatrice. She was a cheap enough diversion.

Early in life, he realized people would do his bidding—no question asked—if his request was accompanied by money, blackmail, or brute force. Of course, people would also respond out of earned loyalty and respect, but those methods took too long. He was not a patient man. He favored plotting and strategizing, not waiting.

Tall and slight of build, he emanated a pale stricken nature reminiscent of a poet, or so he'd been told. And the Percy Shelley approach could be quite effective with women. They were all foolish romantics.

In business and in life, his forte was cleverness and inciting other people to action. Having successfully eliminated the nuisance of conscience and guilt from his psyche, regret and concern for others did not accompany his propensity for taking advantage where and when he could.

A raven landed on a ledge, dislodging a slew of pebbles. The cascading noise interrupted his reflections and he ambled toward Beatrice. She hunkered down with the wariness of a frightened rabbit, trembling as he reached to touch her face. Was she expecting a gentle caress, or the sting of a slap? He liked to keep her guessing.

Roughly, he grabbed a handful of mouse-brown hair at the nape of her neck. Yanking her head back, he stared into her wide-eyed face. Sometimes he hated her—her and all women. You could never fully trust a female. They lived by their emotions, and would betray a man in an instant to save themselves.

As he held Beatrice captive, his prurient desire

rose, then waned. What he wanted was to fulfill his fantasies with Trelayne. How many nights had he tossed and turned, fevered by his passions, reliving their imagined lovemaking repeatedly in his mind? He was trying to beunderstanding, had devised his plans well, and set them in motion years ago. Yet Trelayne remained out of reach.

She toyed with his affections and rebuked his advances, not taking him seriously. Marriage seemed the furthest thing from her mind. But someday that would all change. And as his wife, she would bend to his will. Then he would live out what so far had been only a dream.

Beatrice squirmed in his grasp, and he jerked his hand aside. She half fell, half slid away from him.

"Go prepare something for us to eat," he ordered. "Maybe your fool of a brother will have shown up by the time the food is ready."

"Yes, Lucien. He'll be here soon," she reassured, scrambling to her feet. "I've never known him to miss payment for services rendered."

****

Beatrice hurried toward the inner rooms of the Abbey. She wasn't hungry, but disobeying Lucien in his present mood would only court trouble.

Thankful she didn't have to cook over an open fire, she puttered around the updated kitchen area, daydreaming about who might have lived in this ancient pile of stone. Did royalty, or even a princess, stay within the walls of this fortress? Who had called it home?

What she wouldn't give for a little house of her own, with a garden, and an apple tree. She slammed a bowl down on the table. What use did it serve to think about what might have been and what never could be? Why imagine a world she would never know?

With a sigh of resignation, she added more sticks of wood to the cook stove then poured herself a jigger of gin. Stirring the kettle of soup, a bittersweet smile played crossed her lips. Old man gin was her friend, and opium her comfort. That's what she cared about now, thanks to Lucien.

She must be gone 'round the bend to stay with him. Yet he was handsome in a terrifying way. All that long blonde hair, and those mesmerizing eyes. Pale blue eyes—the color of winter ice. Eyes that could look straight through a person, and make you feel afraid as they pierced your soul and sought out your weakness. The only time she remembered seeing tenderness in Lucien's face was when he was asleep. Yet, as frightening as Lucien could be, Beatrice knew she wouldn't leave him. And it wasn't just because she loved him. Where else could she go? She had no education. True, he didn't love her, using her only for his own satisfaction. But he kept her in pretty clothes, gin, and opium—and occasionally she was shown a small token of human kindness.

She rubbed at the back of her neck. It still burned where he had twisted her hair. Lucien's sexual appetite was what scared her most. Sometimes it was like being taken by Satan himself. That's why he plied her with drugs, to make her more compliant to his demands and desire. That's how her opium habit started. Later he would call her slut and worse, blaming her for not refusing, not preventing him from following through with his wayward compulsions. No doubt it was easier to hate her than himself.

She should run away—far, far away—but she never would. She needed the drugs and a full bottle of flash lightning. And she wanted Lucien, no matter how much he hurt her.

****

Keeping to the dense woods near the Abbey, Bartholomew guided his horse in a circuitous route then gave the agreed-upon call. When Lucien stepped into view and issued the obligatory "all's clear" wave, he urged the animal into the open and cut across the short expanse of meadow.

To keep their association private, they often met at the Abbey, cooking up nefarious plans and business schemes, or just passing time unobserved. Not looking forward to the upcoming encounter, he took his time to dismount, loosen the girth on the saddle, and turn the animal out to graze. Tired and covered with road dust, he ambled closer. Lucien appeared to be in one of his notorious temperamental moods. It would no doubt escalate to roaring ugly when he heard how things had gone wrong in America.

"Where the hell have you been?" Lucien began, before Bartholomew could even catch his breath.

"Don't be gettin' in a lather," he snapped back. "I left the ship at Weymouth when they made port to unload the mail packets. Then I come overland so's it took me a while longer than expected."

"Why the need for such an elaborate itinerary?"

"Because a certain Captain Garrison was also aboard ship, and I didn't want him seein' me make for London."

"Yes, I heard you bungled the job from tip to tail.

What the deuce happened?"

Bloody hell. The cove had already found out. "Well now, Lucien, I'm trail weary and a might hungry," he pointed out, hoping to forestall the abuse he knew was coming.

"You deserve a flogging rather than food," Lucien railed, "but come along to the kitchen."

Grimsby followed meekly, although what he wanted was to punch Lucien in the head. The puff didn't have enough guts or muscle to do his own dirty work, and if things happened to go wrong, he bitched and moaned as if he could have done any better. It weren't a perfect world, a body had to expect a setback now and again.

****

Hearing their approach, Beatrice hid the glass of gin and jumped to busy herself at the stove.

"Beatsie, old nub." Bartholomew gave her a thwack on the rump. "How are you, girl? You got some decent victuals for your dear brother? My stomach's near rubbin' my backbone."

Beatrice couldn't help but be pleased to see her brother. He was her only kin, and in his own way looked after her.

"Hello, Barty." She gave him a smile. "I've got a roasted chicken, veggie soup, and white bread. And there's a pot o' tea already on the table."

"Praise be. That bow wow mutton they served wayside, gave me the mullygrubs."

She watched Lucien take down the jug of rum and two glasses. If the drink mellowed his mood, they might spend another afternoon and evening in the country before returning to the crowded smog-filled streets of London. Maybe even stay overnight.

She was about to join the men at the table, but Lucien caught her by the arm. "Here love," he said, handing her an opium cigarette. "Why don't you go relax in the afternoon sun? You fixed us a fine bit of lunch. You deserve a sit down."

The smile on Lucien's face was innocent, but his painful grip on her wrist told her not to disobey. She grabbed the offering—it was better than food. When he released her, she ambled down the corridor and turned right as if to go to the courtyard. Lucien was watching, she could feel his gaze on her backside. Once beyond his view, she crept around the back hallway to the larder.

The kitchen and pantry shared a common wall. Pulling down a bag of sugar and shifting a sack of potatoes revealed a small hole through which she could see and hear the men sitting by the stove.

"Now, what the hell happened?" Lucien growled. "Why is this Garrison fellow still walking upright?"

"Things went a wee bit awry," her brother hedged.

"A wee bit? You botched the whole job, you cretin."

"It weren't my fault. And I had extra work on account of a sailor what got in the way at a crucial moment. Don't worry," he soothed, with a raised hand. "That one won't talk. He's boxed up pretty as you please. But I was hopin' for a bonus for the extra effort."

"I'm debating on paying you at all, and you've the gall to ask for extra?" The heated glare accompanying Lucien's words could have melted block ice.

"You weren't there, you don't know how hard it

was to pull off what you wanted, especially with all them people millin' about. And I'm getting older," Barty admitted. "I need the money for my retiring years. Much as I'd like to, I can't afford to do work for free out of the goodness of me heart."

"Do stop carrying on. You're a necessary evil in my scheme of things. I'll make it worth your while. You could have at least made sure the partnership papers went unsigned. Or at least retrieved them."

"But I saw the documents blow off the dock into the bay."

"They were ceremonial, just for show. The real ones were signed the night before."

"I'll be damned."

"No doubt you will be. Now spill the particulars," Lucien ordered.

Spellbound, Beatrice listened as Barty explained about the crate he'd rigged and the poor sailor who had tried to interfere.

"At the last minute," he said, lighting his pipe and blowing a cloud, "some little squeaker ran up distracting the Captain. And what with the wind a-blowin' as it were, the crate missed the mark, injuring the girl's parents instead. That Garrison fellow, he's got the luck of a cat. Didn't even suffer a scratch."

"Yes," Lucien agreed, "I met the good Captain a few days ago at Royston Hall. Imagine my surprise. He's poking his American nose into the company business and offering aid and comfort to Trelayne."

"You're a solicitor, ain't there nothing legal you can do?"

"Philip's power of attorney is indisputable, only the girl can act as proxy in the shipping line.

Unfortunately, she's deferring to the Yankee for advice—not me. The man must be dealt with, and Trelayne's dependence upon him eliminated."

Beatrice fumed. Lucien was always running off to see that rich piece of baggage. She hated Trelayne St.Christopher. The silly woman had everything— beauty, money, a proper education. Never bought a dress off the peg or worked a day in her life. She hoped Trelayne's parents died. She hoped Lucien never won her heart. But it sounded like he wanted the trollop now more than ever.

Lucien poured another round of drinks. The conversation waned, and the opium cigarette in her hand seemed to tingle and vie for her attention. Enticed by the urge for a smoke, and the forgetfulness it would bring, she made to leave. Then her brother spoke again.

"I'm itching to have another chance at the Captain," he declared, toying with his glass of rum. "It'll be my pleasure seeing to him. Any other plans on the agenda? You know I hate being idle and I loves counting money."

"I need you to oversee the final opium shipment," Lucien said.

"Piece a cake," Bart assured, "I'm your man." He stretched out his legs, and sipped at his drink.

Lucien's gaze hardened into the frightful expression indicating something nasty was about to happen. He gave Bartholomew's outstretched legs a solid well-placed kick.

"Listen up and listen good," he snarled. "This is the largest investment I have ever made, and I want no mistakes. Not one. Do you hear me? If you slip up again, as you did in America, you won't live long enough to regret it."

Bartholomew sat up rubbing his bruised limb. "All right, gov'nor, no need to be so physical in your explanations."

She wondered why Lucien seemed so nervous over a drug shipment. After all, it wasn't illegal to buy and peddle opium. Even the upper class enjoyed their share. And having successfully avoided the associated pitfalls of robbery, double cross, and general underworld treachery, Lucien anonymously made a tidy profit in his side business.

"Although it isn't a law yet," Lucien said, "there's been talk of restricting opium distribution to the apothecary shops. A black market trade will follow, of course, but it will make matters all the more complicated and risky. Another shipment after this one may be long in coming. Besides, I have special plans for the proceeds, and there is a large crated object onboard of particular interest to me."

"What is it?" Barty leaned forward, replete with curiosity.

"It's instrumental in accomplishing my most daring undertaking yet. For now, that's all you need know."

So, Beatrice thought, Lucien's mind was teeming with new schemes. More danger and thrills for him to feed upon. That was his opium—that and sex. Having heard enough, her hand tightened around the cigarette, and she slid from her hiding place.

****

"I'll take care of things proper this time," Bartholomew promised. "It's personal now between the Captain and me. Besides, who can you trust like you trust me? Who else has committed murder for you, eh?

Our past deeds have made us brothers of the future."

Lucien didn't trust Bartholomew any more than he would trust a total stranger. In fact, he trusted him less. Grimsby literally knew where the bodies were buried. He couldn't take a chance on cutting him loose just yet.

"Both jobs are yours," he conceded. "Our ship is out of Cape Coast Castle, laden from stem to stern with Bombay Magic. It comes to port at Brighton, within the next few weeks. I'll keep you posted. A few pounds in the usual pockets should assure our secrecy, and mollify the authorities regarding inspection and documentation.

"You are to reassign the cargo for distribution as usual, north by rail and to Paris by ship. The profits will be enormous. The special item onboard is to be warehoused here.

"And the Captain? I'll not rest easy until that one's gone under."

"Once the shipment is secured, you may make him your top priority. You have free rein as to the details, just make sure the job gets done right this time."

Deciding to stay the night, Lucien went to find Beatrice. She was sprawled across the mattress face up, fully clothed. Since he was the one who supplied those clothes, he felt no remorse as he rent her over-blouse to the waist. She wore no proper corset, and her ample breasts spilled over the top of her camisole.

In his mind he wanted another, but untamed desire hardened his body demanding release now, and Beatrice was here and wouldn't refuse him. She never did. She never tried to help in his attempt to save himself for the woman he cherished.

Beatrice smiled and reached for him. She was a

temptress. A siren leading him astray, knowingly corrupting him when he should remain pure. She thought to bind him with her willingness to please. Now she would have what she wanted so badly.

He shed his clothes, and slid onto the bed. Her smile faltered as he tore at her skirts and plundered her, first with his fingers then with the part of him driving him beyond control. With animal lust, he consummated the act, unleashing his vengeance against all that was unjust and unfair in his world.

Chapter Seven

Although it was long after dark, and the hour quite late, Trelayne squared her shoulders, blinked a few times to clear her vision, and referred again to her mother's household ledger.

Tomorrow was Michaelmas, a day celebrated at Royston Hall since the 1200's and every detail must be attended to. But her heart wasn't truly in the undertaking. Without her parents, it wouldn't be the same. Still, she was determined to make them proud, determined to conquer the responsibilities thrust upon her in their absence.

The families who lived in the surrounding areas anticipated Michaelmas with great expectation. It was one of the few days each year when they abandoned their cares and concerns. Therefore, the day must be as festive and exciting as it had ever been.

Michaelmas was a day of thanksgiving, hope, and happiness. She was thankful her parents were alive, and hopeful their recovery would be quickly forthcoming, but future happiness seemed an elusive butterfly just beyond reach. According to her novels, its capture could only be achieved with a special someone at one's side. Was Captain Garrison such a man?

Worn out from helping to hang decorations, she slumped down onto a chair, and exhaled a weary sigh.

Her anger for his neglect regarding the accident

had cooled. Originally, she needed someone to blame other than God, or the Fates, or whoever was in charge of these things. Now she wished she had invited him to the festivities, assuming he would be interested in attending. No doubt he fretted over her safety out of a sense of duty, nothing more. He might think their celebration old fashioned, even childish. Just because he took his responsibilities seriously didn't mean he was interested in her personally.

She gained her feet and fussed with the bouquet of flowers on the side table. He probably had a woman waiting for him back in America. What a disturbing thought, why hadn't it occurred to her before? She broke out in a sweat, and it wasn't from her physical labors. What if he were married? They really knew very little about his private life.

As Aunt Abigail breezed into the room, her disturbing contemplations took flight. Her Aunt was an endless well of energy, and a stickler for keeping up the traditions she had known as a child.

"How are we coming with the to-do list?" she asked, peering over her shoulder.

"Thank goodness Cook is familiar with the routine," Trelayne admitted. "She's made hundreds of scones, pies, and pastries for the morning group of revelers.

"Using plenty of blackberries, I hope."

"Bushels of them," she grinned, "all in keeping with the legend."

Apparently, when Satan was banished from Heaven on Michaelmas, he fell into a blackberry bush and cursed and spat upon the brambles, therefore none of the fruit could be picked after tomorrow. Why the plants were deemed usable again the following summer she didn't know.

"Has she prepared a St. Michael's bannock?" Aunt Abigail pressed.

"Indeed. Three cakes in all, as last year we nearly ran out. And she doubled the amount of charwardon and ginger caramels as well. So," Trelayne added with satisfaction, "come the dawning, all that remains is to pick the Michaelmas daisies and prepare the stubble-goose in onion sauce."

Her Aunt gave her a hug. "Fabulous darling. Oh, Millie," she called, to one of the maids. "Adjust that bough of flowers over the window more to the right. That's the ticket. The room looks very grandiloquent. Now hurry along," she encouraged, shepherding the servants out the door, "we must begin on the decorations for the ballroom."

The local tenants would arrive before noon on the morrow, and be escorted with pomp and circumstance into the great banqueting hall. There they would be bidden to help themselves to a resplendent array of food and drink. In turn, the guests would bring a token tithing of their harvest. Wheat or bread, fruits or vegetables, perhaps a precious length of tatted linen. Whatever they could afford without hardship.

More foodstuffs would be prepared than could possibly be eaten, the excess finding its way into pockets or hidden containers brought along by those attending. It was all according to Hoyle when it came to Michaelmas. While this gaiety ran its course, chaos would be in full swing in the kitchen where comestibles would be prepared for the second party to be held later in the evening. The neighboring gentry would attend this soirée, and along with delectable food, there would be music and dancing.

A haunting refrain from a Strauss waltz danced through her mind, wrapping itself around a vision of Captain Garrison. If he were to attend tomorrow, the evening would be complete.

When she thought of him, a river of emotion swept her along, and like a rudderless vessel, she was at the mercy of the current, a waterfall dead ahead, danger and excitement pounding in her chest as she anticipated dropping over the edge. What made one person so heart-stopping attractive, while another mightn't turn her head? The books Penelope supplied failed dismally in explaining the phenomenon—the cause was generally attributed to celestial convergence, or the whim of Cupid, or some such nonsense. There seemed no answer for the intangible question of the ages. Whatever the reason, for her, Captain Garrison had the magic. She felt it whenever he was near.

His presence spurred her to impetuous behavior, such as her outburst upon leaving the phrenologist. The prediction about falling in love with a handsome foreign stranger had popped out of her mouth without due consideration. At the time, it seemed a lark, an innocent game, now she was embarrassed by her reckless action.

She gave a burst of laughter. Spotting him following behind them had been surprisingly easy. He may be an accomplished seaman, and was probably good at blending into his surroundings in the mountains, or on some prairie out west, but in London, he was like a towering oak in a field of dwarf pine. He was taller than nearly every man in the city, and that black American topper only served to increase his height. Such masculine gear—it lent him a dangerous no-nonsense air. And the confident manner in which he walked proclaimed he was a straightforward person, expecting the same from everyone he encountered.

What kind of life had he led, and what were his plans for the future? Snuggling the journal in her arms, she again rued not having invited Walker to the Michaelmas festivities. *Walker*, she supposed it was safe to use his Christian name in the confines of her mind. Like the man, it was a singularly unique name. But to say it out loud would make him too much a reality. A permanent part of her life. She mustn't grow accustomed to having him around, to gazing upon his face, to wishing he would hold her in his arms or against his broad chest as they danced the night away.

"Trelayne, dear. Is everything all right? You look halfway to the moon." Aunt Abigail crossed the room, carrying a tea service for two. Wynona followed, laden with a tray of cheese, fruit, and sliced ham,

"I thought tonight we would eat cozy by the fire," her aunt suggested. "No sense bothering the others with anything formal. Besides, the tables are already set for tomorrow."

Tired to the bone, Trelayne nodded and fought a big unladylike yawn. "It sounds perfect, Auntie. Thank you, Wynona, and thank the entire staff for their efforts. I know they worked hard all day and into the evening. I won't forget what a splendid job they've done."

"You did your share, missy," Wynona reassured, chucking her lovingly under the chin as if she were a child. "Your parents would be proud."

Tears bit at her eyes as she set the journal aside. "I

hope so, Wynona. It's very important to me that they are."

"Don't you doubt it for a moment, Miss Trelayne." The older woman turned to leave, fatigue evident in her step. She was barely out of sight when a knock sounded at the door.

"I'll see to it," Trelayne called, before Wynona could respond. "You'd best go feed Merrick. Tell him the rest of the preparations can wait until morning."

"Bless you, child. Although he never would complain nor admit to it, he must be near starved and ready to drop."

The knock sounded again. Who could possibly be calling at this hour? Not Lucien, she prayed. She was tired, and too preoccupied to respond to his witty banter and fawning attention.

With a burst of strength fueled by irritation, she hauled open the heavy door, and came face to face with Captain Garrison. At the unexpected sight of him her heart lurched, then sped forward double-time. The chill night air rushed in around him, but a flush of heat swept over her from tousled hair to booted toe. He stood staring at her as if he'd never seen her before. Probably in regards to her disheveled appearance. She stared back, eventually finding the presence of mind to close her mouth.

Shadows of the night accentuated the planes of his face, turning his eyes more gray than blue. There was a lonesome quality about him tonight, one she hadn't notice before. Or did her own loneliness simply seek familiar company?

"Pardon my intrusion," he murmured, his gaze locked onto her face. "I realize the hour is unseemly late, but there is a matter that needs your immediate attention."

She clutched one hand to her chest. "Is it Mother and Father? Have they taken a turn?"

Captain Garrison reached to steady her. "No, nothing like that. Dr. Robinson's last report stated they're doing just fine." Taking charge, he gripped her arm, eased her backward into the room, and swung the door shut at his back. "I'm sorry. I didn't mean to upset you."

"You gave me such a fright," she declared, and tugged free of his grip. "Good news rarely arrives unannounced by the dark of night."

"Again I apologize, but I needed to see you."

He dragged his hat from his head and grasped it with both hands like a lad under reprimand, his expression contrite. But he was far from a boy, he was all man, so big and sturdy, emanating that special masculinity so lacking in some of the Englishmen with whom she was acquainted. She wanted to fling herself into his arms, and reassure him nothing he could ever do or say would long cause her to remain annoyed. Then his words sank in. Did his need to see her stem from the same burning desire fueling her delight in seeing him?

"Forgive my manners," she pleaded. "Your arrival took me by surprise, but you're welcome here any time, for any reason. Come in. Please. Aunt Abigail and I were just about to have a bite. Are you hungry? Are you cold? Come enjoy the fire we've got roaring."

Ye gad, she wanted to slap a hand over her mouth to stop the flow of inane words pouring from it. Not waiting for his reply, as if he could have managed to squeeze one in, she turned and fled to the parlor.

"Miss Abigail." He nodded a greeting as he trailed behind her. "A pleasure to see you again, Ma'am."

His voice, spoken in that drawling foreign accent, soothed her even as it stirred something deep inside.

"Always a delight," her aunt replied.

"Perhaps you would care for a glass of port, Captain Garrison," Trelayne offered.

Still speaking without thinking, she drifted over to the wine cabinet.

"You promised to call me Walker."

He followed, and stood so close she could feel the heat from his body more assuredly than the heat from the fire.

"Did I?" She swallowed hard, and turned to face him.

"Yes. And you seemed the type of woman to keep a promise."

A woman...she liked the sound of that. Although she was twenty-one years of age, everyone still sheltered her, treating her as if she were much younger. Ironically, to be recognized as full-grown and able to stand on her own made her knees weak. Of late, she definitely had womanly desires. Then her other promise, the one about keeping an emotional distance between the two of them, popped up in the back of her mind. She ignored it. Here was the excuse to cross the boundary so recklessly devised. Better to break the promise to herself, than the one she'd made to him.

"I've no choice then...Walker." It felt daring to say his name with such abandon.

She glanced up at him through her lashes. Earlier today, she'd gathered her hair into an unflattering bun atop her head. Now a playful tendril maneuvered a wily escape, dipping down in front of her right eye and cheek. He gently brushed it aside and tucked it behind her ear. Although ever so slight, his touch sent a shockwave pounding through her body, the majority of the physical upheaval settling low in her belly.

His gaze drifted lower, taking in her attire. Previously overwhelmed by her labors, she had loosened a few buttons at the throat of her dress and pushed the sleeves up above her elbows.

"I'm sorry, I must look a fright."

"On the contrary. You have a natural loveliness, the rarest kind of beauty. And the most desirable—at least in my humble opinion."

At present, his opinion seemed the most important one in the world. How different Walker was from Lucien. On the rare occasions when he escorted her about, Lucien insisted she wear the latest fashion and hairstyles. And no amount of jewelry ever seemed overdone in his eyes. Did such things not matter to Walker?

Getting a grip, she poured the proffered drink and extended it toward him.

"Your port, Walker."

Heaven help her. Now she couldn't stop using his name. She wanted to shout it from the rooftop, and write it over and over on little scraps of paper like the one hidden in her match box. She liked the way it felt in her mouth and on her tongue. She had never experienced this reaction in the presence of any man; it was mesmerizing and quite pleasing, yet leaving her wanting more, much more.

Her gaze jumped to his face, searching his eyes,

hoping to find a sign she was not acting as big a ninny as she feared. With no indication anything was wrong, he accepted the drink, his fingers grazing hers.

"We must invite Walker to our festivities tomorrow night."

Aunt Abigail's suggestion broke through the schoolgirl trance into which she had slipped—nay fallen. Could her aunt see metaphorical sparks shooting out from her in every direction?

"But of course. You must join us." She pressed her lips together to stop herself from using his name yet again. "It's fancy dress, a banquet, with music and dancing. Do you dance?"

"I've been known to try—on occasion. But I'm not familiar with the steps common here."

"Surely the waltz has come ashore in America."

His face brightened. "Ashore and thriving. I'm partial to waltzing."

"Then you must attend. I shall save the first waltz for you."

"A man would be a fool to refuse such an offer. I'll be there."

Afraid to put her joy at his acceptance into mere words, she glanced away. Then gathering her wits, she remembered to ask why he had come tonight. "What was it you wished to speak to us about? You said it was important."

He set the glass of port aside, untouched, and his expression turned serious. "Are either of you ladies familiar with a man named Bartholomew Grimsby?"

Her aunt gained her feet, a thoughtful expression upon her face. "It doesn't sound familiar. How about you, dear?"

"No, I don't believe I've heard the name before." She stiffened and sucked in a breath. "Is that the man responsible for my parents' injuries?"

"It's possible he had something to do with it."

"How did you come by his name?" Aunt Abigail asked.

"When I checked the manifest for the *Alicia Elaine*'s maiden voyage, he was the only passenger onboard whose nationality was listed as British. All the others were American."

"Is that significant?" Trelayne put in.

"Maybe not," Walker conceded. "But it is curious."

"Would you like us to make inquiries amongst the staff?" Aunt Abigail offered.

"No. We don't want to stampede the herd…start him running," he added at their apparent confusion. "Just keep his moniker in mind, and let me know if you come across any useful information."

"Yes, of course. Is there anything else?" Her aunt placed a comforting arm around Trelayne. "It has been a rather long day, and tomorrow will no doubt follow suite."

Walker shuffled his feet and tightened the grip on his hat. "I know you already have plans to see the Crystal Palace," he began, "but I wrangled invitations for the Queen's special evening celebration. I was wondering if you and Miss Abigail would do me the honor of attending with me."

Trelayne clapped her hands, and levered up and down on her toes. Then remembering where she was, and that her womanly image, so recently hard won, was on the verge of ruination, she contained her excitement.

"How ever did you manage such a coveted prize,"

she asked.

"A few of the vendors were granted invites to see the ceremony, and as Her Majesty has taken a shine to a friend of mine, Mr. Samuel Colt, and the Prince has apparently taken a shine to Sam's pistols, we would be his guests."

She glanced at her aunt who gave an enthusiastic nod of approval.

"Yes, yes. What a marvelous surprise. Thank you for thinking of us." Trelayne could barely believe their good fortune. The Crystal Palace by moonlight, and a viewing of the botanical discovery of the century. More importantly, an opportunity to spend another evening with Walker.

Chapter Eight

Beatrice stormed across the front parlor of Lucien's flat and flung herself into a chair.

"I suppose while you're off with *her,* eating high off the hog and dancing the night away, I'm to sit here all alone with nofin' to do and no one to talk to."

"You'll do as you are told," Lucien growled. Being at odds with Beatrice was becoming tiresome, he was already late and not fashionably so. He mustn't miss the first waltz with Trelayne. "You've had things fairly decent since I took you in. And don't forget, I can put you back where you came from—or worse."

He dangled the pocket watch and fob in front of her, the one he kept for just such occasions. The timepiece held only modest monetary value, its true worth being its ability to strike terror in Beatrice's heart.

Her eyes grew wide, and she snapped her mouth shut stifling any further lamentation.

A rare twinge of guilt seized him, but quickly passed. She was much less haggard and worn than when he'd come across her whoring in a back alley. That was the night he'd discovered the gold watch on her person, obviously stolen from a previous client, his arrival interrupting her opportunity to bag the swag. After confronting her with the evidence, she'd flung herself at his feet, begging for mercy. Thievery could garner many dreadful years in Newgate. But he had not turned her in. And now, the watch was his perfect little bit of blackmail, its delicate golden chain binding her to him with the strength of iron.

"Need I say more?" He snatched the timepiece from in front of her face.

"I'm sorry, Lucien, I just want you to stay with me tonight. I know what you like."

Gaining her feet, she rubbed her bubbies against his chest, and sought to wedge her hand down the front of his trousers. He grew rigid at the possibility of a quick buck and tussle, but there wasn't time. Taking hold of her wrists, he set her aside, then strode over to the metal chest where he kept his valuables. Stowing the watch, he retrieved another item and replaced the lock.

"Don't wait up," he instructed, tossing the cheap bauble her way. "Play with this while I'm gone. There's plenty of gin. What the hell more do you want?"

****

Trelayne fluttered her hand in front of her face then pressed a damp curl into place. Mother had made entertaining look so simple, but to remain gay and the center of attention hours on end was exhausting.

The evening Michaelmas celebration was in full swing, some of the guests having arrived over an hour ago. And with hundreds of candles burning, and so many people gathered together, it was overly warm in the ballroom. The French doors leading to the garden had been removed, but it didn't help one wit. The languid breeze only stirred the heat about rather than relieving it. Still, everyone appeared to be enjoying themselves. At least she thought so until Penelope eased up beside her.

"Laynie," her friend whispered, "the guests are weary and discontent dancing only the polka, mazurka, and schottische. I asked the orchestra to play a waltz, but they refused."

"Oh, they mustn't play a waltz until I give them permission. I'm saving the first one for Walker, and he's yet to arrive."

Did he remember? Would he even care if she drifted across the room with her dreams and her body cozened in the arms of another man? Dismay joined hands with her fatigue.

"Oh, Pen, what if he doesn't attend?"

Her joy for the evening drained away more quickly than champagne from the flutes her guests tipped so eagerly. Then in a huff, she decided what Walker did or didn't do shouldn't matter. She had more important concerns. In fact, her mind was overrun with them. Her mother and father were still far from recovered, Lucien had been pressuring her to solidify their relationship, and although it was Merrick to whom most businessmen deferred, she was determined to properly oversee the shipping line. It was just all too much.

Emotions running wild, tears pricked at the backs of her eyes. This was ridiculous. She was simply overly tired and not thinking clearly. She must give Captain Garrison a little more time. Perhaps he was delayed in town for some reason.

"Please keep dancing, Pen, and reassure the others the waltz is soon to come. I need a moment to catch my breath and clear my head."

Slipping away, she sought the library. The laughter and music faded to a less grating intensity, and she breathed a sigh of relief and roamed about the dimly lit room.

She and her father had passed many an hour together in this room—reading, playing chess, discussing literature and the theatre. She ambled past the huge globe and set it to spinning then grazed her fingers across the carefully framed maps hanging upon the walls. Together they had explored foreign lands, figuratively, of course. What fun it had been planning their imaginary trips. The timetable for passenger ships to Alexandria still lay upon his desk. In the margin a note indicated where one might obtain custom and secure a boat suitable for traveling down the Nile. What special moments they had shared.

She missed her parents so much it was a physical pain, and even with Aunt Abigail to lean upon, she felt horribly alone. To rely more heavily on Lucien was an option, but the idea gave her innards a twist. He was handsome and charming, and he certainly made it abundantly clear he would be at her service—in any capacity. But he was also very secretive and enigmatic at times, and in business, he could be ruthless. At present, it was probably best not to mix business with pleasure.

Then there was the other alternative, working side by side with Walker. That would be the business *of* pleasure, or a pleasurable business. Damn, she was doing it again, conjuring childish idioms at the mere thought of the man. She should never have allowed herself to think of him as anything other than the mysterious Captain Garrison. It was probably for the best if he didn't attend tonight.

Blotting his image from her mind, she idled about

the room turning down the lamps. She mustn't burn oil unnecessarily—economizing was another of father's favorite crusades. With a smile, she crossed the room, moving by sense of touch, circumventing the big desk and overstuffed leather chairs. As she drew near the door, the figure of a man blocked the opening. Cut off from the light in the hallway, it rendered him an ominous faceless shadow. Was it Spring Heeled Jack? She quickly dismissed the crazy notion. He'd not been known to accost people in their homes. She shouldn't have read that gruesome article about him in the *Times*. It had to be one of her guests who stood before her.

"I'm sorry," she said, "but the library is off limits tonight.

The man remained silent, and stepped into the room.

"Who are you? What do you want?"

"I've come to steal your heart, madam. And I warn you, any resistance on your part shall be quite futile."

With relief, she recognized Lucien's voice. "Sweet mother of God," she exclaimed. "You scared me half to death, Lucien."

"Sorry, darling. When I couldn't find you amongst the jubilant crowd I went searching for you."

She retreated farther into the room, and turned up the single lamp she had left burning. Light spilled across Lucien. He cut a dashing figure in his black evening wear, but a feeling of reluctance to go near him niggled at her. She sought the mirror hanging above the fireplace mantel, and with her back to the room, pretended to check her hair and makeup. Lucien's reflection appeared over her shoulder. Before she could move away, he turned her around and they stood toe-to-

toe and face-to-face.

"Lord above," he marveled, "you are magnificently beautiful." His words were as feverish as the hands he placed possessively upon her shoulders. "You shall outshine every woman present here tonight."

Desire was blatant in his eyes, and the smoldering passion in Lucien's voice took her off guard. He'd never looked at her this way before, and while her few previous suitors had offered lovesick expressions, there had been nothing so worldly or pagan or wild in their demeanor. This hinted at territory unknown to her, and for some reason fear overshadowed curiosity.

Before she could distance herself, Lucien took her in his arms, and without question or consent, sought her mouth. The mantelpiece denied her escape from behind, and pressing home the advantage as well as his body, Lucien arched against the length of her. She opened her mouth to chastise him, but he only groaned and tried to thrust his tongue past her lips. His hands dropped lower, coming to rest upon her hips, drawing her ever closer. With a shock she felt his manhood, distinctly aroused. This went beyond playful touching. And although she wished to be found irresistible, the consequences were a bit frightening.

She wrestled free, and raised her hand to strike Lucien's face. He caught her wrist before she could follow through, and they stood as if frozen in time, their lips only inches apart, each of them panting and trying to regain control of their emotions. Lucien recovered first. He stepped away as if she'd turned to flame, too hot to touch.

"Forgive my unspeakably knavish behavior," he apologized. "You drive me senseless. I cannot be near you without wanting all of you. I didn't mean to frighten you. In fact, I wanted to formally ask you to marry me."

At the enormity of Lucien's announcement, her anger withered away. Her life was in complete turmoil, she was on the verge of emotional exhaustion, and he expected her to make the most important decisions of her life. Dumbfounded she stared at him, her mind in a whirl.

A month ago, she would have seriously considered saying yes. Probably would have given in with only slight hesitation. But now uncertainty weighed heavily, and it was all because of Captain Garrison. Her mind was in a tailspin, the situation outrageously impossible, almost laughable. A bubble of mirth at the absurdity of it all grew until it filled her chest and begged for release. She giggled, then hiccoughed, then laughed right out loud. She knew it was improper, but couldn't stop, the champagne spurring her on.

"Lucien," she said, catching her breath and sobering her expression, "I'm flattered and honored by your proposal, really I am. But I can't possibly make such a decision right now.

At her words, his gaze turned cold, his features so hard and unmoving he seemed carved from stone.

"I'm sorry," she added. "You know I care for you. And we have toyed with the idea of marriage. But things are different now. I can't make any commitment to you after everything that has happened of late. And I shall be quite busy with the shipping line. I'm taking an active interest in it, you see."

"But if we were married," he persuaded, with renewed animation, "I could help you run the shipping line. It's hardly a place or a job for a woman. I could be your partner."

"Captain Garrison is my partner. He's been most helpful."

Lucien reared back as if her words had been a physical slap to his person. Teeth clenched, he stared at her.

"Is the good Captain here now?" His eyes narrowed to slits as he awaited her answer.

"No."

"Then I rest my case."

"It's true he's not yet arrived. But… "

"But nothing. He's crude and rude and probably can't find his way here in the dark."

"It's still early," she said wistfully, "and you're being very rude as well."

"It's just that I don't wish to share you with anyone," he pressed. "At least I shall have you all to myself when we visit the Crystal Palace. A unique experience of our own making."

"Oh, dear..."

She hadn't had a chance to tell Lucien about Walker's irresistible invitation scheduled for tomorrow night.

"What?" he queried. "Do not tell me we must again postpone our engagement."

"Captain Garrison managed to acquire invitations for the special evening event. The one being held in honor of the Queen."

The veins in Lucien's neck stood out, and the color drained from his face.

"Lucien, are you all right? Sit down, you look quite ill. Now don't be peevish," she soothed. "How could I say no? It's the opportunity of a lifetime." She put her hand on his arm, intending to guide him to a nearby chair.

"How indeed." He snatched his arm from her grasp as if she were some monstrous beast. "Must you parade yourself in public with this foreign no-account."

"It's just a bit of innocent fun, Lucien. Nothing more."

"The man is an uncouth commoner. I'm surprised you wish to be seen with him."

"That's a horrid thing to say. You know nothing about Walker."

"Walker, is it? You're on a first name basis now. I forbid you to go with him."

"We are not engaged or affianced in any manner. You have no right to bid or forbid me anything. I shall do as I please."

Lucien appeared positively livid. His hand clenched and unclenched as if he thought to strike her.

"You're going to regret your association with this American rabble," he warned. "I guarantee it."

"Your manners are unacceptable tonight in more ways than one. And if this is to be your attitude, I must insist you take your leave."

With a fierce glower, he pushed her out of the way, and made good her request.

Trelayne stood trembling in the middle of the room, wondering what in the world had just happened. Lucien's behavior was shocking and frightening. He had no right to care if Walker was to be her business partner, or if she spent one evening with him at the Crystal Palace. It was just a frolic. Yet he seemed sorely distressed and unreasonably jealous over both possibilities.

The magnitude of his temper-outburst came as a surprise. No doubt her refusal of his marriage proposal had stung—injured male pride and all that. And she shouldn't have laughed, hadn't meant to, it was the situation that was ludicrous, not him. Once he'd had time to reflect on his behavior, he would no doubt apologize, and she would do the same.

Hand at her throat, she tried to regain her composure. Lucien's hungry kisses, and the feel of his body pressed uncensored against hers, had been disconcerting. In her books, such intimate touching was supposed to be thrilling, pure delight. But she hadn't enjoyed it. Perhaps the fault lay with her? Or maybe it depended upon who was doing the touching.

Slipping away to the library had not been the tranquil respite she had envisioned. Employing a piece of letterhead stationary from her father's desk, she fanned her face. What if someone had walked in? Their compromising scene could have led to, if not unwarranted, at least unwanted gossip. Lucien had acted like a different man tonight, showing a side unseen before. Injured pride or not, it was unflattering, and not something she wished to experience again.

With a deep breath to settle her frenzied nerves, she stopped fanning and glanced at the embossed lettering on the page.

Garrison/St.Christopher Shipping
New Bedford - London - Canton - Bombay

Dear generous Father, he had given Walker top billing. It was so like him to be indulgent when he was dealing with someone he trusted and respected. He must think very highly of his new partner. Should she also put her faith in him? It seemed each day brought a new social obligation or demanding business difficulty. It would be quite easy to let someone else do the thinking and decision making….

No, she countered. This was her time to show her parents how capable and intelligent she was. Taking care of herself and the household, even running Poppa's business, were challenges she had to meet. She could do this. She was not the fragile cosseted child her parents insist she remain. They couldn't keep her at home forever, sheltered from all danger and the cruelties of life. Now was her opportunity to take charge and break free, show them what she could do.

Still, there were times, when she yearned to be held in strong loving arms, and be told that everything would be all right—even if it was a lie. Walker came to mind to fulfill those needs.

The clock in the hall struck ten o'clock. Goodness, she'd been away from the festivities far too long. Tongues would wag at her absence. She rushed from the room then her steps faltered. Lucien had abandoned her, and Walker had yet to arrive. She had no formal escort at her own party. Perhaps no one would notice if she just slipped back in and mingled about.

Utilizing the servants' back passageway, she headed toward the kitchen on the far side of the house. She would see how things were going on the way. As the familiar passageway shifted to the right, she recalled the happy hours she had spent playing here when her sister was alive. Even her brother, although declaring himself too old for such folly, couldn't help but occasionally join in the fun. The dark catacomb halls and cubbies were the perfect backdrop for games of hide and seek, and for telling ghostly tales of dragons and demons and monster of varying disposition. It was still a bit eerie and spooky with the muffled sounds of the party pulsing just beyond the walls. It seemed otherworldly, another time and place.

Gaining the small door at the far end of the corridor she paused, her hand upon the knob. The urge to remain hidden in the refuge of childhood memories raced through her. Then common sense won out. She squelched the notion, opened the door, and entered the butlery.

Before she took one step, a tall figure loomed up over her shoulder. Taken by surprise, her blood still running high from Lucien's scandalous behavior, she balled her hands into fists and turned to as if to ward off an attack. In his own defense, Walker slipped one arm around her waist, and drew her up against his chest. An amused smile found shelter beneath his mustache.

"You gave me one heck of a start, little lady, the way you suddenly materialized right in front of me."

"I gave you a start? You nearly scared my hair gray sneaking up behind me."

"That truly would have been unforgivable."

He gazed at the curls framing her face, his expression one of consideration. All the while, his arm held fast, keeping her close, so close she could smell the bayberry soap with which he had washed. So close she could feel the hard muscles of his body and the warmth of his breath. It felt much nicer than when Lucien had held her.

"Your hair is just the right color," he added, with conviction.

"And what color is that, pray tell?"

"The color of chestnuts in the fall, the color of good rich earth that will grow anything a man's heart desires."

Well, she'd never been compared to nuts and dirt before, but somehow the way he said it made it sound like the most sought after compliment in the world.

"Careful, Captain Garrison, you're waxing poetic."

He lowered his arm and stepped back. His expression faltered then took on a harder edge. Now she'd hurt *his* feelings. It seemed her specialty tonight.

"I'm sorry," she amended. "It was a statement of surprise rather than ridicule at your kind compliment.

"Being out to sea offers a man many an hour for wrestling with thoughts and words. Why there's even time for reading books, and reflecting on the contents," he added, sarcasm unmistakable in his speech.

"Again, I'm sorry. I too enjoy reading. It's a wonderful pastime, and has filled many a lonely hour for me."

"It's hard to believe a woman as beautiful as you could ever be lonely."

She studied his face. He seemed serious, not toying with her emotions. She couldn't think of anything to say. It was silly. She'd been told before she was pretty, even beautiful, but it hadn't mattered. Hadn't rendered her speechless.

"Perhaps I'm many things you may find hard to believe," she countered, with a coquettish smile, and high hopes of stirring his interest.

His intense perusal told her she had, but the silence went on so long she began to rue her remark.

"Why are you here in the back kitchen area?" she asked, unable to bear the quiet a moment longer. "Good heavens. Have we run out of food at the buffet? Surely the party hasn't already run amuck."

"I was speaking with Merrick," he explained. "Nothing important," he quickly added, "just a few questions that needed clarifying. And," he grinned, "I was trying to wedge myself into the formalwear he generously loaned me. Merrick said it belonged to their son. It was a true kindness for him to allow me to wear it, although I believe it's a bit out of style."

She cocked her head to one side and gave him the once over. Her heart fluttered at least twice. The fabric strained at all the seams, especially the jacket as it fought valiantly to accommodate the broad expanse of his shoulders and chest. The chest he had recently held her against.

"You look marvelous," she reassured. "Besides, with such a glorious anatomy, who would notice your clothing?" Oh mercy, she meant to think that, not blurt it out.

His grin deepened. He took her hand, placed it in the crook of his arm, and propelled her toward the ballroom.

"Have I missed the first waltz?" he asked, escorting her to the center of the room.

"No," she confirmed. "I've allowed none to be played, and my poor guests are near to the point of exhaustion from quickstepping about the room."

He chuckled, and took a step back, his gaze gliding over her from head to toe. "You appear to have held up beautifully."

As they stood before one another, a hush blanketed the room. It was one tiny moment, filled with a lifetime of anticipation. Coming to her senses, she caught

Penelope's attention and nodded toward the orchestra. Her friend rushed toward the musicians, nearly tripping on the hem of her dress. The lilting strains of Tchaikovsky swirled through the air like a welcoming breeze, and her guests issued playful hurrahs as they hurried to find their partners.

Captain Garrison, male elegance infused with animal-like grace and strength, swept her into his arms—and into a dream come true.

When he placed his hand solidly at the small of her back, a tingling sensation shot straight up her spine to the roots of her hair. The resulting effect was more potent than wine. She was dizzy with desire, giddy with happiness. She must remember to breathe.

They stood so close—only their clothing and the heat of their bodies between them. What a glorious temptation, just beyond reach. Teasing and taunting, it was a fleeting taste of what she yearned to partake of fully.

"I've thought a time or two about holding you in my arms," he admitted, in a husky voice. "It feels even better than I imagined."

"What other thoughts have crossed your mind?" she dared to ask, finding the courage to stare up at him.

His eyes crinkled at the corners, but his gaze held passion as well as amusement. "Things a man ought not discuss with a lady."

Chapter Nine

Beatrice stopped crying and stared forlornly at the "token" Lucien had given her. Compared to the gifts he'd lavished on the little rich bitch in the past, it was nothing to crow about. Then a romantic notion skipped through her mind. If she could garner a snippet of Lucien's hair, and secret it away inside, that would be something special to treasure.

With renewed happiness she eased opened the slender locket. The hinge cracked and the little metallic heart split in two. Her heart felt as broken as the necklace. Then her fist closed around the jagged pieces.

It wasn't fair. That St.Christopher woman had everything, why couldn't she leave Lucien alone? He was all Beatrice wanted in the whole wide world. Just Lucien. But nothing ever workout for her. No one ever listened to what she wanted or needed. So it had been her whole life. She guessed it would be that way until she died.

She threw the necklace against the wall. Not tonight, damn it. Tonight she would do whatever she bloody well pleased.

On the way out, she grabbed her cloak and the money secreted away in the vase by the door. Feeling extravagant, she hailed a hansom cab.

"Royston Hall, out on Killingstone road," she requested, with all the authority of lady born to the manor. "And be quick about it."

The carriage lurched into action, and her anger kept pace. She glanced down at her dress. She couldn't slip in and pretend to be one of the favored guests, but she could spy on them from afar, and watch from behind the scenes. Anything to find out what magical power that woman held over her Lucien.

The rough country road and the churning of the wheels fuelled her ire, bolstering her courage and keeping the audacity of her impetuous action running high. As they rounded a curve, the Manor came into view, an imposing site even at a distance.

"Stop here," she ordered, afraid to get too close. As she paid off the driver, he gave her a sideways glance. "Well, get along with you then," she snapped, his attitude ruffling her feathers. He weren't no better than her. He slapped the reins, sending the horse into a trot.

Sidling off to the side of the road, she sought the welcoming darkness, and with her cape gathered close, edged around the north side of the great house. Near an open window, she paused to inhale the aroma of fine food, expensive cigars, and perfumed ladies. Music drifted through the open doorways into the night, and for a moment, she swayed to the melody—pretending she was a guest rather than a sneak in the night.

At the far side of the house, she slipped through a backdoor and crept silently toward the sound of music coming from ballroom. The garlanded hall was a kaleidoscope of color, laughter, and emotions running high. Hiding in the shadows, she watched and searched for Lucien, praying for a glimpse of the man she loved, yet ruing the fact he would be in the arms of another woman.

There was the uppity Miss St.Christopher, just as beautiful as the miniature Lucien kept of her on the mantelpiece. But she wasn't dancing with Lucien. The man who held her was taller, with dark hair. She couldn't see his face, and she didn't see Lucien anywhere.

"Here now, what you doin' just standing there in the corner?"

She spun around, mouth so dry she could hardly speak. The servant girl facing her carried a tray laden with more food for the buffet table.

"I was to help in the kitchen," Beatrice lied, "but was delayed getting here."

"If you was any later, you needn't have shown up at all. The kitchen's that way." The girl nodded her head indicating the direction. "Uniforms are in the cupboard by the pantry," she added over her shoulder, as she went to deliver the food.

When the girl was out of sight, Beatrice sneaked up a nearby staircase. It had been a long expensive ride to get here, no need to leave so quickly. How irritating that her fib about being a servant had been so readily accepted. It would have been nice to be at least momentarily mistaken for a guest.

She ambled down the hall, peeking into one room after anther. Then coming upon a room unmistakably belonging to the strumpet, she slipped inside, closed the door, and waited for her eyes to adjust to the dim light offered by the moon.

"Saints be praised," she murmured, turning full circle. "This little pigeon has quite the gilded cage."

Cheerful blue and white wallpaper brightened the mood of the room. Ruffled curtains framed two inviting window seats, and the matching dust ruffle, comforter, and canopy were celestial in their gauzy white splendor.

Ambling about, she systematically opened drawers and rifled through letters and papers. Maybe she could uncover something bad about the woman. Something that would make Lucien not like her anymore. Maybe she had secrets too. Or was she as perfect as she seemed?

Unsuccessful, she wandered over to the vanity and plopped down on the little stool in front of the mirror. Her reflection glared back. Dark circles saddened the expression in her eyes, and her hair was mussed and wispy. She sat up straighter, smoothing down the bodice of her dress. At least her heavers were still perky and full, not just a scrawny handful to be easily missed during a grope in the dark. Absentmindedly, she toyed with the collection of pretty matchboxes lining the dresser top. Most held pins or fair tokens, but the heart shaped one held a scrap of paper. She plucked the tiny missive from its porcelain cocoon. She'd been working to improve her reading skills, and although they were shaky at best, this was easy enough to decipher. It was a person's name. The one she'd heard Lucien and Bart arguing about.

Captain Walker Garrison. Mrs. Walker Garrison. Walker, my love. Walker forever. It were the rantings of a schoolgirl. The little twit was in love with this captain fellow. This was good news. But what about Lucien? The silly goose of a woman didn't even want him. Beatrice's protective instinct for the man she loved drove her hatred for Trelayne even higher.

She returned the slip of parchment to its hiding place, her mouth stiff with anger as she drummed her fingers on the dresser top. About to gain her feet, the gleam of gold caught her eye. Half hidden in the folds of the lacy dresser scarf was a filigree chain attached to a perfectly formed heart locket. It was much nicer than the one Lucien had so offhandedly thrown in her direction. She held the locket at her throat, and as the harsh reality of her life faded away, she pretended this was her room, her fine and beautiful possessions.

In a trance, she opened the clasp and fastened the chain around her neck. What was it like to live like this? Loosening a few buttons at the neck of her dress, she smiled into the mirror and swayed to a waltz heard only in her head. The little heart necklace nestled perfectly in the soft mounds of her cleavage.

The pouting and posing ended abruptly as the clicking of heels sounded in the hall. *Oh Lord, don't stop here.* The footsteps were coming closer. They were just outside the room. The knob turned. The chrysalis of fear broken, she sprang to her feet and secreted herself behind a three wing screen near the hearth.

It was the chambermaid. She turned down the bed, filled the wash pitcher with fresh water, and laid out her mistress's nightgown. Then she fluffed at the pillows, and left.

After counting ten, Beatrice scrambled upright and made a beeline to the door. When the coast was clear, she fled down the passageway to the backstairs, and straight out of the house. Leaving the lights and gaiety behind, she ran blindly toward the back of the property.

At the far edge of the garden, she stopped to catch her breath. Adjacent to the area were several ricks of wood, each covered with large oilskins. Shaking from head to toe, she edged between the towering mounds and wrapped her cape around her body. As she snuggled the material in at the throat, her fingers grazed across the gold locket still hanging around her neck.

"Oh Sweet Savior," she exclaimed, in a high-pitched whisper. "I didn't mean to take it. And I can't be returning it either."

Guilt nipped at her conscience. In the past, she'd been reduced to stealing, but only when she was down on her luck and near starving. Shoving the locket into the bodice of her dress, she gave a little gasp as the cold metal came in contact with her bare skin.

She would have to hide it when she got home. God forbid Lucien should see it. Surely he'd recognize it, ask questions, and punish her for leaving the flat. He would never believe she took it by accident. She shivered with dread at the thought of what he might do.

Swallowing her fear, she eased away from the ricks of wood and stared at the winding road leading back to town. Having left in such a dither, she hadn't thought about how she was going to get home. Stupid, stupid, stupid. She would have to hoof it, which would take hours.

Resigned to her fate she made to step forward, but a hand grabbed her shoulder holding her back. She screamed in surprise and turned to face what lurked in the dark. Her breath came in fits and gasps as panic set in.

"It's only me, Beatsie old girl," whispered Bartholomew. "Didn't mean to scare the living daylights out of you. Did you think it was the boogie man come to get you?" He growled and leaped about, amused at her fright.

"You big bloody fool," she screeched, and slapped

at his chest. "You scared me so I near peed my knickers. What are you doin' here anyway?"

"I might ask you the same, luv."

"You go first while I catch my breath."

"Lucien sent me here to keep me ogles on Captain Garrison."

Garrison again. She'd like to meet this man some day. "What you watchin' him for?"

"Just to see where he goes and what he's about. He's living on borrowed time. I got plans for the likes of him. I stepped out here to light a pipe," he added, stuffing a candy wrapper into his pocket.

"Is that who was dancing with the grand lady?"

"Aye. He's spent most of the night with the angelic what lives here."

"Why ain't she dancin' with Lucien?"

"He ain't even here, Beatsie. He's already got home. And he's in as foul a mood as I've ever seen. What are you doing out here? Him coming home and finding you gone is what put his rant over the top before he sent me out."

Fear blasted through her like a bolt of lightning, and she began to sweat. She had planned on returning home before Lucien knew about her escapade. They must have near passed on the road. There would be hell to pay now, delivered by the devil's favorite minion.

"You got a horse, Bart?"

He gave a nod. "He's staked out over yonder in them woods."

"Will you take me home quick as possible?"

"Sure, ducks. I guess Captain Garrison won't be goin' nowhere for a while."

"Thank you. I'd best face the music and get the

arse kicking over and done with."

"More likely you'll be facing the back of Lucien's hand."

"It won't be the first time. I'll tell him I went for a walk. You won't let on you seen me here will you?"

"'Course not," Bart reassured. "Why don't you leave Lucien for good? You deserve better."

"I might deserve better, Bart. But deserving and getting are two very different things. I stay for the same reasons as you. There's nothing else out there for me."

"I got money saved," he revealed. "When this next job is over and done, we'll strike out on our own. We'll get by somehow."

"If only we could, Bart. That'd be a dream come true."

Her brother, big lummox that he was, gently took her hand and led her through the darkness toward the waiting horse.

Chapter Ten

The carriage swung onto the avenue adjacent to Hyde Park, and the Crystal Palace came into view. Like a towering arrangement of earthbound stars, the gleaming glass and metal sparkled in the night—the image forever imprinted on Trelayne's memory.

Her enthusiasm running high, Trelayne grabbed Walker's arm. The intimate action and her squeal of delight forced Aunt Abigail to issue the mandatory cough of disapproval, but the reprimand was followed by a smile the older woman couldn't suppress. Walker chuckled, and patted Trelayne's gloved hand.

They sped past a fountain spewing water 250 feet into the air, wending their way through a collection of statues claiming safe-harbor within the boundaries of the surrounding park. At the geological display, life-size restorations of extinct animals peered back at them in terrifying splendor.

It was a magical evening, and it was all Walker's doing. Reaching the front entrance, they presented their "by special permission only" invitations, and unlike opening day in May, when 26,000 people clamored for a glimpse of the royal family, the anticipation hovering over tonight's select group was wrapped in an almost reverential hush.

"What a magnificent achievement," her aunt murmured. "We are part of history, child, remember this night."

With Walker at her side, how could she forget? It was almost as splendid as dancing in his arms. Edging closer to him, she wondered if he treasured their night together too. Then, realizing she was missing the here and now by fixating on their previous romantic interlude, she took in the sights and sounds, and reveled in the drama of it all.

Along with a towering tree, grand bits and pieces of nearly every country were nestled beneath nine hundred thousand square feet of Birmingham glass. Wooden floors gleamed underfoot, louvers at the top ushered in fresh air, and in the Retiring Rooms, patrons were forming a queue to use George Jenning's revolutionary "necessary convenience." Only a penny per customer.

"No dawdling, ladies," Walker advised, escorting them along. "The Queen is expected at any moment, and we've barely a chance to secure a vantage point from which to enjoy the ceremony."

In a flurry, they hurried past Egyptian sarcophagi, Russian bronzes, and America's Goodyear exhibit of India rubber goods. Not daring to lag behind, she grabbed a handful of fabric from her new dress and hiked it up to keep from tripping. The voluminous skirt swished playfully from side to side even as it threatened to lay her low. Admittedly too long, she had refused to send it back. The ensemble had arrived from the dressmaker late this afternoon, alterations would have meant not wearing it tonight—a thought not worth entertaining. Accented by the matching hat, a miracle of feathers wrought by her favorite milliner and plumassier, this was the long awaited outfit she had intended to wear for Lucien.

Guilt fought for a foothold, but nothing could conquer her delight in the costume's unveiling being instead for Walker. Following the Michaelmas party, feelings for her American sea captain dominated her life, and thoughts of him were the balm desperately needed to sooth the horror elicited by her new nightmare. The one filled with blood and terror. The one in which she was the central character. It was the first disturbing vision she'd had since her parent's accident. And the only one she'd ever had about herself.

With a shiver, she glanced up at Walker. When he was at her side, the nightmare seemed cowed and far less threatening. He made her feel safe and able to overcome anything thrown in her path. Swallowing her fears, she defied the unease. She would let nothing ruin a night holding so much promise.

Walker glanced down at her, giving her hat the once over. He opened his mouth as if to comment, but instead fell silent, and smiled at her. She wasn't sure if he approved of her chapeau, or was suppressing an urge to laugh. He was more of a mystery than any man she had ever known. And perhaps if elegant did not describe him, virile and self-confident surely did. Proud to be on his arm tonight, she wished they might stroll along leisurely, savoring the experience, but they rushed onward like children at the fair—reaching the South American exhibit with only moments spare.

Queen Victoria and Prince Albert, seated majestically beside the display, appeared more than ready for the ceremony to begin. With royal flair, the great woman nodded, and the botanical masterpiece was unveiled. Shiny green leaves, nearly three meters across, drew a murmur of awe from the crowd. Then drenched in moonlight, the exotic white female flower opened. Astonishment turned to delight. Tomorrow at sunset, the mysterious plant would bloom pink, and transform into a male flower.

Jockeying for a better view, Trelayne shifted about. To accommodate her attempt, Walker eased her sideways to stand in front of him. After that, the ceremony became a blur as every fiber of her being was devoted to sensing Captain Garrison's rock solid body at her back.

The essence of manly soap and cologne issued around her, and the warmth of his breath played across the nape of her neck. Without thinking, she leaned back ever so slightly. As if answering the silent call of her body, he pressed forward, sending a desperate yearning coursing through her. These were not the pangs of girlish desires. These were cravings raw and lustful, beyond anything she had ever known. It was an awakening. All previous thoughts of love and romance were reduced to mere watercolor illusions when compared to the dazzling vibrant emotion evoked by simply standing beside Walker.

"The lily pales in comparison to you," he whispered in her ear.

Did he also entertain a reckless thought or two?

Her knees went weak, and a sweet lightness filled her chest. She wished they were alone in the moonlight with no one to see as they slid to the ground, lost in one another's arms.

Suddenly a cheer rose up, jolting her back to reality. She'd missed the entire ceremony. Everyone was clapping as the Queen and her consort took their leave. Still under the spell of enchantment, Trelayne brought her gloved hands together intending to follow suite. Instead, she clasped them in prayer, and gave thanks for such an exceptional evening of newfound delight.

Walker turned her around to face him. The heated expression in his eyes left her fighting for a decent breath. Lips parted, heart pounding, she felt herself being drawn closer and closer to him, and although it was only in wayward thought and delicious contemplation, in her mind, they kissed—long and sweet and passionately.

"Garrison, you old scallywag. You're a sight for these sore eyes."

As if caught doing more than simply staring at one another, they reared back in unison. A tall rambunctious man bore down on them, halted at their side, and slapped Walker on the back.

"Sam Colt," Walker exclaimed, the joy evident in his voice. "You rough ridin' son of a gun. Dressed in such finery, I hardly recognized you. You haven't gone citified on me have you?"

"Hell no. Oh, pardon the language ladies," the fellow begged, with a tip of his hat to her and Aunt Abigail. Then he tugged at his shirt collar, and tried to tame his riotous beard and mustache. "I'm simply out to impress some of the gentry here about in the hopes of procuring financial backing."

Walker nodded in understanding, then introduced his friend. "Samuel Colt, may I present Miss Abigail Royston and Miss Trelayne St.Christopher."

Trelayne extended her hand. "A pleasure to meet

you, Mr. Colt."

Colt gave Walker a strange look then bowed over her hand. She could have sworn there was a questioning expression in the man's eyes, followed by a spark of curiosity.

"Exactly what is this project of yours?" she asked, when he relinquished his hold.

"It's my new Navy revolver, Miss Trelayne. Even more striking than the Army Dragoon—if I say so myself. Here's the one I promised you, Garrison." He liberated a pistol from beneath his frock coat, and held it up for all to see.

"It's a shade lighter than my other weapons," Colt said, hefting the revolver. "Could have used this back in '46, eh friend?"

"It couldn't have hurt," Walker agreed.

The men appeared lost in a shared memory, indicating they were longstanding friends with an intertwined past.

"Is your weapon already in production?" Trelayne asked, breaking the silence.

"It surely is, ma'am," Colt acknowledged, cradling the pistol in his arms. "She's a .36 caliber beauty with a lovely seven and a half inch rifled barrel. A six shot like the Dragoon, but a bit more diminutive in size." As he spoke, the glow of pride and enthusiasm returned to his aura.

"You sound like you're extolling the virtues of a woman rather than a weapon," Walker joked.

"Either one can cause a man considerable pain," Colt ventured. His voice had lost its teasing edge. Walker stood a little taller and glanced down at the floor. Again Colt perused Trelayne with a speculative air.

"How many grains of powder would you recommend?" She issued the question with genuine interest, as well as an attempt at furthering the conversation.

"Around twenty-eight grains," Colt replied. "She's accurate up to fifty yards, depending on who's shootin'. But the most remarkable and innovative aspect of my creation, is the fact all the parts are interchangeable, and preloaded cylinders are available."

"Is that important?" Aunt Abigail interjected.

"Absolutely. It will revolutionize the gun industry. If'n something breaks, you replace that part, not the whole darn pistol. Makes protection available to the common man as well as the rich. The equalizer, it's been called." As he spoke, he broke the pistol down into three parts, barrel, chamber, and frame. Then he quickly reassembled them. "Child's play," he quipped.

"It certainly is a formidable looking piece," Aunt Abigail added. "Will you be in England long, Mr. Colt?"

"Well, I reckon I'll be around a few months."

"You must see your way clear to visit us at Royston Hall," she graciously offered. "When you come, you might bring along a few of those. We've a shooting range outback, and we women pride ourselves on being as proficient as the men. Perhaps you could give me some personal instructions."

Trelayne's eyes widened at her aunt's innuendos. Did she detect a glow of interest as well as adventure in her demeanor?

Samuel handed the pistol off to Walker. "You can depend upon it, dear lady," he promised, ambling closer. "Care to mosey around a bit? There's sights here I've yet to see." Boldly taking her aunt by the elbow, Samuel Colt escorted her to the nearest exhibit.

Stunned and openmouthed, Trelayne stared at Walker.

He shrugged. "Don't look at me. When he puts his mind to it, Samuel has that effect on women." He slid the pistol under his belt, giving him the air of a highwayman, then extended his arm. "Shall we join them?"

"I was hoping you'd ask."

As they turned to follow, a group of onlookers blocked their advance. The rowdy bunch seemed to materialize out of nowhere, crossing their path without care or concern. One man stepped backward, and jostled into her. Off balance, and caught in the too long hem of her dress, she nearly fell on her face. Without missing a heartbeat, Walker gathered her close. Cheek to cheek, a whimper of pleasure escaped her, and she relished the urge to nestle her head against his shoulder.

The group rushed on, leaving them standing alone. She should push Walker away, but she held fast, yearning to wrap her arms around his neck and seduce his mouth with hers. To prevent answering the wicked desire, she pressed the fingertips of her gloved right hand to her lips, creating a barrier not to be crossed.

Walker stepped away from her. "We'd best move on," he suggested, his voice thick with emotion.

She nodded, glancing straight ahead, afraid to meet his gaze; afraid if given half a chance she would drag him off behind a potted palm so they might continue where they had left off. Lord above, she felt positively bold and brash and barely able to contain the shameless ideas threatening her good senses.

In silence, they meandered past McCormick's reaper and a very unromantic hydraulic press. Then to her surprise, Walker tightened his grip on her elbow and urged her off the walkway and into the shadow of one of the hulking iron contraptions.

She felt light headed, and her cheeks grew warm with the unstoppable heat caused by his intense perusal.

"That's some hat you're sporting," he said.

His unexpected comment took her off guard, leaving her confused. "You don't like my new hat?"

"I didn't say I didn't like it, just that it was really something."

"That's a bit vague. *Something* can mean good or bad."

He canted his head and studied her more thoroughly. "It's unique, I'll give you that." He flicked a finger at the bright bow and scarlet ribbons cascading down one side of the creation. "And unexpected."

"Do you like surprises?" she ventured.

"Not generally," he admitted. "But I do like discovering new things, taking my time, savoring each revelation, wondering what will come next.

Capturing her left hand, he toyed with the buttons on her glove. Entranced, she waited restlessly, conjuring naughty images of what he might try to discover next. One by one, he slipped the buttons free, splaying open the soft leather. Cool air slipped beneath the material as he rolled down the top, exposing her skin. The pulse in her wrist jump beneath the pressure of his fingers. Raising her hand to his mouth, he whispered something, but she couldn't catch the words, only the feel of his breath on her bare skin. He lowered her hand, and little by little peeled the kid leather away, turning it inside out, sliding the softness over her knuckles, down her fingers, off the tips. She wished he would undress the rest of her just as completely and slowly—oh so slowly, one little piece of clothing following another.

"Your fingers are cold, Trelayne," he said, cozying her bare hand between his strong warm ones. "But I'll wager there's fire in your heart."

Speechless, she strangled the moan threatening to escape her. There was fire in more than just her heart, and it was near to burning out of control. Was it proper for a woman to ravish a man? For that was exactly what she wished to do.

A hint of smile lingered on his mouth, but his eyes darkened, and there was nothing humorous about the way his gaze made her feel.

She wished to speak, but words escaped her. Rarely at a loss as to what to do or say, she tried to recall what she'd been taught in deportment about keeping up lively conversation and witty dialogue. Nothing came to mind to cover a situation in which her body ruled her mind. All she could think about was what it would be like to kiss this man, make love to this man, be naked beside this man.

"Fires can be dangerous," she murmured.

"Yes," he agreed. "Especially the ones that burn long and slow and incredibly hot."

Illustrations from the books she read in secret seared across her mind—scandalous, wonderful imaginings.

He leaned in closer. She swore he was about to kiss her, could feel his breath and the tiniest tickle of his mustache as his mouth hovered oh so near her lips. Then he straightened, his expression one of confusion, even consternation. He looked like a man delirious with fever, just come to his senses.

"We should find the others," he suggested, releasing her from the spell she was under. It was the last thing she wanted. Couldn't he tell, didn't he know?

"Out of all the wonders here tonight," he reassured, "spending time with you is what I shall remember most."

****

Barefoot and wrapped in a counterpane, Trelayne shuffled across her bedroom and stared out the window. She should go to sleep, but then the evening would be over—an evening of unparalleled experiences.

Walker had almost kissed her. And as they continued to make turn after turn around the Crystal Palace, he had held her ungloved hand rather than her elbow. She couldn't recall what they had seen, but she remembered the feel of his large, strong, and capable hand as she envisioned it touching other parts of her body.

What would it feel like to stroke the forbidden parts of a man, and claim them as one's own? She and Pen had worn thin the pictures in their purloined books and novels. Did all men look the same? The majority of their bodies were beautiful, but their special parts were foreign and rather fiercely grotesque. Craving to put into practice what so far had only been theory, she squirmed with pent up eagerness and mounting desire.

Leaning her forehead against the windowpane, seeking the cool relief it offered, she peered at the night sky. Heavy and full, tonight the moon seemed to lumber rather than sail across the inky blackness. As it now dipped behind the trees, the last of its ethereal glow slanted across the autumnal landscape. It turned the foliage a pearly gray and the cony hopping across the yard to sterling silver. The whole world was enchanted since Captain Walker Garrison had entered her small portion.

A peaceful bliss wrapped around her tighter than the comforter. Then it wavered. It felt wrong to be so contented when her parents were still struggling to recover from their grievous wounds. Yet she knew they would want her to be happy and not moping about growing thin with worry. And they had sent Walker to watch over her—sent him to care for her. It seemed safe and sensible to unquestionably trust him. But was it foolish to undeniably fall in love with him.

There, she'd admitted it. She was falling—no, had fallen—in love with him. The declaration made her feel worse rather than better. She knew next to nothing about him. He was a man of anonymity, a foreigner, a big tall gorgeous American who looked like he had tamed the Wild West single handedly, and then conquered the Seven Seas. She shook her head. No man could live up to such a romantic image. But somehow, in her heart, she thought Captain Garrison would try.

Chapter Eleven

For the second day in a row, Walker idled away his time at the tobacconist.

Fortunately, it was a comfortable atmosphere, granting an unobstructed view of the chocolate shop across the street. It was also a long shot his efforts would be anymore fruitful today than they had been yesterday. Still, what other clues did he have to follow?

All hope hinged on a name scribbled on a boarding roster and the foil wrappers found in New Bedford so many miles away. He supposed it was possible he would never track down the man who had murdered Seaman Barkley and injured Philip and Ophelia. No more attempts had been made on their lives or his. Maybe one killing was enough to satisfy whoever was behind all this.

Either way, it left him with a belly full of discontent. He didn't cotton to loose ends and unsettled scores. Getting to the bottom of all this weighed heavily on his mind. How he felt about Trelayne was also taking its toll. The memory of nearly kissing her flashed through him. He grew hard at the recollection. How he'd burned with the desire to take her in his arms, to kiss her, and do so much more. And unless he was completely adrift at sea, she'd harbored the same intentions.

When this nasty business was put to rest, maybe

courting her properly wasn't completely out of the realm of possibilities. She'd captured his imagination, given him the gift of contemplating the future rather than just the next hour or the next day. There was a great difference between staying alive, and actually wanting to live.

Up the street, a hansom cab turned onto the lane and came into view, and his thoughts jumped back to the present. Straightening to his full height, he stepped closer to the window. Well lookie-there, it was none other than Lucien Lanteen, and he wasn't alone. At the confectionary, the coach drew to a halt and rocked as the larger of the two men stepped down. The stranger headed toward the store as the carriage and Lucien rattled out of sight.

A growl rumbled in the back of Walker's throat. On general principle, Lanteen made his mustache bristle and his hackles rise. The man seemed slippery as a sidewinder, and just as dangerous. And his familiarity with Trelayne was a worry. Did she reciprocate feelings beyond friendship toward the Englishman? Deep down he felt the man was somehow involved, but discrediting him would be difficult. A delicate task demanding solid evidence. Of which he had none.

The thought of a relationship existing between Trelayne and this English dandy put his stomach in a knot, and it was becoming harder to dismiss his own sentiments where Trelayne was concerned. Of course, his feelings should be irrelevant. He was here to protect his partner's daughter, not fall in love with her. Anything else would be dangerous, causing him to lose focus and make mistakes. He couldn't afford to blunder. But not falling in love with Trelayne was one battle he thought he might lose. It had been a long time since feelings like these had stirred his heart and soul. He liked it, and it scared him.

The man re-emerged from the shop, popped a chocolate into his mouth, and tossed the wrapper aside. Walker crossed the street and followed at a discreet distance, snagging the gold embossed foil along the way. His pulse quickened. The wrapper was the same as those he carried. If this man was Grimsby, the puzzle pieces were beginning to fit together nicely. It reinforced the logic Lanteen was involved, but it wasn't solid evidence.

The big burly man with the penchant for sweets looked a nasty piece of work, an unlikely acquaintance for the St.Christopher's uppity solicitor. However, he did fit the role of henchman extremely well.

His quarry lumbered down the walkway and turned in at nearby pub. The sign swinging over the entrance held the image of an angry black bull. Removing his hat, Walker slipped inside and scrunched down on a bench in a shadowed niche behind a timbered upright. The place was all but empty smelling of brew, tobacco, and men who did manual labor for a living. The person he followed swaggered across the room to the table closest to the tavern keeper's station.

"You're a bit early, Grimsby," the grizzled old proprietor quipped. "Ain't even noon."

Walker's gaze narrowed. *It was him.*

"You don't want my business, I'll go elsewhere," Grimsby shot back.

"Ha, you've been banned from nearly every pub in town. The Black Bull's the only one will have you."

"Just give your red rag a holiday, and set me up.

And none of that queer Nantz and crank either. I want the good stuff."

"I takes offense at that," the elderly barkeep snapped. "I don't water my gin. You well know that. If I did, I wouldn't have so many coves losing their grinders and blackening their glims with fighting every Saturday night."

"Aw right, aw right. Please accept my deepest apology," Grimsby sneered. "Now give me a bloody drink. I got a long ride ahead of me."

"Where you heading?" the purveyor asked, as he poured.

"South," came Grimsby's vague answer. "Got me a job down there will pay off big. Maybe big enough to retire."

"That's what you said afore you went to America," the other man razzed

"That didn't exactly work out as planned. And I told you that on the quiet. This time is different."

Grimsby lowered his voice, and Walker missed the next bit of the conversation. Damn. *Keep him talking*, he willed the tavern owner.

"You're full of tales of glory, Bart. I think all that chocolate you eat has rotted your brain as well as your teeth." The man hooted at his own jest, and swiped at the table with a semi-clean rag.

"Aw, what do you know?" Grimsby jeered, at full volume. "I'm glad to be going to Brighton so's I won't have to be ogling your ugly mug or drinking your piss tastin' brew." With that, he drained his glass, threw down a few coins, and stomped out.

When the coast was clear, Walker settled his hat in place and sauntered up to the table Grimsby had vacated. "I could go for a pint," he said. *And hopefully a bit more information.*

The tavern owner eyed him suspiciously, but filled the request.

"That Grimsby's quite the character," Walker said, testing the waters.

"A bad character," came the unexpected response.

"I thought he was a friend of yours," Walker pressed.

"With friends like that a body wouldn't need enemies. That's an interesting topper you got there mister. You from America?"

"That's where I call home," he acknowledged.

The old man nodded. "Our Mr. Grimsby has recently returned from there his very self. Or so he says. That why you asking about him—he get hisself in trouble over there, too?"

"What do you mean, 'too'?" Walker probed.

"Too, is what I mean. It's simple enough," the elder man replied irritably. "He's in trouble everywhere he goes. That's understood. If trouble ain't there waitin' for him when he arrives, he ferrets it out like a pig in a truffle patch. He likes trouble. He invented trouble."

"Slow down." Walker chuckled at the pub keeper's theatrical display. "I get the idea. Do you happen to know where he's going?"

"Where he's goin'? Why he's probably gone lookin' for more trouble. Ha. That's a good one ain't it?"

"Indeed. But I'm serious. The man owes me money, and I heard him say he was into something big with good times coming. I'd like to be there when it happens and get what's due me before he spends it or disappears."

The old man pondered a moment then seemed to come to a conclusion.

"Is it a considerable sum? If it ain't," he advised, not waiting for a reply, "you'd best chalk it up to experience, and leave this one alone. Bartholomew Grimsby's an unpleasant person what will do almost anything for a price, and that includes murder."

Rather than a warning, the words came as music to his ears. Grimsby definitely sounded the culprit responsible for injuring his friends and killing his crewman. The exact why of it was still unclear, but that could be sorted out later. And he knew the ruffian hadn't conjured the plan alone. He appeared suited to following orders rather than conceiving and implementing grand schemes. That's where Lanteen came in. Of course, sharing a carriage ride wasn't proof they collaborated on the crime. What he needed was a witness. Someone who knew they worked side by side in dirty dealings and worse.

"It truly is important," Walker insisted. "A matter of life and death, so to speak."

"Well, you look as if you can take care of yourself. Just don't underestimate the blackguard, or turn your back on him. He mentioned he was going to Brighton to meet a ship coming in from Africa. There's only one port there deep enough to accommodate a vessel of any consequence, so that should narrow down your search. He was a mite secretive about his intentions. Not his usual blowhard self. Maybe it is important."

"How far away is Brighton?"

"About an eight hour trip if you know how to ride and don't dillydally. And if you be considering going by coach, don't. With the roads still rutted from the late summer rains, it'll take you twice as long and you're bound to rattle loose a tooth in the process."

Eight hours. That was a relief. It amazed him England was such a small country. Back home a man could spend months, wandering the southwest territory with nothing for company but coyotes, cutthroats, and cactus.

"Thanks for the information." He laid down twice what he owed and turned to leave.

"Thank *you*," the old man exclaimed, scooping up the money. "And best of luck to ya."

Good luck couldn't hurt, but right now what he really needed was a sturdy mount. They had lots of suitable horseflesh at Royston Hall.

****

"You just missed him," Aunt Abigail explained.

"But why didn't he wait?"

Trelayne couldn't abide women who simpered and whimpered; yet she had to quell the urge to stamp her foot and pout. She was hurt. Walker had come to visit, but couldn't bother to accommodate her schedule and await her return from the nearby Vicarage.

"To be honest, darling, he came about a horse, not you."

"A horse!"

This was even worse news. They'd held hands, feverishly embraced, come a breath away from kissing, and after two days not a word. No courtesy call to prove his good intentions, no treasured trinket. Not even a note to express his feelings for her.

Seeing Walker again was all she could think about. Apparently he had other things on his mind. She flounced across the room, yes flounced, and didn't care.

Well, it was her own fault wasn't it? How silly of her to have so easily fallen prey to her emotions. In a matter of days, she'd allowed Walker to become the center of her world, a world spinning out of control.

Her mind far removed from the charitable duties discussed during her visit with Father Woolsey, she set aside the list of handwritten information he'd supplied.

Perhaps she misunderstood. Surely, Walker had asked about her, left a message regarding expectations of returning this evening to formally call upon her.

"Will Captain Garrison be joining us later?"

"According to Merrick," Aunt Abigail relayed, "he's off to Brighton, and will be gone two or three days. In his absence, he reminded us we should all be on our guard. And he specifically advised you should stay at home."

That bit of news left her torn between happiness at his concern for her safety, and ire at his presuming to dictate her comings and goings.

"I suppose three days isn't all that long," she admitted.

"I got the impression," her aunt confided, "he was following up a new lead regarding the incident with your parents."

Now her emotional scale tilted to the forgiving/grateful side. She had been thinking only of herself. She shouldn't have jumped to conclusions. After all, he *was* on a mission to right the terrible wrongs befallen her family. An image of him slaying dragons and offering himself as her knight-errant-protector flittered through her mind. If properly nurtured, her memories of him from the party and their evening at the Crystal Palace would surely get her through the next few days.

****

Walker glanced around, making sure he hadn't overlooked anything. Then in preparation for an early morning departure, he placed the saddle-pack near the door to his hotel room.

He regretted not speaking to Trelayne before his southbound trip. But if he had, it would only make leaving all the harder, stirring up thoughts best left sleeping. A clear head and quick reflexes were what he needed, not muddled daydreams, his actions slowed by visions of shell-pink lips and warm hazel eyes.

While collecting the horse at the stable, he'd chanced to observe her arriving home from some outing. Knowing she was ensconced at Royston Hall and under Merrick's watchful eye put his mind at ease—although being so close and not touching her put his private parts in an uproar.

Alighting from the coach, she'd disengaged her bonnet, allowing her hair to escape in a free-spirited tumble, the sun adding a burnished glow to her tresses. How he longed to tangle his fingers in those curls. How he longed to do so many things with her—and to her. But for now, desiring her from afar was the best idea. No, make that the only idea. Or better yet, not desiring her at all should be his approach to the matter.

Ambling around the room, he raked his fingers through his hair then unbuttoned his shirt. The chance of getting any sleep tonight seemed slim to none. Still, he needed to try and rest. He unearthed a flask from his pack, and downed a healthy shot of Scotch whiskey. The fiery liquid mellowed in his stomach and spread outward, the warmth soothing the thoughts haranguing his mind.

However, nothing blunted the unrequited need torturing his body.

Chapter Twelve

As night slackened its hold, Bartholomew cinched his coat tighter and jammed his misshapen hat further down over his ears. It always seemed coldest just before dawn.

For him, the road to Brighton was a familiar one, with Oxted and Burgess Hill not far off. He'd already passed Merton and Croydon where unsuspecting villages slumbered peacefully, unaware that one such as he prowled the neighboring fens.

Glancing uneasily back the way he'd come, he patted the old flintlock pistol at his hip. He'd be glad when this particular shipment was safely ashore and stored at Amberley Abbey. There were dangers to worry about in this business, what with pirates and magistrates. Government officials could be bought off to avoid the usual tariffs and troubles, but cutthroats were hard to reason with. And although he'd made a name for himself in the district, and knew a few cullies for hire, he'd be left to his own devises once he reached the coast.

Getting old, that's what the trouble was. It made a man afraid. Afraid he couldn't keep up, afraid of change, afraid things would never change. Lately he felt his time was running out. He wondered if Lucien would truly be satisfied with his latest endeavor. Probably not. The ponies and gambling dens always drained away his fortunes. Betting and greediness seemed as much an addiction for Mr. Lanteen as opium was for Beatrice.

"Bah, you know the truth, Barty old boy," he growled. "Lucien will bleed ya dry of services and anything else he can get. Just as he does with all who come into contact with him."

Thoughts of his sister came to mind—poor old nug. What anguish did she suffer at Lucien's hands? The man harbored a vicious nature and was a randy sonofabitch—never satisfied on that account either. He doubted she would ever run away with him as they'd talked about. Still, Beatrice was better off being Lucien's wagtail than a three-penny upright in a White Chapel back-alley. They all had to do what was necessary to survive.

Too tired to think about it, he yawned and scrunched around trying to find a more comfortable position in the saddle. He'd left London in the wee small hours of the night, and now as his horse plodded along, the rocking motion nearly put him asleep.

Hours later, as fingers of lights splayed up from the eastern horizon, he stopped to breakfast in a small glade. Brighton and Chain Pier weren't far off now, and he'd earned a few minutes out of the saddle. Retrieving bread and hard cheese from his pack, he left his horse to graze, and tucked in beneath the shelter of a large oak. A mound of fallen leaves served as a natural cushion, and he ate his victuals with enthusiasm, wiping his grubby hands on his stained jerkin. Occasionally he took a pull from the silver flask, feloniously procured many years ago. He could no longer remember the face of the unlucky victim. His list of prey had grown too large to commit to memory.

He damped his mug with more Old Tom, and set his thoughts to wandering. They snagged and held on Captain Garrison. Dispatching that foreigner was a chore to look forward to. The mere idea of arranging a painful demise for the Yankee roughneck cheered and invigorated him. He wouldn't get away a second time. Too bad this trip had postponed their destined engagement. Still, if all went well, he'd be back in London soon enough. He grazed his hand across the stubble on his chin and laughed. Sending the Good Captain to his final rest had become a personal challenge, a battle of wits as well as brawn.

****

The sun broke free of the horizon as Walker took his leave on the southbound road to Brighton.

Yesterday afternoon, while procuring the horse, he entrusted the majority of his belongings to Merrick. Now with his hotel bill paid in full, he rode along unencumbered, confident in purpose and destination.

Departing last night had been a consideration, but this proved a better choice. Traveling by the light of day gave him a chance to study the lay of the land. Of course, as predicted, a good night's sleep had been impossible. He'd only gotten snippets of rest interspersed with disconnected thoughts, and absurd arguments about whether he should or shouldn't risk falling in love with Trelayne. He couldn't seem to leave the subject alone. Like a pebble in his boot, it kept begging for attention.

Based purely on logic, the resolution was obvious. But considering the urges in his body and the yearning in his heart, he was leaning toward falling head over heels. Maybe being away for three or four days would put things in perspective.

Touching his St. Brendan medal for safe travel, he kept alert for the bogs Merrick had warned about, wishing this trip over and done. Wishing he were riding away from rather than toward Brighton. He was about to kick the big gelding into a more urgent pace, then reconsidered. A long day's ride lay ahead, and if his mount was to make it in good stead, it wouldn't do to wear him out in the first few miles.

What was the ship's payload, and how would it tie back to the Lanteen? He supposed the squab was good looking in a "need to be mothered" sort of way. But he also reckoned evilness simmered beneath the dashing veneer. And when it boiled over, there would be hell to pay.

Suddenly, he regretted not speaking to Trelayne before hitting the trail. He should have done something more grandiose than sending the souvenir gloves, commemorating their night at the Crystal Palace. The street vender had promised to complete and deliver the pair by currier as soon as possible. Hopefully, she would receive them today.

He patted the pocket of his long coat, and retrieved the kid glove taken from her hand that evening. Soft as her skin, he raised the scrap of leather and inhaled deeply. Her fragrance lingered, sending hot blood surging to his groin. He shifted uncomfortably in the saddle. Lord, how he wanted to make love to her, claim her as his woman. But these were basic emotions, not necessarily related to love. Going it alone was good enough, it was safer not needing anyone, and he'd gotten along all right so far since Katie's death. He was doing just fine. Besides, Trelayne had a life of her own, years in the making. He was a recent interloper—moving too fast where his emotions were concerned.

****

By mid-afternoon, the coastal hamlet came into view, and Walker turned east at Seven Dials then followed Buckingham Place until it merged with the Terminus Road. Winding past the train yards and the clock tower, he took Queen's Road to the pier area. Spotting a local eatery, he decided a well-earned meal sounded soul saving.

Dismounting, he took off his hat and used it to beat the trail dust from his trousers and coat. Then he bought a copy of the *Brighton Gazette*. The lad hawking the papers did so with little enthusiasm, acting as if he would rather be off fishing, enjoying the last warm days of fall. Hat in hand, the newspaper tucked under his arm, he entered the rustic eating establishment.

A middle-aged woman of ample girth sashayed his way. With a high-spirited twinkle in her merry brown eyes, she gave him a thorough perusal.

"Are all the ladies working here as fetching as you?" he teased, shamelessly taking advantage of her interest.

"'Course not, luv," she sparred back. "They only send me out when the customer be a strapping young man needing something pleasant to look at while he fills his belly. What'll you have besides a good gander at me?"

He glanced at the chalkboard on the wall by the kitchen. "The clam-haddock chowder and a mug of spiced wine would be welcome."

"Smart choice," she agreed. "I'll be back in a heartbeat."

He skimmed the newspaper as he waited, trying to get a feel for the town and the people who lived there. It was devoid of anything of interest, and when the waitress returned, placing the food before him, he set the paper aside.

"Looks delicious. Thank you."

"You're welcome, luv. What brings you to our town?" She bent low and swept at imaginary crumbs, offering a playful display of her ample bosom.

"I was hoping they'd were hiring on the docks," he answered, "or perhaps there's a ship ready to sail needs another hand on deck?"

"It'd be a shame sendin' the likes of you out to sea," she bemoaned. "Think of all the lonely ladies you'd be leavin' behind. Why don't ye seek employment in the city? Then you could come by now and again. I'd make sure you got only the best—of everything," she added, with a wink.

Walker gave a bark of laughter, admiring the woman's zest for life.

"If only I had met you sooner," he played along, "before I lost my heart to the sea. I'd be as lonely without the ocean as you pretend you would be without me."

"Well, if there's no changing your mind, you might be visitin' the Wayside this evening. It's out by the docks, and the place most of the recruiting gets done. But be watchin' your step. Many a quarryman frequents there as well as sailors, so the fightin' and fuedin' breaks out regular like. I'd be feeling gawd-awful if I was responsible for sending such a fine specimen as you into any danger."

He appreciated the woman's concern, but from

Shanghai to Montevideo, he'd crossed the thresholds of the roughest establishments in the world. He could take care of himself—in a fair fight. Of course *fair* and the Wayside didn't sound synonymous.

As more customers arrived, his server tore herself from his side to see to their needs. Finished eating, he leaned his chair back against the wall, and tried for the appearance of nonchalance. Then bored with reading the newspaper, he laid down a generous tip and left.

At a reputable stable, he bedded down his mount, and for an extra fee rented a box to stow his few clothes, his hat, and other gear. Then he procured lodging in a less reputable hotel.

When darkness fell, he followed the waitress's directions to the Wayside and lingered in the shadows. Each time the door opened, a rousing combination of merriment and heated arguments escaped into the night.

A group of men materialized out of the fog. Probably quarry workers coming off shift. Most miners were honest God-fearing souls, but this coven looked a motley crew at best.

As the group entered the pub, he eased forward, blending in with the tail end of the ragtag collection. Once inside, he surveyed the layout, veered off to the right, and made for the far end of the bar. With the security of a solid wall to one side, he waited and watched and ordered an ale.

The only two women in the tavern appeared tired and faded. They plied their trade in dimly lit alcoves offering questionable enthusiasm and well practiced skill. All the while, the crowd grew more boisterous and agitated—the scuffles and disagreement more prevalent and serious. A few unfriendly glances were aimed his way.

Beckoning for a refill, he tried some tactful palavering. "To your health friend," he said, after the man set him up.

"I'll watch me own damn health, Yank. And I ain't your friend."

So much for that idea. Although he'd forgone his hat, his appearance and speech still gave him away.

"Truth be told," the man added, "we ain't too partial to your kind around here. Hasn't been all that long since we gandered one another through the sights of a rifle, if you get my drift. Why don't you head back to where you come from?"

"I'd be more than happy to oblige," Walker replied, with forced congeniality. "Fact is, I can't think of anything I'd rather do than to leave your precious little island, but you'll have to accommodate me a job first. I need money to book passage."

"Bloody hell," the barman sputtered. "You want us to feed you, and wipe your arse for you, too?"

Walker ignored the insults. "I heard there's a Mr. Grimsby down here offers short term employment at considerable wage. All a man needs do is work hard and know to keep his mouth shut."

The rotund man's eyes widened slightly then his expression hardened. "You heard wrong," he growled. "There's no Mr. Bartholomew Grimsby here. And there's no high paying jobs. Finish up, mister, and get out. We don't like drinkin' with strange dogs bearing strange notions."

He'd struck a nerve. He hadn't mentioned Grimsby by his first name, but the tavern keeper had. The two obviously knew one another. Refusing to be hurried, he eased back against the wall, returning the defiant stare.

Still chewing on a disagreeable expression, the man headed for the far end of the bar to tend his other patrons. A few minutes later, he beckoned a raggedy lad, spoke to him quietly, and sent him packing.

****

Bartholomew lounged in a private area off the main room of the Wayside. It was a cozy hideaway reserved for special customers. It came with a less tired, less faded girl. And for an extra tip, the poor doxy even pretended she was enjoying herself.

This was the upside of visiting Brighton. By local standards, he was a big fish, treated with grudging respect. And it was as much because of his own notoriety as it was Mr. Lanteen's. Folks here feared him—with good reason. And when need be, they did his bidding.

Tipping the velvet, he put his hands up the girl's skirt, his intentions for sampling her wares fully underway until a knock sounded at the door

"Damnation. It's getting so a man can't even roger a tart without disruption."

Pissed off, he pushed the startled girl to one side, crossed the room, and opened the door a crack to glare at the boy waiting on the other side.

"Better be important for yer interrupting me," he growled.

"Aye sir," the lad reassured him, "Philly said you'd best take heed. Some stranger out front's asking about you."

Philly, the bartender, was a long time acquaintance. He wouldn't send a warning without good cause.

"All right. Good lad. Now get lost."

He glanced at the girl, and grabbed the front of his pants to adjust his private parts. "Keep it warm and keep it wet," he snickered. Enjoying one last leer at the girl's bubbies, he slipped into the dim passageway.

Halfway down the corridor, he turned and faced the wall. Closing one eye, he pressed his face close to the ill-fitting panels. The view over Philly's shoulder into the adjoining barroom came into focus. At first, he didn't see anything out of the ordinary. Then Philly moved his hulky frame, and Bartholomew inhaled sharply. Not twenty feet away sat the bane of his existence. Not believing what he saw, he pulled away from the wall, rubbed his knuckles in his eye sockets, and took another look.

"God's bones. You righteous bastard. Right here in Brighton. It's a one-way trip for you then, Captain. You'll not be returnin' to fair London Town."

****

The evening was not going well. Walker tried engaging a few patrons in conversation, but they ignored him. And although he had a hankering for another ale, the only thing he could garner from the bloated toad of a barkeep was more dirty looks.

After midnight, the bobbery and confusion reached a crescendo then slid into a debauched decline. Tired and downhearted, his optimism bruised around the edges, he admitted temporary defeat and took his leave.

Navigating the avenue toward his hotel room, he put his current troubles out of mind and considered his long-range plans. Was it time to face the real world again? Time to give life another chance?

Since Katie's death, he'd existed in limbo—a void holding no joy, true love, or commitment. He was a ship adrift with no destination. She wouldn't want that for him. It had been nearly five years since that winter's day had changed him forever. Maybe now it was time for another change—one for the better. Trelayne inspired thoughts of the future, as well as igniting his desire to experience the here and now. She had captured his heart, or at least what remained of it. As soon as he returned to London, he aimed to tell her so.

He kicked at a tin can and ambled on. He'd have to stay in Brighton for awhile, canvassing the area. Grimsby was close by—he could almost smell the blackguard. It shouldn't take more than a day or two.

Hands in his pockets, he trudged up the cobbled street toward bed. What was Trelayne doing right now? Sleeping peacefully like the innocent she was, or looking up at the ink-black sky and dazzling display of stars, granting a few moments of her time to think of him. Merrick had damn well better honor his promise to keep her home and safe until his return.

A short way up ahead on the levee, two figures appeared, ending his quixotic ramblings. Keeping a steady pace, he unbuttoned his coat, eased free his revolver, and let his hand hang down at his side. When he angled farther out into the street to gain more room for maneuvering, the two men did the same, and that old familiar foreboding raced through him, stepping up his heart rate. Trouble was brewing, and there wasn't going to be an easy way out of this.

Running footsteps suddenly sounded at his back. They were coming at him from both sides.

"We got you now, you bloody Yank," a voice threatened.

He turned and fired, barely avoiding the length of

chain aimed at his head. The man fell, writhing in pain, the chain slipping from his slackened grip. Head down like a bull, a second man barreled into him, catching him in the stomach, knocking the breath out of him. Walker landed on his back, the stones of the cobbled street bruising muscle and bone. He raised the pistol to fire again, but the man kicked the revolver from his hand, sending it spinning off into the darkness.

Rolling to one side, he gained his feet, and slid free his Green River blade. At the sight of the big knife, the ruffian backed off, momentarily kept at bay. Then the men he'd first seen on the levee drew near. Three to one odds were not promising. He glanced around for his revolver. No luck, it was too dark to see beyond the immediate area. Flipping the knife around, he then sent it arcing end over end toward the man closest to him. The big brute staggered once then dropped to the street, the blade protruding from his chest.

Walker ran forward to retrieve the weapon. Too late. The two other thugs were on him. Aware he was fighting for his life, he took the abuse and kept coming back for more. With sickening repetition, bone hit bone, and bone hit muscle until losing the battle seemed a certainty.

Blood poured from his nose and split lip, and his left eye began to swell shut. His arms ached from giving as well as blocking punches. As he lost his footing, the odds dropped from not promising to grim.

His attackers showed no mercy. Like buzzards on a fresh kill, they circled and closed in, hobnail boots coming at him from every direction. He curled up to protect his vital organs, but nothing shielded him from the hurt raining down upon his body.

At the prospect of his life ending in a dirty backstreet of a foreign country, resentment fueled his near spent energy and he staggered to his feet.

Snarling in disbelief, one of the murderers hit him across the ribs with a piece of planking. The cracking sound turned his stomach, was it board or bone? Gasping for air, he lurched forward two steps—it was bone. A soporific blackness engulfed him as he toppled to the ground. Stunned, he waited for the final blow. He should have told Trelayne he loved her. Now she would never know.

He was slipping away, when a bloodcurdling wail split the night, halting the slide into oblivion. The hair at the nape of his neck stood on end, and even the brutes beating the tar out of him came to attention. As the eerie call rang out a second time, a man built like a grizzly catapulted into view. Walker crawled off to one side, and peered with disbelief through his good eye.

Dressed in cross-gartered pants, wielding a battle-ax as if he knew how to use one, the stranger stalked toward the two hoodlums. This was no defensive maneuver—he was on the attack. Dappled in mist-shrouded lamplight, the man and the scene became an ethereal rendering from a time long ago.

The Norseman's sharp weapon cut one man's throat from ear to ear. Stunned, mouth gaping, the would-be-murderer was dead before he hit the ground.

The other aggressor tried to run, but retreat was futile. The stranger slipped the handle of his ax beneath his belt, scruffed the wretch by the collar and the back of his trousers, and pitched the flailing malefactor off the dock and into the water far below. Dusting hands together as if he'd just tossed out the weekly trash, the colossus straightened and turned in his direction.

No fight left in body or soul, Walker waited. Even on his most promising day, he'd be lucky to best this stranger.

Chapter Thirteen

A few days! What an outrageous lie. Trelayne threw her hairbrush against the wall. Then, ashamed of her childish behavior, she stomped across the room to retrieve it.

Nearly a fortnight had passed since Walker had gone to Brighton. No, since Captain Garrison had gone to Brighton. Oh, what difference did it make what she called him? It didn't change how she felt about him, or stop recollections of each moment they had spent together from eclipsing all her other thoughts.

She would never forget the feel of his strong hand holding hers, or the manly smell of him as he dared to lean close, stopping just short of crossing the boundary to a real kiss, anticipation and yearning raging through her body.

The memories of that evening, too good to resist, goaded a warm happy feeling. Then the romantic image died a tortured death as it crashed head first into the resentment boiling in her belly. Snaring the commemorative gloves he'd sent, she raised her arm to give them the same treatment as her hairbrush. But she couldn't. She'd slept with them every night since their arrival. With a sob, she caressed the leather against her cheek. Where could he be?

Maybe Walker had gone back to America. He was right there on the coast, how simple to just slip away into the night. No. He wouldn't abandon her, he couldn't, he mustn't. Why not, because she was in love with him? Why should that matter? He hardly knew her, and apparently did not find her a bit intriguing. Save for a few bits and pieces of interesting fodder, his past was a mystery and his future unclear. Good heavens, his current whereabouts were not even definite.

Oh mercy, what if he were injured or dead? The blood drained from her head, and she reached for the bedpost to steady herself. She should go to Brighton and search for him. The heroines in her books would jump headfirst into danger and adventure if it meant rescuing their true love. But Merrick would barely allow her a chaperoned visit to town, let alone a trip all the way to Brighton.

What to do, what to do? Lucien might take her, or go in her stead. The picture of Lucien leading an all-out search for Walker wouldn't form in her mind. No, that was not the answer. Besides, Lucien had agreed to take her to visit the poor today. To prevail upon him further was out of the question. Heaven only knew what he would demand in return for a trip to Brighton. Escorting her today was recompense for his outlandish behavior at the Michaelmas party, but he had added the caveat that she must consider the audacious idea of accompanying him to the Holiday Festival at the Bond.

Lucien was unreasonable at times. Still there was a bit of intrigue wrapped in the lonely visage he portrayed as he professed his undying love for her. Unlike some men, who didn't seem to need her at all.

Wistfully setting aside the leather gloves, she sorted through the trinkets covering her dresser top.

Where was her heart necklace? She hadn't seen it for weeks, and the loss of the keepsake added to her discontent. Her mother wore a matching one, it was a connection between them, and she needed to feel that closeness, especially today. Volunteering to distribute necessities to the needy sounded easy enough, but never having done it before, she was a bit nervous.

Mother had often gone on these mini-missions of mercy, and Trelayne was determined to continue the charity work. Running the household and participating in such community events was not only challenging, it was also liberating. Today was her first true venture into the outside world so successfully hidden from her until now.

How different life would have been had her sister lived. Dear Caroline, she missed her so. They had been such a happy family; her death had changed them all. It made Mother and Father fearful, and Branwell reckless. And it left her timid and untrusting in God and Fate and the possibility of happiness without repercussion. And her nightmares did nothing to assuage those qualities.

The mantel clock chimed eight o'clock. Taken by surprise, she abandoned her search for the necklace, and hurried to her armoire. If she were to breakfast and be ready for a day of visitations, she must hurry.

Glancing longingly at the gloves, she rang for the chambermaid. At least Walker had thought about her for one fleeting moment. But it wasn't enough—she wanted more. Her hunger for him gnawed at her soul, even as disappointment battled yearning, vying for the upper hand.

****

Lucien awoke in a surly mood.

Not having been able to come up with a suitable excuse for backing out of his commitment to Trelayne, he must endure a day in London's less affluent, louse-infected neighborhoods.

At least Trelayne had forgiven his outburst and lascivious display at her party. And the true bright spot in this whole dreary business was her promise to consider accompanying him to the Bond—a boon to his plans, a stroke of genius. She must say yes.

Following her refusal of marriage, he no longer knew what to do to win her devotion. His unwavering attention, coupled with exotic flowers and expensive sweets, hadn't done the trick. She always accepted his tokens, but seemingly with reluctance as if motivated purely by the need to not hurt his feeling. Well, no more. He was through being patient, and he was through letting Fate dictate the course of his life. In the future, he would call the tune and pity to those who did not care to dance.

Grimsby's telegraph message had brightened his mood. What a welcome surprise. Captain Garrison's presence in Brighton was unexpected, but it mattered little where the man met his downfall. It appeared he had put up a good fight, and his body was nowhere to be found, but the one surviving murderer swore the captain was dead. Now the only person who stood in the way of his plans was Trelayne.

Lucien rolled over and gave Beatrice a slap on the rump. Before she could wipe the sleep from her eyes, he pushed her unrigged and shivering from the bed.

"Make a cup of tea," he ordered, "and be quick about it. Then lay out my clothes. I don't wish to be late today."

Naked as you please, Beatrice stood before him, her mousy hair a tangle, her doleful brown eyes returning his stare.

"You're going to be with her again ain't you?" she said. "She don't want you, Lucien. She can't show you the kind of appreciation you likes best." As she spoke, Beatrice fondled her diddeys, and traced lazy circles around her nipples.

The brazen display of earthy delights sent a twinge of willingness to his groin. She eyed his erection, and smiled triumphantly. Trailing her hands downward to the mat of curls crowning her thighs, she smiled and stroked herself.

Lucien grabbed her around the waist and tugged her closer to the bed. She leaned over, inviting him to nip at her breasts as she reached to stroke and fondle him. The bitch did know how to please a man.

He forced her head to his loins. She knelt at his side and greedily took him, her hands kneading his chest and thighs. In unison, they groaned with carnal pleasure as she performed her art, quickly bringing him to climax. Drowsy with satisfaction, he nearly fell back to sleep. Then the day's itinerary flashed through his mind. Furious with Beatrice for trying to control him with sex, he shoved her aside and gained his feet.

"You're a dirty puzzle, you heartless slut," he accused. Her eyes widened in surprise. "You're only trying to delay me. Trying to keep me from a woman whose name you're not worthy to speak. All you care about is getting me up your cock alley?"

He grasped her around the throat. "Don't ever forget who is master between us," he warned. "There are several exquisite means of curing disobedience in concubines. It would be my pleasure and your pain should we explore those techniques."

"I'm sorry Lucien," she whispered. "I didn't mean no harm."

"Make the tea," he ordered, releasing her.

She grabbed her robe and fled to the kitchen.

A half hour later, Lucien was on his way, wishing he'd spent the morning under Trelayne's ministrations rather than Beatrice's. Regardless, he did love sex. Like gambling, he could never get enough.

Imagining how it would be with Trelayne, he nearly fell from his horse. Once introduced to the world of sexual delights, she would surely desire them as much as did he. Then his good mood plummeted as he remembered today's agenda, and the inconvenience and disgust he would undoubtedly suffer.

"Blast. What a waste of a good day."

To save riding all the way out to Royston Hall, he was to meet Trelayne's carriage at Beningbrough Hill Road. And as it would appear unseemly for him to travel within, the original plan was for him to ride alongside. This of course was contrary to his intentions. Reaching his destination, he reined in his horse, dismounted, and watched for the old equipage the St.Christopher's called a carriage.

Before long, the antiquated black coach loomed up over an adjacent hill. Why the St.Christophers refused to modernize their transportation was beyond him. This decorative relic bounced and rattled along with bone jarring annoyance. And it looked like something the devil himself would use to patrol the boundaries of Hell.

At least there was one bit of good luck. Jeb manned

the reins, not the tenacious old watchdog Merrick.

As Jeb wrestled the four matched black geldings to a halt, Lucien unsaddled his horse.

"Good morning, sir," the young driver called down. "Anything the matter, sir?"

Jeb's look of worry increased as Lucien threw his tack in the boot of the carriage and tied his horse to the rear frame of the coach.

"My horse has thrown a shoe and bruised his hoof," he explained, the lie rolling off his tongue with practiced ease. "I've no choice but to ride with your mistress." He climbed aboard and shut the door. "Move along now," he ordered, disallowing for any argument.

"Lucien." Trelayne's surprise was apparent as he settled in across from her. "I thought you were to ride alongside."

He explained his horse's condition, and although agreeing to drop the animal off at a nearby hamlet, he refused her suggestion they wait as the mount was re-shod.

"The animal has specific needs, and my preferred farrier is the only one I will allow to work on him."

"Well we certainly must do what is best for the animal," she conceded.

At a nearby village, they accommodated the horse in temporary lodgings, and after slipping the stable boy a few quid to declare there were no rental mounts available, they forged on.

He marveled at the interior of the coach. It was as dreary as the outside. Black-fringed curtains clung to the windows, while old-fashioned brass candle lamps and drip pans tried but failed to brighten each corner. The overall effect was completely dismal. Trelayne was the only gay spot of color. Even dressed in dark burgundy with her hair wrenched back into a chignon, she was beautiful beyond compare. He must insist she wear her hair down when they visited the Bond. On that evening every man in the room must envy him and wish for what he had attained—what he called his own.

She returned his gaze and smiled, or more precisely she beamed with anticipation and enthusiasm. No doubt picturing herself an avenging angel, prepared to swoop down upon the demons of disease, despair, and drunkenness.

"Thank you again for accompanying me, Lucien. I know today will be a glorious experience. Here is my list of addresses from Father Woolsey." She waved a paper containing the information. "We've blankets, soap, candles, dried fruits, and even a few Bibles. Although," she added thoughtfully, "it's my understanding most of the people we shall see today can neither read nor write. That in itself is a tragedy, is it not?"

"Oh quite," he replied, working to suppress his sarcasm. "However, I doubt the inability to read or write is the most pressing concern in their miserable existence. Dying of fever from living in the miasma of their night soil, as well as their animals', is probably higher on their priority list."

"Oh, Lucien, do not be distasteful and pessimistic. I'm sure the area to which we travel cannot possibly be as awful as we have been led to believe. No one could live in such conditions. Most people probably just need encouragement, and the knowledge that some of us truly care about their circumstances. Perhaps they simply need a little advice on managing and running their households."

Familiar with the less glamorous parts of London, Lucien knew the stories were true enough. Smog, filth, and ignorance teamed unchecked there. Yet he supposed it was beyond comprehension to someone who had never witnessed the degradation existing but a few streets away from the grand cathedrals and opulent opera houses. Besides, Trelayne's innocence was one of the qualities he loved best. She was so trusting and easily swayed by high ideals and charitable causes.

"Whatever you say, my dear. I am at your service. Although I still contend you have no business exposing yourself to the disease breeding in these neighborhoods. Your intentions, while valorous, will not protect you from pox and pestilence."

"Should I then let my fears dictate my actions and decide for me what is right or wrong?" she defended, her cheeks colored with passion.

"No, of course not Trelayne, but common sense might serve you better than the common cause."

"Oh, please," she pouted, "let us not bicker. I have been looking forward to this day for nearly a month. I shan't let you spoil it with your mulish bad attitude. Now give me a smile, and try to be more positive."

"You know I will do anything for you darling, and I will try my best not to say *'I told you so,'* yet I fear the occasion will be upon us shortly."

Trelayne leaned forward and peered out the window. Lucien was content just to observe Trelayne.

"Why is it getting darker Lucien? There were no storm clouds in the sky when we departed."

"It's the normal atmosphere here," he enlightened. "The foul brown cloud is created by the poisonous vapors spewing forth from the noxious trades. It blots out the sun, just as it blots out the hopes and dreams of the poor wretches living here. It's no wonder they turn to gin and opium for solace."

"Lucien, you are too hard on these people."

"On the contrary. I'm being practical. One coach full of supplies will not change the reality of the situation. I say let them escape by whatever means they can obtain or afford."

She seemed to consider this information then asked what he had meant by noxious trades.

"Dear Lord, where to start?" He ticked them off on his fingers. "Fell-mongers, tripe boilers, blood dryers, gut scrapers, tanners, glue makers.... They all reside here, from manure and tar works, to sugar refineries and fat extractors, and each trade gives forth its own distinctive by-product of choking smells. The resulting combination is the most horrible conglomeration of odors one can imagine. It's a stench vile enough to generate pestilence."

"But how can anyone stand to live here?" she said, her voice muffled and her expression of distaste barely concealed behind the hand now cupped over her mouth and nose.

"Trapped by circumstance and caged by misfortune, they have little choice."

Like a roving beast, the foul smell crept closer. There were tears in Trelayne's eyes; were they caused by the acrid smell, or sympathy? Probably both.

"Well," she sniffled, lowering her hand, "it's no wonder they're so downtrodden and disinclined to dream of higher aspirations."

Before he could respond, the coach came to an

abrupt halt. Damn. Had they reached their first stop already?

"Move those bleaters and mowers," Jeb issued orders, "and be quick about it. Me coach is sinking in this river of mud you call a street. I can't keep stationary waitin' for ya. We'll soon be up to our hubs."

The baaing of sheep and the mooing of cows issued all around as animals ran in every direction.

Jeb urged the horses back into action. They strained in their traces, but nothing happen. Then there was a sucking sound and the carriage wheels jerked loose from the mud. Without warning, the vehicle surged forward. Trelayne slid from the seat landing unceremoniously on the floor.

"I love women at my feet, dearest, but this is hardly the time or place."

Trelayne rolled her eyes at his lame jest. "For heaven sakes, Lucien, do lend a hand."

He reached to assist her, one hand on her upper arm, the other taking liberties with her thigh. The muscles of one long leg flexed beneath his fingers, and a rush of lusty imaginings made him wince. Oh, to see those long legs naked and spread beneath him.

Trelayne settled back against the squabs and adjusted her shawl. Preoccupied with her mission of mercy, she seemed unaware of the wayward touching

"What in heaven's name are all these animals doing running loose in the city?" she asked, renewing their conversation.

"The same thing they do running loose in the country." This time he just couldn't suppress his sarcasm.

"You know what I mean," she persisted. "I had no

idea people were allowed to keep livestock in their very yards. It does little to improve the smell of things."

"Come winter," he said, flicking a bit of dust from his lapel, "they will probably keep the animals indoors, eating and sleeping right along side of them."

"Mother of mercy, why?" She appeared sickened at the prospect.

"It's the only fresh meat the poor beggars can obtain. The offerings available at the butchers being abominable in both price and condition."

Trelayne stared out window. "This truly is a different world," she whispered. "Even the snatches of conversation drifting by are thick with brogues and so filled with street slang, I can barely understand a sentence spoken."

****

Trelayne's spirits faltered. It was dark and smelly here…and noisy. As they reached one of the few cobbled streets, the clatter of the iron-rimmed wheels, mixed with the sounds of the animals and mongers, created a hideous din. It was enough to give one a case of the jitters. No wonder people threw straw in front of houses when the occupant was ill. Anything to mute the noise and offer ease and quiet to the ailing party. Living in the country, lack of peace and calm had never been an issue.

Entering a mud-filled side avenue, Jeb drew the team to a halt. He scrambled down to assist her, and ended up carrying her through the muck to the front door of the first dwelling. Although grateful for his assistance, from there on out, she insisted on making her own way down the oozing street, one hovel to the next.

Dispensing the supplies as she saw fit was hard reckoning. All the families were one step away from destitution. She could easily leave all the comforts at just one house, but parceling out the items would bring a little happiness to a number of people rather than a great joy to just a one.

But the faces of the children touched her the most. Overly docile and already giving in to their lot in life, they languished in dank rooms, resignation emanating from their dull eyes. They stared at her with vacant looks, not laughing or playing or responding to her smiles and teasing. When she talked to them, they glanced around as if to see to whom she spoke.

Reaching the final house on her list, she was flooded with guilt at being so grateful for her first tour of facing poverty to be finished. The old woman inside gladly accepted the last basket of food and a handful of candles.

"These gifts are from the Altar Society of St. Alban's," Trelayne repeated for the final time, "and the thoughts and prayers of the congregation accompany them."

"Thank you for your kindness, but your prayers be too late for that one." Bent with age and grief, the old lady nodded in the direction of an adjacent room.

Although Lucien tried to stay her actions, Trelayne went to the doorway. As her eyes grew accustomed to the bleak light, she detected a young woman lying in the bed, a near-naked newborn at her breast. The girl was still as a statue, her stare unblinking. Was she even alive? The shallow rise and fall of her chest gave credence she was, but this welcome relief was short lived. The babe she held did not move nor cry, and his little arms and legs seemed unnaturally stiff, his coloring dusky, not pink.

Fighting to remain calm, Trelayne turned back to the old woman. "How long has the baby been....dead?"

"Nearly a day and a half. She will'na let us take him from her arms. She has nothin' warm to bury him in, and she'll not have her Jordie spend all his eternity suffering in the cold ground."

Trelayne glanced back into the room, and her throat tightened with sorrow.

"She hasn't been right since the wee lad died," the old woman lamented, "and after such a terrible birthing it were. She's worried about the resurrection men too. We've no money to pay for a decent burial plot where the babe's body will be left in peace and not stolen for the surgeons to practice on."

Trelayne retrieved a one-pound note from her drawstring purse, and gave it to the tearful woman. "Please take this. Buy him a funeral that will put her mind to rest." She entered the room and eased closer to the bedside, removing her cashmere shawl as she advanced.

"Now then," she said softly. "This will keep little Jordie warm as he sleeps with the angels. He must truly be a special boy if our Lord wanted him back so soon. Come now," she coaxed, extending the shawl closer.

The young woman turned her head toward the sound of her voice. She appeared young of age, but her eyes mirrored a hundred years of pain and anguish. Trelayne almost glanced away. The new mother released one hand from its fierce grip on the infant and shakily reached toward the fine woolen garment. A barely audible "thank you" passed her lips.

The elderly woman retrieved the tiny body from its mother's arms, and carefully swaddled it in the shawl. Rolling onto her side, the girl shook with great sobs and moans, releasing all the grief and sorrow she had been holding back. Trelayne and the older woman quietly left the room.

"Bless you, missy, for what you done. The way she was acting we were afraid we would lose our Bessie as well as the little one. It were most unnatural the way she just stared into the air, clutching that poor dead babe to her breast. She never ate a bite nor spoke a word the past day and a half. And she never shed a tear until now."

Trelayne blinked back tears of her own. "I'm glad I could help."

****

Grasping Trelayne's elbow, Lucien escorted her out of the house and toward the waiting coach.

"Good God, Trelayne. Heaven only knows what the child died from. Do you wish to contract it as well? We are leaving this fever nest immediately, and I'll not listen to any protestation on your part."

None came. In truth, Trelayne appeared stunned to silence. Meeting no resistance, he led her from the nightmare toward the refuge of the carriage. When she wasn't looking, he shoved aside the throng of children begging for coins and kicked at a skinny dog hoping for a stray morsel of food.

"Get us out of here," he barked, to Jeb as he helped her board. "The quickest way possible. Stop for no one."

Social rules forgotten, he sat beside Trelayne. Her chin quivered, and she wouldn't look at him.

"There, there," he crooned, boldly putting one arm across her shoulders. "This is only your first experience with the crueler side of life. You will no doubt grow accustomed to it."

Tears wet her cheeks, and she buried her face against his waiting shoulder.

"How can one ever grow accustomed such pain and sorrow? Perhaps I'm not suited for comforting the poor, or standing strong in the face of their suffering. I thought it would be different."

"But you were wonderful, my pet," he soothed, indulging in a self-satisfied smirk.

In retrospect, the day had not been a total loss after all. Trelayne was broken in spirit and turning to him for solace. Events could not have turned out better.

And this was just the beginning. In less than a week, she would be obliged to negotiate the wages and cargo fees for the *Romney Maiden,* her father's ship. If his plans for sabotage went well, that disastrous experience should be the final blow. With Garrison gone, and her parents still incapacitated, there would be no one to whom she could turn. And he would be there to pick up the pieces.

Chapter Fourteen

His body felt unbelievably heavy, as if cast from lead. Maybe he was dead. But was it Heaven or Hell to which he'd been assigned?

Opening his eyes, Walker peered around. The light from a nearby fire, brighter than a sunburst, nearly struck him blind. Pain shot through his brain, and his stomach heaved. He snapped his eyes closed. It must be the inferno of Hell. Then the comforting aroma of food filled his nostrils. Surely the devil would not offer such tantalizing fare.

"Where am I?" he asked, but only an animal-like croak came out of his mouth.

At his pitiful utterance, someone drew near. Squinting open his eyes, he focused on the hulking form towering over him.

"Praise Odin. You are back from the darkness."

The man's booming voice reverberated from wall to wall, making him cringe.

"I am called Hargis. What is your name, fine fellow?"

A good question. What *was* his name? The pounding in his head increased as he tried to reason out who he was, and what had happened. Having nothing to offer, he remained silent.

Moving only his eyes, he studied the small room. An odd assortment of animal hides, shields, and weaponry covered the walls. The metal gleamed as if newly polished, the intricate designs were of finely wrought patterns and runes. It wasn't Hell—it was Valhalla.

Maybe he was dreaming. He tried to move and the pain took his breath away. He was wide-awake now. Hargis reached to settle him back against the pillows.

Illuminated by lamp glow, the man dwarfed the room, his shadow darkening the walls. A golden beard, mustache, and shoulder-length hair surrounded his piercing blue eyes. He looked like a Norseman, stepped from the pages of *Beowulf.*

"I been calling you Little Hern," the big Viking informed him, "after my brother, Big Hern. You remind me of him. He is dead and buried five years now, gone for a soldier in the old country. He had the fighting spirit just like you."

Hargis touched Walker's brow then stood back and smiled. "Your fever is finally broken. For a while, I feared my possets and poultices were not equal to the seriousness of your injuries. Only in wartime have I seen a man hurt as badly."

Turning, the big man fed more wood to the fire then stirred what was cooking in the pot hanging over the flames.

Walker tried sitting up. Pain slammed through him again. He sucked in a deep breath, regretting the action as what felt like the tips of broken ribs stabbed at muscle and ligament. He collapsed back on the cot, his mind a dizzy blur of urgent questions needing answers, but he couldn't pull together a decent thought.

"You are not ready to be sitting up ways, friend," Hargis pointed out the obvious. "I get for you some water and good hot soup. Don't be worrying about your horse," he added, gathering the bowls and spoons.

The horse? He'd forgotten he even had one.

"I found a ticket for the stables in your pocket. Someone at work knew what it was and where to find the barn. I gave the man money to feed and watch over the animal." He ladled out the soup. "It has been one hell of a few weeks."

A few weeks—good Lord. Again Walker tried to speak, but his tongue, too big and unresponsive, sabotaged the effort. It stuck to the roof of his mouth making even swallowing an effort. Resigned to silence, he ate the soup while casting a covetous stare at the bread and cheese on the cutting board beside Hargis.

"No solid food for you yet friend. Cheese will bind you. You must be up and about before I dare let you eat such fare. You will tell Hargis your name now?"

He still couldn't remember who he was, or what had happened. Only that it seemed vitally important he find out. "Thank you for taking me in," he managed to say, his throat soothed by the hot soup. "I can't remember much of anything," he admitted, scrubbing a hand across his brow, "including my name."

"Maybe it is here on this paper?" Hargis rummaged around in small trunk. "It was also in your pocket. I'm good at many things, but reading is not one of them."

Intrigued, he slowly reached for the proffered parchment. It was a receipt for a hotel in London, signed by a Captain Walker Garrison. Seeing the name in print opened a door in his brain, and the trapped memories slowly fought their way to freedom.

"My name is Walker...Walker Garrison," he muttered. Saying his name aloud prodded his jumble of thoughts into a more logical order.

Relief eased through him as detail after detail fell into place. Then an image of Trelayne blotted out everything else. Was she safe? How long had he been gone? He had to get back to Royston Hall.

"What day is it? How long have I been here?" he demanded, his hand clenched into a fist around the hotel receipt.

"Slow down, Walker Garrison," the man said, and laughed. "Hargis Braunwinson will be trying to answer your questions. I am not sure of the date, but it is fifteen nights since I find you fighting with those men. I helped to even the odds for you."

Unconscious for over two weeks. God only knew what had been happening in London. Everything was going terribly wrong. He'd yet to find proof connecting Grimsby to Lanteen, and now he was useless as a child in taking care of himself, let alone in protecting Trelayne.

"Does anyone know I'm here?"

Hargis shook his head. "No one knows you are alive or where you are. Three of the men who attacked you will bother no one again. The other scurries painfully about the waterfront like an injured rat."

Knowing one of his attackers still lived was good news. The man might have vital information, and a witness, reluctant or not, would be a boon to his mission

"I owe you my life. Again, I thank you."

"Hargis knows what it is like to need a friend. I am glad to help."

Walker glanced at his boots standing beside the bed. One of them held his money for safekeeping.

Intending to give the cash to Hargis, he strained sideways, grabbed up his left boot, and felt inside. Empty. He guessed the man had already helped himself. His gaze shifted to the other man's face.

"Oh ya, ya," Hargis said, with a big grin. "Your fortune is safe." He pried up a floorboard, revealing a tin box beneath the planking. Liberating the currency from the box he handed it over. "You should not hide your money in your boots," he said, with reprimand. "If a bad person knocks you out, he will most likely steal your shoes."

Walker felt ashamed for having doubted the big man. In his attempt to protect the St.Christopher family, it had become second nature for him to mistrust everyone.

"I beg your pardon, Hargis. You have been more than generous, and how do I repay you? I treat you with suspicion and prejudgment." He extended the fist full of currency, but Hargis refused to take it.

"I work for my money," the other man said. "When you know Hargis better, you will see I can be a loyal companion. And when you feel better, we will go to town. Then you can buy me a drink, and we will have a merry time with the women." The man's laughter again filled the room.

"How long have you been in England?" Walker asked.

"Only one half and two months. I am trying to go to America. That is where you are from I think. But I had only enough money to get this far, and now I work for the Queen of England." Walker raised a brow at that information. "We rebuild the Royal Pavilion near here," Hargis clarified. "It will be truly wonderful. And, I am one of the few men on the crew who works unafraid in the banqueting hall."

"The others fear the room?"

"Oh, ya. It is haunted by the ghost of Mary Gunn, the Brighton Bather. But alive or dead, Hargis does not run from beautiful young women. Besides, they pay me extra to work in there. Soon I will have enough to sail to America and start a new life in the new country."

"What trade do you claim?" Walker asked.

"I am king of the forge, blacksmith you call it. I turn iron into knives and swords. Or I can change silver into anything you want, something to adorn your clothes, or perhaps a trinket to please your special lady."

"Did you make all of the things?" he questioned, nodding toward the wall.

"Ya, I have done so, and there is much more at home in Norway. I cannot bring it all. I have here my finest work to show what I can do. Also, these things are good company. A piece of me is in each piece of work. What is it you do, Walker Garrison, besides fighting vandals who outnumber you?"

"I build sailing ships, like the one you hope to take to America. In fact, I know a few sea captains who make port in Brighton. As soon as I'm well enough, I'll arrange passage for you on one of them."

"I will be appreciating your help. For now though, we put another poultice to your wounds. Then you get some sleep. Tomorrow you must try to get up. It will be a hard day's work so you had best rest tonight."

How could he rest with anxiety chewing at his conscience? He'd screwed up. Left Trelayne with no one but Merrick to look after her. A sense of panic squeezed at his chest, and he couldn't catch his breath. He must recover as quickly as possible, but judging by the way he felt, it might be a while before he could fend for himself. He should alert Merrick to the situation, but risking a written or telegraphed communication seemed unwise. Someone wanted him dead, and he wasn't about to give them another chance. All he could do was wait—something he was not very good at.

Hargis re-wrapped his wounds, the herbs soothing his unhealed flesh, and he marveled at Hargis' gentle touch. He'd seen the big man knock an opponent cold with one blow. Yet those same hands had sewn his torn body together with stitches tiny and precise enough to rival the finest embroidery.

As he was thinking about how good a shot of whiskey would taste, Hargis grabbed a jug and poured out two portions of blood red liquid.

"Here," his new friend offered. "This will make the pain sleep. Then you can sleep too. I will have some as well," he added, "because I am such a damn good nurse. To Odin."

Hargis swallowed his portion in one gulp, and stood by in anticipation.

Walker tossed down his share. At first nothing happened. Then a burning sensation exploded in his belly and spread outward. It made his eyes water. Coughing and sputtering, his arms wrapped around his chest to splint his ribs, he tried to catch his breath. Hargis laughed at the sight of him, showing no remorse at having caused his distress.

"Good stuff, aye," Hargis added. "You get used to it. This is what keeps us warm in a Norwegian blizzard."

Still laughing, Hargis dampened down the fire, and put out the oil lamp. Then he crawled between the covers of the sleeping pallet situated across the room.

"Be seein' you in the morning, Walker Garrison. Maybe then you can tell Hargis who is Trelayne. Day after day, you been asking for her."

Chapter Fifteen

Trelayne paused outside the Vicarage, her mission today more rudimentary. Deliver the donation she carried, and flee before the Vicar recruited her for another round of visitations.

The human misery thriving in the backstreets of London had been terrible to witness, and her lack of resolve to return soon, left her feeling ashamed. *Small steps*, she reminded, or rather *small doses.* Chin up, she gained the entryway and lifted the brass knocker just as the portal opened and old Father Woolsey all but collided with her.

"Bless my soul, Mistress Trelayne, how good to see you. Did we have an appointment?" He peered at her over his spectacles, his thin white hair fluttered around his head, his brow puckered in confusion. "Or perhaps you've come to procure another list of those in need."

"No," she denied, too loudly. "I mean, not this time. I've come to offer coinage rather than time. With Mother and Father still in America I'm afraid my days are filled to overflowing. Running Poppa's shipping company is terribly complicated, and although Wynona and Merrick are invaluable, there are things around the estate demanding my personal attention and…"

She clamped her mouth shut to stop the flow of prattle spilling forth to cover her unease. Oh, why couldn't she be more like Mother and Aunt Abigail? They were the ones with courage and fortitude. They faced trials and tribulations so fearlessly.

"Of course, my dear. Calm yourself. Come inside and we'll have a spot of tea."

"I didn't mean to inconvenience you. Obviously you were on your way out." Did her weak-willed character hover about her like an apparition?

"Nonsense, child," he reassured, leading her to the parlor. "I was merely going for my constitutional. Oh, Mrs. Casterbean," he called, in a kindly voice.

A gray-haired roly-poly woman popped up at the door. "Yes, your grace. What can I be doing for you?" Pink cheeked, a sparkle in her eyes, she smiled and wiped her hands on an embroidered tea towel.

"If you can see your way clear," the Vicar said, "a pot of tea and a biscuit or two would be most appreciated."

"I'll be on it straight away," she promised, retreating from view.

"About that donation," Father Woolsey said, as they settled into wingback chairs by the hearth. "Pardon my being so forward," he added, unabashed, "but we sorely need the money. Our latest project is for the children. Poor pips, they suffer the most."

The vision of little Jordie and his grief-stricken mother still haunted her, and liberating the money, she pressed it into his hands "Yes," she said barely above a whisper, "for the children."

"I take it your tour of making rounds went well?"

She swallowed back the words of protest. "It was very…enlightening. Have you read Dr. Hunter's recent article in the *Lancet*?" she asked, changing the subject.

Her father subscribed to many journals, and she had leafed through this one only yesterday.

"An excellent discourse," Father Woolsey acknowledged. "He's proven the relationship between poverty and disease. Still, to elevate the habits of the masses to a more healthful way of life is a long way off."

At his words, her stomach knotted. "Isn't there some means to help them with more expediency? Cannot the government force change upon the people? After all, it's for their own good?"

"A worthy thought. But who decides how much force is appropriate? As it is, the common man complains about too much Parliamentary intervention. If we dictate the factory owner must refuse work to women who are with child, these women will see it as being denied employment when they need it most." He shook his head. "Protecting the child without further burdening the parent is a conundrum."

"We could start by educating the groups most affected," she countered. "People usually make mistakes out of ignorance, not choice."

Father Woolsey veritably beamed at her. "Quite perceptive. Education is our greatest weapon. We've recently discovered many of the infant fatalities listed as malnutrition and respiratory distress are actually deaths caused by accidental overdoses of opium and laudanum."

"They give opium to children?" The outrageous possibility nearly brought her out of her chair.

"Oh, yes indeed. In copious amounts. Mother's Friend, Godfrey's Cordial, Atkinson's Royal Infants Preservative, call it what you will, they all result in the infant wasting away from starvation. And all the while, the parents do not see the correlation between the drug and the deaths. They give it to the children so they sleep at night, and the people who tend the children while the parents work use it to make the babies less troublesome by day. The poor mites are being dosed around the clock."

"But it's just common sense," she murmured.

"Common to us, but not to them. One druggist in Nottingham admitted he sold four hundred gallons of laudanum annually. 'Tis a shocking amount." He fell silent, but his countenance brightened as the housekeeper delivered the tea. "Thank you, Mrs. Casterbean. The biscuits look delicious."

"You're welcome. Now don't be spoiling your noontime fare by eating too many," the elderly woman clucked on the way out. "There's corned beef today, your favorite."

Trelayne served the tea, indulged in a sip, and ponder the predicament.

It sounded hopeless, her donation a mere pittance in the face of such overwhelming need. They must raise more money, much, much more. She would be sure to sponsor a booth at the next charity bazaar.

"At the least," she persisted remembering the squalor, "something could be done to eliminate the dirt and grime permeating their houses."

"They have no water for cleaning purposes. They queue up at the commons for hours—in all sorts of weather—for water barely enough to meet their drinking and cooking needs. One can hardly expect them to take such a hard-earned staple and use it to scrub walls and floors."

"But surely their clothes…"

He raised a hand, staving off her question.

"Sadder still, if they use the water to wash their clothes, what do they wear while the wet articles dry? Many have but one set of threadbare coverings."

There seemed no answer to the never-ending problems.

"We have made great strides," he reassured. "But what we need most is to alter political philosophies, proving the poor are not indolent, self-indulgent, or immoral."

"Then we must effect change through legislation. I shall compose my letter this afternoon. What topics are of the greatest importance?"

"Two things come foremost to mind," the old Vicar said, his enthusiasm remarkably undiminished. "First, we must force a ban on infant insurance. That will help prevent child murder for the sake of burial money."

She nearly choked on a biscuit. "This truly happens?"

"Cruelty and greed are found in all walks of life, Trelayne. The starving and downtrodden are no exception. Money does strange things to people—the having of it, the lack of it, and especially the wanting of it."

Heaven help her. How could she have lived so long never recognizing the existence of this alternate world, its customs as unfamiliar to her as a foreign country? It was a land with its own language, with a set of fearful rules and consequences. She understood the reason her parents sought to protect her, but keeping her isolated also left her unprepared for the challenges she now faced.

"What is the second issue we must address?" She carefully swallowed, steeling herself for the answer.

"We need laws to control the sale and use of the opium. It's a sinful drug, and has nearly brought the Chinese empire to its knees. Their misfortune must not become ours."

Finally, here was a subject she could attack with zeal. But what difference would one letter make?

"Right now," he encouraged, as if privy to her doubts, "you may feel like a tiny pebble cast into the rushing stream of despair. But many pebbles mortised together by God's love and direction can build a stalwart dam capable of stopping that stream."

As she considered the contents of the letter she would write, the housekeeper peeked into the room. "Pardon the interruption, Father. I was to be reminding you there is a christening to follow your noon repast."

"Yes, right you are." He gained his feet. "Thank you, Mrs. Casterbean. I'll be along momentarily."

The Vicar walked Trelayne to the door. "God bless you and keep you," he said with sincerity as she took her leave. "I know you've had many burdens to bear lately. And I'm gladdened to see you have been strengthened by your sorrow and hardships rather than embittered by them."

As the coach swayed its way home over the rutted fall roads, she thought how wrong Father Woolsey was. She wasn't strong at all, or for that matter high-minded. Until recently, she had only thought about the poor when she accidentally crossed paths with them in town. And she had yet to learn how to put her money to proper use. Even restoring Amberley Abbey would be a labor for her enjoyment, a tribute to her heritage, not society.

More often, her thoughts were engaged in wondering what the newest fashion might be, or when she might see Captain Garrison again...if ever. But this new approach to championing the downtrodden was inspiring and revitalizing. She could hardly wait to put pen to paper. The trick, of course, was to be polite as well as mordacious. Unfortunately, she was much better at the latter.

If only Walker were here. With his help, they would construct a dynamic letter with an irrefutable masculine appeal. These days, animated statements offered by women only succeeded in labeling the woman a hysterical female, her cause looked upon as trivial. But a man's opinion was a different matter. Regardless of how obscure, over reactive, or outlandish his view might be, a man was at least given a chance to state his case. Society was frustratingly biased.

****

As Royston Hall came into view, she noticed Lucien's horse tethered out front. For once, she welcomed his intrusion. He could assist with the letter.

Jeb swung down from up top the coach, and walked her to the door.

"I'm sorry, Miss Trelayne," Wynona greeted at the foyer. "Mr. Lucien insists on seeing you. He declared he was determined to wait even if it took all day. He was adamant. Said if I did not grant him entrance, he would sit upon the front steps lamenting his treatment right out loud. He's been ornery since he was young," she insisted, "and he's not improved with age. He's in the dayroom if you care."

"Would you like me to *assist* him off the estate,

Miss Trelayne?" Jeb offered, a gleam of anticipation in his eyes.

"No, thank you. We mustn't take Mr. Lanteen too seriously. If we show our discontent it will simply encourage his roguish behavior. I will see him in the library."

"As you wish, dear," Wynona said, "but keep your eyes as well as the door open. If you ask me, Mr. Lucien has too many wild ideas in his head. Your Aunt Abigail went to town with her friend, Lady Morton, and Merrick's seeing to the drainage ditch in the fields to the north, but I'll be near at hand."

While Trelayne waited, it struck her she must break off her relationship with Lucien. This resolution was not based upon what may or may not happen with Captain Garrison, more so it was based upon how Walker made her feel regardless of whether he would ever become a part of her future.

Her relationship with Lucien would never go beyond platonic. She could see that now. The thought of being with him did not set her mind to whirling and her heart to fluttering. And during his absence, she did not grieve and yearn for him body and soul. She didn't think about him at all. Occasionally, when they were together, he aroused lustful needs and piqued her curiosity about doing *it*, but that wasn't love. It was unfair to lead him on. She would never be satisfied with Lucien.

As he entered the room, she gave a start. "Oh. I didn't hear you come in. I guess I was daydreaming."

"Dreams of me, one would hope," he said, rushing to her side. "Every moment I waited for you seemed an hour. But the time was well spent. You are a vision."

171

She slid her hand free from his grasp. "I see your horse has recovered," she pointed out, not falling prey to his flowery speech.

"Yes, quite. But dash the horse, let me look at you. You are my life's breath."

"Good heavens. I'm not sure I'm up to such a responsibility." She couldn't help but smile. It was hard not to be pleased with such glowing compliments. Knowing she shouldn't, she did take pleasure in Lucien's attention. "Since you prize me so highly," she teased, "perhaps you would be willing to assist me in writing a letter to Parliament. I could use a man's point of view on the subject."

"But of course. Pray tell, upon what subject do you expound?"

"I've just returned from a visit with Father Woolsey, and…"

"Great Scott," he interrupted, "do not tell me you are contemplating another outing to the residue of society."

"Possibly," she admitted. "But today I believe wielding the pen will prove to be more effective. Our topic is laudanum and opium."

Was it her imagination or did Lucien pale at her words? Surely it was just a trick of the afternoon light.

"The misuse of these compounds is causing large scale devastation," she pressed. "The drugs worsening the problems under which these people already suffer, offering only pipedreams. I intend to write to Parliament to encourage regulation of such dangerous medicine. Why, little babies are actually dying from it."

"What makes you think I know anything about opium?" Lucien asked. His expression remained calm, but he gave a nervous tug to his cravat.

"I should hardly think you do, but you are very good at being persuasive. I need your help in phrasing a sensible and powerful letter. A masculine approach to solving the problem will lend more credence to my protest. It must fire the imaginations of all those stodgy old men of the Queen's court."

"If that is what you desire, than let us begin immediately. I am flattered to be your anonymous inspiration."

For nearly two hours, they collaborated on the missive. They laughed, co-conspirators exchanging witticisms and glances of camaraderie. Yet in the back of her mind, thoughts of Walker colored her sensibilities. She both rued and treasured the day Walker had entered her life, and she continued to vacillate between pining for him and being furious with his unceremonious disappearance. At present, she was peeved at him, as well as at herself for a giving a tinker's damn. Overwrought and frustrated, she flirted outrageously with Lucien, totally disregarding her previous pledge to keep him at bay and break off seeing him in the future.

****

There she sat, the picture of heroic innocence, lips pursed as she steadfastly concentrated upon a particularly difficult passage. It was all Lucien could do not to shove the writing materials aside, lean Trelayne over the desk, and have his way with her.

To keep from following through with his desires, he clasped his hands behind his back and paced about the room. The plight of the poor didn't tug at his heart strings. If babies were dying, who cared? It was

Nature's way of killing off the unwanted. And what of the parents' addiction? The more they spent satisfying their cravings, the more money he saw in his coffers. Even stricter regulation caused him no fear. If anything, it would create a black-market trade, driving prices higher.

He had nothing to lose and everything to gain by assisting Trelayne in her endeavor. With any luck, his fabrication of concern would serve to raise him to a higher esteem in her eyes. The eyes of the one he desired so passionately. After they were married, of course, he would never allow her be so outspoken and independent.

Standing at her side and feigning interest in her letter, Lucian tried to peer down the front of her dress.

"For heaven's sake, Lucien," she cried, in annoyance, having caught him peeking. "Whatever has come over you? We are trying to save little children from the horrors of poverty and disease and all you can think about is looking down my dress. Can you not behave like a gentleman instead of a child yourself? I should insist you leave."

"Forgive me," he begged.

"The need for that seems all too frequent lately," she pointed out.

"I told you before, my willpower and fortitude are no match for your charms. Clear thinking, nay propriety of any sort, is hopelessly unattainable."

****

She shook her head at his Byronic platitudes. If only it were the elusive Captain Garrison who spoke such words and sought such liberties. Bother and damnation, she was doing it again—escaping into a make believe world revolving around an American enigma rather than reality. Curse the man anyway.

"Trelayne?"

Her thoughts snapped back to the present, and she stared up at Lucien. More and more he overstepped the boundaries of acceptable behavior, but this time she would keep her temper, and turn the incident to her advantage.

"I will forgive you your ill mannered ogling, if you will agree to go with me again next month on rounds for the church. A few extra comforts will be just the thing to brighten Christmas for those in need."

Lucien appeared as if she had just asked him to down a tankard of pond water. Then his expression changed.

"I will agree to go under one condition," he said, daring to counter-bargain her request. "Consent to accompany me to the Festival at the Bond. You promised to consider my offer. Do say yes."

"I did consider your offer, and I must decline. All manner of debauchery and nonsense takes place there. I've been told it is one of the most notorious clubs in all London."

"Pure rumor," he refuted. "There is no true danger there. I shall ensure we have a positively proper and boring evening. A few dances, perhaps an elegant meal. And I promise to take you home the moment you desire to leave."

"I don't know, Lucien. I should not, and you know it."

"I see. You are quick to explore how the poor live, and to wallow in their mire, but you will not even think to experience the pleasures and delights of high society.

You, my dear, are a reverse snob."

This theory gave her pause. Before making her rounds for the church, she had been frightfully ignorant of how the less fortunate lived. Was she being closed-minded now about the upper strata of society? Besides, it would be the last thing she could do to please Lucien before telling him they had no future together. Based on his reaction to her refusal of his marriage proposal, she could only imagine what kind of row terminating their relationship completely was going to cause. Going to the Bond would cushion the blow, and leave him with a fond memory.

Of course, Merrick and Wynona would never allow her out of the house at night with Lucien. She would need to manufacture a story about being with Penelope.

Her heart pounded. To attempt such a charade was contrary to the usual rules of deportment she followed. On the other hand, taking over the duties of both her parents had taken its toll. A little gaiety would go a long way in compensating for the stressful demands that seemed so overwhelming of late. What could it hurt?

"I accept your daring proposal. But you must be the consummate gentleman and keep your promise about taking me home when I desire to leave."

The happiness on Lucien's face was hard to ignore. How frightful to realize she had such a commanding effect upon his mood.

"It's just for a lark, Lucien. Nothing serious, no strings attached."

"Whatever you say, my darling."

****

After Lucien took his leave, Trelayne sat embroidering by the hearth, and her mind drifted from one subject to the next.

After creating a final draft of the letter, she'd spent nearly an hour with Merrick, reviewing tomorrow's proceedings for the *Romney Maiden*. She admired Merrick and trusted to his wisdom, and was grateful for the faith he placed in her. Following their conversation, she felt confident, even optimistic, about negotiating the wages and cargo fares for the newly arrived ship.

Merrick would accompany her to the docks, but remain in the background. There was no reason why the crew and merchants should be opposed to her offers. That is, once they accepted the idea of dealing with a woman. What could go wrong? And later, she would write to her parents detailing the affair. They would be proud of her achievement, and less worried about her and the company.

Abandoning the embroidery in her lap, she stared at the flames in the fireplace. Merrick admitted he was worried about Walker's long absence. Had something dreadful happened to him? Surely he was safe. Walker was the most capable man she had ever met.

He must come back, because regardless of his feelings for her, she could no longer imagine the world without him.

Chapter Sixteen

The morning arrived swiftly on the heels of a restless night.

As their coach made its way down Little Tower Hill, Trelayne's sparse breakfast fought for a foothold in her stomach. Face it, she was scared.

What had seemed easily attainable last evening in the muted comfort of her home, felt less certain by the glaring light of day. Much hinged upon the outcome of this transaction—proper and equitable pay for her employees, her credibility at running the partnership, even her pride. More importantly, it would either bolster her confidence or lay low her capacity to face the responsibilities piling up against her day by day.

The warehouses came into view, the sight anything but encouraging. High walls kept the sunlight at bay, the bricks and mortar cutting off the view to the south. Today, St. Katherine's Dock was a dismal place, the oppressive atmosphere cluttered with dirt and debris. It even smelled unhealthy.

She clasped her hands in prayer, but it was too late now for petitioning God, they had reached Irongate Wharf.

"You'll do just fine," Merrick reassured, handing her down from the carriage. "Just keep your head, and don't allow 'em to bully you into anything your gut tells you ain't right."

As Merrick's words struck home, she realized how many of life's situations offered only two choices—fight or flight. Since she couldn't leave, she would fight her fear, and if necessary, the men awaiting her arrival. As determination flared, it lit an ember of courage in her heart. Her hackles rose, and the physical reaction transformed foreboding into eagerness. Unlike the overwhelming situation surrounding the destitute children, today's challenge was something over which she had control. Something she could sink her teeth into, on her terms, in her territory.

As they boarded the *Romney Maiden*, the grand vessel rocked gently in her berth. Up ahead, men of varying social status assembled on the main deck and crowds formed along the loading area. It was almost as if today's event had been publicized.

Reaching the foredeck, she assumed her "entering a ballroom" demeanor, and while doing her best to avoid coils of rope and other seafaring equipment, she moved along as regally as possible. If they wanted a show, she would bloody well give them one. A murmur passed through the crowd, and she glanced toward the docks. To her surprise, several faces appeared sullen, her gracious smile returned with angry jeers.

"Send us a man to do a man's job," a voice rang out.

Her steps faltered, and she searched the faces in the crowd. The message had been loud and clear, but the person responsible remained anonymous, and the statement acted as a catalyst, touching off a round of heckling comments. Merrick's stern continence appeared to be the only thing preventing the crowd from turning completely ugly. Thank goodness the men in her father's employ remained steadfast.

After locating the Commissioner of Trade Unions, Merrick escorted her to the bargaining tables. At her approach, the pudgy red-faced man appeared flustered and confused by the negative peer pressure issuing around him.

Merrick made the introductions. "Mr. Abernathy, may I present Miss Trelayne St.Christopher."

"Oh, dear me. Dear, dear me." The little man mopped the sweat from his brow with a huge white handkerchief.

Hope for support from that quarter quickly disintegrated. The scared rabbit of a man would be too afraid to back her cause. She was on her own to drive a hard bargain with the buyers. Yet if her crew were to receive anything above their flat wages she must procure a good price. The bonus money was what paid their way and encouraged them to be the reliable men they were. They had worked hard, made this voyage safely and in record time. They deserved to be rewarded for their efforts. As Merrick retired to the background, she took her seat and silently vowed not to let them down.

Ignoring the leers and attitudes of superiority, she waited for the negotiations to begin. But after several minutes of proposals and rejections, she could bear no more. Leaping to her feet, shaking with anger, she fought to control her temper. "This is preposterous. I know what a fair price for this shipment should be, and I'll not take a shilling less."

"The way I see it, Missy," countered one self-serving buyer, "you don't have much choice."

"Oh, but I do, gentlemen. Before I allow you to

manipulate me in such a manner, I shall burn this shipment while it is still crated, and pay my men their wages from my estate. Think it over, kind sirs. The Navigation Act of '49 grants foreigners the right to carry British cargo, and the St.Christopher shipping line is now the Garrison/ St.Christopher line. We are twice as big and will soon be doing twice the business—in England, America, and around the world. When next you need our ships for transport out of London, I shall be setting the prices, and I won't forget today."

She flicked a gaze at Merrick. He grinned and gave her a nod of encouragement. The smug expressions faded from the faces of the men, replaced by concerned speculation. The crewmembers within earshot of the conversation offered their support.

The tide was turning in her favor, success nearly within her grasp, then two men roughly jostled into Merrick and laid hands on him. A third brandished a knife and held it at his throat.

"Are you going to hide behind a woman's skirt?" the man with the knife taunted the crewmen. "Ya bunch of seafarin' pansies. What make of men are ye? She's just a snip of a girl, what can she gain for you? Why you'd be better off to take yer money in cargo. You won't be seein' no bonus this trip."

Discontent rippled through the crowd, and good sense became scarce. A man tore open a cargo crate, grabbing at merchandise, throwing it about. Good Lord, what was happening? The crew appeared equally shocked. The men creating the mayhem were not sailors. They shouldn't even be on deck.

The crowd dockside scrambled about fighting to retrieve the booty as it landed at their feet. You could almost smell mass hysteria in the air. Now they were attempting to board ship. It was like being in the middle of a pirate raid.

Outnumbered and out-muscled, Merrick was at a loss to gain his freedom. In desperation, she glanced around the deck and spied a trunk marked for Samuel Colt. A smile pulled at her lips. She sidled closer, pulled free the lock pin, and lifted the lid. Gun parts and more—just what she'd hoped for.

Recalling Sam's demonstration at the Crystal Palace, she gathered the necessary items, and pulse racing slipped the preloaded cylinder into place. Replacing the barrel assembly, she drove home the wedge by tapping it on the side of the crate. Her hands shook so badly she could hardly seat the firing caps. When all was in place, she pulled back the hammer and turned to face the man with the knife.

"Let him go—now," she challenged. "Lay down that knife, or lay down your life. The decision is yours."

The ruffian stared at the bore of the gun then glared at her. She didn't know why, but now her hand was rock steady, and with unconscious effort she assumed the stance she'd been taught to use when handling a firearm.

The man snarled in defeat, lowered the knife, and high-tailed it through the crowd. The other two hooligans released Merrick and followed suit. As the weight of the heavy pistol took its toll, she was about to set the weapon aside. Then she recognized another crate of interest.

The markings indicated it came from Persia, and she wagered it contained the magnificent carpet noted on the ship's manifest. The rug had been specially ordered for one of the richest men in London. He would be furious if anything happened to his long awaited prize, and the buyer sent to collect it for him would be held accountable.

She fired a shot over the bow of the ship, bringing the anarchy to a swift conclusion.

"I'm willing to resume bidding if you will grant me an honest price," she offered. "I'm also willing to start destroying this entire cargo, beginning with one very expensive carpet." With the pistol trained dead center on the crate, she awaited their answer.

Clamoring around the table, the buyers were eager to begin again. She sat down, cradling the pistol in her lap. This time, prices soared beyond her wildest imaginings. The exuberant crew sang her praises, and gave her three cheers.

Having completed the paperwork, she wandered over to the seaward side of the great vessel and stood gazing out upon the water. Why had the crowd been so agitated? And who were the men attacking Merrick and encouraging the insurrection? It was all very curious.

As puzzlement faded, she stood taller, and the thrill of victory quickened her pulse. She had held fast, had represented the St.Christopher name with honor. If only Walker had been here to witness her success. Would he have been proud of her? Wish it or not, his opinion mattered to her.

Gripping the rail, she studied the seagulls soaring overhead. Walker had spent near a lifetime viewing the world from the deck of a ship; she could almost feel his presence at her side—see his rugged profile as he faced into the wind.

Where was he? He'd been gone too long. Ire at his

absence had once again shifted to concern, leaving her emotions in tatters. Maybe she was overreacting. After all, the man had sailed the world over, and heaven only knew the escapades in which he had engaged. So far he had managed to remain unscathed. Surely, a simple trip to Brighton wouldn't be his undoing.

****

While Hargis was at work, Walker prowled the immediate vicinity, scrounging for wood and anything else they could burn for fuel.

The process was slow and painful. Simple activities, once taken for granted, took on the dimension of major accomplishments leaving his self-image near as damaged as his body. He couldn't abide being weak and dependent, it made him feel less of a man.

His outer wounds were healing cleanly, adding three new scars to his collection. But his insides were slower to mend. He'd finally quit urinating blood, thanks to the mysterious concoctions Hargis insisted he drink. Yet while the hours seemed to drag on, the days were flying by. How soon until he was fit to travel?

He tossed a piece of planking into the cart. When he became too downhearted, Hargis cajoled or bullied him out of the doldrums. His friend also countermanded any delusions of grandeur. Yesterday, he proclaimed himself ready to return to London, but Hargis insisted it was too soon. Adamant and overconfident, he'd challenged Hargis to a mock battle. Thoughts of an immediate departure were quickly reversed. But ready or not, he must leave soon.

Back at the shack, he unloaded the burnable material into a box in the corner. He'd failed Trelayne, had let her down, and it tore at his heart, pride, and conscience. His battered body was proof there was danger afoot, a condition he would gladly suffer again if it meant keeping her safe, keeping all eyes on him, but gut instinct told him this wasn't the case. Grimsby and Lanteen were responsible for this mayhem and murder, he felt it in his broken bones, and now they would list him as dead and turn their attention elsewhere.

"How goes your day, Walker Garrison?' Hargis greeted, coming home for the evening. "I got a surprise for you."

Without explanation, he motioned Walker to the abandoned smokehouse behind their hut. When his eyes grew accustomed to the dim light, Walker saw something hanging from one of the meat hooks attached to the rafters. Close inspection revealed the wriggling object to be a man. He threw Hargis a questioning look.

"I found the lone survivor of the four men who attacked you. It was a hard choice which way to hang him," Hargis growled, "by the feet or by the neck."

The cutthroat, trussed like a Christmas goose, revolved upside down, and as he came around full circle, his gaze focused on Walker and his eyes widen in recognition.

"You…you're dead," he stuttered.

"Almost," he countered, drawing closer, the urge for retaliation coursing through his body. "Who hired you to kill me?" he asked, his voice stone-cold, his hands balled into fists.

"Nobody," the man whined.

"So the four of you were just walking along and it occurred to you it would be a damn good time beating me to a bloody pulp."

"That's it, gov'nor, exactly. I wouldn't lie to you."

"I'd say lying would come rather natural to a man who would take money for murder."

"I think he needs encouragement," Hargis said, starting a fire in the little woodstove. "I hear smoked English pig be very tasty."

"We Yanks like nothing better," Walker agreed, going along with the ploy. "Of course, the best meat is cooked long and slow. Why, it could take days to get it just right. Let me lend you a hand so we can close this place up and relax outside in the cool evening air."

"Good idea, friend. I would rather be tending a red hot forge than be left in here when this fire takes hold."

"Now wait a bloody minute," the dangling man shrieked. "You can't be doin' this to one of the Queen's citizens. You cut me down, you foreign devils."

"Did you hear something?" Hargis asked, cupping one hand to his ear.

"Just a squealing pig-like sound," Walker replied.

The room was small, the heat fierce, and sweat beaded off all three men as hickory smoke filled the confined area. Walker coughed, setting his ribs to burning and aching, and he and Hargis made for the door. Surprisingly, the man remained silent. Was this no-account actually willing to die rather than reveal his employer? This kind of loyalty, or more likely fear, said something for the man who had hired him.

"I'll talk," the rabble relented, his face red as a beet. "Cut me down, for God's sake, cut me down."

Hargis raised a questioning brow. At Walker's nod, he produced a large knife and sliced sideways through the rope. With a thud and a curse, their prisoner dropped to the floor.

After closing down the stove, Hargis kicked and rolled the evil little man closer to the door where all three could breathe easier.

"I'll tell you whatever you want to know, just untie me. Get me out of here."

"Not yet," Walker insisted. "Talk first. Then we'll discuss your accommodations. Who hired the four of you to kill me?"

"Ah, sweet Jesus save me," the fellow trembled and pleaded. "If I tell you he'll kill me he will."

"And I'll kill you if you don't tell," Walker bluffed.

"It was Grimsby what hired us, Bartholomew Grimsby."

"And for whom does Grimsby work?" Walker asked. A well-aimed prod with the toe of his boot helping matters along.

"He works for Lucien Lanteen. They transport goods and do a bit of smuggling, whatever will turn a profit. Legal or illegal, they don't much care. And, they ain't particular about eliminating whoever gets in their way."

Finally, his suspicions were confirmed, but he felt no relief or satisfaction, rather the news revived his worst fears. He pictured Trelayne at Royston Hall, alone and at the mercy of Lucien with only Merrick and Wynona to keep watch over her.

"And...." Walker pressed, his voice rough with the anger building in his chest.

Hargis sighed, stepped to the stove, and stirred the coals back into flames.

"All right, all right. All the else I knows is Lucien received a recent shipment of opium. A large shipment and they be keepin' it down here."

"In Brighton?" Walker interrupted.

"No, no, just somewhere close to Brighton. A warehouse or an old inn. I can't recall. I was never there meself. But Lanteen's got a right regular scheme what includes marrying some girl. And there's something else in the works as has not been revealed to the likes of me."

Marriage… Was Lanteen mad enough to believe Trelayne would agree to marry him? What if Trelayne viewed Lucien in an entirely different light? She didn't know he ruined peoples' lives by selling smuggled drugs, nor did she know Lucien had been willing to kill him and injure her parents in order to prevent the merger of the shipping lines. She thought of him as a longtime friend and advisor, unaware he possessed a greedy, perverted, and most generally unhinged side to his nature.

He should have confided in her more readily. Trusted her to be sensible and mature. He had hesitated because he feared she wouldn't believe him. Feared he might drive her into the arms of whoever had been responsible for all this madness, and now it looked as if may have done just that.

"What else?" he hollered, frantic at the thought of Trelayne being under Lucien's control.

"Nothin' else. That's all."

"I don't believe you. Think harder. You must know more. I don't care if it's only idle gossip or speculation. Tell me everything." Fists raised, he towered over the man.

"I'm tryin' to think, really I am. All I remember is they stay at that inn or winery when they come down here and he's obsessed with the lass, nearly mad for her. I don't know another word. I swear. Except Mr. Lanteen likes gamblin', good clothes, and seein' things suffer."

"I think the pig's done squealing," Hargis said, "but it's your call."

Walker turned away. "I agree, but we'll have to keep him here a few more days until I'm fit to travel. If we turn him over to the Constable tonight, word may leak out I'm still alive, and I'd like to keep that quiet until I'm back in London. Thank you, Hargis." He threw one arm across the big Norwegian's shoulder. "You're a man among men and a friend indeed. Come outside where we can finish making plans."

"Hey. Wait a minute," the Englishman cried. "You can't just leave me here tied up."

"Why not?" Hargis growled. "You be quiet and ponder you are lucky to be alive. If it were up to Hargis you would be standing before Odin for what you done to my friend. Remember, he is the nice one and he is leaving soon. Then you will have only me to decide if you live or die."

Damping down the stove, they closed the smokehouse door, wedged a large board up against the latch, and left the man trussed and stewing in his own thoughts. When true darkness fell, Walker donned local costume to obscure his identity, and they went to town.

Along the docks, he located a ship from New Bedford. Arranging free passage to America for Hargis, he left a promissory note and letter with the Captain, and instructed Hargis to find Dr. Nathan Robinson when he made port. The letter advised Nate to honor the promissory note and treat Hargis with all due respect and assistance.

The arrangements completed, the temptation to seal the deal with a drink was too great to ignore. They slipped into a pub called the Pick and Shovel, a quarry men's hang out. Walker kept to the shadows and watched in amusement as Hargis became involved in a wrestling contest. His friend took on every challenger, and beat all comers. In payment for the entertainment, the tavern-keeper gave Hargis complimentary ale, which he heartily consumed.

Hargis slammed down his current empty tankard and grinned. "Enough fighting. Now is time for loving."

A pair of lovelies, impressed by Hargis' strength, sidled up and vied for his attention. "Which one of us pleases you most?" the dark-haired girl asked, trying to force him to make a choice.

"I like you both," he declared.

He picked one girl up under each arm, and amidst their shrieks of laughter, headed for the private backrooms of the establishment. Walker snorted in amusement and continued to lay low.

It would probably take two of them to satisfy the big Goliath.

When a third girl strolled his way, he smiled and shook his head. She ambled off to find a more willing prospect, and he passed off his lack of interest as a result of his injuries, but in his heart he knew the real reason was because he yearned for only one woman, and there could be no substitute.

Heaven only knew what Trelayne must think of him. He'd been gone nearly a month. Would she turn to Lanteen for comfort and amusement? Merrick indicated she'd led a rather sheltered existence, but a need for adventure and a willful spirit were a part of her too. He'd seen it in her eyes and felt it pulsing in her body when he kissed her wrist.

The more he brooded, the more restless he became. He should leave for London tonight, but the last train was gone.

Then he'd damn well go by horse. He glanced out the window. There was no moon to light the way, and it was threatening snow, or at least sleet. With a sharp wind blowing out of the north, the going would be treacherous for man and beast.

So what? He'd ridden in worse conditions, but over trails he knew well and only when he'd been of sound body. To suffer a re-injury due to poor judgment would only succeed in making matters worse. The reasonable thing to do was to wait a few more days, renew his vigor, and go north by rail as planned.

Logically, he knew this—emotionally he was unconvinced.

Once before, he'd been too late to save the woman he loved.

He couldn't survive going through that again.

To build up his strength, he ordered a huge meal from the barmaid and ate every scrap. Then as the night slipped away, he waited with good humor for his friend.

Smiling from ear to ear, Hargis returned from his trysting and threw himself down onto the seat.

"I take it a good time was had by all," Walker said.

Hargis, still as bright eyed and energetic as a young colt, nodded and ordered more ale.

"Does nothing wear out that hulking body of yours?"

"It would take more than two small English girls to tire Hargis out. I learned about love from big hearty Scandinavian women."

For Walker, *one* small soft English girl would be more than enough to fill his desires.

Chapter Seventeen

Trelayne lay across her bed, starring up at the ceiling, absentmindedly toying with a lock of her hair. It was three days since the incident on the *Romney Maiden*, and the weather had turned damp and chilly. Tonight, angry clouds again filled the sky, the smell of snow was in the air, and her mood was equally as dismal.

Having acted in haste, she now regretted her decision at leisure. Tonight was The Bond Street Consortium Gala. She never should have agreed to go. She should have arranged to meet Lucien on more neutral ground for their heart-to-heart talk. But everything was arranged, it was too late now, and truly she wished to put their discussion behind her.

Lucien's presence had become almost smothering. He seemed to know her every move, showing up at the most unlikely places.

The other day, he'd appeared at her dressmaker's. Not the usual venue for a man to seek. Another time, they crossed paths near Father Woolsey's priory. Lucien had insisted he was simply passing by. But passing by to what? The Vicarage was rurally located and not really on the way to anything of interest. Maybe, she should chance his ire, and simply refuse to go. He would be furious, of course, but would eventually recover from his disappointment. Besides, as she intended to break off their fabricated-relationship, what difference would it make in the long run?

Of course, since she *was* soon to break his heart, this was the last consideration she could show him. She guessed it was either lie to Lucien about being sick, or lie to Aunt Abigail as to where she was going tonight. When she had casually mentioned The Bond, her guardian had launched into a surprisingly puritanical lecture regarding the disreputable aspects of the establishment. An exposé on those who frequented such places had scathingly followed, but it piqued her interest rather than deterring her.

Ever since Walker's absence, her aunt had become as overprotective as Mother and Father. It was tiresome being told what to do and when to do it. She felt ready to burst with an unknown energy, and even her nightmare, obviously a warning of some sort, didn't cow her spirits.

Penelope understood. She knew how it felt to be intoxicated with curiosity about life—about men. How it felt to be filled with unstoppable passion, your soul seeking answers to questions of the heart. Penelope knew what it was like to yearn irrepressibly for someone.

Melancholy consumed her, and it was the elusive Captain Garrison's fault. He'd ruined her for any other man. She had dared to gaze into his eyes, losing her sense of direction while wrapped in his embrace. Wanting someone so very much, and not being with him, was self-inflicted torture. Where in heaven's name could he be? Unless he had done so by choice, it hardly seemed likely he could disappear so completely. Even the runners Merrick sent to Brighton couldn't find him.

She reached for the gloves she now kept close at hand, grazing the leather along her temple, her cheek, her throat, all the while imagining it was Walker's touch. But pretending wasn't enough, she wanted the real thing.

Setting his gift aside, she gained her feet and paced the room, wringing her hands, her back stiff with concern and indecision. Then she made up her mind as to what to do, and it felt as if she'd been holding her breath and could once more breathe deeply. If by tomorrow, there was no news regarding Walker, she would insist Merrick take her to Brighton. And tonight, as planned, she would set the record straight with Lucien, severing all ties. She wished not to go at all, but knew he would keep hounding her until they settled the matter. Surely she could put on a good face for just one evening. Although in truth, knowing she must wait until tomorrow to search for Walker left her straining at the leash, her nerves on edge, and her mood anything but gay.

A tapping noise sent her racing across the room. She jerked open the door.

"Mercy me," Penelope gasped. "You're in a dither. I've obviously arrived just in time."

Trelayne grabbed her friend's arm, hustled her into the room, and closed the door.

"I'm going to do it," she declared.

"Do *it*?"

"Oh, heaven's no. Not that *it*. What I mean is I've definitely decided to accompany Lucien to The Bond."

Penelope heaved a sigh of relief. "You had me terrified for a moment. Of late you're too bold and daring for your own good. I can't imagine what you will do next. Besides, if you do *it*, it must be with Captain Garrison."

"As he's still missing, I hardly think the occasion will arise any time soon. I'm worried about him. But perhaps I shouldn't be. After all, we've not declared are feelings for one another, maybe it's not my concern where he goes, or how long he stays away."

"Oh, bunkum and balderdash." Penelope blurted. "You're in love with him."

She stared at her friend, thinking to deny her statement, but she could no more deceive Pen than herself.

"Yes, oh yes, I am in love with him…desperately. But it's unrequited and it's breaking my heart. I thought to be giddy with happiness, aglow with joy, instead I'm miserable and lackluster at best.

"But unrequited love is supposed to be romantic."

"Well, it isn't, I assure you. It's not at all like in the stories we read. It's tearing me apart, I'm in emotional shreds."

"Still you can't be sure of his intentions. You've not spoken to him about such things, or given him a chance to profess his feelings."

"You're right, of course. And on the morrow I intend to remedy that situation by going in search of him, although I don't know how I'm going to wait that long. Already this seems the longest night of my life. I was going to cancel, but if I don't keep busy I shall be reduced to a sweet madness, never to recover. And I must resolve my issues with Lucien."

"Well, then," Penelope said, leading her to the wardrobe, "if you are to soldier on this evening, you shall do so in style."

The first dress Trelayne held up received a negative shake of the head from her friend. Dropping it on the floor, she grabbed another. "Are you clear on what to say when Aunt Abigail asks where we are going?" she asked.

"I have it rehearsed to perfection. No, that one won't do either," Penelope clucked. "Here try the lavender one. You had better be on your guard tonight," her friend added. "If anything goes awry, your very reputation will be at stake, tarnished and talked about from here to Cornwall."

"What is the worst that could happen, Pen? Lucien will protect me from true harm. He's in love with me, why would he allow anything to ruin my name or character. Besides, if we are to emulate the women we read about, we must occasionally throw caution to the wind."

"I'm just worried you're turning caution loose in a maelstrom," Penelope said. "And remember, many of those books we read end in tragedy."

"A valid point," she agreed. "I promise to make it an early evening, just staying long enough to appease Lucien, and to speak to him honestly about my decision regarding our relationship."

"Good. No more lectures." Her friend couldn't suppress a giggle. "It does sound wickedly exciting. Truth be told, I'm jealous as can be. You must tell me everything. What the women wore, what flirtatious games they played, and to what pagan tunes they dared to dance."

Trelayne hugged Penelope. "I'll not leave out one glorious detail."

****

As the coach sped away into the night, Trelayne settled back against the seat and pulled together an expression of cheerfulness. Her emotions were ratcheted to a fevered pitch, but not because she was looking forward to their outing. All she could think about was Walker. Was he safe? Did he miss her as much as she missed him?

Lucien near inhaled the sight of her, not even remembering to make polite conversation for her entertainment. Apparently the lavender gown was a good choice, the white silk rose pinned at the bodice the perfect touch to mask the worry and distraction overwhelming all her senses.

"Do tell me about tonight's festivities, Lucien," she said, seeking a diversion from the thoughts racing through her mind in the deafening silence.

"What? Yes, of course." He shook his head as if coming out of a trance. "The Bond is a world unto itself," he began, "where magnificent chandeliers twinkle overhead, and towering palms and exotic plants create an atmosphere of mystery."

He paused, as if to allow her to paint the image in her mind, but all she could see was Walker's face.

"The cuisine is unparalleled, the wine cellar extensive" he added. "And one of the finest small orchestras in London presides over the ballroom. But the gaming parlor is the main attraction, overflowing with merriment and high stakes betting."

"It sounds fascinating," she said, trying to be attentive, "and not nearly as sinful as I was led to believe. Why, I'm almost disappointed."

"Neither of us shall be disappointed tonight, my love," Lucien promised. "When you experience the excitement and ambiance to be had, you will be carried away to another time and place."

Handing her down from the coach, Lucien paid the driver, then sporting an elegant walking stick, grandly escorted her into the club.

The interior was resplendent, the room emotionally charged. Men laughed, their women clinging overtly to them. Cigar smoke swirled through the air, transformed into a dreamy haze by the twinkling light from the chandeliers, and ethereal music completed the ambiance, seducing her senses, leaving her dizzy. For Penelope's sake, she tried to focus and make note of specifics.

The women's gowns showed a daring amount of décolletage. They could not possibly be employing corsets or proper undergarments.

"Oh, Lucien, I'm dressed completely wrong for such an event. Maybe we should leave," she added, grabbing at the excuse to make a quick exit.

"Nonsense, Trelayne. You are an enchanting breath of fresh air, an innocent amongst the garish and used women normally available here. Does not every man turn his head as we walk by? All of their eyes are upon you with desire, and upon me with envy. I would not trade places with any one of them."

So much for that idea. They meandered across the lobby toward an area constructed for serving refreshments.

"Sit here, darling," he suggested, holding a chair for her. "We must have champagne for so memorable evening. Promise not to look too fetching in my absence," he added, leaning his walking stick against the table, "lest upon my return, I must fight my way through a league of men surrounding you."

Obviously well known, Lucien signed for the drinks as several people recognized him and vied for attention. He cut a dashing figure tonight, but it was not the sight of him, nor the near palpable energy vibrating in the air that made her heart race. It was the thought of seeing Walker tomorrow. If he were her companion, she would be content to sit by the fire, reading, or embroidering. He would be all the excitement she needed.

With nothing better to do, she people-watched, and was not impressed with what she saw. The men openly leered at her. One depraved fellow blew her a kiss as he fondled the bosom of the woman at his side. Beneath their painted smiles, the women appeared sad, their doleful eyes lamenting *I was young once, too.*

Alarmed by such a display, she twisted in her chair searching for Lucien. Where was he? She did not wish to be left alone any longer. It seemed beneath the glitter of gold and the sound of laughter, there lurked cold hard iron and bitter memories. About to panic, she exhaled a sigh of relief as he returned.

"Forgive me for leaving you unattended so long." He took to the chair at her side and handed her a glass. "A toast to your beauty and my gratitude for your company."

In an attempt to recapture her original bravado, she heartily complied.

"Have another sip," he insisted, although he didn't touch the contents of his own glass.

She followed his suggestion, enjoying the warm serenity spreading through her body.

After a few moments, he rose and held out his

hand. "Shall we try our luck at the tables? You're sure to charm the dice as readily as you have all the men in the room."

"Lucien," she said, trying to make herself heard above the merriment. "We really must talk."

He extended his hand closer, the other holding a full glass of champagne. "I can't hear you, darling. Come along, the night is young, and so are we, let's enjoy the fun,"

Seeing little option, she gained her feet then reached for Lucien to steady herself. Good heavens. She'd often sampled wines and champagne at parties and formal dinners, but nothing ever affected her so quickly or so drastically.

Relying upon his arm for support, they ambled about the room. His casual conversation suddenly seemed profound, his humorous stories amazingly witty. At the gaming tables, she was persuaded to try her hand with the dice. All went well until Lucien plied her with more drink. Then her concentration became scattered, the numbers and score completely eluding her.

"Lucien, I feel so light headed. Do be a pet and let us sit down for a moment."

"Of course," he obliged, his voice filled with concern. "You look pale. Have you eaten today?"

"Very little," she confessed, as he directed her to a more quiet setting.

Properly seated, the wooziness eased, leaving her oddly contented. She glanced around. They were in a small room, a very compromising, very private room. The dimly lit compartment sported oversized cushions and soft fur throws. One part of her brain sent out signals of alarm, another part found the quiet atmosphere a panacea of welcoming comfort, so appealing to her swirling thoughts.

Lucien sat at her side, apprehension furrowing his brow. My, but he looked so serious. Tonight he treated her like royalty. Maybe he wasn't such an unsuitable match for her after all. No, that was all wrong. What was she thinking? But he was being sweet, and she felt sorry knowing they would be parting forever after tonight. She gave him an innocent kiss on the cheek, then the strange giddiness she'd felt before struck again, and she laughingly fell back against the pillows. Her body was reacting before she could reason what she was doing. This was not the proper order of things.

"I'll order food." Rising, Lucien headed for the door. "We can relax here until you are feeling yourself again."

She must collect her thoughts. Being alone with Lucien in this private room was highly improbable, no not improbable...improper...that was it, highly improper. She wondered at her confusion then with a sigh stared at the flocked wallpaper. The colors seemed so bright, the patterns swirling about as if they were alive.

"The comestibles will be here shortly," he reassured, returning with more sparkling wine.

His eyes appeared a deeper blue, almost smoldering. With a brazen half-smile, he poured more champagne and eased down upon the settee.

"You've never looked more beautiful, Trelayne," he crooned.

He pressed the glass of bubbly to her lips. Without thinking, she drank it in, along with his compliments.

Boldly, he kissed her, his tongue gently probing. She should be shocked—was indeed shocked, but thoughts would not become actions. A knock on the door gave her a jolt. Leaning away she blushed furiously.

Lucien laughed, and went to answer the call.

The waiter placed a tray upon a nearby table. Again, Lucien signed for the order, but he also gave the lad a large handful of coins. The boy glanced over at her, grinned up at Lucien, and retrieved a small placard from his uniform pocket. He hung the sign by its brass chain on the outside handle, and taking his leave, firmly pulled the door shut.

She should protest, and demand to leave immediately, but her body felt so languid, and her thoughts soared beyond serious contemplation. As the sound of the orchestra seeped into the room, she closed her eyes. She was supposed to talk to Lucien, but all the things she had planned to say were jumbled in her mind, hovering just beyond her grasp.

Where was he? She opened her eyes. There he was, standing near the tray, his back toward her. He seemed to be organizing the food.

Repairing to her side, he offered a strawberry tipped with powdered sugar. She really should eat something. He placed it in her mouth. It tasted a bit odd, but went down easily. She had a second one, then another.

"You must have some too," she insisted.

"No," he declined, restraining her hand as she attempted to feed him in kind. "You're all the sustenance I need."

The food, rather than making her stronger and clearing her mind, left her feeling all the more fainty and floaty. It wasn't exactly a bad sensation. In fact it was rather pleasing. Every inch of her skin tingled, the music felt as if it came from inside of her, and the cushions were soft as clouds.

"Oh, Lucien, I don't know what's come over me. I can barely catch my breath. Could you open a window?"

"Sorry, darling. The windows are locked tight. The proprietor wouldn't want anyone sneaking in uninvited or sneaking out without paying."

"Yes, of course. How clever of him."

It all made good sense, but the room was stifling. In a haze, she pushed the off-the-shoulder sleeve farther down upon her arm. Lucien trailed a finger along the exposed skin.

"If you are truly in distress, my dear, perhaps I should loosen a button or two on your dress."

No…he mustn't. She struggled to put her protest into words, but only a garbled sentence passed her lips. Experienced fingers released several button closures, and her dress gapped, revealing her corset. Lucien grazed his hand across the mounds of her breasts. Alarmed at his behavior, she found the strength to push him away.

"Easy, darling." He shushed her as if she were a child.

Stroking her hair, he rocked her back and forth. Now his touch was reassuring rather than threatening. Everything was all right. Everything was marvelous.

"Rest your head on my shoulder, sweet. Don't fight the pleasure surrounding you."

Closing her eyes, she complied and her thoughts turned to colors, every fiber of her being pulsed with a life of its own. She heard the rustle of fabric, it sounded far away. Lucien slipped his hand beneath her skirts, he touched her knee and inched his way upward.

In the foggy far reaches of her mind, her instinct for self-preservation cried for him to stop. But her arms felt too heavy to lift and wouldn't respond, but how was that possible when she was floating, so light, so carefree. Yes, delightfully carefree, there was no need for alarm. Walker wouldn't hurt her. Visions of her wild and wonderful Sea Captain flashed through her mind. She opened her eyes... It was blonde hair that met her gaze, not Walker's dark thick mane. Something was wrong

With monumental effort, she rallied "Lucien," she breathed, "we mustn't."

He eased back, giving her a comforting smile. "Whatever you wish, my love. There's no rush. We've all the time in the world. Do have another strawberry."

Chapter Eighteen

Walker shifted the knife and scabbard to a more comfortable position on his belt. Hargis had designed the weapon to replace his Green River blade lost in the fight. This one was smaller, and more suited for concealment in the city, but it was just as deadly. Standing on the stoop outside Lucien's flat, he had a dark craving to christen it in blood.

Edging closer, he listened at the door. It was quiet as a tomb inside. Damn. It would be just his luck no one was home—delaying his satisfaction for revenge. Upon his return from Brighton, Walker had stopped at Royston Hall. At first, he'd been alarmed to find Trelayne was not present then reassured after being told she was with her friend Penelope. With that worry off his mind, it left the way clear for him to search out Lanteen.

He pounded on the door. The sound echoed through the rooms beyond. Again and again he slammed his fist against the wood. Shockwaves of pain reverberated through his barely healed body, but pretending the oak panel was Lanteen's face, pain became pleasure.

****

Beatrice heard the summons and quit sobbing long enough to glance in the direction of the front door. Maybe Lucien had changed his mind. Maybe he had come home instead of keeping his assignation with *her*.

For one happy moment, she clung to the sliver of hope. Then it occurred to her—if Lucien had returned he wouldn't knock, he would use his key.

Slumping back upon the bed, she lay listening to the persistent commotion. Finally, curiosity and concern got the better of her. What if the caller was involved in Lucien's business dealings? Slipping from the bed, she straightened her crumpled dress, and padded across the room. If she didn't respond, and it caused him to lose money, she would pay dearly for her poor judgment.

"Who's there? What you be wanting?" She pressed close in order to hear the reply.

"I've a message for Mr. Lanteen."

"He's not home, go away."

"I've a package for him too, Miss."

"Well, leave it outside and get on with you."

"Please, you don't understand. You must sign the receipt. That's the rules, and I'll be punished if they ain't followed. I'll lose me job, or at least get a good beatin'. Please, Miss. It won't take but a moment."

The voice sounded so sincere, and knowing what it felt like to taste the master's whip, Beatrice took pity and unbolted the door. The man revealed gave her a start. Coo, he was a handsome rascal. She couldn't imagine anyone giving him a beating. He was hardy and manly, not pretty like Lucien. And he was tall, towering over her by a good foot. His eyes had a kindness about them although they appeared commanding as well. Entranced by the sight of him, it took a moment before she realized he wasn't carrying a parcel.

"Say, where's this important package you want me to sign for?" As she inspected him more closely, appreciation turned to apprehension.

The man remained silent as if pondering his next move. Her suspicion rose, and gut instinct roared something was wrong. She tried to slam the door shut, but he easily pushed it back and forced his way in. Turning, she searched for a likely weapon.

"I'm not here to hurt you." He stood his ground as if trying to gain her trust.

"Who are you? What'd you want?"

"I'm Captain Walker Garrison. I need your help…please."

Recognition of his name momentarily overtook fear. So, this was the amazing Captain Garrison. The man Lucien hated and that hussy Trelayne loved. His speech had reverted to American, but wasn't he ever so polite, asking for her help, not an order but a request. That was a switch.

"What could I know that would help the likes of you?"

****

Walker hesitated. If Lucien was in love with Trelayne, why was this woman here and very much at home in his residence? A residence where no expense had been spared. Even the china upon the table was exquisite. Set only for one, it seemed safe to assume the lady intended to dine alone tonight.

As he pondered the situation, he studied the rest of the room. A painting hanging over the fireplace caught his attention. The scene was that of an old monastery or gatehouse, the rendering flanked by ornate sconces. A lace mantel cloth beneath it, gave the arrangement an alter-like appearance.

He drew closer. The brass plate at the bottom of the picture indicated the structure was Amberley Abbey. Odd Lucien would have such a fascination for an old monastic ruin. His gaze roamed sideways and held fast as it snagged on a miniature of Trelayne, displayed in a singularly beautiful filigreed frame. How revolting. Lucien had her likeness over which to weave his vile dreams and plans. Lovingly, he picked up the tiny portrait and turned it over. An inscription added to the silver work read, *Queen of my desires, Abbess of my soul.* By all that was holy, what was that supposed to mean? Resisting the urge to slip the treasure into his pocket, he precisely replaced the miniature, his fingers lingering on the image.

From the corner of his eye, he caught the woman backing out of the room. She inadvertently brushed against an end table, and the crystal figurines on top collided. The soft tinkling sound broke the silence in the room bringing her up short.

"You'll never make it to the door before me," he challenged. "Where is Lanteen? I really must know."

"He's out on the town," the woman snapped, holding her ground, "and I don't know when he'll be back."

Was she miffed at having been left behind? That could work to his advantage. "Had a fight did you? Is that why you're here alone?"

"It's none of your business why I'm here. And once he figures out she ain't all he dreamed her to be, he'll come back to me."

"She?"

The woman nodded at the mantel.

A sick feeling gripped his stomach. "Good God, is he with her now?"

"So what? It don't mean nothin'."

How could this be? Was Merrick lying to him, or had Trelayne lied to Merrick? He stalked across the room. If she was with Lanteen, she was in over her head and setting into motion circumstances she might not be able to control.

"Where are they? Her life may be in danger."

"In danger. That's a good one. He won't hurt her none," she snarled. "He's infatuated with the skinny bitch."

"Be careful how you speak about the woman I love," he growled back. "Those two should not be together, not now, not ever."

"Sweet mother of God," the woman bristled. "So you're in love with her, too." After a moment, a calculating expression replaced her angry grimace.

"My name's Beatrice," she offered. "Maybe we can help each other."

"In what manner?"

"Well, you want the girl, and I want Lucien. It's simple as that. You sees the girl is out of the way, and then Lucien will be mine again."

After getting past the idea that anyone actually wanted Lanteen, Walker considered the offer.

"But you got to promise me one thing," she added, fear evident in her voice. "If I help you, Lucien must never find out."

Although he did not trust this woman, he saw no reason not to promise what she asked. "Your part in any plan devised will remain a secret—unless you betray me or Miss St.Christopher. Then you'll have more than

Lucien to contend with."

The woman blanched. Had he come on too strong? As she appeared to weigh the pros and cons, her gaze flickered over to the miniature of Trelayne. She clenched her jaw, and the color rushed back into her cheeks, jealousy apparently conquering fear.

"I'll help you. But what assurance do I have you won't tell on me one way or the other."

"Only my word."

Beatrice gave a sniff of sarcasm.

"Ma'am," he persuaded, "if I were the malicious untrustworthy type, I would be, at this very moment, beating the daylights and information out of you. I have no interest in and nothing to gain by betraying you. Where are they?"

"They're at The Bond." The words burst from her lips as if their immediate escape was the only way to ensure they would be heard before she lost her nerve.

"What and where is the Bond?" he demanded.

"The Bond Street Gentlemen's Consortium. A men's club what allows women on certain evenings. Many a misadventure takes place there in the wee small hours of the night. I've been there once or twice me-self," she added, with pride.

"How do I get there?" Walker asked, heading for the door, his anxiety rising with every step.

"It's rather 'round about from here," Beatrice hedged, following close behind.

He halted and turned around. The woman was trying to keep some control of the situation, but he couldn't have her tagging along and getting in the way.

"I'd prefer to go by myself," he said.

"And just how do you plan to find her? It's a large

establishment, open to patrons only, and Lucien has many friends there. You can't go charging in like some white knight expecting to carry off your fair maiden without a fight. A romantic notion, but poorly advised."

"What do you suggest?" he grudgingly asked. "Tell me quickly, I fear time is of the essence."

"I know the ins and outs of the place, even the private rooms where Lucien likes to frequent. I'll get to your woman and bring her out to you. Lucien will think she has abandoned him and then he will come back here to me. The rest is up to you. Keep the little princess away from my Lucien. Take her off to America, or anyplace far from here. You'll have what you want, and things will be like they was for me."

Unable to come up with a superior plan, he agreed. To induce Lucien away from Trelayne long enough for Beatrice to do as she promised, he suggested they leave a message for him in the lobby of the establishment. Tearing off the letterhead of the fine parchment found in the desk, he wrote the note for Lanteen, then a second missive.

Dearest Trelayne,

You are in danger. I await you outside and will explain all once you are safely in my arms. Trust no one, other than the woman who delivers this note—and her guardedly.

Devotedly, Capt. W. Garrison

He folded the memo, but was reluctant to let it go. What if the woman gave the note to Lucien rather than Trelayne?

"I'll not betray you," she said, with insight and surprising kindness. "It will all work out. Don't you see, it must. I can't go on no longer the way things are."

She snatched both papers and stuffed them into the bodice of her dress. There was despair in Beatrice's eyes. She must have had a lousy life if getting Lucien back was the most important thing she had to live for. It was frightening to think of him as anyone's hope or salvation.

Walker smiled. "I have faith you will do what is right, and not just what is to your own advantage."

She nodded, but her own smile trembled as she jammed her feet into soft leather boots and flung a cape about her shoulders.

"Do not fail me," he added as they took their leave. "You hold in your hands the fate of many people. And you'd best choose wisely tonight in all matters, for your fate is among them as well."

At the street, the sound of coach wheels on cobblestone echoed through the night. When the carriage materialized out of the fog, Walker flagged it down and they were off.

"Don't be getting impatient for us," Beatrice said, as they halted at the servants' entrance of the Bond. "It may take a while to play out all of the drama about to unfold."

"I understand," he said, his lips pressed into a determined line. Waiting was going to be pure hell.

"You really do love the rich little baggage, don't ya?" she threw over her shoulder, and hurried off.

"Move on driver," he ground out. Beatrice's last words left him feeling desperate in a dozen different ways.

They circled around to the front of the building, and it was all he could do not to leap from the coach and proceed with the ill-advised frontal attack—

previously discussed and rejected. Instead, he directed the coachman to secure a discreet position a few streets away where he sat in the deafening silence, fighting to remain calm.

The sides of the carriage seemed to draw ever closer, and remaining inactive and sequestered was an effort requiring all his concentration. He was a man of action. This idle waiting went against the grain. For the second time, he checked the load on his pistol and the time on his pocket watch. What seemed an eternity was in reality only a few minutes.

Touching the St. Brendan medal at his neck, he implored the saint to watch over Trelayne, for tonight she surely swam in uncharted waters. Then, sitting there in the dark, it occurred to him there was only one way to make good Philip's request to keep Trelayne safe. What would she think of such a plan?

****

Lost to the shadows, Beatrice pressed back against the brick wall a few paces from the back door. Used by the kitchen help, and bolted from the inside, there was nothing for it but to wait.

Flushed with excitement, she hardly noticed the cold. It had been a long time since she had felt this alive. She was about to do something important, motivated by the intent to do what was right and good for the greater whole. At least the greater whole as she knew it.

The door creaked opened, and a lad came out lugging two buckets of food scraps to add to the heap already piled high. While his back was turned, she sneaked forward and gained entrance.

Inside, she drew up her hood to conceal her

identity, sought out the manager, and delivered the urgent message intended for Lucien. Waiting in an alcove near the private rooms, she saw the house-page head off to deliver the note. A moment later, Lucien stormed past in the direction of the reception area—a scowl on his face, the note in one hand, his walking stick in the other.

As soon as he was out of sight, she began knocking on doors. She needn't look in any other area. Regrettably, she knew Lucien would already have Trelayne isolated in one of the luxurious side rooms—already plying his charms and reaping his rewards.

Her first attempt garnered a masculine voice advising her to go away or risk bodily harm. Undaunted, she rapped on the second door. When silence followed, she knocked again. This time she heard a weak female voice. Easing opened the door she peered inside. There she was, the silly woman, draped over the cushions and furs. Her dress undone and gapping, her hair disheveled, her eyes glassy and overly bright.

"Miss Trelayne, you must come with me," Beatrice began, and hurried forward.

"Penelope?" Trelayne made a halfhearted attempt to sit up. "I'm so glad you've come. I'm frightfully confused."

Beatrice extended her hand. Trelayne reached for it, missed, and slid down the mountain of pillows to land in a heap at Beatrice's feet.

"Bloody hell." She bent over to right Trelayne and study her more closely. "Are you drunk, girl?"

"Definitely not," Trelayne protested. "And you are not Penelope. But," she added politely, "it was terribly nice of you to stop by."

Beatrice rolled her eyes. She had been prepared to face a stubborn Trelayne, an arrogant Trelayne, even a snobbish, angry, disbelieving Trelayne. But she had not been ready for the drugged, helpless, childlike Trelayne before her now. This was an unanticipated complication.

She squatted down and buttoned up the back of the lace dress. As her rough hands fingered the expensive material, she was overcome with envy and resentment. If she lured Trelayne into the street, and left her to fend for herself, in her present condition she was unlikely to survive the night.

Especially if left in the neighborhood Beatrice had in mind.

Then she remembered the Captain's words of trust. He was a man who would move mountains for the woman he loved, and his strength and goodness was contagious.

For a moment, Beatrice sat motionless imagining what might have been, and the shard of decency buried deep in her abused soul surfaced long enough to point her back toward the compassionate direction.

When Trelayne babbled incoherently, Beatrice examined her eyes more closely.

"God's bones." She was trepanned as well as bleezed. Lucien had been overly liberal in the amount of opium doled out to the girl. She was near unconscious, and they needed to get a move on.

Efforts to get Trelayne up and walking proved unsuccessful. Maybe if she gave her the letter, it would bring her around.

"Here," Beatrice said, pressing the note into the

other woman's hands. "It's from your friend, Captain Garrison."

Trelayne took the paper and stared at it as if she'd been struck illiterate.

Chapter Nineteen

Beatrice gritted her teeth in irritation. Grabbing the useless note, she stuffed it back into the bodice of her dress. "Wake up girl," she demanded, giving Trelayne a good shake. "You must come with me."

"I do not wish to go anywhere for any reason," came the petulant reply, as she crawled back onto the cushions. "I am much too tired, and it is quite comfortable here. Who are you? Did you already tell me? Have a strawberry, dear. They're delicious with champagne."

Before Trelayne could latch onto another piece of fruit, Beatrice snatched up the tray and set it aside. Then temptation won out and she sampled the fare. The food was heavily laced with drugs. She downed two more pieces, and although not partial to highfalutin bubbly wine, drained a full glass of champagne in three gulps. That was better. Summoning her patience, she tried again, but the situation was going awry in a hand basket.

"Look, ducks. I'm a friend of Captain Garrison's. He's ever so handsome and waiting for you just up the row. Now come along like a good little lamb. We must leave, really we must." As she spoke, Beatrice hauled Trelayne to her feet, and bundled her in the fine cloak waiting at hand.

"Walker? Is he here?" Bleary-eyed Trelayne

glanced around.

"By the Saints. I'd have better luck with a two year old. Captain Garrison isn't *here*—he's waiting outside. We must go to him, straight away."

This time, Walker's name had a charmed effect, and Trelayne became more attentive and focused.

"Come then," she coaxed, trying to make a game of it, "let's find Walker."

She shoved Trelayne toward the door. Checking to make sure the way was clear, she took a deep breath and dragged her charge into the dimly lit hallway. Music and laughter echoed off to the left, and Trelayne turned to follow the sounds of gaiety. Beatrice grabbed her none too gently, and redirected her forward momentum toward the door leading to the alleyway.

Once outside, Beatrice heaved a sigh of relief. The chill night air seemed to revive Trelayne, and a more pinkish hue colored her previously pale lips and cheeks. She no longer appeared to be on the verge of unconsciousness.

"Have you any idea where we be?" she asked, with high expectations.

Solemnly and thoughtfully Trelayne glanced around. "It's terribly cold," she said with concern. "Is it York we've come to visit?"

Beatrice groaned. Trelayne broke into a fit of laughter.

The alleyway opened out onto Rampling Street, a bustling thoroughfare not far from Upper Sydenham Road. Cajoling the woman into the stream of pedestrians, she expertly threaded a path through the surprisingly heavy crowd. In a matter of minutes, they were off the busy avenue and into a quiet side street.

The carriage and Captain Garrison waited just up ahead. They were almost there. They were going to make it. Then Beatrice heard a commotion across the way.

She hustled Trelayne into an alleyway, and peering around the edge of the building, spotted a man across the street. He stepped into the halo of a gas street lamp, glancing first right, then left, and her heart near stopped. She knew that blonde hair and recognized his stance—Lucien. He'd already discovered their ploy. Heaven help her. What was she to do now? This venture was likely to be her doom rather than her salvation.

He turned in their direction, and made as if to cross the street. This was the end. He'd never forgive her if he knew she was party to Trelayne's escape. Tears wet her cheeks. Served her right for trying to help, for thinking she could outsmart the devil.

Just as she'd given up all hope, a figure leaped out of the mist and grabbed Lucien from behind. Cape swirling, fire shooting from his fingertips, the fiend let loose with a terrible howl. It was Spring Heeled Jack. Beatrice swallowed a scream, and with Trelayne in tow, she dragged her up the street at a run.

Nearly at the coach, she glanced back. Poor Lucien, set upon by that vile creature. Employing his walking stick, he seemed to be holding his own. No doubt he was madder than a hatter over tonight's events, and spoiling for a fight. Spring Heeled Jack clawed at the air with talon-tipped gloves as Lucien flung him sideways up against the wall. Even at this distance she heard a growl of surprise and rage as the boogieman leaped upon the stone ledge and made for the nearby rooftop. Agile as a chimneysweep, he scrambled over the slippery shingles and disappeared into the night.

Beatrice wretched open the carriage door, shoved Trelayne inside, and clambered up behind her. Huddled on the floor out of sight, she prayed they hadn't been seen.

"What are you doing?" the Captain roared. "And what in God's name is wrong with Miss St.Christopher?"

He scooped up his unconscious sweetheart, and gathered her against his chest. Even in the dark, his expression gave Beatrice the shivers.

"Damn it, woman, what have you done to her? Or was it Lucien?" he added, his voice sharp with anger.

"Get a bloody move on," she advised, avoiding his questions. "And as for Lucien, he's just down the street. If it weren't for Spring Heeled Jack he'd have seen us."

"To the Royal Lambeth Hotel," the Captain called to the driver. "What has that marauding monster got to do with anything?"

As he fawned over his true love, she explained the near miss. "Guess that's the first time old Jack ever came to anybody's rescue," she added, but the captain listened halfheartedly.

"Trelayne, can you hear me?" he prodded. When no response ensued, he pinned Beatrice in place with a deadly glare.

"She's only had a bit too much to drink," she lied. "Just let her rest a spell."

After seeing Walker's full-on fury, she wasn't about to let him know the love of his life had nearly been drugged to the point of overdose. It would only make more trouble for her and dear Lucien.

"That had better be the truth," he challenged, with a dark scowl.

"I swear on the relics it is. I've no reason to lie to you. Blimey, I'm the one took all the chances so far, so don't be ranting and railing at me."

"You're correct. I am sorry. I appreciate your help" He retrieved several coins and handed them to her. "You did the right and admirable thing. Thank you, Beatrice, I'm in your debt."

Surprised at being treated kindly, she remained silent all the way to the ritzy hotel. But when the good Captain prepared to carry his precious woman through the front door of the lobby, she felt compelled to speak.

"You'd best take her in the back way," she advised. "It's probably too late to salvage her reputation, but you might at least try."

****

As the carriage bearing Beatrice disappeared into the night, Walker considered the advice and changed course. Trelayne probably had suffered irreparable social disgrace, which reaffirmed his idea as to what they must do next.

Gaining access to his room via the backstairs, he placed her on the bed near the hearth. She appeared so small and fragile, her form lost in the depth and width of the huge four-poster. Yards of the gossamer dress she wore billowed about, encasing her pale figure in an angelic lavender mist.

The pulse at the side of her throat was too slow, her breathing too shallow. He eased back the lid of one eye—the pupil was unresponsive to light. He'd seen many a stinking drunk sailor on at least three continents, none of them acted like this. He had also seen the opium dens of Hong Kong and Canton. Beatrice had lied. Her lowlife consort had drugged her.

"Wake up, Trelayne. Open your eyes."

Suppressing the animal instinct for immediate retribution, he fought off the need to track down Lanteen. Not even the pleasure of beating the hell out of the man could induce him to leave the side of the woman he loved. The words echoed through his mind. It was true, he did love her. Being away from Trelayne for the past pain-filled weeks had been a mental torture rivaling the physical agonies of his body. And the thought of seeing her tonight had been a psychological restorative to rival any of Hargis' potions.

He wet a cloth with water and pressed it to her forehead and wrists. She began to shiver, and he threw more wood on the fire—enough to warm a castle keep. Sweat poured off of him, but she still shook violently. Stripping off his shirt, he slipped into bed, and gathered her close to his bare chest.

"Come on back to me, darlin'," he urged. "Don't leave me. You mustn't."

Trelayne touched a deeper chord within him than any woman he'd met since losing Katie. He couldn't explain why—had quit trying. What mattered was the realization he was ready to risk all, ready to gather the tattered pieces of his heart and offer them to her. Hoping it was enough, hoping a future with the woman in his arms would be his redemption from the barren world through which he had traveled for far too many years.

She turned toward him and nestled closer. Her body felt warmer, her respirations deeper and more regular. Her eyelids fluttered open, and smiling sweetly, she reached out to touch his cheek.

"It's really you," she murmured. "I thought I must be a dreaming, but my dreams are never blessed with handsome men and passionate interludes."

She made a weak attempt to kiss his lips. He turned his head aside. Once he tasted her fully, he would never be able to stop. She didn't know what she was doing, was under the influence of opium and alcohol.

As she played one hand across his bare chest, he gritted his teeth and tried to think of something else, but all he conjured were lusty images of what they would do together. Fingers tangled in his hair, she pressed closer, her body imploring him to want what he knew they might regret in the morning. When his full-blown erection, begging for hard use, took control of body, mind, and soul, his noble intentions faltered.

"Trelayne," he groaned, with his last ounce of self-control.

"We have to talk."

The words sound ludicrous, talking was the last thing he wanted to do with her.

"No talk. Just kiss me," she whispered. "And hold me and make love to me."

"I'd like nothing more, but I'm here to take care of you, not take advantage of you. Listen to me."

"No, no, no. I won't listen," she shrieked, putting her hands to her ears. She was out of control again, nearly hysterical.

He took her hands from her ears and lowered them. She responded to his touch, her eyes not so wild, the pulse in her wrist once more regular and strong.

"Listen to me," he insisted. "Lucien drugged you,

you're not thinking clearly."

"Lucien?" She rose up on one elbow and glanced around, her brow puckered in confusion. "It wasn't anything like I thought it would be," she said, sagging back onto the mattress at his side.

His stomach knotted, and fury replaced passionate aspirations. "Did he touch you, force you to do things you didn't want to do?"

"What? Oh no, nothing, really, just a kiss," she reassured, her speech slurred. "I meant the Bond, the evening, the adventure. It was nothing I thought it would be. Not romantic at all. Not even fun. All because you weren't there."

He blew out a breath of relief. Thank the Lord Lucien hadn't …damn, he couldn't even think about it.

Again she ran her hand across his bare chest then laid her head upon his shoulder. He wanted nothing more than to show her what making love could really be like. But the very idea was unconscionable. Although somewhat more lucid, she was still woozy and not thinking clearly, and if he took her here and now, he'd be no better than Lanteen.

She sighed, long and slow, and curled up like a kitten, her eyes closed, a sweet smile upon her lips.

"Trelayne," he said, and gave her a little jostle.

"Hmmm," came her drowsy response.

"Tomorrow, we're getting married."

Chapter Twenty

Her head felt twice its normal size, and empty of everything accept excruciating pain. With the greatest of care, Trelayne opened her eyes. Where was she? Worse yet, what had happened last night? It was a blank, or at least a dark fuzzy blur.

She concentrated harder. Jagged thoughts surfaced out of the black abyss making her feel worse, which hadn't seemed possible. Fist clutched against her stomach, she chanced a look around, and her eyes widened in wonder. There was someone asleep on the nearby divan—it was Captain Garrison. More bits and pieces dropped painfully into place, images of kissing him and holding his shirtless body next to hers. Oh, Good Lord. Had she finally done *it* and didn't even remember? That would be the ultimate irony. But she didn't feel any different. Surely she would.

In a panic, she ran her hands along her hips and torso. Although loosened, her clothes were properly in place. Only her shoes and hose were missing. Easing the covers aside, she slid from the bed. The room tilted riotously. After a moment of concerted effort, she gained her balance, tiptoed forward, and stood staring down at Walker.

Fully clothed, he sprawled upon the couch in childlike innocence, one long leg hanging over the side. His shirt was unbuttoned exposing a sinful glimpse of his chest and abdomen. She inched closer and stopped just short of touching the sprinkling of dark hair accentuating his rippling physique. The top of his pants hung loose around his trim waist, there would be just enough room to slip one's hand inside…

With a mutter, he shifted position. The unbuttoned shirt slid sideways, gaping further open. Her initial rush of delight turned to alarm as a wicked, barely healed, scar showed on his ribcage.

Dropping to her knees, she reached to soothe the tortured flesh then held fast, again not daring to touch him.

"Good morning, Miss St.Christopher."

She leaped to her feet, regretting the energetic movement as the world swam before her punctuated by streaks of bright lights. "What happened to you?" she asked, cradling her pounding head in one hand. "Is this why you were gone so long?"

Walker swung his legs off the divan, gained his feet, and jammed his shirt into his pants. "Only death or injury would have kept me away," he said, towering over her. "Don't you know that by now? And it seems I returned just in time. What in God's name were you thinking, Trelayne? Lucien had plans for you last evening involving more than dinner and dancing."

She backed away. His sudden dark attitude took her by surprise, raising her defenses. Going to the Bond with Lucien had been a terrible mistake. She knew that now, and didn't need a reprimand or to be made to feel the fool. "It's no business of yours who I see or what I do."

"Oh, but it is. Your father made it my business when he bade me watch over his daughter and keep her safe. I thought it sounded a reasonable request until we met. While I applaud and admire you being a high-spirited filly, your adventurous nature leaves me quaking in my boots. That's why we're to be married as soon as possible. It's the only way to keep you from further harm and repair the damage already done."

Stunned, she stood in open-mouthed wonder. It sounded more like a plan to throw her into jeopardy. Still, as the notion sank in, part of her thrilled to the idea. Married to Captain Walker Garrison. Her daydream fulfilled, no longer a fantasy, and the thought of him making love to her almost buckled her knees. Then her stubborn streak reared its head. How dare he presume she wanted to be married to anyone, let alone to him?

"I do not wish to marry you. But I appreciate the proposal."

"I'm not asking you. I'm telling you. That is what is to be done. No doubt half the uppity folks you know are already spreading well-seasoned gossip regarding your escapade of last night. Someone of importance must have seen you at the Consortium, or crossed paths with you as you stumbled down the street in a drugged and tipsy condition. And if that is not enough to sway your decision, you just spent the night with me in this hotel room."

A sick feeling washed over her, but it was not the lasting effects of overindulgence. She truly had made a muddle of things. Walker was correct. Her reputation was in tatters. She was almost glad her parents weren't here to witness her disgrace. And oh damnation, Aunt Abigail was going to have a prize winning tizzy-fit.

"Don't look so horrified," Walker said, misinterpreting her expression. "It will be in name only.

And we can have it all annulled once things settle down and you decide what you truly wish to do."

In name only—disappointment danced around that revelation. "I must return home at once and let everyone know I'm all right."

"I sent a message to Royston Hall last evening, and received a reply early this morning. All are in agreement you will follow my instructions to rectify this situation. Your aunt has given us her blessings, and suggested we go to a place called Gretna Greene to have this matter taken care of immediately."

Rectify the situation? Have this matter taken care of immediately? It sounded more like she was to have an ugly wart removed, not celebrate what should be the wedding day of her dreams. Hands clenched at her side she glared at him.

"I will do no such thing," she gritted. "And you can't make me."

"No, I can't make you. But there is little choice, unless you'd rather marry Lanteen. He's the one who put your reputation in peril. I'm sure he would oblige. Although I believe his consort Beatrice would have my scalp if you do."

Beatrice… The name sounded familiar. Another image of what transpired last evening played across her mind. "Was she the woman who came to me at the Bond? The one who led me to you? I thought the woman was in your employ. What do you insinuate?"

"Beatrice did me the favor of secreting you out of the establishment, but it was for her own gain. She's Lucien's lover. And I take it she has been for quite some time."

His lover? She heard the words, understood the

concept, but couldn't realize their importance. This morning was making as little sense as last evening.

"He drugged you with opium, Trelayne. He planned to seduce you or worse."

Opium. That's why she had felt so uninhibited, and had not been able to come to her own defense. As a picture of what might have happened became clear, she clenched a fist to her stomach. All this time she thought Lucien her friend, had trusted him, but he had betrayed her on every level. He'd planned her ruination all along to force her into the marriage she had refused. But if he had a lover—poor thing. Men were inexplicable as well as despicable.

She stumbled across the room, grabbing her shoes and stockings along the way. Walker was correct. Marriage was the only option.

****

The coach was old, and the road to Gretna Greene filled with ruts, the combination devastating to both her head and her bottom.

Refusing to look at Walker, Trelayne stared out the window. It wasn't because she didn't want to look at him. Who wouldn't? The Colt revolver and knife he carried were suitable substitutes for a saber and pistol. And with his hair disheveled and a shadow of a beard glorifying the mustache she so loved, his appearance alluded to all the drama and romantic nonsense of a highwayman. And he may as well have kidnapped her as she was being whisked off to be married by circumstance rather than choice. If he hadn't insisted it was all for show, the picture would be complete.

In name only… Would he really be able to keep his hands off of her? If he did, it would be a piteous blow to her self-esteem, adding rejection to the wounds already caused by Lucien's betrayal.

"Will we be there soon?" she asked, and rearranged her position accommodating a new set of bruises on her derriere.

He flashed a boyish lopsided smile. The expression dimpled one cheek and crinkled the corners of both eyes. "Anxious for the proceedings to begin?" he teased.

"Anxious to be out of this rustic carriage," she snapped, glaring at him.

His expression sobered, and sadness seemed to cloud his blue/gray eyes. "Marriage isn't the worst thing that can happen to a person, Trelayne."

"And you would know this because…"

"Because I was married once myself."

Married. She was stunned. This wretched day was plagued with one shocking disclosure tumbling downhill after another. Then it occurred to her how little she knew about the man she was to wed. A flurry of questions flashed through her mind. What had his wife been like? Why did he use the past tense? Had they been madly in love?

"Did she leave you because you were too often gone adventuring, and had a girl in every port?"

"No. She died."

Trelayne pressed back against the seat, horrified at her faux pas. "I'm sorry, Walker," she whispered.

"As am I. But it's your future which demands our concern, not my past."

Averting her gaze she stared unseeing at the scenery sliding by. A tear slipped from one eye. Angry with herself for her thoughtless words and foolish suppositions, she roughly swiped it away with the back of her hand.

"I've made a terrible muddle of things," she confessed. "And I'm sorry you are being forced to defend my honor. Since your arrival, you've been nothing but kind. You deserve better."

Walker levered up from the seat, lurched across the moving coach, and resettled himself at her side. "What people deserve and what they get are generally two different matters. And as far as muddling things about, I've done my share as well."

He eased one arm across her shoulder, and his offer of unbidden comfort set loose the floodgates. All the sorrow she felt regarding her parent's injuries, coupled with the loneliness she had endured of late, blanketed her in darkness. Surrendering to his warmth, she clung to his solid reassuring form, and as they sped northward on what should have been the most joyous day of her life, she cried harder than she had ever cried before.

****

"I now pronounce you man and wife. You may kiss the bride."

Walker gave Trelayne a simple peck on the cheek, but the visions romping through his mind hardened his body rather than his resolve not to touch her. Fighting to keep the burning need in check, he studied her face. Was it his imagination, or did she appear disappointed by his lack of ardor? Guilt stabbed at his gut. That felt real enough. He had married her to keep her safe. At least that had been the idea. Now he wondered if that wasn't what he wanted all along. Too late to worry over the whys and wherefores. The deed was done.

When Trelayne remained unmoving, he took her

arm and escorted her from the chapel. "This way, Mrs. Garrison," he said, forcing a lightness into his voice he didn't feel.

An image of Katie flittered across his mind, the only Mrs. Garrison he'd ever thought to love and cherish as a wife. It was as if her spirit hovered near, her voice just beyond his hearing. It was a joyful feeling, as if she were happy for him. That was a comfort.

Truth be told, he was glad about being a husband once again. The role had always appealed to him. Glancing sideways, he caught sight of his new wife's stony expression. Apparently, Trelayne was not as thrilled by the condition.

"It will be all right," he promised, and somehow he would make it so.

The inn where their bridal suite awaited was but a short walk through a nearby overgrown garden. Although the towering vegetation struggled to hold onto the last vestiges of a riotous summer bloom and a peaceful autumnal farewell, it seemed as desolate as their situation.

"It's too late to travel home tonight," he said, feeling the need to explain the room, and the necessity to share it. Home—that sounded strange. He supposed he would be living at Royston Hall. For show if for nothing else.

"I'm glad," she said quietly.

Her mood, unreadable, did not match her words. He supposed only time would reveal how she really felt.

Their love nest was a spacious well-appointed accommodation, worth the price he'd paid to secure it.

A fire burned cheerfully in the fireplace, and the small table by the window held a late evening repast. A curtained-off section held a huge four-poster bed, a dressing room, and marvels of marvels, a water closet.

Avoiding the sleeping area, he directed her toward the settee. She dropped down upon it with an expression of total defeat. He'd never seen her like this, not even on the day he'd arrived with the bad tidings of her parent's accident.

He sat at her side, and took her hands in his. They were ice cold. He should add more wood to the fire, but didn't want to let her go.

"This must not have been what you envisioned for your wedding day," he began. "If things hadn't gone sour in Brighton, I would have been in London to stop you. Been there to occupy your time so you wouldn't have entertained the idea of endangering yourself in such a misadventure."

She sat up and stared at him in wide-eyed wonder. "How gallant. You think this is your fault? I doubted you, was infuriated by your long absence. It was childish and petty, and no one is to blame but me." She reached up and smoothed her fingers across his mustache. "I've wanted to do that since the first day you came to Royston Hall."

The simple caress broke his ironclad promise to keep his distance. He drew her close and kissed her— slowly, deeply, savoring what before had only been contemplation. Then he released her. "And I've wanted to do that on several occasions."

"I wish you hadn't waited so long." Her warm breath teased across his neck and ear as she leaned against him. "I don't want to be married in name only," she murmured. "Make love to me, Walker. We've every right."

Her bold proposal took him by surprise. Often enough he'd imagined what he'd like to do with her and to her. But it would change things immensely. The marriage had been designed to restore her reputation. If they made love, it would be extremely hard, perhaps impossible to annul or revoke the contract. This had not been part of the plan.

"You're not thinking clearly," he warned. "What you suggest will drastically change both out lives."

"I should hope for the better and not the worse. Either way, as stated in our vows, we must stay together until death do us part. When you were gone to Brighton, I pined for you, and when I was not infuriated with you, I was ill with worry. I didn't realize until you were gone, I had already given you my heart, now you must come take the rest of me. I want to know you in every way, be yours in every way.

She rested her hand upon his thigh then grazed her fingers across his crotch.

Damn good intensions, they would go to plan B.

****

Trelayne could no longer resist the desire torturing her body. She wanted—needed to be made love to. The craving gripped her more mightily than last evening's opium and champagne. It was beyond a physical craving, it was an outcry of the soul.

Like a rushing river, the prurient information secretly researched with Penelope flooded her mind, drowning out all other thought and reason. She touched Walker, knowing her ministrations were pushing him over the line. His mouth found hers, this time rough with need, exploring and conquering her mouth, a portent of what was to come when they truly joined. Nothing had ever seemed so right.

Unbuttoning his shirt, she eased her hands beneath the fabric and traced the contours of his body, her palms grazing his nipples. With a groan, he slid his hands to the back of her dress. Tiny pearl buttons flew in every direction as he made short work of the obstinate fastenings. Yielding to her appeal, it seemed nothing would now deter him from what he wanted— from what they both wanted.

She had abandoned her corset this morning, and now with the bedraggled lavender dress fabric out of the way, he set to work removing her camisole. Cool air licked at her skin, colliding with the hot need burning in her belly. It nearly stole her breath away. Walker nuzzled her neck, rained kisses downward to her collarbone, his hands firmly cupping her breast. She held onto him tightly, the only thing solid in a world gone spinning out of control.

The part of her yet unexplored grew tight and pulsing. What would it be like when he touched her there? At the mere thought, wetness was added to the aching delight, and she sighed and rubbed her body against his.

He drew back, cold fear replacing the warmth of his caress. Had he changed his mind? Then he rose from the divan, tugged her upright, and swept her off her feet.

Renewed eagerness rushed through her as he laid her down in the middle of the bed. Standing before her, his gaze never leaving her face, he proceeded to remove his clothing. In record time, he was down to his trousers and boots. Glorious to look upon, twinges of anticipation accentuated the space between her legs, already begging for relief.

Turning, he leaned back against the bed, tugged off his boots, then dropped his breeches. When he turned back, her eyes widened at the sight of him, big and hard and ready to fulfill all her expectations.

Easing onto the bed, he stretched out beside her and tugged at the dress material gathered about her waist. Frantically, she shimmied free of the fabric, snagging her pantaloons along the way. Extricated from those as well, she offered up her naked body to his sight and touch.

"You're every bit as beautiful as I dreamed you would be," he whispered.

Had she really filled his musing? He had certainly overtaken her daydreams. Thoughts of him even tamed her most recent nightmare, banishing the monster to a dark inaccessible corner.

"Have you often thought about me then?"

"On many a lonely night," he admitted.

As if she were made of porcelain, he glided a curled finger along her cheek.

Taking his hand in hers, she slid it down to cover one of her breasts, and with a moan arched up against his palm. Tonight, she didn't wish to be cherished, she wanted to be ravished. As if reading her mind, he slid his other hand between her thighs, turning her moan to a gasp.

Leaning over, he captured her mouth, his tongue and fingers probing, exploring, delighting—arousing her body to near delirium. Then stilling his motions, he pressed his cheek against hers. "The first time hurts," he said softly, stroking her without hesitation, "but only for a little while."

"I don't care. I need you, all of you."

No words did he speak as his thumb pressed against the nub that pulsed at the apex of her thighs. She rubbed against his hand and wrapped her arms around his neck. It felt better than she ever imagined. He played her body with skill and patience as if she were a fine instrument and he knew exactly what song waited in her soul to be set free. As she spiraled into a world that existed only for the two of them, he eased her legs apart and covered her body with his. She could feel the tip of him, hard and ready, touching her, tempting her, easing forward, now retreating.

"Wrap your legs around me," he urged.

She did as he asked, taking him in a bit farther, ebbing and flowing—again and again. Each time more of him joined with her, each time more of her belonged to him. Bearing his weight on his forearms he framed her face with his hands and crushed his mouth against hers. Then with a groan and a shudder he gave her full measure. Pain replaced what had felt so good, and a tear slipped from her eye. He stilled his movements and kissed it away. As he began to ease out of her, she grabbed his backside with both hands and thrust upward keeping him in place. The thought of him inside of her renewed desire, a balm to the sting, a spark to the embers waiting to burst into flame and burn out of control. She never wanted to let him go.

"Don't stop," she pleaded, "don't ever stop."

He set the pace, tantalizingly slow, and with each stroke she expanded, opening like a flower. Greedily, she took him in without hesitation. Then their tempo increased like the crescendo of a waltz, and she felt as if she were spinning faster and faster. There was nothing dainty about it now, only animal passion, hard and powerful. Moans of delight gathering volume and intensity, the demands of their bodies overruling all else. Gasping for breath, she knew she was moments away from something wonderful, something she wanted with every fiber of her being.

"Oh, Walker," she screamed in delight.

Where their bodies joined as one, a throbbing explosion of unknown pleasure peaked and spread outward. It curled her toes and near stopped her heartbeat.

Walker groaned out something unintelligible and slammed into her, crushing her into the mattress, penetrating deeper, grinding his hips against her. Then he collapsed on top of her. Still big and hard and filling her fully, she pulsed and contracted around him.

"We've done it now, Trelayne," he said, his voice calm yet somehow filled with concern. "There'll be no easy way to break this marriage."

"Yes," she murmured, "we've certainly have done *it*. And *it* was wonderful."

Chapter Twenty-One

Lucien threw the figurine against the wall, sending a cloud of splintered glass arching through the air. In the rays of the morning sun, it flittered downward like crystal rain.

Beatrice jumped and scurried from the room. She was smart to do so. Following another night of debauchery, he had a roaring hangover, and it was all because of Trelayne's betrayal. This morning he sought someone, anyone, upon whom to take out his frustration and pain. Yes, pain. A torturous agony. On the evening of the Gala, Trelayne had sneaked away in the night like a common whore, leaving him standing stupefied and unfulfilled.

At first, in shock and disbelief, he thought she might have wandered off while he answered the bogus summons and waited like a fool at the front desk. But he knew she had been too incapacitated. Then he entertained the idea Spring Heeled Jack had gotten to her. But that didn't make sense either. It had been a well-planned scheme, and someone had been her accomplice.

Yesterday morning he'd gone to Royston Hall only to be told she had gone away with her aunt. Another lie. Old Merrick, tightlipped as ever, offered no further information. So last night he'd gone on a bender, trying to forget, trying to save his sanity.

She had to have returned by now. Grabbing his coat, he slammed out of the flat. He'd get to the bottom of this yet. It was early morning and a not a suitable hour for a gentleman to visit. Who gave a damn? Not him. Not any more. He was through trying to do things according to protocol. Admittedly, he and Trelayne shouldn't have been together at the Bond in the first place; still, he would demand an answer for her reprehensible behavior.

****

Dismounting, he secured his horse adjacent to the carriage waiting outside of Trelayne's home. As he charged toward the house, the door opened and a woman took her leave, a spring in her step, a great silly smile upon her lips. It was Penelope, Trelayne's closest friend. The woman was a nuisance, and had been a constant stumbling block in his campaign.

"Miss Penelope," he said, forcing a civil tone into his voice. "You look as lovely as ever."

"Thank you, Mr. Lanteen." She paused, and although it seemed impossible, her smile broadened. "If you've come to see Miss Trelayne, I'm afraid you shall be disappointed. She isn't here."

"Still not in residence? Perhaps you would know when she is expected to return."

"It's rather difficult to say," Penelope all but squealed, her hands clasped at chest-level as if to contain her excitement. "She's on her honeymoon."

He staggered backward. Surely he'd heard incorrectly. "I don't understand," he managed to utter.

"She's run off to Gretna Green with Captain Garrison."

Fury grappled with disbelief, exploding in his

brain, blurring the world around him. He could barely suppress the bellow of rage clamoring for release in his throat. Fist clenched, he took a step forward. Penelope reared back, gripped her skirt with both hands, and fled to her waiting carriage.

Inhaling several deep breaths in an effort to stave off complete madness, he watched the billowing clouds of dust erupt in the wake of her coach as it raced down the lane. Married—the bitch. And to Garrison. But he was supposed to be dead. Grimsby had failed again.

He stormed about, first one direction then another, trying to talk himself down from incapacitating rage to mere hateful revenge. If she wouldn't come to him a virgin, she would come to him a widow. One way or another, he would still have her.

****

Married…she was married. She was Mrs. Walker Garrison. And last night they had made mad passionate love. She was ecstatic, felt as if she had discovered the most well kept secret in the world. No one else could possibly know such joy.

She opened her eyes and peered around the bridal suite. A glimmer of morning sunlight peeked through the curtain lace, promising a beautiful day, surely a good portent for a beautiful life. Shifting her gaze to the sitting area, she spotted an array of food waiting on the nearby table—but it wasn't food for which she hungered.

She reached for Walker. He wasn't there. Had it been a dream? She jerked upright and squirmed in discomfort. The space between her legs where last night's ecstasy had ruled now burned and hurt. Was this the price one paid every time for the delight of coupling? Or was it just because it was her first time? It had better be the latter because she planned on many repeat performances.

Where was her man, her husband, her lover? She pushed aside the covers and eased from the bed. Wrapped in a quilt, she padded across the thick Persian carpet in the sleeping area and glanced through the archway to the sitting room. There he was, standing before the hearth. Dressed only in trousers, he bent to add more wood to the fire. The muscles of his shoulders and back flexed as he performed the simple task, and at the sight of his near naked body, a shock of remembered images and newfound delights feathered through her.

He glanced up, straightened, and smiled. When a knock sounded at the door, his expression turned to a quirky grin. Without a word of explanation, he went to answer the summons. Not wishing to be caught undressed, she scurried to the water closet, leaving the door ajar to watch through the crack.

Two men entered, lumbering beneath the weight of a copper-bathing tub. Several women followed, carrying buckets of steaming hot water.

"Over here, beside the hearth," Walker instructed. The women filled the tub near to overflowing, all the while giggling and casting sideways glances about the room.

"Thank you. We'll not be needing anything else this morning."

Walker followed the little group as they left, handing out shillings as if they were farthings, before shutting and locking the door behind them.

Still ensconced in the water closet, she took the

opportunity for morning relief then raked a comb through her tangle of hair. As she stared at her reflection in the mirror, a sudden shyness overwhelmed her. What had seemed so natural last evening in the dark, took on new proportions in the light of day. Would Walker still find her irresistible, still want her as much as she wanted him?

A whisper of a knock sounded upon the door. "Come, Mrs. Garrison, before the water gets cold."

She peered out. He reached in, took her by the hand, and led her toward the tub. Tugging the quilt from around her body, he left her standing naked—naked and praying not to be found lacking. His gaze meandered the length of her. A half-smile possessed his mouth, and a heated expression flamed in his eyes.

"Marriage agrees with you, wife," he said. "You look even more beautiful this morning."

A wave of relief washed over her, and she smiled back. He'd known just the right thing to say. Even though it had been an arranged marriage—a testimony to his honor for saving hers—she had a feeling spending the rest of her life with this man might be the best thing ever to happen to her.

"It's you that agrees with me," she countered, "not the institution of marriage."

Playing her hands across his chest, she delighted in the feel of short dark hair beneath her palms, and renewed hunger for his body pounded through hers. Apparently, raw desire was an emotion requiring frequent feeding.

Their gazes locked, and she wanted to jump headfirst into the blue/gray depths, wanted to see the world from his side. He captured her face between his hands, and swooping forward took her lips by storm, his mouth demanding. His hands slid downward to her arms, now around to her backside. She pressed her hips against his, and felt his hardness through his trousers. He nuzzled her neck, and there was no mistaking his enthusiasm as she rubbed up against him.

As if inspired by her response, he slid to his knees, wedged one hand between her thighs, and dotted little kisses across her belly. His mustache grazed and tickled, and head back, she smiled and held him close, running her fingers through his hair, tousling, twisting, near pulling as she reveled in the spasms of delight racing through her midsection.

When he stroked the tender skin leading to the depths of her body, she nearly lost her footing. Just in time, he scrambled to his feet, cradled her in his arms, and lowered her into the tub. Like a warm ocean, the water sluiced over her, soothing yet invigorating. The soreness between her legs eased, and her nipples hardened as she leaned back and floated in the warm liquid embrace.

Walker knelt at her side. Employing a large sponge, he explored a random path down, around, and across her body. Watching her face, he wedged the nubby fibers between her thighs, massaging and rasping, stimulating the place that now throbbed with desire rather than discomfort.

She floundered, the water reaching her chin, but he slid his free arm beneath her shoulders holding her up, holding her in place. "Be easy, Mrs. Garrison," he cautioned, nipping at the lobe of her ear and gently tonguing the rim. "Put yourself completely in my hands." Hands that were doing wondrous things to her body.

She relaxed and her hips rose. Abandoning the sponge, he sought to please her with his touch. For a moment the pain returned then her body responded, opening for him, opening for the pleasure she wanted and remembered. He stroked her gently then demandingly. Leaning over the tub, he sought her lips, plundering her mouth as his fingers slid in and out, conquering her body.

The hot water heightened the pleasure, and his thumb teased on the outside, roughing the point where all delight blossomed and grew. Nothing she'd read in a book compared to the rapture overtaking her now.

Walker eased back, watching her, his breath coming faster as if pleasing her was pleasing him. Hot desire ripped through her from the top of her head to tips of her toes.

Out of control, she gripped the sides of the tub, thrusting her hips upward. Drawing her hard against his chest, Walker brought her over the horizon for which she reached.

Panting and moaning she clung to him as he rocked her back to reality.

"Oh, Walker. I thought for a moment I might die and I didn't care."

"That was just the beginning," he said against her cheek. "Now we shall make proper love." Liberating her from the tub, he carried her toward the bed.

"But I'm soaking wet," she sputtered.

"I intend to lick you dry," he informed her. "Then kiss you wet again."

He tossed her onto the middle of the bed. She shrieked with laugher, but sobered as he removed his trousers. The sight of him hard and purposeful again took her by surprise. He was magnificent, and just the thought of having him inside of her made desire return full blown.

He eased onto the foot of the bed, and as promised, licked a path along her body. Toes, ankles, calves, knees. Working his way upward, his head between her thighs, he kissed what before had only known the stroke of his hand and the male part of him. This was wickedly wonderful. Would he let her do the same to him? He nuzzled and nipped and nibbled at her, his mustache tickling in the most marvelous way. Then with a growl he covered her body with his. She bent her knees and raised her hips, seeking to draw him closer. The tip of him probed gently, but he didn't enter her. He kissed her cheek and whispered in her ear.

"To please you is a greater need than my own desire. Does this please you, Trelayne?" Over and over, he nearly entered her then drew back, taunting her with what she knew was to come, tormenting her with anticipation until she begged him to continue.

"Don't be cruel. You're torturing me and you know it. I want all of you, now."

She dug her fingernails into his back and thrust upward. This time he delivered the full length, leaving her gasping, a guttural cry curled in her throat.

Bodies wet with lover's passion, they caught up the primal rhythm, meeting one another in frenzied enthusiasm. He plunged deeper, pushed harder, adding an extraordinary grinding twist that excited the magical spot between her legs. She screamed in delight. He groaned out his release. Then they collapsed on the bed side by side—sigh by sigh.

Chapter Twenty-Two

The honeymoon was over, but only geographically speaking. After returning to Royston Hall, the love they shared was growing even stronger, and the love they made outshone anything Trelayne ever imagined. This delirium, coupled with the recent news of her parents' continued progress, wrapped her in happiness.

Upon their return, nearly one week ago, Aunt Abigail had taken one look at them and proclaimed it was obviously anything but a marriage of convenience. As this did not seem to come as a surprise, Trelayne had her suspicions this had been expected all along.

"Have you crossed paths yet with Lucien?" Penelope asked.

"No," Trelayne admitted, "and part of me wishes I had. It would give me great pleasure to rebuke him for the horrible way he has treated me. He deserves a dressing down of the highest magnitude."

"What wretched news to learn he had a paramour stashed away all this time. He was so infatuated with you, Laynie, it's hard to believe he had a trollop on the side."

"No doubt he is with her now, and I am the furthest thing from his mind."

"Don't be too sure. The day I told him you'd run off with the Captain, he looked a man about to do someone bodily harm. There was revenge in his eyes."

At the memory, Penelope's fair complexion managed to pale even more. "You'd best stay clear of him," she added.

"I hardly imagine I will see him anytime soon. Besides, I'm much too happy to dwell on him and the pain he's caused. Oh, Pen, it's so wonderful to be in love. We must find you a suitable husband posthaste."

"I'm all for that idea. But I have only one possibility, and no sure prospects. You must describe your wedding night again. And this time don't leave anything out. Pretend you're reading to me from one of our books." Her friend gave a nod, and an encouraging smile. "Oh, don't look so shocked, I freely admit I'm living vicariously through your eyes. Or should I say your body."

Trelayne laughed. "Making love is a beautiful experience. Sometimes gentle and sweet like a meandering stream in a wooded glen, drifting along to a delightful ending. Other times wild and passionate like a roaring river, crashing and thundering down a canyon, leaving one fearful of survival. Either way it's beyond pleasurable—it's divine rapture. For those few moments, nothing else matters." She was breathless at the remembering. "I don't know why the suffragette material makes it sound like a hideous chore to be borne with martyr-like fortitude.

"He's so good to me, Pen, and pleasures me as much as he expects me to pleasure him. And I've learned a few things that weren't in the books," she added, in a whisper. "When you're married, too, we can compare notes, but I dare not tell you now."

"I'm near faint with anticipation," Penelope sighed, gripping the arm of the divan. "I don't know how much longer I can endure this virginal existence. Every fiber of my being cries out for a man's touch, a man's body."

"Telling tales out of school, ladies?"

At the sound of Walker's voice, both women jumped. Penelope's fair skin now flamed scarlet to match the silk rose pinned to the neck of her dress. Trelayne scrambled to her feet, and ran to her husband.

"We didn't hear you come in," she said, grinning up at him.

"Obviously."

He wrapped his arms around her, making sure their bodies touched in all the right places, and although the fire in his eyes said he wanted more, he bowed to social necessity and sweetly kissed her cheek.

"Are you not acquainted with any handsome Americans who would be interested in someone as charming and desirable as Penelope?"

"Not in England," Walker chuckled, "except for Sam Colt. And he's a scallywag and a sweet-talker. I'm afraid his intentions might be opposite to what Miss Penelope is expecting in a man."

"That's not a very nice way to talk about your friend," she scolded.

"It's no news to Sam he's a bit of a bounder. Don't get me wrong," he added at her pout. "I admire him and would trust him with my life. In fact, on several occasions I have."

"That's better." She smiled, splaying her hands upon the lapels of his woolen jacket. When he pretended to be humbled by her make-believe badgering she enjoyed it immensely. "Besides," she added. "I think Aunt Abigail has designs on him."

At the mention of his friend, Walker seemed

reflective, and she wanted to press him for more information. Their history went back many years, encompassing a large part of his life, a part that remained a void, a missing chapter. After learning he'd been married, and his first wife had died, she hadn't inquired about Walker's past, fearing to open old wounds. But a person was the sum total of that through which they had lived, and he had turned out a strong and giving person. To know how he had come to be so was important to her.

She held his gaze, hoping hers expressed the love in her heart growing for him day by day. He smiled, setting aside whatever thoughts had been rambling around in his head.

At their continued silence, Penelope rose. "Don't forget the Chinese bazaar Saturday next," she reminded, heading toward the parlor door.

"What?"

Trelayne turned in the circle of Walker's embrace. She hadn't meant to ignore her friend, but when Walker was near, he had the knack of making the rest of the world disappear.

"The bazaar," Penelope repeated, "to raise money for the London Orphan Asylum at Clapton."

"Oh, of course. I'll meet you there. Don't leave, Pen."

"Truly I must," she insisted, with a shy smile and a jaunty wave of her gloved hand. "Until then. And don't bother, I'll see myself out."

When they were alone, Walker led her out of the French doors, through the garden, and down a flagstone path. The recent bout of particularly warm weather made it hard to believe it was well into November with winter waiting in the wings.

"We need to discuss a few business matters," he informed her, as they entered the secluded solarium.

They settled onto a bench in a sheltered nook, side by side, his arm around her, the sun shining through the glass panels warming them nicely. It was a moment to treasure. Resting her hands in her lap she marveled at the simple joy of having such a wonderful man in her life. The more time they spent together, the more she realized how very fortunate she was, at least in this capacity of her life.

"As your husband," he began, "I have access to your property and funds, but you are still the only one who can sign proxy for the shipping line. I've brought home several documents requiring your attention. The difficulty lies with the fact that Lanteen would normally handle the legal aspects of the transactions."

"Can we not seek another solicitor?" She squirmed in place, made uncomfortable by even the thought of the man. "Although I would sincerely enjoy reading him the riot act, I really don't wish to see Lucien again."

Walker grinned at her. "Don't get all riled up. I understand. I just wanted to clear everything with you first. I'm glad you're washing your hands of Lanteen. He's involved in some dark and devious dealings, and although it would be just my word against his, I know he had something to do with your parents' accident."

"Walker, surely not." She sat up, horrified at the very idea. "That is unthinkable. Why did you not mention this before, and why would he do such a thing?"

"For you, Trelayne. I've come to the conclusion

he's not of sound mind. You've become his obsession—have been his obsession. I put off telling you because you seemed so happy of late, and I wanted you to enjoy a few more days of innocent fun." He urged her back to his side and held her close. "I'm only informing you now for your own safety."

"If you believe he has done something so egregious, we must go to the authorities."

"I have. But the magistrate refuses to bring charges against him. Lanteen is a solicitor in surprisingly good standing. And I'm an American, with my only witness a questionable dockside ruffian being held in Brighton. I've no sure way of connecting him to that Grimsby fellow or your parents' accident or my attack. We can only hope our marriage put an end to Lanteen's mania, and he will back off and set his sights elsewhere."

"He wouldn't dare come near me now, not with you as my protector."

She curled against his shoulder. Here in his arms it seemed impossible anything could hurt her. She grazed her fingers across the medallion Walker wore beneath his shirt. When they made love he took it off, but on most other occasions it hung from the chain around his neck.

"Why do you wear this?" she asked, tapping a finger against the metal nestled beneath the fabric.

"It's a rendering of St. Brendan. He watches over sailors and travelers."

"But he's an Irish saint."

"We knew him in the Old Country too."

"The Old Country? You're from America, the farthest thing from the Old Country."

"I wasn't born there."

She sat up, and stared at him in surprise. "My husband is a man of mystery. You know all about me, but I know so little of you. Tell me everything."

The contemplative smile she'd seen earlier recaptured his mouth. "I don't know the first thing about you," he protested. "What were you like as a schoolgirl in pigtails? What was the name of your first pony? Did they send you away to boarding school where you attempted to run away at every chance?"

She made a face then laughed. "I would not be caught dead in pigtails, even at the age of nine. My pony's name was Midge. And I was tutored at home, so there wasn't any place to run from or to. Although I did find a cave in the hills to the south where I spent a great deal of time playing and hiding.

"I'm terribly good at embroidery," she added, "not so good at singing or playing the piano, can carry on a decent conversation in four languages, and I love heart-wrenching poetry and one amazing American sea captain. So there you have it, all the pertinent information regarding my life. Now it's your turn."

"What do you want to know?" he hedged, rather than listing off the highlights.

"Where are you really from? And how did you come to be in America? Let's start with that."

"I was born in Flanders," he began. "My dad worked the coal mines, and my mother cleaned rich peoples' houses. One day there was an explosion in the mines, and my father was killed along with fifteen other men."

"Oh, Walker, I'm so sorry." She touched his cheek, wishing a simple caress could erase the pain no doubt evoked by such memories.

"It was a long time ago," he said, capturing and holding her hand "Fortunately, Father had been setting money aside with the intentions of one day taking all of us to America. And brokenhearted though she was, Mother bravely fulfilled that wish for him. We settled in Massachusetts. At the time I was ten years old, and my brother was seven."

"You have a brother? Another revelation. Where is he? Is he a sea captain too?"

Walker shook his head. "Hardly. His name is Trenton. He's in Colorado, and he hates the water. He was seasick every moment of the voyage over. Never wanted to see another ship, barge, or boat. He sought the West for the same reason I took to the ocean— they're both places where a man can see forever and breathe clean air."

"You love being out of doors, don't you?"

"Yes, for me it's a necessity. As children, before the accident, we worked in the mines too. It was a sinister and fearful place, and after our father died, we were terrified to go back into that manmade hell."

"Do you miss your brother? I miss mine. And my sister."

"Now you have me at the disadvantage. I never knew you had a sister."

"Her name was Caroline. I idolized her. She was older then me, perfect in deportment and all the required accomplishments. And she was so good to me. Always patient, as I tagged along behind her. Then she died of typhoid fever, and my parents became obsessed with protecting me from all possible harm. But they merely succeeded in trapping me in perpetual childhood."

"And yet you have risen to the occasion in their absence."

"A willful nature cannot be so easily suppressed."

"I'll remember that," he said with a chuckle. "And yes, I do miss Trenton."

"I suppose having him visit is out of the question?" she mused.

"Only if we can figure some way for him to ride a horse from Colorado to here."

"I'll work on that," she promised. "Trenton," she mused. "You both have unusual names."

"Again my mother's doing. Walker was her family name before marriage, and Trenton was her mother's maiden name. She was a stickler for keeping the family history alive and well."

"She sounds a most interesting and courageous lady. She must come and stay with us."

"That would be wonderful, but I'm afraid impossible. She died several years ago."

Hearing of all the tragedy that had befallen him filled her with sadness. "That's why you named the ship after your mother, to honor her. My poor darling, you've suffered the loss of many loved ones, even your...." She stopped short of saying the word, hadn't meant to bring up the subject.

"Katie," he said. "Her name was Katie. And although not alike in coloring, you are quite like her in spirit," he revealed, and tightened his embrace. "Charging ahead full-sail when the need calls for it. Helping those less fortunate."

She almost cringed at his kind words. Her charitable rounds to the poor hadn't been her most shining moment, but she did plan on helping out at the up coming bazaar. His Katie sounded a woman of enviable character.

"If it wouldn't hurt too much, can you tell me how she died?"

Instantly, she regretted the question. Of course it would hurt—she was probing too deeply. But the sun dipped lower, leaving them in shadows, allowing them to share parts of their souls more difficult to reveal in the bright light of day. Walker proved his faith and trust in her by answering.

"Being kind of heart," he began, "she went to take food to an elderly couple who lived on a small farm outside of New Bedford. It had been a bad summer and a worse winter. The old folks' crops had failed, leaving them with few provisions, and with a snowstorm coming, she knew the husband wouldn't be able to get out and hunt for several days. The storm hit sooner than expected, and she never made it back home. I nearly lost my life searching for her. I was crazed and frozen stiff when Sam Colt tracked me down. He lived near us back then and saved me from suffering the same fate as Katie. There were times I wished he hadn't."

She didn't know what to say. Could not even imagine what it was like for him to lose someone he obviously loved so very much.

"I should have gone with her," he added, the words barely audible.

"But then you might have died too." The sentence was out before she could stop it.

What would she do if Walker were taken from her? It was incomprehensible. She was glad he had not succumbed to the deadly storm. Or perhaps if he had gone with his wife, they would both have survived.

Then he would still be with Katie and wouldn't belong to her now. Guilt knifed straight to her heart, and she glanced away. Katie's death and his suffering were a high price to pay for having Walker in her life.

He curled a finger beneath her chin and their gazes met. "I never thought to be this happy again, Trelayne. That's what matters. The past we cannot change, and the future is not always ours to command. The here and now is all we have, and I'm very grateful for you being a part of it. I wasted so many years looking back and never believing I could find happiness again, never even trying.

"I realize our marriage was a matter of necessity," he continued, "and your wedding day not what you had envisioned, but I do love you, and I will try to be the best possible husband to you. What started out a scandalous disaster can be our blessing in disguise."

She turned, blanketing his body with hers. Supported by his broad chest, she marveled at his strength as he held her in place. "I love you too," she breathed, against his neck. Sliding one hand downward, she pressed her palm against his crotch, and felt him harden.

"And by the way, I loved my wedding day, or more precisely my wedding night. And even if I could, I wouldn't change a thing." She nibbled at his ear. "I too promise to honor our vows, and be the best possible wife—in every way."

As true darkness wrapped them in seclusion, Trelayne slid to her knees between Walker's thighs. Her husband had taught her many wondrous things about making love. She enjoyed pleasuring him in this manner, loved the taste of him, the subtle control she held over him as she drove him to madness with her mouth. It was an unselfish act, asking nothing in return, and this evening he deserved special attention and consideration. He must fully realize how much he meant to her.

Slowly, she slipped the buttons free on his trousers.

With a groan, he cradled her head with one hand, and eased back against the bench.

Chapter Twenty-Three

As evening shadows washed the room, Beatrice finished packing the last of the crates waiting by the door. Lucien ambled about his flat, his footsteps echoing loudly in the vacant rooms. They only needed to secure one more piece of precious cargo before they headed for Amberley Abbey.

The last of the opium had been sold at a terrific profit, and employing jaw-clenching restraint, he'd steered clear of the gambling dens, keeping every penny of it liquid and available for their adventure.

He would be far from sad to depart London. The town held only bad memories and unfulfilled dreams. Paris was the place to be. Innovative, unrestrained, "*La Ville-Lumière,*" The City of Light. Everything would look brighter there.

"Are we to be married before or after we go to Paris," Beatrice asked, her voice all a-tremble with happiness.

"I think after," he returned. Poor woman, she still believed the lies he fed her. She would never see the shores of France, let alone Paris. "Be patient and do as you are told," he added. "You shall have your just reward."

Just reward indeed. Somehow, she'd been involved in Trelayne's disappearance from the Bond on the night of the Gala. Of that, he was sure. He'd found the necklace she'd hidden in the vase by the door, the one Trelayne used to wear. At some point, they had obviously been in contact with one anther. Careful not to tip his hand, he'd left the bauble in place. Confronting Beatrice with what he knew and forcing the truth out of her would be counterproductive. In fact, the two women's previous interaction would work to his advantage.

A smile crimped his mouth. It had been years since he'd been this excited about running a scheme. It gave him a heady rush of exhilaration, something rarely experienced lately in this jaded world. But while anticipation was titillating, fulfillment was gratifying.

"Come along, Beatrice" he said, reaching to fondle her breasts. "We'd best make the most of tonight. Tomorrow promises to be an eventful day."

****

Before the scream was fully born, Trelayne felt Walker's arms around her. The dream was back, prowling the backstreets of her mind as if it owned the territory free and clear. It had been too much to hope it would stay away forever. During the day, Walker protected every aspect of her being, but even his love and strength couldn't subdue the otherworldly in the dead of night.

"What is it? What's the matter?" He drew the covers up over her quaking body.

"A dream," she whispered, "just a dream. I've had it before."

"Not just a dream by the way you're trembling."

Walker was correct—it was a hideous nightmare. Although it had been several weeks since the bloody specter had disturbed her sleep, it now returned in even more glaring detail.

"Tell me about it."

"I dare not. I never tell anyone my dreams."

"Maybe you should."

"But to put words to it might give it life," she said, offering up her rote answer.

"Or," he pointed out, "take away its power."

She swallowed hard. That's what Aunt Abigail always said. She slumped back upon the bed. Maybe with Walker warm and near, she might be able to do as he suggested. It would be a great relief to share the mental burden, something she had never had the nerve to do before.

He settled at her side. Then as if to make her feel less awkward, he nonchalantly bent one arm up behind his head, leaned back against the pillows, and closed his eyes.

Taking a deep breath, she screwed up her courage and took the chance.

"In the dream," she began, "I'm trapped in a small room. The walls are made of stone, it's damp and poorly lit, and it smells fetid." She shivered at the memory and inched closer. "A tapestry hangs on the wall, but it doesn't add warmth or comfort. The vaulted ceiling makes one hope for stained-glass windows, anything to break the dark evil atmosphere hovering there, but no natural light penetrates the tomb-like chamber."

Knowing what was coming next, she buried her head against his chest—seeking the heat of his body and the steady beating of his heart. He lowered his arm and cinched her closer.

"Go on," he encouraged.

She raised her head. His eyes were open now, steadfastly returning her gaze. She tried to gage his reaction to her recitation. His expression held only concern, no mockery, or condescension.

She swallowed hard, lowered her head against his chest, and continued. "Then a crashing ensues, followed by a sparkle of light, and the cubit begins to fill with blood.

The dark ruby liquid sucks me down into a deadly embrace. Thick and warm and unrelenting, it covers my body and face, forcing its way into my nose and mouth." Her breath came in fits and gasps. "Then when I think all is lost, I wake up—clawing my way back from the edge of death."

He turned toward her, crossing one leg up over her thighs and hip, partially covering her body as if to shield her. Having torn the hateful apparition apart in her mind, she did feel a little better.

"After I met you, and fell in love," she said, "I was hoping the nightmares would stop."

"Then you've had other dreams of such a disturbing nature?"

"Sometimes."

"Even as a child?"

"It was different then. When I was small, I had good dreams, sometimes prophetic, but for happy reasons—such as knowing when a relative was coming to visit, or when a mare might foal. Then there was a good long while with no dreams at all. I was sad because some of them were so much fun. About a year ago, I started having ugly visions. I had one about my parents being hurt, and it was terrifyingly correct. That's why this one frightens me so much. Since we've been together, you've filled my world with happiness and pleasure, I thought these wretched specters had given up torturing me and gone away. But now...."

"I must be falling down on the job," he joked, stroking her neck.

She wanted to respond, but was too upset. Simple distraction wasn't going to resolve her problem. He seemed to realize gentle teasing wasn't the answer. "Do you fear this dream is prophetic as well?"

"Yes. No. I don't know. I certainly hope not."

"What can I do to help?"

His willingness to fix the problem eased the tension from her body. He took her seriously, not chiding or laughing at her fearful dilemma.

"Just what you're doing now. Hold me. Tell me everything will be all right."

He hugged her tighter. "Everything will be all right."

He said it with such conviction she could almost believed it was true. Turning to more fully face him, she pressed her hips up against his. The part of him that still held her fascination twitched against her belly.

It was a long time until morning. Perhaps a little distraction wasn't such a bad idea after all.

****

The day dawned clear and brisk, full of promise and sunny expectation, with no room for nightmares or gloomy thoughts. It was the perfect day for the charity bazaar.

The booth Trelayne managed with Penelope, open now for an hour, was drawing quite a crowd. Their custom was sheet music for the *Hebrides Overture,* signed by Mendelssohn himself, and they were selling faster than roasted chestnuts on a cold winter's eve. Of course the signature was false and everyone knew it was a forgery—that being the whole hilarious point.

Up the row, you could purchase a snippet of wax, supposedly a discard from Madame Tussaud's Exhibition, or a paper flower complete with certification stating it had been *grown* at Kew Gardens. It was all a lark providing items to be dragged out for amusement at future dinner parties.

She reached to straighten the stack of papers, brought up short when Penelope gripped her arm with the strength of a bricklayer.

"Laynie, there he is. Isn't he wonderful?"

She craned her neck to follow her friend's line of sight.

"Don't look," Pen warned. "He'll see us gawking, and think me ever so immature."

"If I don't look how can I see how wonderful he is? And who he is."

"His name is Jeffrey Lancaster. He's the son of Hubert P. Lancaster."

"The Lancasters of High Wycombe?"

"The very same. They have a huge bit of property with tons of sheep and a thriving woolen mill. Jeffrey doesn't often visit London. I didn't expect to see him today. He must have remembered me mentioning the bazaar at the Queen's concert. Oh mercy," her friend squeaked, blushing furiously. "He's coming this way."

"Good morning, Miss Penelope. You're looking more appealing than a lamb in springtime."

Penelope made a happy sound, coquettishly playing with the ribbons on her cloak. Trelayne tried to keep from laughing. A lamb in springtime? Well, she supposed it was a rather endearing image. The two smitten souls stood mutely staring at one another. It would seem Pen had finally found her Mr. Rochester. Charlotte Bronte would be pleased.

"I'm Trelayne Garrison," she put in, amused at the couple's charming lack of social etiquette. It must be love.

Pen and her would-be suitor finally tore their gazes from one another and took note of the world around them.

"Jeffrey Lancaster, at your service." He bowed in a quaint old-fashioned manner, and Trelayne understood why Penelope would be entranced by the young man. He was sweetly good-looking, and seemed steeped in romantic notions. Even the way he dressed expressed traditions of a by-gone era.

"I'm so pleased to meet you, Jeffrey. Have you tried the new confection called ice cream? Penelope has been going on about it all morning." Pen shot her a confused look, but not breaking stride, Trelayne rambled on. "The two of you had best go purchase some before it is lost to the heat of the day."

"I shan't leave you alone to man the booth," Pen protested.

"Yes, you shall," she insisted. "The crowd has thinned since they opened the ring-toss game across from us. I'll be fine. Please, go, enjoy yourselves."

More easily convinced, Jeffery offered his arm. Penelope accepted, and together they strolled off into the milling throng. Trelayne was so happy for her friend. They made a decidedly perfect couple. She could envision a huge red barn, filled with fragrant hay, Jeffery reading poetry to Penelope as she wove a garland of wild flowers—bunnies hopping by, and those adorable lambs cavorting about. Penelope never cared for city life. She would be happy playing the mistress of a thriving rural legacy.

As a woman approached the stall, Trelayne's smile froze. There was something familiar about the person. With a shock she realized it was Lucien's paramour—the woman who had rescued her from the Bond. Mixed feelings wrapped around her. She recalled Walker telling her the woman's name was Beatrice. The doxy had done her a good turn that evening. Still, Trelayne was miffed Lucien had kept familiar with this woman the whole time he had been courting her. Whether one wanted the man or not, it was difficult to realize he was dabbling on the side. Making small talk with Beatrice sounded uncomfortable at best.

"Thank you for supporting our efforts to raise money for the orphans," she began, keeping it on a business level.

"Don't you recognize me, Miss Trelayne? Or I should say Mrs. Garrison."

"Yes, I do. I just thought to ignore the fact."

"Well, that ain't no way to be talkin'. I mean you no harm."

She supposed it really wasn't this woman's fault for being seduced by Lucien. He could be charming and irresistible when he so desired.

"I'm sorry. Did you wish to purchase a copy of sheet music?"

"Me, sheet music? Not hardly. I come to give you a message from my fiancé."

"Lucien?"

"Yes, Lucien. I'm soon to be Mrs. Lanteen. You

see it all worked out as planned. You have your Captain and I have Lucien."

She was shocked to realize Lucien was actually going to marry this woman. He always maligned people who were uneducated and from what he considered the lower classes. This was a complete turn-about. Maybe he had changed his ways. For Beatrice's sake, she prayed so.

"Congratulations. I hope the two of you will be very happy."

"Well, that's why I come. Lucien wants to say good-bye as it were. Wish you well and all."

"That's not necessary. Tell him thank you for the felicitations and extend mine to him. I don't think having him visit Royston Hall is a good idea."

"But he's here now. Just over there in that grove of elm wood. It won't take but a minute."

Considering the malicious acts Lucien had committed against her and her parents, Trelayne knew she couldn't face him and long remain civil.

"I'm afraid it's out of the question."

"Please," Beatrice begged. "Let him get this off his chest so's we can be happy with no undone business between the two of you standin' between the two of us."

She felt herself weakening. Beatrice sounded desperate to start her new life free of bad feelings or omens. It was a relatively small request, and to dampen the spark of love, regardless of how incongruous it may seem, was disconcerting. Out of pity for Beatrice, she wavered. And as Lucien would most likely never be legally brought to justice, she could at least tell him off good and proper.

She glanced around. Penelope and Jeffery were long gone. Well, no matter. The ring-toss competition was still in full swing, monopolizing all the customers. Surely it would be all right to slip away for a few moments.

She gave Beatrice a nod of consent, and snuggling into the cloak Walker had given her this morning, she stepped from behind the booth. Like a big hug, the warm wool cozened her, and she thought again how lucky she was to have Walker as her husband. It wasn't her birthday, or their anniversary, or any special occasion. He had surprised her with the present for no other reason than wanting to see her "beautiful face" framed by the exquisite burgundy shade.

When they were almost to the thicket of trees, she noticed a large brutal-looking man lounging beside the horses, but she didn't see Lucien. Maybe this wasn't such a good idea after all. Sensing alarm, she slowed her pace then halted.

"I've changed my mind. I really must return to the bazaar. It was irresponsible of me to leave the booth unattended."

"But we're nearly there, ducks," Beatrice encouraged. "Lucien? Where are you?"

The door to the carriage swung open, and Lucien stepped down. Dressed smartly from head to toe in somber black, he'd never looked more handsome, or more dangerous.

But his stare gave her chills. The expression in his pale blue eyes was cold as ice. There was nothing warm or pleasant about his demeanor. His manner held no intention to please or amuse as before when he was with her. A full-fledged shiver ran through her. Lucien really had changed, and not for the better.

He ambled forward, took her by the elbow, and escorted her closer to the conveyance. She snatched free of his grip.

"How is married life?" he sneered.

"Wonderful," she breathed. "I hear you are soon to be married as well."

"Something like that. Shall we drink to both our future happiness? Grimsby," he ordered with a snap his fingers.

Grimsby...that was the name of the man who had injured her parents and sought to murder Walker. The ruffian sauntered forth with a bottle of champagne and two glasses. She shrank back.

"I've no time for a toast, I really must be going."

Coming ever closer, the man scared the daylights out of her. As panic set in, she stumbled backward then turned to run.

"Yes, you must be going," Lucien agreed. "But not back to the bazaar."

His henchman threw down the champagne and glasses, grabbed her around the waist, and wrestled her up off the ground. Kicking out with her feet, she tried to break free, but he hurled her into the coach. With a painful bounce, she settled onto the floorboards then scrabbled up onto her hands and knees.

Hampered by her skirts and cloak, she floundered about unable to gain purchase. Lucien leaped in after her, nearly stepping on her hands. He grabbed her and flung her up onto the far seat. Her head hit the side of the coach, and she saw stars.

"Say, what goes on here," Beatrice demanded.

"Shut up and get onboard or I'll leave you behind."

The carriage sagged as the woman followed orders. The door banged shut, and the coach lurched into action. Trelayne grabbed at the handle, attempting to gain freedom, but Lucien backhanded her. Pain shot through her jaw, and the metallic taste of blood permeated her mouth. She tried to scream, but he presses a damp cloth against her face, muffling the sound and restricting her movements.

Fighting hard, she turned her head from side to side, her heart pounded painfully in her chest, and her arms and legs were weak and rubbery. She clawed at the fabric and his hands—desperate for a breath of air. Then the sickeningly sweet odor over-powered her, and she floated into the blackness.

Chapter Twenty-Four

Dusky shadows eased closer to Royston Hall, but nothing eased the panic threatening to overtake Walker's mind. At wits' end, he raked his hand through his hair and paced the length of the dayroom.

"I'm so sorry. I don't know what happened," Penelope repeated, swiping at the tears on her cheeks. "Like I said, when Jeffery and I returned to the booth, Laynie was gone. It was a madhouse with all the crowds and gaiety. We asked, but no one saw anything suspicious. She just wasn't there."

Wynona slipped her arm around the young woman and gave her a hug. "It's not your fault, dear. Come along to the kitchen." She glanced at Walker, and at his nod of consent, led the girl away. "We'll get you some tea and a bite to eat."

Walker clenched his jaw to keep from howling in frustration. As he turned and headed for the door, Sam Colt blocked his path and shoved him back into the room.

"Settle down," Colt advised. "Now's the time for straight thinkin' and straight shootin', not acting crazy and going off half cocked."

Thank the Lord that Sam was still in London. Unplanned, but as promised, he'd dropped by this morning to give Abigail a shooting lessen. Then the missive proclaiming trouble at the docks had arrived.

Sam and he had gone to check things out, but it had been a red herring. Nothing was amiss. Upon their return, they had found Penelope in her present condition, and Trelayne gone missing.

"Where can she be?" Abigail clutched at her bosom and eased down onto the settee. "Do you suppose Spring Heeled Jack could have gotten to her? He was seen in the area the night before."

"That doesn't seem right," Merrick put in. "He mainly strikes at night. Besides, the depraved creature is being blamed for everything from folks taking ill to hens not laying. We mustn't fall pray to the same hysteria."

"I agree. My money's on Lanteen," Walker ground out. "The business down at the wharf today was a diversion. There wasn't any trouble brewing there, but it kept us occupied for hours. I'm guessing, in a depraved bit of irony, he sent the note claiming an emergency just like the one I sent to spirit Trelayne away from him at the Bond."

"So where does that leave us?" Sam put in. "We went by the scoundrel's flat on the way back from the docks, and by the looks of things, he's clean gone out of there."

"If he gave up his lodgings," Walker concluded, "I don't think he is still in London. He might not even be in England." That realization increased his panic. "He could be anywhere, with the whole world in which to hide."

As he took to pacing again, he smoothed his mustache in a habit of worry and contemplation. There had to be a connection between Trelayne's disappearance and Lanteen vacating his premises, but in which direction would he head? It was anybody's guess.

"What is this place?" he asked, halting before a painting on the west wall.

"It's Amberley Abbey," Abigail explained. "The property belongs to Trelayne, or rather to the both of you now. My father willed it to her."

He'd never before taken note of the artwork. It was a small landscape, painted, by all appearances, by someone in the family. Although viewed from a different angle, the resemblance struck home, the connection unmistakable.

"Where is it exactly?"

"Approximately 30 kilometers northwest of Brighton."

"That's where she is."

"But why would you think such a thing?"

"Lanteen had a similar painting at his place."

"It's rather a famous site for artists. It could be a coincidence."

"I don't think so. It was hung with near shrine-like reverence. And one of the Brighton river rats who tried to kill me said Lanteen had a place near there where he holed up. A warehouse or monastery. This has to be it.

"Come on, Sam. Time to saddle up and hit the trail."

As he headed for the door to the room, everyone leapt into action.

"I'll have Jeb ready two horses," Merrick said, and hurried off.

"I'll help Cook pack food for the journey," Abigail offered.

He and Sam took the stairs two at a time. Reaching

his and Trelayne's room, Walker flipped up the lid of a large beleaguered trunk and dragged out clothing and accouterments. In a matter of minutes, he was outfitted in his long black duster, two Colt revolvers, his new knife, and his big black hat. Sam grabbed up similar attire. The clothes were a little big on his friend, but they'd do.

Within the hour, they were on the road, but as darkness fell, so did the rain, slowing them down.

"Damn English weather," Sam groused. "Ain't seen the sun shine more than fifteen minutes in a row since I've been here. You sure your gal's at this abbey place?"

"I'm sure."

He considered Trelayne's recent nightmare. It fit in perfectly with the image inspired by the painting. There wasn't a doubt in his mind Lanteen had taken her to that medieval stronghold. The man was a lunatic, a dramatic but dangerous lunatic. He would even execute evil with flair.

What if Trelayne's dream came true before he could get there? Trelayne had given him another chance at love, another chance at a life worth living. He couldn't lose her.

He gripped the fanciful English saddle tighter with his thighs, and kicked the horse into a canter. On this trip south, speed took precedent over sparing his mount.

****

Trelayne opened her eyes and cringed.

In the dim room, the light from the candles seemed brighter than the center of the sun. Pain pounded in her head, and her stomach felt queasy. Whatever they'd used to knock her out produced the most wretched lingering effects. Lord, she felt awful.

Lying motionless on the small cot, she shifted her gaze, and fear, hot and liquid, raced through her veins. This was the chamber in her dream. She sobbed, and wanted to scream, but she knew no one would hear her.

In her nightmare she was up and walking around. Maybe if she remained prone nothing would happen. But that was no good. She had to find a way out of this room, had to figure out where Lucien had taken her.

What time was it? How long had she been unconscious? Everything was all turned around in her mind. As the nausea subsided, she eased upright onto the side of the raised pallet. Her stomach gave a healthy rumble. Several hours must have past for her to be this hungry.

She gained her feet then froze. Someone was outside the room. The latch rattled and the door creaked open, the sound rending the silence of the small chamber.

"Ah, you're awake." Lucien stepped inside and closed the door at his back.

"What is this place?" she demanded, probing for information relative to escaping.

"Don't recognize your own landholding? We're at Amberley. I see by your shocked expression you never discovered this room. How fitting that I should know of it and not you. I love this ancient relic more than you ever did, and had such glorious plans for it." There was a far away look in his eyes. "It should have been mine. But all that is ruined now."

"You must let me go, Lucien."

"Must I? I don't see why."

"I'm married to Captain Garrison. I belong to him.

You've no right to keep me here."

"No right?" Ruddy spots of anger highlighted his cheekbones. "I have every right. I am the one who has done your bidding year after year, showering you with gifts as I listened to you prattle on and on about the poor underclass and orphans. You spared them more attention than you gave to me. And I am the one who stood humbly by while your father treated me like a mere employee and never a suitor with possibilities. Now, I am your only possibility."

"But Walker will not rest until he finds me. What purpose does it serve to keep up this charade? We all have dreams, but sometimes they are not fulfilled."

At least she hoped this one would not be.

"I doubt he will look for us in France."

"France…the country is one step away from revolt. Paris is in turmoil."

"All the more exciting. And the more easily one can become lost in the crowd."

"Or crushed in the rush—even killed. This is madness. I won't go with you."

"But you will. Either upright and awake, or unconscious, a repeat performance of your journey here. The choice is yours."

Anger renewed her fighting spirit. If she were a man, she would show him another choice, one with well-aimed punches. "This is unworthy of you, Lucien," she said, fists clenched at her sides

"No, *you* are unworthy of me. But although you are now used goods, the devil take me, I still want you."

"The devil take you indeed. What you've done to my family and me cannot be overlooked. You have overstepped every boundary and committed unforgivable acts. I shall hate you forever."

He glared at her. The feral brightness in his eyes played off the blue ice as a menacing smile creased his face. Walker was correct—Lucien was demented. Swallowing hard, she held her ground.

"I see you need more time to reflect upon your situation and limited options. We've still a few hours before the crossing."

"I will pray the waters are too rough for setting sail."

He chuckled as if privy to a jest that bespoke of her foolishness. "The temperament of the sea will not inhibit our excursion."

Turning, he opened the door to leave. She raced across the room—too late to hold him back or squeeze through to freedom. Slumping in defeat, she heard the latch fell back in place—declaring her once more a prisoner.

There had been a glimmer of light in the passageway. It must be morning. She had slept the entire night away. What difference this made to her situation was moot, but somehow it helped to organize her thoughts.

Ignoring another protest from her empty stomach, she walked the perimeter of the enclosure, running her hands over the cold stone wall, seeking another door or passageway. How odd no one knew about this secret room. Leave it to Lucien to discover the macabre chamber, secrets and subterfuge being his specialty. Standing dejected in the middle of the room, she wrapped her arms across her chest for warmth. He could have at least allowed her to keep her cloak.

A tear trickled down her cheek. Had it only been

yesterday morning Walker had given it to her? Having it near would have meant more than warmth. It would be his love surrounding her.

****

Beatrice snuggled the burgundy wool about her. It was cold on the parapet, but the view was breathtaking, and Lucien had bid her wait here for him.

She wondered if Bart was all right. She missed him already. He'd left this morning for the coast, and by now was well on his way to Paris by ship. He would insure their baggage and household items arrived safely, and secure suitable accommodations.

With a contented sigh, she pictured a cozy flat in the heart of the foreign city. One with tall ceilings, sunlight filtering in through leaded glass windows. Maybe a flower box on a little wrought iron balcony. Oh, it was going to be wonderful. She had never been happier. She'd make Lucien a good wife.

But what about *her*?

What a surprise when Lucien forced Trelayne to come along, rather than saying goodbye like he promised. This boded ill, and her old feelings of hatred for the woman flared hot and well remembered. Maybe he wanted to teach her a lesson for running off with the Captain. Maybe just frighten her and give her a bit of torturin' then let her find her own way back to Royston Hall. What other reason could there be for her to be here? The trek home would be a long and dangerous one. Maybe she would die along the way. That thought cheered her. If nothing else, it would be a cold walk without her expensive cloak.

She petted the fine wool and felt for the necklace hidden beneath the fabric of her dress. After Lucien's proposal, she'd taken to secretly wearing the heart locket, pretending he had given it to her as a token of his love. A smile softened her face. Just think of all the beautiful Parisian fashions soon to be hers. Lucien said they would be leaving shortly. She hoped he knew what he was doing.

****

Bolstered by anger, Trelayne ripped the threadbare tapestry from the wall and draped it around her shivering body. Then she stared in open-mouthed wonder at the partition revealed. Rather than stone, it was damp moldering wood. She moved closer to examine the find. What was on the other side? If she could break through the barrier, she might escape before Lucien returned.

Flinging aside the tapestry, she grabbed one of the tall wrought iron candleholders, and using it as a battering ram, attacked the planking. A section of the panel splintered, and the glass drip cup shattered, sending shards spiraling through the air. Not having expected such a volatile reaction, she dropped the twisted iron, stumbled backward, and covered her head with her arms.

Reflected in the light of the other candle, the twinkling fragments mirrored her dream. Something terrible had been set in motion. Stunned and shaking, she held her breath, waiting for what was surely to come next. A slab of wood broke loose at the top of the partition and crashed to the ground. Then what had been held back for centuries by the rotting timber came pouring out. Dark and red, it gushed through the opening, pooling on the floor, filling up the small chamber.

The depth of the foul liquid was already knee-deep. In a panic, she lunged toward the door, but her foot caught on the abandoned candleholder, and arms splayed wide, she fell to the floor. The putrid liquid was rising quickly. She tried to lever upright, but her hand slipped sideways landing her flat on her back. The wave of red horror sloshed over her, covering her face, stifling her breath, and her screams for help.

Thrashing about in three feet of thick crimson liquid, she floundered into a sitting position, sobbing and gasping for air. As the initial deluge tapered off, the flood reduced down to a trickle. She wasn't going to drown after all.

Cupping her hands, she scooped up a bit of the liquid and sniffed it. A bubble of mirth rose in her chest. It was wine, not blood. Hooting with relief, she splashed about in the very old, very sour, decanted Bordeaux. The hidden chamber shared a common wall with the vats in the winery. Too bad it was unfit for drinking.

How ironic, all this time she had been terrified of her grisly nightmare, when in reality it was trying to show her the way out of one.

Staggering to her feet, she sloshed over to the hole in the wall and stuck her head through the opening. The vat was tall, but the well placed wooden crosspieces offered a feasible path upward, and the room at the top promised light and a way out.

She scraped at the residue clinging to her arms then wrung the wine from her skirt and petticoats. The blood-red stains would never come out. She must look as if she'd barely survived the most brutal of attacks. Gathering the ruined fabric, she drew it up between her legs, and giving it a twist, tucked the material up under her cloth belt. Then she crawled through the jagged breech.

As she began the ascent, recollections of her tree climbing days surfaced. For once, trying to keep up with her brother Branwell would come in handy.

Chapter Twenty-Five

As Amberley Abbey came into view, the clouds finally gave way to the sun. They had ridden all night, stopping only once to eat, rest the horses, and relieve themselves.

"How about we circle them trees and come in from the far side?" Sam suggested.

"Sounds like a good plan." Walker nodded. "Although riled up as I am, I'd rather charge the place full-bore, guns blazing."

"I know, friend, but Trelayne could be hurt."

"That's the only reason I'm not following through with the urge. It looks like something's going on topside. Do you see someone up there?"

"I do. Gonna make getting close unobserved a might tricky."

"We could try a diversion," Walker offered, "but I'd rather the two of us stick together."

"I agree. We'll have to take our chances, and hope experience wins out over a superior tactical position."

****

Her freedom gained, Trelayne was at a loss as to what to do next.

Adjusting her clothing, she prowled around the lower level of the abbey but couldn't find the coach or even one horse in the stable. How did Lucien plan to get to the coast in order to board a ship? And with no horse available, how did she plan to get away? If she left on foot, Lucien could easily track her down. Then she'd be right back where she started. At least now she had the advantage of surprise. To gain the upper hand on Lucien and render him senseless would make a great difference in her choices and chances.

Armed with a sturdy stick to use as a club, she abandoned the ground floor and gained the stairs leading toward the upper levels. Muffled voices filtered down from the rooftop, staying her ascent. Who was with him? Beatrice most likely. Or maybe Grimsby, that frightful hooligan who had driven the carriage. If they were all together, the jig was up. She couldn't face down all three of them. Still, she couldn't just stand there doing nothing. Realizing she had no choice, she tightened her grip on the club, and crept up the stone steps.

The top of the abbey was in the shape of a large square, edged with a low crenellated wall. A round tower speared up out of the middle, and lesser stone formations and collapsed partitions created random nooks, wind blocks, and shade. Huddled in the shadows, she peeked around a pile of rock. Beatrice and Lucien stood talking. Good, that made just two to one, and maybe Beatrice could be convinced to offer aid. No doubt the woman would be glad to see her gone, and as far away from Lucien as possible.

She shivered as a stiff breeze sprang up, plastering her wet wine-soaked dress against her body. She longed for her cloak—the one Beatrice was wearing. Lucien barked out a command then headed for the stairway. Scurrying sideways along the stone barrier, she waited until he passed, his footfalls in the stairway fading to silence. Now was her chance to speak to Beatrice and gain her assistance.

Setting the club aside, she stepped out into the open. "Beatrice," she called. "I need your help."

The woman gasped, her eyes wide with surprise. Then her expression transformed into one of horror. "Lord almighty, look at the blood. He's killed you, and you be a ghostly apparition."

Too late Trelayne realized her bedraggled hair and scarlet-stained clothes were frightening Beatrice.

"No, you don't understand."

She rushed forward, trying to reach the other woman before she made a commotion or started screaming.

"I didn't really want you dead," Beatrice cried tripping backward. "Keep away, keep away."

"Don't be afraid. Just give me my darn cloak, and we can talk."

Tangled together in the billowing fabric, they stood face to face on the precipice of the wall.

****

Gaining the edge of the trees, Walker and Sam paused to consider their next move. The Abbey was at least a hundred yards away, and the land between here and there was open field, uphill all the way.

"Looks like we'll just have to—" Walker stopped mid-sentence as a flash of burgundy at the top of the Abbey snared his attention. It was the same color as the cloak he'd given Trelayne yesterday. His mood spiraled upward at having found her. Then agonizing disbelief shredded all hope.

"Oh, God, no."

She tumbled over the side of the parapet. Caught

by the wind, the cape flapped and fluttered erratically like the fatal dance of a rare butterfly. Heart pumping, his breath trapped in his chest, he kicked his horse into action and galloped toward a destination he wished he'd never reach.

Reining in hard, he skidded to a stop, launched himself out of the saddle, and ran forward. Bile rose in his throat as he knelt beside the crumpled body. A knot of sorrow constricted his breathing as he gathered his beloved into his arms. She was wearing her golden heart necklace. The one matching Ophelia's. By all that was holy, how could the hand of destiny be so brutal as to see him suffer such a tragedy of heart and mind twice in one Lifetime?

The hood of the cloak slid to one side. He forced himself to gaze upon her face. Shock and surprise replaced dread, nearly knocking him senseless. It was Beatrice, not Trelayne.

He sobbed with relief then struggled with guilt for being so pleased to find it was someone other than his wife. Poor Beatrice. He knew she'd had a hard life. Now it had ended in a terrible death. Easing her broken body to the ground, he closed her eyes, and wrapped the wool around her. As he removed the heart locket and slipped it into his breast pocket, alarm returned full force. Why was Beatrice wearing Trelayne's cloak and jewelry? Where was his wife? What had they done to her?

He scrambled to his feet. Sam hurried to his side and gripped his shoulder as if to offer comfort.

"It isn't her, Sam. It's Lanteen's woman. Trelayne must be inside somewhere. There's no time left for highfalutin' strategies, or worrying about being quiet, we're going in."

Pistols in hand, they stormed the Abbey. Halfway there, a shot rang out, missing Sam by a frog's hair. Taking cover behind the capstone of an old cistern, they fired back. Two additional shots kept them pinned in place.

****

Trelayne clamped both hands over her mouth, stifling the scream threatening to tear from her throat. Then screwing up her courage, she peered over the edge of the wall, knowing what she would find, but still needing to look.

"Oh, Beatrice, I'm sorry," she whispered and reached out, tears burning in the back of her eyes. She hadn't meant for anything like this to happen.

Dazed and confused as to what to do next, she clung to the wall and tried to calm the wild beating of her heart. Then she recalled having heard gunfire. It must be Walker—he'd come for her. She must go to him. Sprinting across the ramparts toward the stairs, she crashed into Lucien.

"Here you are, my dove," he said, wild-eyed and panting from running up the steps. "I see you took time for a hearty sampling of the monks' wine."

He slammed the door shut at his back and wedged a rock up against it. Then pistol in hand, he wrapped one arm around her, jerked her up against his chest, and licked her cheek.

"Not a terribly good vintage," he noted. "Aged a bit too long. Where's Beatrice?" He grabbed her by the arm and towed her back the way she'd come.

Trelayne pointed to the low wall. "She fell. It was an accident."

"What the deuce." He dragged her closer to see for himself.

A grimace of sadness captured his visage then his expression brightened. "Well, she wasn't to come with us anyway. Move along."

"Walker is here, isn't he?" she goaded. "He's found me, and now your plans are ruined."

"On the contrary. He's here but nothing has changed. Everything is ready. We leave immediately."

He prodded her in the back with the muzzle of the pistol. Refusing to capitulate, she dug in her heels and balked.

"You'd best co-operate," he threatened, "unless you'd like to join poor Beatrice."

By the look in his eyes, she feared he meant every word. Giving in she followed. Besides, it didn't matter; there wasn't anywhere to go. They were trapped on top of the abbey. Lucien had made a grave error. There was no way off the roof other than down the steps. He had a weapon though. That was a worry. After the exchange of gunfire Walker would be aware Lucien was armed, but that wouldn't stop her brave Captain from rushing to her rescue.

As they made their way around to the far side of the tower, the optimism she harbored dissolved away. Dumbfounded, she stopped dead in her tracks. A huge flying balloon awaited on the far side of the central tower. As if in a trance, she drew closer, mesmerized, as well as terrified by the grandeur of the orb.

Lucien lovingly ran his hand over the varnished silk. "Exquisite, isn't she," he crooned. "State of the art, as well as a work of art. And it cost a pretty penny, I'll tell you."

Predominately blue, the sides were embellished with signs of the zodiac, fleur-de-lis, and the frightful faces of lions and eagles. Only the splendor of the balloon rivaled her fear of it.

"It took five hours to fill," he said with pride, kicking aside the still smoldering remains of wood. "But we've finished just in time."

This was lunacy. She glanced around, seeking the quickest route to the steps and freedom.

"Even the gods are with us," he declared, "it's a perfect day for flying. Tonight we dine in Paris."

As if equally anxious to take to the sky, the monstrous globe fought the tether keeping it earthbound.

"We'll never make it. It's too far. You don't know the first thing about aeronautics."

"Oh, but I do. I spent nearly a month with Charles Green. Took a crash course in ballooning as it were. Oops, poor choice of words. And it is not too far. Fifteen years ago, Green went all the way from Vauxhall Gardens to Nassau in one night. Why, we'll be in France in a jiffy, ready to start a new life in a new country."

With a crazed look upon his face, Lucien muscled her closer to the towering monstrosity. This could only end in disaster. It was true there had been a few successful crossings. But others had tried, and many had died.

"I can't swim," she uttered, doubting it would make a difference to Lucien.

"One must hope there'll be no necessity for swimming. Now climb aboard, and we'll be off."

The fragile wicker undercarriage appeared barely

large enough for two. She struggled in his grasp. "I won't go. I would rather die here."

Agitated at her refusal, Lucian waved the pistol in her face, all too ready to make her commitment come true.

"Do as I say or we shall both regret it. No matter what it takes, Trelayne, I'll not be thwarted at this juncture. Perhaps I should give you more chloroform. Magical stuff that, although it does leave one with a wretched headache, or so I'm told."

What should she do? Unconscious she'd be in no position to help herself or to escape when Walker breeched the rooftop. She gritted her teeth, and taking as much time as possible, climbed aboard. *Hurry Walker, she prayed, hurry.*

Lucien scrambled in beside her, jammed the pistol into the waistband of his trousers, and reached to untie the tether. She yelped in surprise and grabbed the basket-rail as the craft lifted off with a jolt. Immediately caught in a cross-breeze, it lurched sideways, trailing a long second line behind.

As they drifted along just above the surface of the roof, she caught a movement from the corner of her eye. It was Walker and another man she couldn't make out. Gripping Lucien by the lapels, she garnered his attention, making sure his back was toward the approaching men. At the run, and never breaking stride, Walker shed his hat and coat.

"Lucien, it isn't too late. Let me go."

He snarled, and pulled free of her grip.

"I know you were involved in my parents' accident," she divulged, trying to shock him into rational thinking. "And I can only assume you tried to sabotage the negotiations of the *Romney Maiden*. Save yourself. Go to Paris. Just let me go free."

He remained silent, lost in the delusion they could run away and begin some idyllic life together.

As they drifted near the edge of the rooftop, her expectations for a quick rescue were dashed. Walker was too far away. Not meaning to, she groaned in defeat. Perceiving the change in her demeanor, Lucien glanced back over his shoulder. Then with a hiss of anger, he shoved her aside, and went for his pistol.

She grabbed his arm. The weapon discharged, sending a bullet through the floor of the wicker basket. Their struggle set the gondola to swinging wildly. Lucien lost his footing, and she struck out again, knocking the gun from his hand. It fell from the basket, clattering onto the rooftop. One leg over the side, she tried to follow suit. Too late—there was nothing beneath them now but a long sheer drop to the ground. Lucien grabbed her by the hair, and yanked her back inside the basket.

Walker, running at top speed, kept coming toward them. He must stop, it was pointless, he couldn't reach them now. Then what he had in mind became apparent, and she screamed in alarm.

"It's too dangerous. Don't do it."

Her words of caution were flung wide by the wind as Walker leaped off the roof and grabbed the trail-rope.

Seizing the edge of the basket, she leaned over trying to catch a glimpse of her husband as he dangled far below. His added weight caused the balloon to lose altitude, and they dipped closer to the tree-covered terrain. Branches smashed into Walker as he worked to haul himself, hand over hand, upward toward the basket. All the while, Lucien worked at untying the rope from the inside, but the tension on the sisal was too great, and he couldn't work the knot.

Down below a man was running along the west wall of the Abbey. She recognized him now—it was Sam Colt. He mounted one of the tethered horses, caught the reins of the other, and chased after them. Renewed expectations for a happy ending quivered in her breast until Lucien tore the sleeve off her dress. At first she thought he was attacking her then she realized it was a far worse scenario. He wrapped the fabric around his hand and ripped a metal brace off the funnel used to direct the scorching-hot air into the balloon. Employing the still glowing metal he worked to sear through the rope upon which Walker dangled. It was a slow process, but promised eventual success. She wrestled with him, trying to slow his progress.

A cold blast of wind sent them rushing toward the coast. The atmosphere nearer the ocean was blustery, their path chaotic. The basket tipped from side to side, causing Walker to swing riotously beneath them. At least he was no longer battered by the trees. But as the balloon's shadow flittered crossed the sandy beach and slipped beyond the shoreline, her palms began to sweat. They were heading straight out to sea.

The rope Lucian labored over smoldered, and then burned halfway through. She pummeled his back and slapped at the line trying to put out the sparks. Ignoring her assault, he began sawing the line with the jagged edge of metal.

Peering over the edge of the basket, she squinted against the rush of air coming at her full force. They were gaining altitude. Her panic increased, and she decided when the rope holding Walker broke, she would be on it too. Better to die with Walker than live without him. Hiking up her skirts, she shimmied over the edge of the basket, and with one hand still on the top rail she reached for the twisted hemp draped over the side. Wedging one foot in the cross-rigging beneath the basket she secured a tenuous position.

Walker grappled up the last few feet. His hand clasped the calf of her left leg then her thigh.

"What in God's name are you doing? Get back onboard," he ordered, coming face to face with her. The sight of the bloody cuts and dark bruises on his face and hands made her wince.

They clung to one another near the bottom of the basket. "The rope is almost burned through," she warned. "It won't last much longer."

He slid his foot in the rigging beside hers, and wrapped one arm around her.

Without thinking, she glanced down. Then she snapped her eyes shut, and began to shake. She wanted to be strong, but all she could think of was how they were never going to raise a family, or grow old together.

She began to cry, couldn't stop, the hysteria welling up in her chest.

"Can you swim?" he asked.

"Not a stroke," she uttered, between great sobs, eyes still closed.

"Not to worry," he said, "the drop will probably kill us."

At his sarcasm, she gave him a horrified look, as well as her full attention.

"That's better," he said, with the grin she so favored. "Do you trust me?"

"Always and forever," she sniffled.

Reaching down with one hand, he pulled off his left boot and then the right. Freeing a pistol from its holster, he fired at the balloon.

The air began to leak out, sending them on a wild descent. Visions of a wet crash landing flooded her thoughts. Then the rope broke, and her mind went blank.

She buried her face against Walker's shoulder. He held her tight and wrapped his legs around her. They plummeted like a rock, hit the water, and went under.

Having no idea which way was up, she thrashed about, sucking in saltwater. Strong hands pushed her to the surface, and sputtering and choking she gulped great breaths of air as Walker bobbed up beside her.

"Hang on," he instructed, dog paddling to keep them both afloat, "and try not to drown me."

He swam for shore, one powerful stroke after another. She held onto his belt, barely keeping her head above water as he dragged them toward land. The tide was out, offering a sandy beach rather than deadly rocks, and the waves were surprisingly cooperative.

Sam Colt was waiting. He slogged through the shallows, helping them to their feet and shepherding them to dry land.

"Enjoy the ride?" Sam asked, slapping Walker on the back.

"The view was nice, but the accommodations lacking."

"Glad you're all right, Mrs. Garrison," Sam said, handing over his coat.

Walker snuggled it around her, and in unison, they turned toward the horizon to search for the balloon.

"I'll be damned," Walker said, and pointed. "He's losing altitude, but still airborne."

Chapter Twenty-Six

Trelayne's physical injuries, being relatively minor, quickly healed. The scars on her mind ran deeper, her emotions slower to recover.

At first she feared to leave the house. And when they weren't in bed together, she insisted on knowing every minute where Walker was and if he was safe. Ever patient, he finally convinced her that allowing her fear to rule her life was keeping her as much a prisoner as Lanteen ever could.

Taking Walker's advice, she worked hard at relegating thoughts of Lucien to the wasteland of her mind. There was nary a word regarding his whereabouts, or if he had even survived his maniacal escape. Walker was correct. There was too much happiness in her world to spend one moment on unsettling reflections. Her parents were making great progress, and now she discovered her best friend was soon to be married.

"Oh Pen," she laughed, clapping her hands, "what positively splendid news. I'm so happy for you and Jeffery. A winter wedding sounds beautiful,"

"Are you sorry you didn't have a proper wedding of your own?" Penelope asked. "One with all the trimmings?"

She thought about it for a moment then shook her head. "Perhaps a few more flowers and a suitable dress would have been nice," she admitted. "But being whisked away to Gretna Greene was utterly romantic. Just like in the books we used too read."

"Used to? You mean we have to stop reading them now?"

"No, of course not. If we don't keep reading, we won't keep learning. But we must take care our husbands never find them, lest they think we are dissatisfied or dreaming of another man while in their arms. They're funny that way."

"I'm afraid of the first time," Pen admitted. "You promise it didn't hurt over much?"

"Only a little. And only for a little while." She squirmed on the settee recalling the first time Walker had made love to her—or as he put it, the first time they shared lust and desire. "You want it so badly," she confessed, "the trepidation gets lost in the passion."

Penelope leaped up, starry eyed and flighty as a hummingbird. "You must help me with the wedding plans, Laynie. You have brilliant ideas, and this way it will be partly your wedding, too."

"Yes, of course. Thank you Pen, it sounds wonderful. I'd love to be your co-conspirator." She gained her feet, and arm in arm the women ambled to the front door. "Can't you stay a little while longer?"

"I dare not. Madame Bodane has just received a new shipment of tulle. And before the best of the collection is taken, I must select what is to be used for my veil. Come visit later this week. The sketches she prepared are divine. It's to be a wedding gown beyond compare." Penelope's voice held a dreamy quality, and her eyes shone with visions of her perfect wedding and her perfect future.

"I'm sure it will be the best of the season, and I promise to see you soon."

She gave her friend a hug and a farewell peck on the cheek then watched and waved as Penelope took to her carriage. Alone and left to her own devices she wandered through the house. It was quiet as a mausoleum. Where was everyone?

"Do you know where Aunt Abigail might be?" she asked Merrick, as he sat reviewing tenant records in the east wing.

"I believe," he replied, with a grin, "she's enjoying a carriage ride with Mr. Colt."

"Do tell." Her aunt was seeing quit a bit of Samuel Colt. His visits put a glow in her cheeks and spring in her step. "And Walker? Has he gone to town?"

The older man looked up. "He rode out to inspect the lower forty. He seems to like the out-of-doors. I expect he misses being at sea, Miss Trelayne...I mean Mrs. Garrison."

"Oh Merrick, you mustn't call me Mrs. Garrison. It makes me feel ancient. Besides, you and Wynona are family. Simply call me Trelayne. Please," she added at his contrary expression. "I insist."

"It isn't the natural order of things," he grumbled. "And you know I'm a stickler for orderliness."

"Well, at least give it a try. Do you think the Captain misses his former lifestyle?"

Merrick considered his answer before speaking. "He's the kind of man accustomed to open spaces, and if I may say so, to adventuring."

His words rang true. She hadn't thought enough about what their marriage meant to Walker in this respect, or what he had given up. How selfish. She just assumed he was happy living here at Royston Hall. But perhaps he wasn't. Perhaps his needs and desires were not being met. A prickle of unease poked at her. Walker was a man of action—he'd been a soldier and a sailor. How dull for him to worry over whether or not the crops were growing properly, or how disappointing for him to monitor the docks and watch the ships leave port without him.

"He's probably back by now," Merrick said. "Most likely in the stable."

She grinned and snared her old wool cloak on the run. At the barn, she silently slipped inside and paused. After the noontime glare, the atmosphere seemed muted. Dust motes twirled through the streaks of sunlight boldly spearing between cracks and holes. It was very quiet, not the usual melody of snorting, stomping, and hay munching. After a moment, her eyes adjusted to the dim light, and she spotted Walker.

His back to her, he brushed the only horse in the stable, crooning to the beast as he worked. She held back to admire his broad-shouldered physique. He was so big and tall and solid. She still marveled every time he held her in the shelter of his embrace. He was her fortress.

Having tossed aside his tweed jacket, he stood clad only in shirt, vest, tight breeches, and those rugged American boots—of which he seemed to have an unending supply. She liked that he maintained his own style. His big black hat and tickly mustache were two of her favorite things about him, although at present, thoughts of the rest of his body and the desire to see it here and now, took precedence. She pressed her thighs together to ease the throbbing brought on by her thoughts. She could never get enough of loving him, and prayed he felt the same.

Quiet as her cat, she sneaked up behind him and slipped her arms around his waist. With no hint of surprise, he continued brushing the horse. Nudging her hips against his backside, she slid her hands lower, covering his crotch. The brushing stopped, and what lay beneath his trousers came alive and alert.

"Is that you, Mrs. Garrison?" he asked, over his shoulder.

"Well, I should hope so. Who did you think it was?"

"There was a quite fetching maid traveling with the tin monger. They came by only this morning. I thought perhaps she'd returned alone for more than pleasant conversation."

"You rogue. What a wretched thing to say. Besides, the woman who travels with Mr. Brisbane is no maiden. She's at least forty years old, and the way she's always complaining about her chilblains, she would never survive a tussle with you."

"A tussle? Is that what they're calling it now days?"

"A proper rogering then," she dared to say.

He turned to face her.

"What unexpected vocabulary from such sweet lips."

Dipping his head, he captured her mouth with his, stifling further discussion. He dropped the currycomb, and grazed one hand across the bodice of her dress—quickening her heartbeat. They were kissing in the daylight, right here in the barn. It was outrageous, it was daring. What if they were caught?

Coming up for air, he eased her away from his chest, and smiled down at her. The horse whickered and bobbed his head as if in approval.

She glanced around. "Where are Jeb and all the other horses?"

"The farrier is here. Except for Mr. Darcy, Jeb's taken the lot to the far paddock for trimming and shoeing. They'll be at it for hours."

He slid one hand down to the apex of her thighs and pressed his fingers into the yards of fabric, finding the spot that led to bliss and the point of no return.

"I can think of something I'd like to be doing for the next few hours," he said.

With a come-hither look, she braced her hands against his chest as he rubbed between her legs and nuzzled her neck. A moan stuttered in her throat, and eyes closed, she was once more transported to a world holding only pleasure.

Shifting his hands, he gripped her bottom, held her close, and propelled her backward across the stable toward a mound of hay. His gaze never leaving her face, he loosened the clasp on her cloak. The garment tumbled to the ground, coming to rest beside the woolen jacket he'd abandoned earlier.

Taking her hands, he dropped to one knee, encouraging her to follow. The fragrant smell of grass-hay billowed around them as they stretched out side by side. Before he could distract her beyond her capacity to think clearly, she levered upward and boldly shifted to straddle his thighs.

Perched astride his body, her hands on his chest, she stared down at his wonderful face, and when he gave her that crooked smile that said he intended to make love to her no holds barred, a tremor quivered through her. He reached to make good his objective, but she captured his hands, and stayed the action.

"What's the matter, too good to do it in the barn?" he teased.

She released his wrists, and stroked the bulge below his belt. "I'll show you good—and better," she shot back. "But I want to talk to you first."

"Talk," he sputtered, "with you touching me like that, I can barely think, let alone talk."

"I wanted to be sure I had your full attention," she explained.

"Undivided."

"Are you happy here?" she asked.

"Delirious."

He eased his hands under her skirts and worked his way between the folds of material. Seeking and finding her pantaloons, he gently rent the seam in the crotch and proceeded to explore with his fingers what lay beneath the fragile material.

"I'm serious," she gasped, barely able to talk now herself. "I don't ever want you to regret marrying me. I don't want you to yearn for the sea or anything but me."

"I love you Trelayne, and I'm yearning only for you—burning only for you,"

"Are you sure?"

"Yes." His hands stilled, resting on her thighs. "Traveling the world and being at sea was a good life, but a hard one. Now I've got the memories to last me forever with none of the adversity."

"But what about New Bedford? I know you miss it. I see it in your eyes every time you speak of America."

"I do miss Massachusetts," he admitted, "and

someday we'll travel there, and I'll show you my house. We'll share the adventure together. To return by myself would make me unbearably lonely. And if you said you couldn't or wouldn't go with me, I would stay here forever. Wherever we are together is home. Now be a good wife and unbutton my trousers."

Rather than obey his direct order, she unbuttoned his vest and shirt, smoothed the linen aside, and grazed her hands across the wide plane of his torso. He watched her every move, the expression in his eyes hazy with contentment. When she finally reached for his belt and undid his trousers, he bucked his hips upward in anticipation and the part of him now belonging to her sprung forth big and full and ready to take her to a place she coveted more and more.

Just the thought of what was to come made her wet, and taking the initiative, she crawled forward and hovered above him. Guiding the most needful part of him through the opening rent in her pantaloons, she slid downward in one, slow, delicious movement.

"Oh, God, Trelayne," he groaned.

Savoring the feel of him deep inside of her, she dug her fingernails into his bare chest.

"So it's hot lust you want today, and not sweet gentle loving."

"Yes," she breathed, rocking back and forth.

He let her move at will. It was exhilarating to be in control, to set the pace and conquer the male beast. She rode the man-animal without a care for his desires, lost in a world of gratification, although her enjoyment always seemed a please him as well.

Suddenly he spanned her waist with his hands, and lifting her off his body, set her aside.

"What are you doing?" she cried, scrambling to her hands and knees atop the abandoned coat and cloak. She wanted more, wanted to scream with disappointment and unfulfilled need.

"Walker," she keened and panted.

"Shhh, little tiger, we aren't done yet."

Kneeling behind her, he brushed her skirts aside, and tearing the opening in her pantaloons larger, he took her from behind. She twisted her fingers in the wool, bracing her body as he slammed against her, forcing the air from her lungs and a moan from her throat. He took command now. Gripping the fabric of her dress in one hand, he held her in place then sliding the other hand around to the front, he sought the delicate spot he so skillfully tortured to perfection.

They had never done *this* before—it felt naughty—it felt wonderful. Each slow, deliberate, driving force sent a wave of animal hunger rippling through her body. Each groan escaping Walker raised her desire.

Moans became guttural cries. Uninhibited, she arched her bottom taking in the full length of him, and clawing at the wool, head back, she writhed with pleasure. The sweat of rising need dampened the inside of her thighs, and flushed with a craving that could wait no longer, she cried out and went over the edge. Wrapped in a release more overwhelming than ever before, she lost contact with the world around her. Walker grabbed her around the waist with both hands, and with one last forceful thrust, followed her to the end delight, leaving them both panting.

With a playful growl, he bent over her, and nuzzled and nipped at the back of her neck.

Then they smelled the smoke.

****

Lucien tossed the empty bucket of lamp oil aside, and watched the flames curl up the north wall of the stable. She was a bitch in heat. Just now he'd seen her screwing the good Captain like an animal.

On the outside looking in, he'd watched through the cracks in the barn. He felt like a beggar boy denied entrance to a fine restaurant—hungry for what he could never have, watching the man he hated partake of a feast that should have been his.

How could he ever have thought her worthy of his love and devotion? She was no better than a common whore. No better than Beatrice. He missed Beatrice, more than he ever imagined he would. Now he had no one—other than the voices in his head.

Limping away from the heat and smoke, he took shelter by the corncrib. His body, broken and bruised, throbbed and ached and he rubbed his thigh to ease the pain. When the balloon had gone down, he'd been dragged for miles along the rocky coast, tangled in the ropes, no escape from the agonizing battering of his face, left hand, and left leg. He'd languished in the night barely alive, wishing to die. But a fisherman had found him on the shore the next morning. And like it or not, he'd lived. Now, a monster scraped raw and scarred for life, he was the ugly hideous part of society he had always scorned and hated.

Clasping his head in his hands, he tried to make the pain stop. It was agony, greater than any he had known existed. And it kept getting worse. The voices trapped in the pain told him it was her fault, and she deserved to die. She had refuted their bright and glowing love, turning it into a dark malicious cloud. It was a putrid caul poisoning his thoughts, leading him to this end. Now she would suffer the pain he felt.

****

Walker leaped up, dragging Trelayne to her feet. They jammed their clothing into place and ran to the walk-through door. It was locked.

Catching the scent of smoke, Mister Darcy reared up, snapping the lead on his halter. Frightened by the acrid smell, the poor beast charged about, first one way then the other, knocking over feed bins, hay forks, and wheelbarrows.

"Stay behind me," Walker ordered, as he tossed his vest aside and slipped free of his shirt.

One hand resting on his back, she kept pace as he stepped closer to the horse.

"It's all right, old boy. Calm down, Mister Darcy. Good boy."

For one split-second, the horse paused and turned toward the familiar voice. Walker grabbed the halter, slid the shirt over the horse's face, and tucked the tails of fabric beneath the leather straps. The horse reared one more time, nearly jerking Walker off his feet, but he held tight not relinquishing his hold. Then the animal pawed the ground and stood trembling.

Trelayne ran to the sliding barn door and pulled with all her might. It wouldn't budge. The smoke was drifting lower creating a swirling cloud of choking fumes. Through the haze she saw flames on the roof. If it caved in, they were dead, no mistake.

"Trelayne..."

She hurried back to her husband's side. He took her right hand and placed what remained of the lead in it. "Take him over to the big door. A little fresh air should be seeping in around it. I'm going to try and break down the walk-through."

Tears burned in her eyes from the smoke, and from the fear they may not survive this ordeal. She didn't want to leave his side, but knew she must. "I love you," she whispered.

"I love you, too." He kissed her forehead, and smoothed her hair back from her face. "We're going to be all right," he added, and eased her on her way. "Don't try to hold him, tie him up. He may get out of control again when he hears the noise I'm about to make."

With his face still covered, Mister Darcy followed obediently.

Using an iron crow, Walker levered the hinges on the door. Built to withstand the abuse of rambunctious livestock, it was solid built, and wasn't about to give way easily.

When the roof creaked, Trelayne cringed, expecting the wooden beams to come crashing down at any moment. How could this have happened? Surely someone would see the smoke and come to help.

"Easy, Mr. Darcy," she soothed, petting the nervous gelding. "My husband will save us. He's very resourceful and brave and handsome, and oh dear Lord, please don't let it end like this."

Trying to filter the smoke from the air, she buried her face in the horse's mane.

Chapter Twenty-Seven

The hinges burst loose on the wooden door, and Walker wrenched open the portal only to shove it back into place. A wall of flames waited on the other side. Someone had piled tree limbs and debris against the opening, creating a barrier Hell would have been proud to call to its own. With the exit rendered useless, he groped a path back across the stable, trying to tamp down his fear, hoping it didn't show in his face

"It's no good going that way. We might be able to get out through the roof."

"But what about Mister Darcy? We can't leave him here. I won't leave him here."

He hadn't brought along his pistol today. An amateur mistake. He was becoming too comfortable in this civilized environment. He slid his hand to the hilt of the knife Hargis had made for him. That would be a horror. Having no compassionate means of dispatching the beast, he supposed it was all for one and one for all.

Optimism fading fast, he wrestled again with the sliding door. It remained jammed tight, but at least no roaring infernal met his gaze as he peered through a nearby crack.

"Maybe we could tunnel beneath the door," she suggested.

"Good idea."

As he turned to search for an implement with

which to dig, Trelayne was seized by a coughing fit, and the horse snorted snot and slobber. There wasn't time for trenching. Before long they wouldn't be able to breathe.

"I'm going up top," he said. "No matter what happens, you must stay right here. I'll drop down on the outside and open the doors."

****

"It's too dangerous. There are already flames up there."

"It's the only way."

"Wait."

She took off her petticoat and tore it into strips. After wetting the fabric in the water trough, they tied one piece across Walker's mouth and nose and wrapped the others around and around his hands.

Their gazes locked, and he chucked her under the chin. The expression in his eyes said he wouldn't let the magic die, wouldn't let this be the end.

Wringing her hands, tears streaming down her cheeks, she watched Walker climb the ladder to the haymow. Then his image disappeared in the smoke billowing down from above.

Pounding ensued followed by a flash of daylight. Fresh air streaked in through the new opening, offering relief. Then fear returned tenfold as the downdraft breathed life into all the pockets of smoldering hay. Fire leaped up from all sides creeping closer. Grabbing a bucket, she sloshed water over the horse, herself, and the ground around them.

Her chest ached from the smoke, and from the deep sobs she couldn't hold back. A prayer on her lips, she remembered being a little girl and playing in the barn.

She remembered when Mister Darcy had been foaled, and how her father had laughed good-naturedly when she insisted on naming him after a character in one of her favorite novels. No, no, no. Didn't people about to die have their lives flash before them? She must think of the future, not the past. A future where her parents were recovered and returned home. A future where she was big with child—Walker beaming at the prospect of being a father. Just the other night, she'd had such a dream. What a surprise and delight to have such a happy vision.

The gelding trembled, and she hugged him close. His eyes remained covered, but he needed no vision to grasp the dire circumstances. Sweat trickled down between her breasts. Her back felt scorched, the air so hot it hurt to even think of taking another breath. Walker coming to her rescue was the only thing keeping paralyzing fear at bay.

Dizzy and at the breaking point, she leaned against the door and nearly fell on her face as it slid sideways. Merrick gathered her close, ushering her out into the fresh air. Jeb surged forward to lead Mister Darcy to safety.

Wynona was there too. Trelayne grasped the cup of water she offered, downing the cooling liquid in great gulps. When she could think straight, she glanced around. Where was Walker? Why wasn't he at her side? Then she noticed the upturned faces of the people gathered around. She followed suit, and gasped in shock. He was still on the roof. And he wasn't alone.

Walker stood tall, holding his position on the near wall. The fabric once used to cover his mouth was pushed down around his neck. "So you survived your ill-fated balloon ride," he acknowledged.

"More or less," Lucien replied, as he limped forward and steadied himself against a smoldering upright. "But the two of you won't survive this conflagration."

"Again, your plan seems a bit poorly thought out. My wife is safe and I intend to join her shortly."

Lucien peered over the side of the roof. "How unfortunate," he spat, his gaze boring into her. "It appears I'll have to be satisfied with seeing only you die a torturous death. She can watch. It will no doubt be even more painful to her than dying."

Lucien drew a large pistol from the waistband of his trousers and aimed the muzzle directly at Walker's bare chest.

Trelayne dropped the cup and made to run forward. Merrick grabbed her around the waist and held her in place. "Leave it be," he insisted. "Don't be distracting him. He's accustomed to ship's riggings and high places and dealing with scallywags."

Bowing to Merrick's wisdom, and trusting to Walker's fortitude, she choked back the desire to call out his name. A hush fell over the crowd, leaving only the sound of groaning timbers and the crackle of flames to fill the air.

As if trying to erase his pain, or an unwanted memory, Lucien shuddered and scrubbed his free hand across his face. Off balance, he fought for better footing.

"Don't do this, Lanteen," Walker called across to him. "Come down with me. We'll get medical treatment for your wounds, and sort this all out."

Someone handed Wynona a quilt. "Mr. Lanteen's

truly lost his mind," she whispered, slipping the counterpane around Trelayne.

"He never had far to go," Merrick muttered.

"That's true enough," Wynona agreed. "But how did he come to be so mangled about the body?"

"It must have happened when the balloon went down," Trelayne murmured. "We thought him dead, or safely arrived in France."

A mirthless grin contorted Lucien's face, and even from this distance, the madness in his eyes was feverishly bright. The beam the two men shared cracked and sagged and she jumped and took a step forward.

"You're not thinking clearly. Don't you see it's over?" Walker said.

"Nothing is over until I say it is. And I'm not crazy," Lucian bellowed. "You're the ones who don't see. This was the only way. We were all to die together. Now you've ruined that as well."

Silently, Walker unwound the strips of petticoat from his neck and hands. Then calmly and methodically, he tied them end-to-end.

"Any last words of love for the fair Trelayne, betrayer of my heart and soul," Lucien lamented. He cradled his head in one hand and snarled in pain, his voice that of a wounded animal.

The sun was hot, the nearby flames even hotter, but the words chilled her to the bone. Something bad was about to happen.

Staring up at the sky, Lucien leaped up and down. The beam broke, and both men dropped from sight, falling into the burning abyss once called the barn.

Trelayne clutched Wynona, and amidst the hellish

red glow and blistering heat, the world seemed frozen in time. She wanted to scream, thought she was screaming, but all she could hear was her pulse pounding in her ears, and all she could feel was the wild beating of her heart.

A mumble from the crowd drew her attention, and she glimpsed a thin ribbon of white looped around the lightning rod. A hand reached up beside the fragile safety line to grasp the metal bar. Then the top of Walker's head appeared as he hoisted himself onto what was left of the roof. Grasping the makeshift cloth rope, he half-crawled half-walked over to the edge. A man with a ladder ran forward. Seconds later, Walker was on the ground and at her side.

She buried her face against his chest, weeping with joy. He hugged her close until a series of wracking coughs beset him and he staggered to one side. She eased up under his right arm, and lending her shoulder for support, led him to a bench. Dropping to her knees at his side, she clung to him.

"We're all right now, love," he reassured her, and stroked her hair, "we're all right now."

With a great whoosh, the last of the roof collapsed and the flames leaped up nearly as high as the old oak on the other side of the water ditch. A bucket brigade was in full swing, but the attempt was useless. Thankfully, the building was surrounded by dirt-filled paddocks. With no vegetation growing near to the structure, the inferno was contained as it burned wildly and without pause.

"Poor Lucien," she whispered. "What a dreadful way to die."

"He was badly broken in body and soul," Walker

affirmed. "He didn't want to live any more. I could see it in his eyes."

She rose up on her knees, and eased her arms around his neck. "When I thought you had fallen to your death, I didn't want to live either."

"Hush now. Don't think about it anymore," he said softly. "We're both safe, and we have our whole life ahead of us. A good and happy life, with adventures to seek and happy dreams to fulfill."

Chapter Twenty-Eight

Two months later—off the coast of America:

Their opportunity for adventure came sooner than expected.

All of Trelayne's Christmas wishes came true. Jeffery and Penelope's opulent wedding had taken place without a hitch. The new barn, completed shortly thereafter, was ready before the truly cold temperatures set in. And her parents were almost fully recovered. The last happy revelation prompted her and Walker's journey to America.

For twenty days they had been at one another's side—eating royally, sleeping late, and despite the winter weather, promenading the deck at all hours of the day and night. Better still, they made love at all hours of the day and night. It was the true honeymoon previously denied to them, and once Trelayne found her sea legs, she was enthralled with the wildness of the ocean and the fascinating beauty of the night sky.

This morning, wrapped in her new fur-lined cape, she leaned against the starboard rail on the *Alicia Elaine* and counted her blessings while watching the dolphins swim alongside the ship. Walker stood at her back, protecting her from the wind, his solid form her anchor when the ship hit a rough spot or pitched and rolled.

315

Tipping her head back on his shoulder, she glimpsed the maze of lines and sails towering overhead behind him. A stunning arrangement of deliberate chaos, the forest of masts carried one hundred thousand square feet of canvas, and each sail had its own name and purpose. Last evening in the moonlight, Walker had pointed out the ones called Stargazer, Moonraker, and Cloudscraper.

She gazed again upon the sea, grateful for a peek into this corner of his world. She had never felt closer to him. And while she might be Walker's wife, the sea would always be his mistress, and she understood why. No woman could be more captivating or enchanting. It seemed once a man fell in love with the sea, you'd lost that part of him forever. But if the mysterious deep was his only distraction, she would not complain.

"A penny for your thoughts," he whispered, in her ear.

Where to start…"I marvel at the changes wrought upon my life in so short a span of time," she admitted.

He pressed closer. "You've been confronted with many obligations and harrowing experiences," he agreed. "I'm so proud of the way you've faced each challenge."

"The changes haven't all been challenges," she corrected. "Having you in my life is a gift requiring no effort at all on my part. And before long, we will have our first child."

He slipped his hands inside her cloak, splaying his fingers across her belly. "I thought you were toying with me when you described your dream on New Year's Day."

"I had it again last night," she laughed.

"Perambulator after perambulator, parading by, filled with little smiling faces."

"That's one dream I'm glad to help make come true."

After learning she was with child, he hovered over her like a protective archangel, and she loved the attention—she loved him. What would she ever do without him?

"Begging your pardon, Captain Garrison," a voice interrupted. "May I speak with you, please?"

The golden moment broken, Walker released her. She sighed as the warmth surrounding her slipped away and they turned in unison to find Captain Parker awaiting their attention. On this voyage, Walker traveled as a passenger. No captain's quarters for them. Instead they were granted the finest traveling accommodations, their every need seen to. And rather than being saddled with the burden of running a ship, Walker was afforded a carefree journey. Something he hadn't experienced in a good long while.

"Yes, Parker," Walker acknowledged. "What might I do for you?"

"Just wanted to alert you regarding a small matter. Seems we may have a stowaway on board."

"What makes you think so?" Walker asked.

"Just the usual. Missing food from the larder, a stolen blanket. Little things such as that."

"I see." Walker's expression transformed from mildly curious to obviously concerned.

"Perhaps one of the crew took the food," she put in.

"Oh, no, Ma'am," Captain Parker countered. "On board ship, the taking of food from the larder, guns from the armory, or rum from the medical locker be hanging offenses."

His words stunned her. The shock must have shown on her face.

Walker placed one hand at the small of her back to steady her. "It sounds harsh, love, but I assure you its quite necessary. Some voyages can last a year or more, during which time dire circumstances can arise to push men beyond endurance and clear thinking. Rules such as these, ruthless as they seem, can mean the difference between the crew's survival and sure death."

Again she wondered at the kind of life he'd led upon the sea. To be isolated for months on end, trapped in a world unto itself, the prevailing law and one's own existence governed by the integrity of those around you. It rather crushed the romantic illusion she had built up over the last few weeks.

"Thank you for the information, Captain Parker," Walker recognized. "We shall keep our eyes open, and alert you should we come across any useful information."

"I'd be obliged." Parker nodded then headed toward the top deck.

Misgiving tiptoed down her spine, and the odd feeling of being watched niggled at the back of her mind. "Do you suppose someone really did stow away on the ship?" she asked, glancing around.

"It's possible. Most likely a young lad with aspirations of being a cabin boy. Better a hard life at sea with three meals a day, than a hard life on dry land with an empty belly. He'll probably present himself at port and beg for a job. Or it could simply be someone with high hopes of making a new life in America. Either way, Mrs. Garrison, you're not to worry," he encouraged. "Let's go below and have some of that tea you like. I'll even have a cup."

She gave a chuckle, knowing what a concession this was. Walker remained a staunch coffee drinker, not something terribly common in her family. She supposed she would have to learn to prepare the dreadful concoction.

"How can I turn down such an offer?" she laughed. "Watching you choke down chamomile tea always brightens my day."

"When we reach New Bedford," he declared, giving credence to her thoughts. "I'm brewing up the biggest pot of coffee you've ever seen, eggshells and all. After we see your parents, of course," he amended. "That's first on the agenda."

Being with her mother and father was a much anticipated joy. She'd waited so long for this day. "I'm terribly excited to see them. Thank you for arranging to have all of their needs met, and then some. I know such good care was paramount in speeding their recovery."

"You're welcome. Now come along. I've detailed plans for entertaining you until we make port."

"Does it involve more than watching you drink tea?" she teased, knowing exactly what was on his mind.

"Oh quite."

As snowflakes swirled around in fairytale fashion, he gently seized the edges of her fur-trimmed hood, drew her close, and kissed her lips.

****

Gripping Trelayne's elbow, Walker carefully escorted her along the icy dock of the New Bedford harbor.

It was snowing in earnest now, and by the look of the sky, it would get worse before it was done. He touched the St. Brendan medal, giving thanks for their safe crossing and for being on dry land. Then a familiar twinge of discontent wended through him. The harbor brought back recollections of the day Philip and Ophelia had been hurt. And the snow reminded him of the day he'd lost Katie.

Trelayne grappled onward, nary a misstep or hesitation. In spirit she was so much like Kathleen. They would have liked one another, or perhaps he just hoped it would be true because he wanted to have Katie's blessing for going on with his life without her. To do so was harder than he'd imagined. Starting over was a daunting task, and if not for Trelayne, and the love he felt for her and from her, it would never have been possible. It was not easy giving oneself over to deep emotion. He knew first hand the pain of losing someone when they became your whole world—became your reason for living—and then were gone forever.

As they entered the hospital, she gazed up at him and smiled. He was so proud to be her husband—and still fevered at the thought of being her lover.

A man in a white coat sauntered forward, his hand outstretched and reaching for Walker's.

"The lost sheep has returned to the fold," he declared with a grin.

"This is Dr. Nathan Robinson," Walker introduced, as he vigorously shook the man's hand. "He runs this amazing facility, and claims my beating him at chess is due to his compassion and not my skill. Nate, my wife,

Trelayne."

"I'm honored to meet you, Mrs. Garrison. You're obviously a good influence on this old rascal. I've never seen Walker looking so well."

Trelayne beamed at the praise. "Thank you, Doctor, for the kind words, and for all you've done for my parents."

"Come this way," Nate offered, escorting them down the hall. "They're eagerly awaiting your arrival, bags packed and ready to go."

As they entered the solarium, Trelayne broke away and ran forward to hug and kiss first her father and then her mother. Left standing alone, Walker felt lost and a bit jealous. Then a smile wove its way across his face as it occurred to him he would soon be a parent too. Hopefully his own child would someday show him such love and devotion.

"You look wonderful, Trelayne. Are you happy, dear?" Ophelia asked.

"Ecstatic," Trelayne replied, taking to a small stool at her mother's side. "And seeing the two of you is the answer to my prayers."

Philip St.Christopher gained his feet, and with the help of a cane, ambled forward.

"Good to see you, Walker. According to the letters we've been receiving, we are in you debt. It sounds like keeping Trelayne safe and getting to the bottom of this whole affair was quite the formidable task."

"We do seem to attract misadventure wherever we go. But keeping Trelayne from harm is as important to me as it is to the two of you. I hope you both understand that, sir."

"We do," Philip nodded. "The marriage came as a

bit of a surprise, but a good one. And from the look of things, that task has proved less formidable for you."

"Not a task, Philip," he corrected, "a joy."

"And soon, Poppa, there will be even more joy when you become a grandfather."

"What?" Ophelia squealed, in unladylike fashion. "Are you sure?"

"Yes, Mother. And if my dream comes true, this will be the first of many."

"Oh, darling. You aren't still having nightmares, are you?" Ophelia worried.

"Of course not, Mother. Only happy prophesies now. And Aunt Abigail secretly confirmed my future with her gypsy friend."

Ophelia gave a sputtering laugh. "So she's still living precariously. How is my sister? She must be lonely with Branwell gone to India and the two of you here."

Walker grinned, amused by what he knew was coming.

"She's had a gentleman caller recently," Trelayne revealed. "He's an American," she added. "And they're very hard to resist."

Chapter Twenty-Nine

Trelayne had been awake for hours, rambling around the house. Still requiring rest, her parents remained asleep in one of the other three bedrooms.

Her husband's New Bedford home was large, rugged, and sturdy. Just like him—just like this bold America. And although somewhat modest in size by English standards, the house was well appointed, an eclectic collection of items from around the world.

In the library, Walker's spirit was definitely the driving force, revealing part of the story behind the man. Decidedly masculine, it was infused with the aroma of leather, polished wood, and tobacco. A huge fireplace dominated one wall. A large map of America presided over another. And all available space in between was taken up by bookshelves, framed artwork, and Native Indian items.

Keeping company with the rifles and swords were painted buffalo robes, war shirts, moccasins, and spears. It seemed a room full of wonders where a little boy could dream. Yet the big roll top desk, littered with papers, declared work relative to a full-grown man also took place here.

Work—that's where Walker was at present, down at the docks seeing to business, but he'd assured her, he'd not be home late. And he promised they would have a festive evening meal to celebrate her parent's first full day out of the hospital.

She trailed her fingertips along the edge of the desk, and inhaled deeply of his essence so imbedded in the room. Then with a smile upon her lips, she wandered down the hallway to the kitchen.

"Exactly what will we be serving tonight?" she asked the man sitting at the table.

Willie Mathews seemed to be the only "servant" Walker employed. Willie was a long time friend, and being too old for sea duty, was now a landlocked butler, valet, and handyman.

"Aye, good morning to you, Mrs. Garrison. Let's see now," he considered, and cleared his throat. "We'll be havin' wild turkey with stuffing and gravy, sweet potato pie, Indian corn pudding, and cherry cobbler." The little bulldog of a man rattled off the menu with pride and anticipation.

"And several pots of coffee," she threw in, with a grin.

"Dang blast," he swore. "Oh, beggin' your pardon. I just remembered we're out of coffee beans. That won't do."

"Where must I go to purchase some?" she volunteered, wanting to be sure her husband had his favorite hot beverage on hand.

"Well now, it's snowing pretty hard, Mrs. Garrison, and the store's a goodly walk from here. I'm thinkin' the Captain wouldn't want you out on such a day."

"Nonsense," she countered, feeling up for a good challenge. "We have snow in England, too, you know."

Despite her bravado, a quick glance out the window gave her pause. Although offering brief periods of respite, the billowy white flakes fell with determination. It was piling up quickly, adding a layer of pristine white to the old brown-tinged mounds already heaped up along the streets and walkways. Not to worry. She wanted to do this for Walker, wanted to contribute to the meal he was so intent upon serving them tonight.

"I'd best be goin' with you," Willie offered, setting aside the silverware he'd been polishing.

"No, please don't interrupt your work. Besides, when Mother and Father awaken they'll want breakfast, and you know where everything is and what's available. Please," she implored, fastening her cloak. "Just tell me the directions to the shop,"

Willie met her request as she unearthed a woolen cap from a trunk in the front hall and snugged it into place. Tugging on a pair of matching mittens, she opened the door and stepped out onto the porch.

"I ain't feelin' good about you goin' off by yourself, as it were," Willie called after her. "The weather here about can change in a heartbeat, and not for the better."

"I'll be fine," she called back. "Really I will."

The cold made her catch her breath, but it felt good to be outside in the fresh air. Watching for icy patches, she stepped along with a lightheartedness that came from being truly happy—happy with her husband, happy with her life, happy with the thought of simply completing this innocent little mission to procure something important for Walker.

A burst of wind at her back pushed her along, and her smile broadened. See, even the elements were on her side. Although, she had to concede, the devious cold had already found passage through her layers of clothing, and her toes were tingly. No matter. There was the store just up ahead.

Gratefully, she hurried inside, quickly shutting the door against the swirl of snow following in her wake.

"Mercy," she laughed, and made her way to the counter.

The shop was small, but cheerful and immaculately clean with shelves full of various blends of coffee. A big shiny machine stood at the ready to grind out special orders if what was available didn't meet one's needs. It hadn't occurred to her there would be so many choices.

"Oh, dear."

Crestfallen, her gaze flitted around the room. She had no idea what Walker's favorite variety might be. Perhaps the man behind the counter would know.

"Good day," she began. "I'm Captain Garrison's wife. Might you be familiar with my husband's preferred blend?"

"Glad to meet you, Mrs. Garrison. I'm Andrew Benson. He usually requests Java—with just a hint of Turkish and a kiss of Brazilian."

"How extraordinary. It sounds as if you're creating a perfume rather than coffee."

"To some the aroma is nearly as pleasing, the flavor like nectar."

"Very poetic," she said, and smiled. "I promise to work on my appreciation for the infusion. Would you make some up for me, please?"

"I heard the Captain had returned, and I have some right here."

"Why, thank you. Is it possible for you to put that

on our account? I've left the house without a pence to my name."

"A wedding gift to the both of you," the shopkeeper offered, handing her the canvas bag of fragrant beans.

"How very kind. Again, thank you."

"Captain Garrison is well respected in these parts. And without his ships," he added with a smile and a shrug, "the coffee wouldn't get here in the first place. Enjoy."

"I will." Following such glowing praise for her husband, her heart soared. "We will," she corrected, and took her leave.

Heady with pride and her love for Walker, she set off for home. That would take some getting used to, thinking of Walker's house as home. Everything here seemed so different, yet people everywhere had the same hopes and dreams, the same fears and regrets. She supposed where one was born, or to where they eventually strayed, was one of life's many mysteries. A year ago she could never have imagined being happily married, joyfully pregnant, and so very far away from England. Yet here she was.

Beginning to feel the cold in earnest, she quickened her pace, glad her destination was not far. Willie's prediction had come true, the weather had taken a turn. A blast of wind sent a blinding white veil across her path, limiting her vision to only a few feet. It whipped the once soft and fluffy flakes into needle sharp sleet and came at her from every direction. Struggling to keep her footing, she bent into the wind.

"Carriage ride, ma'am?" a voice rang out.

It was silly, she had less than two blocks left to

travel, but the going was near impossible. Why not ride? Once home, surely Willie would have money on hand to pay for the service.

"Yes, thank you," she agreed, and clamored aboard the old fashioned transport. With a sigh of relief she settled back against the hard wooden seat. Then leaning forward, she called through the open space behind the driver. "I'm only going a short distance to the big house on the hill," she instructed.

"I know where you're going, Mrs. Garrison."

Again, the glow of pride warmed her. Did everyone in town know Walker? He seemed almost to be an icon in New Bedford. As they drew closer to the house, she adjusted her woolen hat and gathered her cloak in preparation for the descent from the coach and the dash to the house. But rather than slowing down, the carriage picked up speed.

"No, you've made a mistake. You're passing the house."

"There's been no mistake, Mrs. Garrison. Just a difference of opinion regarding your destination."

"Who are you? What are you talking about? I insist you stop the coach."

She pushed opened the door and contemplated jumping. Then thoughts of the baby ruled out such an option. As she reached for the door to slam it back shut, the bag of coffee slid from her lap onto the street. The canvas pouch struck a stone and burst open spewing out the beans—leaving a stain dark as blood in the pure white snow.

****

Walker managed to get away from work earlier than anticipated. Rather than taking the chance of coming dockside during the horrendous blow, two of his ships were riding out the storm at sea. He tried not to view their misfortune as his good luck, but damn he was pleased to be heading home early.

Home…he hadn't imagined he would miss New Bedford so much. But his trip to England had reinforced his love of America, and his fondness for his seaside house.

Disregarding the ice, he bounded up the front steps, skidded to the door, and chuckling at his own boyish enthusiasm, entered his house.

"Willie," he called, striding down the hall. "How are preparations going for tonight's dinner?" He rubbed his hands together in anticipation. "Why don't I smell that turkey roasting?"

Gaining the kitchen, he stopped short. Willie and Trelayne's parents sat around the table looking solemn as undertakers. Something was dreadfully wrong. The only one missing was Trelayne.

"What's happened? Where is she?"

"She went out for coffee beans," Willie said, "and ain't come back."

A shock of heat flashed through him. Then a cold sweat broke out on his chest. Panic squeezed at his heart just as it had the day she'd been kidnapped from the charity bazaar. But that was crazy, Lucien was dead, and who else would want to harm her? There had to be a logical reason for her having gone missing.

"When?"

"A little over an hour ago. I shouldn't have let her go alone, but she wouldn't take no for an answer. Said you had to have your coffee tonight."

His coffee? *It was his fault she'd gone out.* Now a

barge-load of guilt was added to his concern. He turned to leave. "I'll go check at the shop."

"Already did," Willie said, stopping him. "Mr. Benson said she'd been there and gone. I was just figurin' to go lookin' for her in the other direction," he added, wrestling on a sheepskin coat and a tattered beaver-skin hat.

Willie at his side, Walker retraced his steps to the street. Squinting through the blinding white, he tried to push his fears aside as flashes of losing Katie in a blizzard clawed through his mind adding past terror to the present. Pacing north along the road, he spotted the torn canvas bag and heap of coffee beans. She'd been so close to home, but had kept going. Willie pointed out the barely discernible carriage tracks.

"She left on foot," Willie said, "but the weather wasn't so bad when she set out."

It didn't make sense. Had she been walking and someone picked her up? Had she taken the carriage by choice? Where was his wife, was she cold, was she frightened? And what about the baby? Anger now replaced his fear. The urge to tear something or someone to pieces brought a rush of energy surging through his body.

He searched for a coach to summon so they might follow the trail before it was completely gone, but the street was deserted. Anyone with half a wit was inside, and most likely hunkered down in front of a roaring fire. He headed back toward the house and the stable where he kept two mounts.

"Come on, Willie. No use trying to follow on foot. We'll get the horses and head north—it's our only hope."

Almost to the front steps, he heard someone calling his name.

He turned to see a lone figure materialize out of the curtain of white. It was a lad, bundled up from head to toe, waving a letter as he stumbled along. Walker caught the youngster as he careened to an exhausted halt. It was Jimmy Thompson, the baker's son. The family lived on the other end of town. Jimmy looked near frozen—the letter iced into his mitten-clad hand. Picking the boy up, he carried him into the house.

Extracting the letter from his grip, he let Mrs. St.Christopher lead the boy to the hearth to warm him up.

Willie peered over his shoulder. "What's it say, Captain."

The parchment was wet and the ink smeared, but he was able to make out the heart-stopping message.

If you wants to see your woman again, come
to the old mill north of town at 5 P.M. Come alone.

"I don't get it," Willie said. "Why ain't they askin' for ransom?"

"A good question, Willie." He turned toward the boy. "Jimmy, what did the person look like who gave you the letter?"

Jimmy screwed up his face in thought as he stood dripping by the hearth. "He were on the burly side and mean looking. And he talked funny, like Mr. Northrop who runs that shop what sells them fancy gewgaws from England."

With a start Walker realized it sounded a lot like Bartholomew Grimsby. Adding in Captain Parker's suspicion about there being a stowaway onboard the *Alicia Elaine*, it tied in perfectly. Damn the son of a bitch. In England, rumor had it he was still in France, but he'd been right there the entire trip, watching their every move, spying on them, waiting and plotting. Now he had Trelayne, and that meant he had Walker too.

"You were correct," he said to Willie. "This isn't a matter of money. It's a matter of unfinished business. Deadly, unfinished, business."

Chapter Thirty

As the carriage skidded to a halt, Trelayne flung the door open and scrambled to the ground. The snow was deep, the footing slippery, her escape short lived. The man driving the coach caught her by the hood of her cloak, and near choking the life out of her, dragged her toward a hulking building.

Inside, he shoved her into a chair, and with but a few quick turns of a waiting rope, secured her firmly to the piece of furniture. She kicked and struggled, her attempts useless. Seemingly amused at her futile efforts, he laughed and lit an oil lamp.

Realizing she was accomplishing little other than exhausting herself and providing entertainment, she stopped struggling, trying to slow her racing heart as she studied her surroundings.

The building was a deserted mill, the massive wooden wheels and cogs silent and draped with cobwebs. Torn burlap bags lay heaped in one corner, a pile of moldering wheat in another. A rat squeaked and took cover as the man walked toward a table to set the lamp down beside a pipe and a bottle of rum. As he took to the chair, the glow of light washed across his face. She knew him. He'd been with Lucien the day of the charity bazaar. It was Grimsby, the man Walker had long sought but could never make pay for his crimes.

Disoriented, as if reliving a nightmare, she glanced

around half expecting Lucien to materialize out of the dark. But he was dead, and she was here in America, and this was to be a special night with her family and husband.

"What do you want, Mr. Grimsby?" she snapped, angry with this man for disrupting her life. "If it's money you're after, you could have selected better accommodations to await the transaction."

"So you've recognized me," he said, the pride evident in his voice. "No, it's not money for which I've come, but recompense of a more personal nature. This is where it all started, and this is where it will end. The good Captain has escaped death twice, once right here in New Bedford, and once in Brighton. But as the saying goes, the third time's the charm."

At his inference, the blood drained from her head leaving her dizzy and sick at her stomach. He didn't want money. He didn't want her. He only wanted her husband. And Walker would surely come—she was the perfect bait. She and the baby. This monster must never realize he had two bargaining chips.

"What have you against him?" she pressed, trying to reason out his obsession with murdering the man she loved.

Grimsby uncorked the bottle, took a healthy swig, and wiped the back of his hand across his mouth. "It's a matter of principle," he barked, slamming the bottle down on the tabletop. He sounded belligerent, and she guessed this was not his first nip of the day. "I don't like leaving unfinished business. And it's a matter of loyalty. Because of him two of my boys in Brighton are dead, and one's in jail. And I'm also doing it for Beatsie."

Beatsie? He must mean Beatrice, Lucien's mistress.

"I remember her. What was she to you?" If she kept him talking, maybe she could learn something useful to turn his intentions.

"She was my sister. And from what I hear you helped her off the top of that Abbey."

"No, it's not true. It was an accident. I wished her no harm. You weren't there, how could you know?"

"I ran into Lucien before he burned up in your barn. He denied it was his fault, and that leaves you. It did my heart good to see what he'd become. Just deserts if ever there was any." He grabbed the bottle and took another pull. "In the end he were no better than me. And he were no smarter. Now I'm going to finish what he couldn't. I'm gonna kill the Captain, and give you a taste of what it's like to lose someone you love."

"He won't come for me," she lied. "We had a terrible fight. I hate it here in America—didn't want to come in the first place. I'm going back as soon as the weather permits."

"Ha, that's a good one, Mrs. Garrison. I seen the two of you aboard ship, cooing and petting like the lovers you are."

"You were the stowaway."

"That I was. No use wasting good money when you can get the ride for free."

"Oh, I wish they'd caught you and thrown you overboard."

"If wishes were horses the postman would ride," he chortled. "Now shut yer yap and stop prattling."

She fell silent, and the stillness of the cavernous

building was unnerving. A tomb or mausoleum couldn't be more inhospitable. Then the wind switched direction, making her jump as it spattered sleet along the north side of the millhouse. It grated and scraped against the wood like sand blasting out of a hot desert, but it was far from hot. She shivered with cold, wishing this night to be over, yet dreading what it might bring.

****

"The note said to come alone," Walker pointed out, changing into warmer clothes.

"Well, I ain't staying behind," Willie insisted. "I was with you when that mizzen mast broke and they dug the two of us out of the rubble, and I been with you through a dozen other hair-raising experiences. I'll hang back and stay out of the way."

"All right," Walker conceded. He wouldn't mind having another gun along. There was no guarantee Grimsby was in this alone. "But you stay low. I don't want you getting hurt. You're not as young as you used to be."

"Of course I ain't as young as I used to be. That's an impossibility. What kind of thing is that to say? Here," he tossed a pair of fur-lined gloves at Walker. "It's cold enough out there to freeze the balls off a brass monkey," he muttered.

"Just be careful," Walker reiterated, trying to stem the verbal tidal wave Willie was wont to unleash when he was wound up and heading into danger or adventure.

Dressed for foul weather, and armed sufficiently, they led the horses to the street and mounted up. The packed snow on the road had turned to ice, and as the animals fought for purchase, the going was slow.

"Let's see if the footing's any more stable off the

road," he hollered, over the wind.

They swung to the right. The sun dropped low, playing tricks with the shadows. His horse found solid ground, but Willie's mount stumbled in a ditch, sending Willie flying. A tree stump abruptly stopped his trajectory.

Walker vaulted out of the saddle, and crouched at his friend's side.

"Dammit to hell," Willie gritted, "caught me in the ribs. I'm guessing I broke two or three, but I can still ride."

"No you can't, and no you won't"

As gently as possibly he helped Willie to his feet. Each step was an agony, and his old friend couldn't stifle the groans of pain.

"Just a little farther, Willie. You can do it. I don't have time to take you all the way back to the house, and I'm not about to leave you to freeze in the snow. That nearby church will have to do."

He settled his friend in the back pew. "Looks like there's an evening meeting going on. When it's over, someone ought to be kind enough to fetch Dr. Robinson, or at least get you back home."

"You can't abandon me in a dad-blamed church. I ain't a Methodist. Why, this is worse then the time you left me sittin' at that temperance meeting so's you could sweet talk that gal handing out fliers. She was the only one around young enough not to remember the Revolutionary War."

"I'll make it up to you when this is over."

"Oh, get on with you then," he gritted, "and watch your back."

Willie offered up his pistol. Walker took it, and

hurried back into the storm. Going it alone would be dicey, but maybe it was for the best. He glanced at the clock tower, barely able to make out the hands on the face. The 5 P.M. deadline was drawing close. He pushed his horse as fast as he dared. Ever optimistic, he led Willie's mount for Trelayne to ride home.

He slowed his pace and squinted. The mill came into sight, grim and looming in the muted glow of the setting sun. The river, where it wasn't frozen, ran along the back of the building, the north side was piled high with drifted snow. Not even considering a frontal approach, he headed for the south wall.

Reduced to an opaque disk, the sun dropped out of sight. The cold increased, but the wind died down. It was so dead silent, he felt as if he'd gone deaf. No matter, the snow would muffle his movements. Riding as close to the building as he dared, he dismounted and tried to tie up the horses, but couldn't. Frozen solid, the reins were useless. He herded the pair behind a tall thicket, and hoped they would stay put.

Pistol at the ready, he broke a trail through the deep snow, exertion soon taking its toll. Halfway there, he could feel his heart pounding in his chest, and the air whooshed through his lungs with the sound of a forge bellows.

Why did this keep happening to the two of them? Every time he thought they were finally safe with only happiness ahead, something extraordinary waylaid their plans. Their road to happiness had been repeatedly sidetracked by misadventure and mortal danger. It was a hell of a way to start their life together. Please, God, he prayed, let their future be boring and mundane, littered only with children, good times, and good friends.

Reaching the building, he pressed his back flat against the rough boards, held a moment to catch his breath, then edged sideways until he was even with a crack leaking light from within. Peering through the opening, he gritted his teeth and choked back a growl of rage. Trelayne was trussed up and tied to a chair. With a start, he realized she was wearing Katie's mittens and wool cap. The sight threw him for a moment. Memories of Kathleen rushed at him, confusing him, yet giving him strength. At least Trelayne appeared alert and uninjured.

Grimsby, a portrait of evil framed by brute determination, sat at a table contentedly smoking a pipe and biding his time He wouldn't underestimate the man. Although not a genius, he was crafty. And if not solid brains, he was solid muscle—mean and strong as a corn-fed bull.

His gaze tripped around the shadowed interior. There didn't seem to be any of Grimsby's henchmen in attendance. It was too easy. Quickly, he surveyed the area outside. Other than his, there were no footprints in the pristine carpet of white. He must be missing something. Grimsby liked to play games, outsmart his quarry, devise uncommon methods of accomplishing his dirty deeds. There was something more here than met the eye.

Regardless of whatever the blackguard was up to, Walker needed to do something quickly. He was cold to the bone, and could only imagine Trelayne was, too. Trelayne and the child she carried. He imagined the poor little mite shivering inside her.

He studied her again, wishing he could somehow

let her know he was here, and she was going to be all right. Then he saw it. There was a rope around Trelayne's throat, the tail end disappearing upward. It was probably tied to the hoist used to move grain to the sack floor in the top of the mill. But the building was derelict and long out of commission. Could parts of it still be operational? Maybe Grimsby planned to use counterweights or gravity. If he rushed in, it might set something into motion he'd not be able to stop.

It seemed he had little choice but to surrender, giving Grimsby what he wanted in exchange for what Walker couldn't live without.

****

Ever since this horrid man had placed the rope around her neck, she'd been afraid to move, afraid to take a deep breath. It escaped her how the apparatus to which it was attached worked, but she had no doubt it was designed to efficiently end her life. Carefully, she licked her lips, and tried not to shudder. This waiting was agony, yet its culmination promised to be worse.

Maybe she should tell him about the baby, maybe he would take pity on her. Moving only her eyes, she glanced in his direction. Grimsby checked his pocket watch and grinned, the image sent a chill down her spine. He would show no pity.

Why hadn't she had a dream of forewarning about this, one of her standard hideous nightmares? Lately there had only been those splendid visions of babies and happiness. Maybe that meant everything was going to turn out all right. She had to cling to that, had to have faith Walker would rescue her yet once again.

The main door creaked open. With great caution, she canted her head. Walker's outline filled the opening, a dark visage against the backdrop of white snow. Relief for salvation smashed headfirst into fear for his safety. Should she warn him Grimsby was intent on killing him? Her mouth felt dry as dust; besides, Walker would assume the man was armed and deadly. A wave of nausea slogged through her stomach. She'd best remain quiet, and try not to be sick

Their nemesis gained his feet and rattled forth the small saber he carried at his side. With a pistol in his other hand he strode toward her. "Do come in, Captain. Nice of you to be on time."

"Untie her," Walker demanded, taking a menacing step forward.

"All in good time, Captain. Hold where you are and drop your weapon."

Walker's pistol clattered to the floor.

"And your other one," Grimsby ordered, positioning the saber crosswise on a separate rope near the one wrapped around her throat. "One cut of this and the hoist takes her up by that slender white neck."

As if weighing rage against logic, Walker clenched and unclenched his fists. Then he produced a second gun and tossed it aside.

"Excellent. Now over to the pit wheel if you please."

"I'll not move an inch until you release my wife."

"You're hardly in a position to make demands," Grimsby sneered. He sawed through a few strands of rope. Unable to suppress an involuntary whimper, she sat up taller as if it might somehow aid her condition.

With a curse, Walker complied, striding toward the massive intermeshing of wheels and cogs. A small heap of straw littered the floor, and he took his place in the center of it.

Grimsby sprinted forward. Walker braced for an attack but none came. Howling with glee, Bartholomew muscled a large stone over the edge of the pit leading to the river. A rope attached to the stone, looped up over a rafter, the other end lay hidden beneath the hay. Drawing tight, the hemp encircled Walker's ankles jerking him off his feet and up into the air.

****

As his world turned upside down, Walker heard Trelayne scream. Swinging to and fro, he fought to orient himself, fought to make sure she was safe. Grimsby doubled over with laughter.

Unbuttoning his hide coat, Walker let it fall to the ground. Now he had room to maneuver. Now he had a chance of reaching the sharp bladed knife attached to his belt at the small of his back. It was hidden by the sheepskin vest he wore. All he needed was for Grimsby to turn his back.

"Now the real fun begins, Captain," the other man said. He ambled forward, kicked the straw back into a pile, and set a match to it. "I hear you used a similar method of entertainment on one of my lads back in England."

"Close enough. But not for the same purpose."

"Nor for the same results," Grimsby added. "There'll be no saving you."

"Please," Trelayne begged. "Don't hurt him. This is madness."

"Madness?" Grimsby spun around to face her. "Madness is me considering to let you live. I sees now the both of you will have to go. But which one first. That's the questions. Maybe both together."

342

Grimsby plucked at the rope holding back the counterweight to the hemp around Trelayne's neck. The chair rocked and she shrieked, the depth of her fear spearing straight to his heart. Twisting slowly above the flames, Walker fought the panic overtaking his senses. He had to focus on one thing at a time, not worry about what might happen, but deal with what was happening.

The burning straw produced more smoke than fire, and although it blinded and choked him, it also provided cover for his actions. Bending at the waist, he grabbed his pants leg, and hand over hand, hauled himself up. Grasping the rope snared around his ankles, he retrieved his knife with his other hand and sawed at the knot. His feet came free and he righted himself and dropped to the ground.

Straw flew in all directions, sparks hurtling into the air. As Grimsby turned, Walker lunged at the man. Trelayne screamed. The sound cut brutally short as the rope tightened around her throat. To his horror, he saw the chair began to rise into the air.

"No," he bellowed.

Never missing a step, he slammed his fist into Grimsby's surprised face. The man went sprawling, his pistol clattered across the floor out of reach. Walker slashed at the rope with his knife. Trelayne and the chair crashed back to the floor. Her head sagged forward. Had she fainted? He prayed it wasn't anything worse as he slid the noose from her neck.

Hearing a scuffling at his back he turned in time to ward off Grimsby's renewed attack. The man rushed forward, saber in hand. Deflecting the blow with his knife, metal hit metal as they both fought for their lives.

The ineffectual flames died down, but the smoke

billowed around the two of them, adding an apocalyptic touch to the atmosphere, and to an outcome holding certain death for one of them.

The fury of seeing his wife nearly hanged infused Walker with strength beyond measure. Seething with vengeance greater than anything he had ever known, he pursued his quarry. Realizing he'd lost the upper hand, Grimsby retreated. Never lessening the attack, never wavering in his desire to see this man dead, Walker kept going at him. The battle swiftly fell to his favor.

Grimsby staggered backward. His foot caught on the edge of the pit housing near the big wheel. He teetered on the lip, eyes wide, hands grasping at air. Then he fell. His cry of surprise echoed sharply and ended abruptly. Walker peered down the shaft. The ice beneath the mill wasn't fully formed. Grimsby had fallen through into the water to drown or freeze to death. Either remedy suited Walker.

He ran back to Trelayne. She was still unresponsive. Releasing all her bonds, he bundled her in his coat and left by the side door. He must get her to a doctor, or at least to a warm fire. Hoping the horses were still on the far side of the mill, he headed in that direction.

The snow collected on his shoulders and neck, soaking through his vest. He couldn't feel his feet or legs. His face was numb, his arms frozen around the only thing in his life that mattered to him. Keep moving, his brain screamed out. If you stop you're dead. Even worse, Trelayne and his child would be dead.

The wind had returned full force, kicking up the snow on the ground to mingle with the relentless powder falling from the sky.

The effect was disorienting. He glanced back. Big as it was, he could no longer see the mill. He wasn't sure which way to go. Anger wrapped around his fear and frustration. He glanced down at Trelayne, or was it Katie. Again, the cap and mittens confused him. It had been a night like this in which Kathleen had perished, but this time would be different. He refused to allow history to repeat itself.

Clenching his teeth to keep them from chattering, he staggered on. He thought again of the wee babe growing inside Trelayne. Was it still safe, still warm? How unfair if it were to die before ever drawing a breath.

From the corner of his eye he thought he saw movement. Yes, it was a figure motioning him closer. It was a woman with blond hair. She was smiling, dressed only in a thin fluttering gown. It was impossible. He closed his eyes and shook his head, but when he looked again, she was still there. He made to follow then stopped. It wasn't the right direction. He should go back the other way. She was leading him closer to the river, away from the horses. Or maybe she was correct, he didn't know anymore, couldn't think straight.

She seemed so real, looked a lot like Katie—he really was losing his mind. Now she begged him to follow. Trusting to the memory of the woman who had once shared his life, he lurched toward the apparition. As he drew near she disappeared. He howled with rage at having been so deceived, the sound blunted by the wall of snow and wind. Then he saw a glimmer of light. Following the dim beacon, he came to a shack. With a foot that felt like a block of ice, he kicked at the door.

Chapter Thirty-One

"She looks better this morning," Hargis said.

"Yes, she does," Walker agreed from where he sat at Trelayne's side. "Much better."

Last night, it had given Walker an unnerving jolt when the door to the snug little shack opened, and he came face to face with Hargis. For a moment it compounded his confusion, then the warmth from the hearth-fire, and the familiar aroma of barley soup, convinced him it wasn't his imagination.

It was a bit harder convincing himself the woman who had led him to the shack was Katie in spirit form. But what or who else could it have been? It's what he decided to believe. He was certain if he'd gone any other direction, they wouldn't have survived the night. And it made him feel good to think she was watching over him from the great beyond. She had helped to save Trelayne, so it seemed she sanctioned his new life, affirming she wished him to be happy.

"I heard on the docks you had come home," Hargis said, "and I was hoping to see you soon, but not last night in the middle of a blizzard."

"You've done well for yourself," Walker acknowledged. "I'm glad."

"I owe much to you," Hargis said. "When I reached New Bedford, your friend Dr. Robinson honored your note. I set up my shop here in the mill annex, and soon I

346

will purchase a place in town and sell my finer items wrought in silver. Then I can pay you back."

"You owe me nothing. You've saved my life twice now. And Trelayne's as well. I'm the one who owes you more than I can ever repay."

Walker studied Trelayne's peaceful expression. Last evening, before falling back into an exhausted sleep, she awakened long enough to have a bit of soup. Her throat was sore inside and out, but other than that, nothing seemed seriously wrong with her.

"Walker?" she said, in a sleepy voice.

He leaned over and kissed her forehead. "Yes, love. I'm right here."

"Is it over? Are we safe?"

"Everything is all right now," he reassured.

"You're not just saying that, are you?" She rose up on her elbows and glanced around. "But where are we? And who is that man? He looks like a Viking. Am I dreaming?"

Walker smiled. "That's Hargis, a good friend with an uncanny knack for saving my hide. And in this case, yours, too."

"I remember. You told me he helped you in Brighton when you were so terribly injured. But that was in England, not America, I'm all befuddled. Oh dear, what of Mother and Father? They must be worried sick, and they are barely recovered."

"They know you're safe and we will be home later today. Hargis lives here now, everything is as it should be, you aren't confused."

"Has the horrible storm ceased?"

"Oh, ya," Hargis put in. "The sky is clear and the wind tamed. This was just a little squall. In Norway we have much worse."

"I'll take your word for it," she grinned. "And thank you for helping us."

"I will always be glad to help you and your husband. I am here in America because of his kindness. He is a good man."

"Yes," Trelayne agreed. "A very good man."

****

Glad to be alive, Trelayne laughed with abandon as they sailed over the snow in a sleigh Hargis had made. Miraculously fit, and anxious for a run, the two horses had weathered the blizzard on the south side of the mill. Now as they flew past the hulking structure, she turned away and slipped her hand into the crook of Walker's arm.

The authorities had already come and gone. Bartholomew Grimsby's body had been found, and they could rest assured he would bother no one again. But she didn't want to think about that. She wanted to marvel at how blue the sky was, and how quickly the weather had changed from near fatal to fantastic.

They didn't go directly to Walker's house, instead they skirted the town, and she was captivated by the landscape spreading out before her. Here in America, freedom seemed a tangible spirit, a living entity. She could feel it in the countryside, in the wide-open expanses that seemed to go on forever, in the thick forests promising wild game and firewood and lumber for building a future. This land had helped shape her husband's spirit, his very essence. She recalled the crowded dirty London backstreets seen on her rounds for Father Woolsey. The sadness and desperation felt a world a way. Here hard work seemed to result in a better way of life. This was a land of hope.

On the crest of a hill overlooking the ocean, Walker brought the sleigh to a halt. The horses stamped their feet, snorting out great puffs of frosty breath as the bells on their traces jangled in the boundless silence. An extraordinary scene, made perfect because Walker was at her side.

She sighed, and offered a quick prayer of thanks then studied his face. "Right now, this very moment, I am happier than I have ever been. I love you, Walker. I love our child yet to be born, and I love all the beautiful possibilities stretching out before us. I even love the thought of growing old with you."

"Don't rush us too quickly into rocking chairs on the porch," he teased.

Slipping his hand inside her cloak, he grazed his hand across the bodice of her dress. Her breasts, made ample by her pregnancy, strained against the fabric, and her nipples hardened and ached for him. Right on queue, the rest of her body reacted hot and ready, responding to his touch, to his need for her, to the knowledge of how much he loved her.

A girlish giggle escaped her. She truly believed he could forever make her feel young and wild and beautiful, so beautiful. But she needed to hear the words. "You promise you will love me even when I'm old and gray?" she pressed, as he nuzzled her neck.

"Yes, always. I am besotted and hopelessly in love with you. And I plan to stay that way. My mission, to fulfill your every dream. Only the good ones, of course," he corrected.

"Only the good ones," she murmured against his neck.

Epilogue

New Bedford, Massachusetts

Their son was born midsummer, a strapping young lad, drawing his first breath in the land of the free and the home of the brave.

Rather than returning to England, everyone had agreed to extend their stay in New Bedford. Trelayne's father was interested in seeing the workings of this exciting foreign country, and her mother was ever happy to be at his side and to be near Trelayne and their first grandchild.

This morning, in a rare quiet moment while they were both still abed, Trelayne yawned and snuggled closer to Walker, seeking his warmth in the early hours before dawn.

"We can't keep calling him 'the baby,'" she said languidly. "He really must have a name."

"You're right, of course, but regardless of what we choose, someone's feelings will be hurt."

"Yes, I know," she agreed, silently reviewing the possibilities in her head.

There was Phillip for her father, Bertram for his father, Samuel for Walker's best friend, William who had been sorely injured trying to rescue her while she was pregnant, and of course Hargis.

She toyed with the silver rattle so delicately

wrought by the big Scandinavian.

Much as she liked the man, and was grateful to him, she wasn't about to name her child Hargis. It sounded much too close to haggis.

"We could name him Walker," she suggested.

"No." He shook his head, his tone indicating he was adamant about the decision. "I'm not much on saddling a child with the name of the father, or any relative. Let destiny declare who he will be as he follows a journey of his own making."

He reached over to the nightstand, snared his St. Brendan medal, and made to slip the silver chain over his head.

Before he could follow through, she caught the filigreed strands between her fingers, staying his actions.

"We shall call him Brendan," she declared, studying the holy figure.

Walker smiled and hugged her. "A perfect choice. If my son is anything like his mother, he will definitely need watching over."

"And if he's anything like his father," she countered, "he will grow up to be a great man, with adventures to follow and grand dreams beyond our imagining."

"He's also going to need a brother or sister," Walker pointed out.

Rather than putting the chain and medallion around his neck, he placed it back upon the bedside table.

"Is that so?" Playfully, she pushed at his chest then glanced over at her son sleeping peacefully nearby. Her sweetest of dreams was coming true. She had her hero of a husband, and was joyfully working on that gaggle of children.

"Would you like a daughter this time, or another son?" she asked, gliding her fingers across his belly.

"Right now, all I want is you."

Author's Notes

The Crystal Palace

The Crystal Palace, known as The Great Exhibition if 1851, was designed by Joseph Paxton who received a knighthood in recognition of his work. But the idea was the brainchild of Prince Albert. During Queen Victoria's visit, she complained about the infestation of sparrows. The Duke of Wellington suggested sparrow hawks—problem solved.

Nearly six million people wandered through the 990,000 square foot creation which housed examples from 14,000 exhibitors. The displays included almost every marvel of the Victorian age, including pottery, porcelain, ironwork, furniture, perfumes, pianos, firearms, fabrics, steam hammers, hydraulic presses and even the odd house or two. The invention of cast plate glass allowed for the clear walls and ceiling which earned the structure its name—the Crystal Palace. It housed a living elm tree, a twenty-seven-foot crystal fountain, and had the first major installation of public toilets in the Retiring Rooms.

The mid-nineteenth century saw the birth of the industrial revolution and the beginning of the modern era and was the forerunner of future Worlds. The Great Exhibition was just the beginning. To quote Charlotte Brontë, "Its grandeur does not consist in *one* thing, but in the unique assemblage of *all* things. Whatever human industry has created you find here."

After the exhibition ended in 1854 it was moved from Hyde Park to a park in Penge Common near Sydenham Hill. It stood there until it burned down in 1936, the glow of which was seen across eight counties.

The Amazon lily

Victoria Amazonica grows in the region of central Brazil. The immense leaves (sometimes exceeding seven feet in diameter) are the largest of all known aquatic plants and float on the surface of hidden ponds and lagoons deep in the forest tributaries of the Amazon River. The stems can reach as much as eighteen feet.

Discovered by British explorers in 1801, it was named after the British Queen Victoria, but it was nearly fifty years later when it was first brought to bloom in "captivity" in England. The lilies are night blooming, scenting evening air with a pineapple-like fragrance. The first night flower, a magnificent white female flower, appears one day then turns into a pink male flower the next day. Rather than by bees, they are generally pollinated by several species of beetles.

Spring Heel Jack

Spring Heel Jack was a real nineteenth-century phenomenon, and like Jack the Ripper, never captured or identified. As an interesting aside, Bigfoot was also reported to have been first spotted in Canada in the mid 1830s. Immortalized in books, plays, and newspaper clippings, Spring Heel Jack is regarded as one of Britain's patron saints of the supernatural. Modern day theorists have suggested he was an alien.

Opium use in 1851

Prior to the 1868 Pharmacy Act, which restricted the sale of opium to professional pharmacists, anyone could legally trade in, or use, opium products. Blatant usage is reflected in the literature of the day, and opium in one form or another was seen in all levels of society.

Pills, penny sticks, Godfrey's Cordial for babies, and a mixture of opium and alcohol (laudanum) were the most common forms in use.

Historical Disclaimer!

Although preloaded gun cylinders were a possibility (as used by my heroine onboard the *Romney Maiden*) they were often very unreliable when put to use, and it is highly doubtful Colt would have included preloaded gun cylinders in his shipment of gun parts from America to England for the exhibit.

General Overview

The Victorian Era appears to have been an age of wonderment and enlightenment, thwarted by superstition and the inability of the male gender and religious factors to surrender tired-out tradition to common sense and the common cause.

A word about the author...

Gini Rifkin lives in Colorado with a Noah's Ark of abandoned farm animals. When not writing or tending "the herd," she enjoys volunteering at the local historical society, especially on days when full costumes are encouraged.

Family and friends are her greatest treasure, and they're delighted with her new hobby—learning the art of baking pies and pastries.